LOVE AND MURDER
on Rocky Neck

MARIA GRACE FURTADO

iUniverse, Inc.
New York   Bloomington

Love and Murder on Rocky Neck

Copyright © 2010 Maria Grace Furtado

iUniverse books may be ordered through booksellers or by contacting:

iUniverse
1663 Liberty Drive
Bloomington, IN 47403
www.iuniverse.com
1-800-Authors (1-800-288-4677)

ISBN: 978-1-4502-5503-5 (pbk)
ISBN: 978-1-4502-5504-2 (ebk)

Printed in the United States of America

iUniverse rev. date: 10/04/2010

For Karen and Kirby, for your love and encouragement.
Thanks for loving my stories.
For mom, dad and Margaret, for your love and support.
And for Zoe and Bette, for watching out for me from up above.

Empty pockets never held anyone back.
Only empty heads and empty hearts can do that.

NORMAN VINCENT PEALE

Chapter 1

Nina hurriedly packed her one good bag with trembling fingers. She could hear her brother-in-law as he settled onto the sofa in the living room, the ancient springs of the rust-colored couch creaking under his heavy weight. He had come home early from work, supposedly because he was coming down with the flu ... again. Nina listened as Bob picked up the phone and dialed. She remained still as she heard his gruff, lifeless voice repeat the feeble explanation he had used so many times before. Just more excuses, thought Nina. And she knew what her sister's response would be, too. She rolled her eyes, recalling the eight beers Bob had consumed last night while whooping and hooting loudly at the contestants of the Miss Florida Hawaiian Tropic Pageant. A shiver wracked her already-tense body as she tried not to think about Bob, a grotesque vision in his too-tight white tank top, licking his thick lips between gulps from his tall can of Budweiser.

Nina glanced eagerly at her watch, more grateful than ever that her cab would soon arrive. Twenty minutes. Thank God. This would be the last time she would be in this place. She mentally tallied the cost of the cab ride, carefully counting the approximate minutes it would take to get from the duplex to the bus station. Probably about ten dollars, she estimated. A minute later, Nina looked at her watch again. She was anxious to get going, to get started with her new life. If the cab didn't arrive soon, it was going to be close. Luckily, last night her eagerness had gotten the best of her, and she had found herself in the bus station carefully ticking off the dollars as she handed them to the attendant behind the counter. Well, at least her new life was prepaid via Greyhound. The first leg, anyway.

Nina opened the rumpled envelope and carefully pulled out the stiff new driver's license. She looked at her solemn face staring back, the strange new name typed permanently in place. She had felt things getting out of control a month ago and her instincts had kicked in. So she had dialed the number she had known about long ago but had never called, asking in a tentative voice how much it would cost for a new license. She had lost hers, she had explained. Nina looked at it for a moment. She read the name again, as she had done so many times before. The first and last name, a combination of her two favorite soap opera characters, almost sounded familiar as she practiced them. Nora Mason. She tried not to giggle, feeling at once silly and scared as she thought about the new, unpaved road ahead of her.

She unsnapped her slightly worn Louis Vuitton wallet, the one she had eagerly snatched up at her favorite consignment shop, and pushed opened the stiff, unused slot, carefully sliding in her new identification. Nora Mason. She thought about her soap opera stars' characteristics. Beautiful. Dramatic. Well dressed. Wealthy. And lucky in love. Perfect. Like the life she had always wanted and would finally make for herself. She was determined this go-around. No more wasting time. She would be focused. And she would get what she wanted. No matter how, or where, she had to start.

Nina thought about the day ahead of her. It would be a long one. She had finally chosen a short knit black skirt that highlighted her lean, muscular legs. The coordinating black-and-white striped cap sleeve T-shirt was fitted and flattered her narrow waist. Her leather sandals completed the ensemble. Her light blonde, shoulder length hair had been brushed carefully and tucked behind her ears. At least she could look good for the journey, she thought. She might be riding a bus, but she didn't have to look as poor as she really was. Her mother's quote came to mind again. A quote, Nina realized, she had long ago memorized and would repeat often, especially in times of trouble when she stumbled, finding herself again off course.

"Empty pockets never held anyone back. Only empty heads and empty hearts can do that."

Her mother had carefully copied the quote, in her perfect English teacher's script, into her goodbye letter--the letter she had left for Nina, along with a birthday card and a one hundred-dollar bill on the night of her sixteenth birthday. It was the same letter Nina had carried downstairs and read in disbelief to her sister while tears streamed down her cheeks, a look of anguish on her young face. The two had sat on the loveseat, hugging, each trying to imagine how their mother could drive off into the night in the family car, leaving them to fend for themselves. The pain had always remained there, fresh as the first day's wounds. And they both had suffered, financially as well as emotionally, each taking care of herself and each other as best they could.

Nancy, at the ripe old age of twenty, had taken two jobs and worked around-the-clock. This resulted in her being too tired to live her life as a normal twenty-year old, too wary to search for love. Nina, on the other hand, possessed both worldliness and innocence at sixteen. And she worked as many hours as she could after school, to purchase the right clothes and make certain her social calendar was always over-stuffed, though it was usually with countless, mostly inappropriate, dates in the hope of finding Mr. Right. They had both smiled proudly when Nina graduated from high school, her diploma tucked under her arm as they entered the TGI Friday's where Nancy worked. And they had even splurged on a celebratory lunch, which ended just two hours before Nancy's shift would start.

Sweet Sixteen thought Nina again, her mind jumping back to that fateful night her mother had abandoned them. It certainly hadn't been the way most of her other classmates had celebrated it. But then again, she had always known she wasn't part of a normal family. It was something she had realized since turning eleven, on the dark day her father had walked out. Her sister had explained to Nina that he wasn't coming back. Nina cringed now, still remembering her mother, always perfectly dressed, her hair stylish, waiting for the day her husband would return. Yes, he missed them, her mother had always insisted. And, yes, he would be back. Soon. But that day had never come. And then everything had changed. The letter had revealed their mother was ready to find her own happiness, and unfortunately, she couldn't take them with her. Being on their own would build character, their mother had explained. And they were old enough to take care of themselves, she had insisted.

Kids, Nina had later realized, would have discouraged her mother's new boyfriends and future husbands. Their childhood had ended, just as their mother's new single adventure had begun.

Nina mentally shook off the thoughts that hadn't permeated her mind for over a year. No negative thoughts, she reminded herself. Positive thoughts. She switched her concentration to what she would do once she arrived in her new hometown. She felt a jolt of excitement, her newfound hope causing her face to flush. After getting off the bus in Boston, she would buy a train ticket for the Commuter Rail ... The Purple Line, as the operator had referred to it. Once she got off the train, she would call a cab. This was key, Nina reminded herself. She couldn't be seen looking destitute and dragging all her worldly possessions around town. She would have to make a good first impression. She'd call a cab to take her to an inn or hotel, get some dinner and the local paper and then start planning her new life. A new job, a new place to live. A cottage, thought Nina. She had always wanted a cottage by the sea. She wondered how much that would cost. She smiled, the first real smile in almost a week. The first real smile since Tom had fired her.

Though it was another hot and humid day in Fort Lauderdale, Nina felt the goose bumps, the rows suddenly prominent along her neck and arms. She hugged herself, trying to prevent the nausea from rising in her tightened throat. She forced herself to take a deep breath. Nina still hadn't processed what had happened. And why. She should have known better. Tom, her former boss and now ex lover, hadn't even given her a chance to explain. She had called and stopped by the store as well as followed him to his beachside condo. But he had turned a deaf ear, saying only that no matter her intentions, she had broken the law. The fear began to rise inside her again. What if he called the police? No, he wouldn't do that, she tried to reason. He had fired her and ended their relationship. Knowing his temper, that would probably be enough, thought Nina. He probably felt vindicated.

Nina had set her shoulders squarely, her resolve evident on her well-chiseled features and in her cornflower-blue eyes. Her well-honed survival instincts had suddenly taken center stage, and she vowed that she would get through this. That she would start over. Except this time, she thought, it would be without her sister, Nancy. She was instantly sad. At least, Nina thought thankfully, she would be rid of the suffocating dead weight that had become permanently attached to their family, her brother-in-law.

Nina opened the billfold compartment of her wallet, carefully pulling out the thin stack of twenty-dollar bills. She counted slowly. Twenty. Forty. Sixty. Eighty. One Hundred. One Hundred Twenty. One Hundred Forty. One Hundred Sixty. One. Two. It was less than she had hoped. One hundred and sixty two dollars. She would turn over a new leaf with one hundred and sixty two dollars. Nina sighed nervously and carefully placed the bills back into her wallet. She pulled out the sealed envelope from her purse and walked over to the worn nightstand before placing it upright and facing the doorway. She wanted to be certain Nancy would see it immediately upon entering the room. On the outside, she had written her sister's name, and inside she had placed a note explaining that she needed a new start, that she had lost her job, and that she and Tom had broken up. At least that was partially true, thought Nina. She was too embarrassed to share all of the gory details. Besides, Nina admitted, Nancy would worry enough that she was leaving and would be on her own. She didn't need to know the rest.

Nina included a forwarding address--a post office box that she had arranged for through the Gloucester Post Office, pending her arrival and signing of the paperwork.

The last paragraph of the letter included her long-ago-memorized quote:

> *Nancy, I love you. Please take care of yourself, and always remember:*
>
> *"Empty pockets never held anyone back. Only empty heads and empty hearts can do that."*
>
> *With Love,*
>
> *Your Sister, Nina.*
>
> *P.S. I left a gift for you.*

Nina took out the separate sealed envelope from her purse, which contained four hundred dollars--the equivalent of half of next month's rent. She had closed her account yesterday, asking for four hundred dollars in ten-dollar bills. The annoyed teller had eyed her suspiciously.

Nina slipped the envelope under the worn quilt of the twin bed, the hiding place where she and her sister had always left notes or cash for each other, away from Bob's eager hands and suspecting eyes. Nancy would have a better chance this way, thought Nina. If she had to dip into the rent money, most likely to buy extra beer for Bob on nights when he was especially ornery, then at least she could dole it out slowly. Nina sighed, her heart heavy with worry at the thought of leaving her sister. She reminded herself that Nancy loved Bob, even with all of his faults. And she knew that her sister would never leave him.

Nina's thoughts shifted back to her task. She made a mental note of everything she would need and had taken care of. Her bag … yes. The letter and money for her sister …yes. Her own money and new license … yes. Her bus ticket … yes. The boxes she would have her sister send to her new post office box … yes. Nina looked at the half dozen boxes in the corner, all of which were carefully sealed with the word Fragile printed in permanent marker. Nancy would add her new address and post office box number when she had a chance to send them off. She lifted her chin. She was ready. Ready for her new life.

Nina checked her watch again. Ten minutes to take off. She heard the loud honk of the taxi horn and jumped unexpectedly. She took one final look around the room then quickly walked through the narrow kitchen past Bob, her eyes glued to the old metal screen door and her impending freedom just past it. She held her suitcase in one hand and clutched her purse and bus ticket in the other. Bob started to speak. She hesitated then pushed at the thin metal frame of the door, not looking back or attempting to explain as she stepped into the bright sunlight.

Chapter 2

Remy stood at the podium, her gleaming, almost-black hair hanging exactly to the middle of her perfectly aligned back. She leaned forward slightly and grabbed her light blue Coach bag, the golden-olive skin of her hand shining softly under the podium's reading lamp. Thank God, she thought. She was going to be able to spend the afternoon on her deck after all. The season hadn't gotten into full swing yet here on Rocky Neck. And the lunch shifts at the Rocky Neck Grille were neither exciting nor financially rewarding. Not yet, anyway. She crossed her fingers, hoping that what Evan, the owner, had assured her was true. That the area would be swarming with artists, tourists, old and new money, and fun. Shit, thought Remy, this town had charm, but what she really needed was to inject a little excitement into her life.

Ever since she had left San Francisco six weeks ago, Remy had felt a gloom that had by now become her constant companion. The breakup, damn it! When was she going to start feeling better? About herself. About her life. And when, exactly, would she feel the sense of satisfaction from working, and making a living for herself … and all that other crap that her grandmother had praised? Now that she had to work. Now that her grandmother had shut her off. Too much frivolous spending, she had proclaimed during Remy's last visit to the family home on Nob Hill. She had waved Remy off, dismissing her abruptly as if she were done with her for the moment. Remy had looked around the mansion as her grandmother lectured her. She had wanted to protest. She had been angry yet slightly amused, not believing what was happening. She had wanted to proclaim that she had learned her frivolous ways from her parents. And that, yes, the apple hadn't fallen far from the tree. But she hadn't dared. Remy hadn't dared to anger her grandmother even further.

She punched the time clock awkwardly, an experience she still found humiliating. She walked outside, careful not to dig her light blue narrow-heeled slingbacks into the large gaps in the dock. Walking along the wharf and uneven cobblestone roads would take a little getting used to, she reminded herself. But she could handle it. She had always worn her newest and most expensive clothes while walking around her native San Francisco, even while walking up the steepest hills. It had just taken a little practice. Remy stopped for a moment, pulled out her cell phone and checked the screen. No messages. Good. At least she might get a little break from the calls. The I'm-so-sorry-I-hurt-you calls she had been getting since her hasty exodus.

Remy looked around, taking in the beauty of the quaint and eccentric village known as Rocky Neck. She had searched the web before her move, trying to decide where she could go to disappear for a little while, to take a break from her breakup. She had surfed for countless nights, finally settling on this place after being charmed by what she learned. The Neck, as the locals called it, was the oldest working artist's colony in the country. It was a famous place, known for its magnificent and picturesque coves on the stunning rocky coast of Gloucester, Massachusetts. Thousands of truly talented artists flocked there every year, mesmerized by its infamous light. And countless artists-at-heart followed suit, enveloped by their magical surroundings and returning to make their pilgrimage every year.

And though the winters kept even the most avid nature lovers inside, the other three seasons on Rocky Neck turned out day-after-perfect-day of sparkling sunlit skies, a gloriously windswept flower-lined coastline, and all variations of briny and interesting characters-in-residence. And they all gathered on the tiny colony in order to find themselves, fill their dreams, and feed their souls.

Late night was famous as well. All of the restaurants, which numbered a mere half-dozen in any given season, sported romantic lighting and fresh-from-the-sea culinary indulgences. The evening entertainment was always guaranteed to be equally memorable, and it ranged from a classically-trained piano player crooning Bobby Darin hits at his sing-along piano bar, to a sultry jazz singer and his four-piece band entertaining the throngs in the salty dockside air.

The countless art galleries buzzed with late-night excitement, too, as the artists-turned-salespeople worked to make a living as they coaxed their tipsy patrons, many with tales of struggle and woe. Once midnight rolled around, however, most of the artists would turn in their sales skills for gallon-size gimlets, mingling or dancing under the stars among the tourists and locals.

Remy had been charmed. She liked the ruggedness of it. She pictured herself leaning on a gleaming mahogany bar while sipping an Absolut Apple Martini, her Chanel scarf hanging expertly from her neck as she stood sandwiched between a starving artist wearing perfectly-wrinkled linen and a brawny fisherman slouching casually in an aged cable knit sweater. It would be the perfect place, she had decided, to mingle with other eccentric, adventure-seeking souls.

*   *   *

Remy opened the car door then touched the black leather seat of her convertible Saab. Good. Not too hot. She would have to start putting the top up soon, now that summer was around the corner. She lit a cigarette, then grabbed the wide black leather headband from her glove compartment and slid it over her forehead and behind her ears. At least her mother wouldn't be nagging her about smoking, a nasty habit she had taken up again since the breakup. She grabbed her black Persol sunglasses from their case, slipped them on then checked her reflection in the rear view mirror. "Fucking Audrey Hepburn Perfect," she said aloud. "All dressed up and no where to go," she mumbled in a slightly irritated tone. She checked for traffic, pushed it into first gear, then expertly pulled her usual U-turn, speeding down Rocky Neck Avenue as if she were very late for a dinner party.

As Remy cruised into third, out of the corner of her eye, she saw the two admirers. She smiled, a beauty queen smile she had learned so many years ago from her mother. She had been perfectly trained. Her mother had thrown her the perfect coming-out party. How ironic, thought Remy, in more ways than one. Then she had attended the perfect East Coast College, Simmons, her mother's alma mater. She would love Boston, her mother had promised. Simmons was where her mother had met Daddy while he was attending MIT. After graduating, Remy had bounced around the New England coast, wondering all the while what the hell she was going to do with her Liberal Arts degree. After taking an entire year off and wasting too many hours at too many bars in Newport with her newfound East Coast friends, she had gone back home to the West Coast to be with the family. She had acquired a high profile, low-paying art gallery job, and then she had promptly fallen in love. And she had been happy, so she thought, until that fateful day when she had been unceremoniously dumped, in front of anyone who was anyone on Nob Hill. It had been humiliation on a grand scale. Remy felt herself flush. She clicked on the stereo, hoping for some distraction during her brief drive home.

She slowed as she approached downtown, the red brick building that housed her loft appearing suddenly on the waterside. Remy rumbled into her parking space, glad to be home for the afternoon. She would make a pitcher of Apple Martinis, she thought. And she would try on her new Prada print canvas slingbacks that had just arrived, along with a new D & G striped swimsuit from one of her favorite stores, Neiman Marcus. She should look hot in it now. Now that she had lost fourteen pounds as a result of her breakup. She slammed her car door, not caring that she had left the top down. She stepped up her pace, eager to slip inside and into a cool martini.

Chapter 3

Nina looked at the calendar in her checkbook for a brief moment before placing it back into her purse. Almost eight weeks had passed since she had arrived on this tiny strip of land. She had gotten off the bus that first day, practically bounding off the last step, eager to shed her previous life and start a new one here on Rocky Neck. She had loved it immediately, feeling right at home among its quirky characters. On the day of her arrival, she had been one of the first off the bus, her hopes for the future packed with her limited but elegant wardrobe into her one good leather bag.

She had been cautiously optimistic since her arrival, careful to keep her hopes and dreams close to her heart. She was starting over. No one needed to make judgements based on the lurid details of her past. Nina thought back to that local bar near the duplex, the one she had wandered into the night before she had left Fort Lauderdale. She had been close to desperate, trying to decide where she would go once she had realized there was nothing to salvage from the wreck that had become her life. She had just come from the T-shirt shop she had managed, and she had tried unsuccessfully to explain to Tom what had happened. He had refused to speak to her, asking her to leave before he decided to call the cops and tell them all about it. Nina had almost stumbled toward home, speechless, until the sounds of laughter billowing from the propped open door called to her. She had been just one block from her final destination. She had looked up at the window, eyeing the words, "Charlie's Skiff," on an antique sign that appeared to have weathered too many tropical storms before being brought inside and propped in the tiny window.

On a whim, Nina had stepped inside and had slid onto a worn leather stool. She had ordered as soon as the bartender made his way toward her. "Rum and coke, please." Nina tried to breathe, first taking a shallow breath, as if to test that she was still alive, then a deeper one. She had sat quietly, trying not to draw attention to herself, her body lifeless, while she gulped her drink. Once an hour had gone by and she had made some progress with her third drink, Nina made her way to the restroom. As she stepped into the moderately clean stall, she glanced toward the floor. The vivid brochure, filled with photographs of the ocean and happy visitors, lay at her feet. The captions beckoned to her, first as a slow whisper then as a loud call as Nina read: *"Glorious Rocky Neck, the Country's Oldest Working Artist's Colony, Located in the Historic Seaport of Gloucester, Massachusetts, Welcomes You … to Explore its Magic."*

Nina picked up the brochure, her hands trembling. This was her sign, she assumed. The divine intervention for which she had been secretly hoping and praying every day for over a year. And this, she decided, would be where she would start her new life. A place she had never seen nor heard of before. Where she didn't know a single soul. Thanks be to God.

She had dialed the number that had been pasted on the wall beside the pay phone, listed just below Oceanside Taxi 24-Hour Service. The bus station operator had answered in an unfriendly nasal tone, "Greyhound. How can I direct your call?" Nina's excitement had grown as she waited for the operator to complete her memorized greeting.

"Yes. I need to get to … Rocky Neck … Gloucester, Massachusetts." She took careful note as the reservationist explained how long it would take her to get to her new life. She would take a bus to Boston, then a train to Gloucester, Massachusetts. "Fine," Nina had replied. "I'd like to get a one-way ticket. What time do you close?"

The next afternoon she had sat on the train, watching the unfamiliar scenery as it flew by. This was the last leg of her journey, she thought, her anticipation high, even as nagging feelings about deserting her sister crept into her mind. Her sister, Nancy, was a woman trapped in a life that would probably never change, and she was married to a man she felt she didn't deserve. And Nina had watched while Nancy waited on her husband hand and foot, obsessed with fulfilling his every unreasonable wish and hoping all the while that she was loved by him, even just a little. Nina grimaced, sad that Nancy had never seemed to want or need more. She, on the other hand, would never have that kind of relationship with a man again. And she would never fall in love with a man like that.

*   *   *

"Miss, can I pay for this check here?" The irritated voice of the annoyed tourist jolted Nina back to reality. She watched as the heavyset woman stared at her. "And could I get a receipt for that?" she added.

"Yes, certainly, Nina assured her. "My name is … " Nina fought the urge once again, though she was getting more accustomed to her new name. "I'm, Nora. How was everything?"

The woman seemed to relax, her irritation now forgotten. "Great. Thank you. That was the best lobster I've ever had."

Nina printed the receipt, handing it to the woman along with her change. She smiled, "Good, I'm glad you enjoyed it. Are you in town for the day, or … ?" Nina feigned interest as the woman told her story, as everyone seemed to do. Everyone except her.

"Well, we'll see you again soon, then. Thanks for coming in." Nina relaxed her tired jaw, watching as the woman made her way through the lounge and to the deck outside. She was glad she was only helping at the cash register today. At least she didn't have to be so damn nice at the Hostess Station. God, it was hard being this charming all the time, she thought. Well, she reminded herself, the old Nina might be tired and bitchy, but the new Nora was always happy to talk to a tourist, cranky or not. She shook off her irritation as she thought about the last eight weeks.

Nora had started working at the Rocky Neck Grille just two days after arriving. Once stepping off the train, she had taken a cab to a local bed and breakfast the cab driver had recommended. She had decided to rent the generic but clean room for a month, hoping it would be enough time to get on her feet. Nora had been frugal, spending her money on groceries at the Stop and Shop only when she really needed to. And she had taken advantage of the complimentary lunch offered to employees, ordering it after every shift and taking it home to be split into two servings.

Each week, she would cash her check, carefully counting out the bills, then placing almost all of the money in the growing roll that was wrapped tightly with a rubber band and hidden in a compartment of her gray toiletry bag. Once the day had arrived when Nora knew she could afford to find a more permanent home, she had sat down with the newspaper, highlighter in hand, imagining her perfect cottage. And someone had smiled upon her the day she found it.

She had reassuringly smiled at the professor and his wife, promising them she would treat their home as if it were her own. And once they had confirmed her employment, she had rushed over to sign the lease, not wanting anything to get in the way of her finally realized plan. Her landlords had left the next day, ready to start their year living abroad in the French countryside, ecstatic to have someone to watch over their beloved belongings. Someone who appeared to be as particular as they were, so they thought.

After working at the restaurant for only a few weeks, Nora had decided she hated waiting tables, and though it paid less, hostessing was at least a little more dignified. It most definitely would showcase her looks and clothing more than waitressing ever would. And she wouldn't smell like fried seafood and salad dressing, her skin damp with perspiration and her hair unspectacular in its regulation tight ponytail.

They were very particular here, she had soon realized. Evan, the owner, was a stickler for details, including how all the girls wore their hair. She had found out early on that Evan's mother had sold the business to him two years earlier, after she finally married into her new husband's old funeral home fortune. The O'Neill Funeral Homes had turned out to be a perfect resting-place for the newly crowned Mrs. Francine O'Neill, and she took great pride in letting everyone know that. Even after acquiring her ridiculously fat bank account, she had still insisted on selling the restaurant to her son at top dollar.

Once taking ownership, Evan had vowed to his staff and to all who knew him that he would make this restaurant *the* place for locals and tourists alike. He had always hated the way his mother and stepfather had run the restaurant, with too-high tourist prices and too-fried tourist meals. The Rocky Neck Grille was now becoming a hangout for fishermen, professionals, artists, and tourists. The décor was tasteful, the meals were tasty seaside fare, and the members of the staff were good, too. Something hard to come by in the restaurant business. And it seemed apparent that Nora was Evan's prize pupil.

Nora thought about Evan. She could always tell when a man liked her ... usually before he did. Evan was always kind to her, treating her with kid gloves. Even on the days when he was in a foul mood, sometimes critiquing other members of the staff, he couldn't ever seem to look into Nora's crystal blue eyes and say anything unpleasant. She looked around the restaurant from her podium-like hostess station, which she had gone back to between cashing out guests. Nora tried to relax, knowing she'd have a break between the lunch and dinner shifts. She reached into her purse, pulling out the concert tickets as she watched Evan approach. Nora stared at the two tickets, pretending not to notice him.

Evan drew closer, his usual lack of confidence with women painfully evident. Though he could be ruthless with a vendor or critical in admonishing a late employee, he was secretly very shy. He watched Nora, feasting his eyes on the curve of her neck and her lightly tanned back. The light blue linen sleeveless dress she wore was one of his favorites, and he could barely stifle a smile as he drew closer.

"Hi, Nora, how was the lunch shift?" Evan glanced into her eyes for a brief moment then looked down. He settled on pretending to be fascinated by the gleaming, just-polished hardwood floor.

"It was fine," Nora replied. "A little slow, but I think it was the cloudy weather today." Nora folded her arms, half-hiding the concert tickets. She continued in her sexiest voice. "But it was fine."

"I'm sure it'll pick up as soon as next weekend rolls around," Evan replied. "As soon as the Fourth of July hits, all hell will break loose. You'll be tired of all the crowds before the summer's over." Evan was careful never to use the word tourist. He felt it was practically a derogatory term, probably because he had heard his mother constantly complain about them after one-too-many martinis, which was just about every night of the entire summer season for the last twenty years.

"I'm sure it'll get busy," Nora answered as she caught Evan's eye. She slowly looked away toward the harbor pleasantly stuffed with boats and houses dotting the rocky horizon behind them. Nora stared at the cove. This was her favorite angle, from the hostess station in the dining room. She admired the array of boats, from yachts to schooners to fishing boats and dinghies. She imagined the lives of the sailors aboard them. Gleaming white yachts, reflecting all of the harbor's magical light, enormous in the tiny harbor. A bright blue fishing boat called Gracie Ann, sitting peacefully while seagulls circled around its perimeter. Alongside it, a gleaming green-hulled sailboat was unfurling its sails. And dozens of sail and powerboats, ranging from miniscule to impressive, bobbed playfully on their moorings, while overhead, countless eager seagulls casually circled the lively scene.

Evan mistook Nora's silence for lack of interest. He turned back to his task at hand, quickly beginning his perfunctory afternoon routine of wiping down the lunch menus with a moist bar towel. He was meticulous with this task as he was with every detail in the restaurant. He had winced every time his mother had stuffed dirty, ketchup-spattered menus into the menu rack without cleaning them. Evan's menus, on the other hand, were perfectly sanitized, smelling slightly of lemon. He insisted on this small yet important detail, after every lunch and dinner shift.

"I'll be in the office if anyone needs me.'" Evan started walking away, his feeling of rejection showing slightly on his smoothly-shaven face.

Nora stared at the concert tickets. The large logo, a royal blue and green wave design, announced the event: <u>Cape Ann Summer Concert Series presents: A Midsummer Night's Concert Starring The Smooth Blues Quartet</u>.

Nora had never really been interested in jazz or blues, but she thought it would be a great way to add a little bit of class to her empty social calendar. Since she had landed here on Rocky Neck, she hadn't found it as easy as she had expected to meet the right men. Not only was her work schedule limiting, but add to that keeping the house perfect, going out to do laundry, and not knowing the bars where she would be comfortable, and that meant a still-empty dating roster. Should she get Evan to ask her to this event, she wondered? It might turn out to be romantic. Or, she admitted, what if Evan didn't take the hint? Maybe he wouldn't even step up to the plate. Then she would certainly be embarrassed, especially if she was obvious in trying to invite him. Evan was going to be a little tougher than she had thought.

Nora watched as Evan made his way back to his office. Though he possessed a somewhat lean runner's frame, he had a rugged air to him. And though his dress was usually somewhat casual, the way most business people dressed on the North Shore, his choices were always impeccable. His hair was kept short and was almost military like. And when given the chance, Nora couldn't help but stare into his green-flecked golden colored eyes. She estimated that he was of average height, probably about 5'10" and she had, on more than one occasion, admired his shoulders and forearms, which were fit and seemingly muscular, probably from having spent the last twenty years working in the restaurant. Nora felt the familiar rumblings stir inside her. She thought about the passion that she imagined deep within Evan. She was convinced that it lay undiscovered until now and buried under his shy demeanor and conservative nature.

Nora looked around the restaurant, realizing that the remaining crew had punched out after their lunch shift. She made her way over to Evan's office, approaching slowly, listening for stirrings from within. She looked around then pressed herself to the closed door. Betty, the Office Manager, was speaking in low tones. Over the last two months, Nora had noticed this same type of exchange on a daily basis, after every lunch and dinner shift. Nora pressed her ear closer, trying to grasp their conversation.

Everyone was aware of Betty's devotion to Evan. She had often been heard bragging to the staff that in the two years she had worked for him, she had never missed even one shift. Evan seemed to appreciate her, Nora admitted, and she was certain that if a flu epidemic ever struck the entire restaurant, Betty would be the one to be wheeled into work on a stretcher in order to be by Evan's side.

Nora tried to listen again, then grimaced, realizing she couldn't decipher a single sentence. She hesitated, her hand held up to the door before she knocked gently. Nora waited, not hearing anything, not even the usual whispered tones. She knocked again. A few seconds passed, then Betty opened the door slowly, peering out as she did so. She stared at Nora, obviously annoyed to have been interrupted.

Betty kept the door only slightly ajar, turning back to Evan and speaking in a loud, brash tone, "I'm runnin' out for a bit. I'll be back for the dinner shift." She looked Nora up and down then continued. "In about forty-five minutes."

Nora watched as Betty let herself out and walked past her. As Evan looked up from his desk, Nora flashed him a nervous smile, suddenly questioning herself, wondering if she would seem foolish and too eager. She leaned in the doorway, forcing herself to smile more widely, waiting for Evan to invite her in. "Hi. I'm … sorry. Am I interrupting?"

Nora watched as Evan's eyes wandered from her slightly pink, perfectly lipsticked mouth to the curve of her neck. She watched his gaze as it traveled down to her breasts for a quick moment. She saw him flush, suddenly feeling that she had made the right decision. Evan caught himself, then switched his gaze to the calculator and column of numbers directly in front of him.

He cleared his throat, attempting to sound casual, "No, no problem. What can I get you?"

Nora was enjoying his attempt at being casual. She had seen this from many men before. He was trying hard. That was good.

"Evan," Nora explained in a low voice, "Have you ever been to the Cape Ann Summer Concert Series?" She surprised herself with her lack of finesse but plodded on. "Do you have any interest in going? I have two tickets and thought it would be a fun thing to do." There was a long silence. Nora continued, now doubting her decision, "I mean … not as a date, of course. Just a nice casual night between friends."

Evan's look seemed to be one of disappointment. Maybe Nora's date wasn't able to make it, he thought, and she couldn't get rid of the tickets. He pondered the question for a moment longer, the silence between them thick and uncomfortable. So, what kind of invitation was this exactly, he asked himself? Was she pretending it was a friend thing in order to sound casual, or is that what she really wanted? He glanced back over at her, trying to decipher her cryptic invitation. Women never thought of him as a serious date, he admitted. Instead, they always wanted him as the perfect social event escort.

Evan tried to catch Nora's eye. "It sounds … interesting. But my schedule's already getting really busy. And this coming weekend is when the season's officially going into full swing." His voice dragged, making it obvious he wasn't certain of what he was saying. He continued,

"Thanks for thinking of me, but I'm going to have to pass." He looked away, uncomfortable with having said no.

Nora flushed suddenly, not expecting to be turned down. How dare he, she thought. He wasn't even that good looking. She had dated much better-looking guys. Richer guys. And he was saying *no* to her? What the hell was wrong with him? He should be so lucky. She stifled a sarcastic reply and instead smiled and leaned forward, gently kissing him on the cheek, her lips lingering noticeably. She thought about her new perfume, which was floating lightly in the air between them.

"That's alright." She cleared her throat uncomfortably. "I understand."

Nora turned toward the door, willing Evan to watch her as she walked away. "I'm going to head home," she replied. She wavered slightly, praying that he would feel instant remorse as he watched her walking out of the room.

Evan sat speechless and flushed. He didn't want to be used again, he reminded himself. He knew he had done the right thing. But why did he feel so regretful? He felt even more unbalanced around Nora than he usually did around women. Damn it. Why did he let her make him feel so flustered? He thought for a moment about her beautiful skin, her brilliant blue eyes almost a shock against the rose of her cheeks. He got up and closed the door to his office, leaning against it and breathing deeply, the scent of Nora's perfume still lingering. Evan forced himself to go back to his work. When he closed up, he drove his usual route home, past Nora's cottage, his heart pounding, secretly wondering what she was doing and with whom.

Chapter 4

Nora awoke the following morning feeling slightly nervous. And she didn't know why, exactly. Why was she so worked up about going to some small-town concert in the park? Because, she admitted, it wasn't the concert. It was the fact that she was going alone. And that was something that made her very uncomfortable. Nora wasn't accustomed to going anywhere alone. And she hated to start now, in a new town. Well, she would have to get over it.

Though Nora had gone without while growing up, she had always been the girl the other local girls had envied. She had learned, at an early age, the secret to managing boys, then men, through her flawless good looks and impeccable clothes. Most of the girls didn't have dates on Friday nights, as Nora did, so they traveled through the mall in packs, always seeming to harbor envy and a cruel word for her.

On the surface, Nora later realized, she seemed to be quite the bitch. She was 5'5" and had a petite build. On a bad day, she weighed all of 110 lbs., and she was always stylish in whatever she wore. In addition, Nora had developed quite the taste for fashion, which included not only her clothes but also her up-to-the-minute accessories, her impeccable hairstyle, and her slightly snobbish demeanor. She was the envy of every local girl, and the wet dream of almost every boy. But no one realized how much work it was to appear that perfect on the surface, and unfortunately, it was all she really had. No girls were waiting to hang out with her, and no boys were promising marriage.

Nora stood in front of her closet, telling herself it would be alright.

What would she wear, she asked herself, that would have the most impact on a man?

*   *   *

Nora closed the door of her closet, then stood in front of her full-length mirror, making a mental check of her ensemble. The dress was a pink linen, with thin straps, fitted and just above the knee. Her coordinating off-white leather sandals accentuated her toned legs. Yes, she admitted. Sexy, but not over the top. She grabbed her purse and headed for the front door with newfound excitement. After walking four blocks, she turned onto the dead end street where she had last parked her dull gray Chevy Nova.

She opened the enormous door, which she always kept unlocked, then slammed it behind her, grimacing at the thunderous metal thud. Well, at least she owned a car. Her first, she had admitted to the salesperson, when she had purchased it last month. She pumped the gas pedal, as she thought she was supposed to do, then turned the key in the ignition. She stared straight ahead as the thick plume of gray smoke drifted into the dark blue sky. Nora's cheeks reddened as she realized that she might be frightening her neighbors as they stared out into the smoke-filled dead end street. She heard the engine as it prepared to stall, then quickly gave it some gas and coerced it from park into drive. Nora put it into drive, thankful there was no car parked immediately in front of hers. She ignored the squeal of the tires as she stepped hard on the gas. Nora guided the vehicle off Rocky Neck, taking a left onto East Main Street toward downtown. She allowed herself a smile as she felt her newfound independence. She took a deep breath of the fresh ocean air, reveling in the new fragrance that had been foreign to her until recently. Even the ocean smelled differently here, admitted Nora. Not like the hot, salty air of Fort Lauderdale often filled with the scent of the nearby bars and restaurants. Here, the air had a purity, a cool early morning scent, often filled with the deep ocean, mollusk tinged fragrance that was Rocky Neck. Nora admired the perfectly striped blue sky, marveling at its brightness. She focused toward the harbor as she slowed in the downtown traffic, noting the hints of a soon-to-be tangerine sunset. Nora slowed to a near stop as she passed the Port Side bar, noting the streets congested with tourists circling and vying for a parking spot. The air was starting to cool, and Nora took in the view of the bustling harbor as she coasted down the hill toward The Boulevard. She watched the horizon, as the throng of boats flooded the entrance to the harbor, all trying to make their way under the bridge while it was still open, their final destination the Gloucester Marina and their awaiting cocktails beyond.

Her anticipation surged as she neared Stage Fort Park, the location for the concert. She pulled into the first, street-level lot, praying that a parking spot would be available so she wouldn't have to endure the embarrassment of driving through the park and past the throng of attendees toward one of the lower lots.

Nora's pulse quickened as she spied a makeshift parking spot. Half on the grass, closest to the baseball field, but it would do, she determined. She braced herself, swinging wide, pretending not to hear the squealing as she squeezed in beside the new SUV. Please, she prayed, please fit. She brought the car to a sudden stop, throwing it into park and getting out simultaneously, careful not to bump the shining black vehicle parked beside her dull one. Phew, she thought, relieved. Nora slammed the door quickly behind her, eager to reach the grandstand and pavilion not yet visible at the top of the hill. She walked briskly, trying to put some distance between her and her car.

She dropped her keys into her purse, then turned as she heard the slightly familiar voice, "Aren't you going to lock your car?" Nora continued to scan the nearby passersby as she tried to identify the voice. "Hey Nora, aren't you going to lock your car?"

Nora stopped dead in her tracks, finally realizing who was speaking. She turned as she spotted Christian's handsome face as he came up behind her. He approached quickly, his strides long and smooth. He was even more handsome without his waiter's uniform on, thought Nora. She remembered asking him how old he was the first day he had started. Even then, his confident air impressed her. Not bad for a college junior, she thought. She had found out that he was home from the University of Vermont for the summer. His mother and stepfather had a summer cottage on The Back Shore, the first and only *real* place of honor for the idle rich of Gloucester, according to restaurant gossip. And, his outrageous good looks and family money happened to be a winning and much sought-after combination among the Gloucester, college, and restaurant sets. Too bad, thought Nora. He would always be twelve years younger than she was. And that was something she could never overcome. Plus, she admitted, her competition would be society girls named Buffy who were nineteen or twenty and had the bottomless bank accounts she could not even begin to imagine.

Nora pretended to be surprised as she watched him admire her. "Oh, hi. It's Christian, right?" She gave him a devilish look. "How are you?"

Christian smiled. His dimpled grin was so disarming thought Nora. "I'm great, but aren't you going to lock your car?"

Nora admired his innocence. "No, I don't usually lock it." She almost wanted to laugh. She felt her face flush, imaging what Christian had probably driven here tonight, hoping it wasn't the shiny new SUV parked next to her lackluster gray one. Nora watched as Christian smiled, another Oscar-winning version guaranteed to melt the hearts and panties of young girls everywhere. "Are you meeting somebody?" he asked, almost sheepishly. She had seen that look before. It was one she had used too many times herself, and she knew full well that it was intended as an attempt at shyness and innocence.

Nora tried to think of a clever reply. "No, actually. I ... wanted to get out. And this sort of sounded interesting." She continued, "How about you?"

Christian looked around before answering. "It's my mom's fiftieth. And for her birthday, she said she wanted to come to this concert with my dad and me and then have cocktails and dinner in town. So here I am."

Nora noted Christian's air of sarcasm and lack of interest. She could tell he thought this event was definitely too old. She suddenly felt slightly embarrassed. "So, you're not here of your own free will then?"

Christian's grin was his answer as he held out his arm, which Nora grabbed, trying to be casual as she did so. They flirted innocently, then she allowed him to lead her through the thickening crowds. As they strolled up the hill, Nora leaned in so that Christian could wonder if it was in fact her breast that his right forearm was grazing. Indeed it was, thought Nora. She was feeling charitable today. She carefully turned her head up toward his smooth, tan face, his dimples catalog-perfect and almost irresistible. Nora stared at his eyes, noting the familiar bad-boy quality she adored.

He's too young, Nora reminded herself. He wouldn't be ready for marriage for at least another ten years. And that meant she would be wasting her time. Plus, she had to admit. He was out of her league. But, damn. He was a Ralph Lauren model in the flesh. His sexy, slightly disheveled look only added to his charm. Nora admired his clothes for a moment, her eyes searching through every article hungrily. His white linen long-sleeve shirt was appropriately slightly wrinkled, and his tan linen pants were professionally creased and permanently cuffed. His rich brown leather boat shoes were definitely not run-of-the-mill starter models, and even his ankles were sexy as they showed occasionally when his pant legs swayed in the early evening breeze.

As they approached the bandstand area, the crowd grew even larger. Christian grabbed Nora's hand, leading her through the bevy of couples and groups of singles and families waiting patiently for the concert to begin.

The emcee approached the microphone. He was dressed in a crisp navy summer suit, white shirt, and red-and-navy-striped tie. His speech was dramatic, "Ladies and Gentlemen. Welcome to the Cape Ann Summer Concert Series. Our concert will begin in approximately fifteen minutes. Please take your seats."

Christian stopped and looked around, slowly surveying the crowd while trying to locate his parents in the swelling group of familiar and not-so-familiar faces. "My parents said they'd be near the bandstand, but that could be anywhere." He looked at Nora. "I thought I could introduce you to them, and then maybe we could go up to the cocktail area and do our own thing for a little while."

Nora was surprised by Christian's self-assured attitude, which she found surprising at his young age. But maybe that's the instant boost of confidence being wealthy gives you, she thought, envying him. She would never know what it had been liking growing up in his world, and more importantly, he could never imagine what it had been like for her, growing up as she had.

Christian flashed Nora a warm, almost comforting smile. He moved closer, putting his hand on the small of her back. She felt the surge of excitement, surprised by how his touch had affected her. He bent down slightly as he leaned toward the soft skin on the nape of her neck. "Let's get out of here," he whispered. "We can catch up with my parents later. Maybe during intermission."

Christian guided Nora effortlessly to the refreshment area. As they reached the bar that had been set up under a large elm tree, Nora wondered if he would be bold enough to order cocktails. Yes, she thought. Of course, he would. She was certain it had never even crossed his mind that he was underage, not since the day he had been born into his privileged Back Shore mansion. Nora tried to imagine what it looked like.

"Would you like a glass of champagne?" He asked confidently, interrupting her thoughts.

Nora laughed to herself, but she couldn't resist. "Absolutely. Please."

Christian scanned the makeshift bar, spotted the domestic bottles, then pointed toward the champagne bucket containing the magnum with the familiar orange label. He faced the bartender confidently as he ordered. "Two glasses of Veuve Clicquot, please."

Perhaps it was his poised air, or his award-winning smile, but Nora noticed that the bartender didn't hesitate, even as he scanned Christian's face, then popped the cork, expertly pouring the two glasses of amber liquid. Nora loved good champagne. Especially when she was sharing it with a sexy man. Christian casually pulled a fifty-dollar bill from his wallet, presented it to the bartender and waited for change, then left a generous gratuity in the silver tip bowl. He turned toward Nora and smoothly extended an arm. Nora grabbed the fluted glass, admiring her champagne as the late afternoon sun shone through the sparkling miniscule bubbles.

"To summers on Cape Ann," Christian toasted in a husky, confident voice. Nora raised her glass, then took a long, lingering sip. As she intentionally licked her lips and started to speak, Nora heard yet another familiar voice.

"Hi. I ... hope I'm not interrupting."

Nora turned quickly with her glass in hand, almost tipping the effervescent liquid.

Evan stepped toward Nora, continuing his conversation, obviously surprised and uncomfortable, "I just wanted to say a quick hello."

Nora stood speechless, as Christian wrapped his arm possessively around her waist. She flinched slightly, feeling instantly awkward.

Evan filled the silence. "Betty offered to man the fort for a little while … " He cleared his throat. "And I thought I'd come down and check it out." Evan looked at each of them suspiciously.

Nora finally spoke. "I'm so glad." She glanced toward Evan, then Christian.

"I see you two are doing the same." Evan looked toward the ocean as he spoke, pretending to be fascinated by the boats on the horizon.

Another awkward silence ensued as Nora tried to catch Evan's eye. He looked casual yet very deliberate in his tan chino shorts and light blue button-down oxford, Nora thought. The cuffs of his sleeves were turned once, showing his strong tan wrists.

"Yes, this is nice. My first time," Nora remarked, abandoning her initial impulse to try explaining to Evan what very much looked like a date. But then again, thought Nora, maybe she would let Evan draw his own conclusions. It might keep things interesting. If it didn't completely backfire.

Christian seemed to be enjoying Evan's awkwardness. He finally spoke, his eyes darting back carefully between Evan and Nora, "We were enjoying a glass of champagne. Would you like to join us?"

Evan tried to hide his agitation. He knew all the details about his employees, including the almost trivial ones. He knew that Christian was a Junior at the University of Vermont. That his father, who had attended high school with Evan, was from very old money. And that Christian was not only very privileged … but definitely under age. If not for the fear of appearing envious of a college kid, Evan would have shut him off, telling the bartender what he hadn't cared to notice.

And what was Nora thinking? Evan flushed, realizing the awkwardness of the situation. Oh, God, he thought. He knew how it looked. As if he were eagerly chasing Nora like a pathetic puppy dog. And what was worse, he was competing with a privileged college kid who happened to be his employee. He thought about Nora for a brief moment, admitting to himself how beautiful she looked and how attracted he was to her.

Nora saw the embarrassment as it settled onto Evan's reddened face. He stared at each one of them for a brief moment, first Christian, then

Nora. His voice sounded a bit strained as he said the words, "You kids enjoy yourselves, but don't have too much champagne. You're both on the schedule tomorrow, and I need you there in good condition. We're expecting some important guests for dinner."

He turned and quickly headed toward the lot. It was the first time Evan had ever shown frustration or anger toward Nora. God ... how he hated that she could get the best of him. Especially in front of Christian.

Nora and Christian stood, frozen for a moment, as they watched Evan retreat. They were both suddenly very aware that they needed to be careful. Evan had just reminded them that they were his employees. And if they weren't considerate of that fact and got involved, it would make for one long summer. Nora was instantly fearful as she thought back to her nightmare in Florida. She knew what she wanted, and she knew what she had to do. The game of seduction was satisfying, admitted Nora, especially if the stakes were high. But the prize had to be worth it. And she wasn't sure yet, about Evan. She hoped he would be worth her while. Christian, on the other hand, would do her no good. She had made a promise to herself, and it was one she intended to keep, which included staying away from anything that slightly resembled trouble, though she might be tempted.

Evan headed back to Rocky Neck, angry for having embarrassed himself. He had wanted to go with his instincts, which obviously had been completely wrong. Shit, he thought. He had just been the backup in case she hadn't found somebody better to invite. Apparently, Nora had worked it out, finding the date she was looking for.

He parked his freshly washed Land Rover, slamming the door as he got out. He made his way toward the kitchen by way of the service entrance. Women, he reminded himself, were hurtful, selfish creatures, ready to humiliate you at a moment's notice. It was how his mother operated ... how she always made him feel. To this day, he always felt uncertain, trying too hard to please, dreading the times she would call in the middle of a busy shift, eager to second guess him, asking him questions she was sure would make him doubt himself and how he ran his business. After he had been sufficiently pummeled, she would call again, her words seemingly innocent, ready to offer him praise and reassuring him he had imagined her hostility. And reminding him she couldn't live without him. How he hated his mother when she treated him like that. and right now he almost hated Nora as well.

*   *   *

Nora flirted with Christian until intermission then quickly decided she had had enough of his award-winning boyish charm. She suddenly had no desire to mingle with what she assumed would be his outrageously well-groomed and extremely proper parents. This flirtation with Christian was interesting, but she needed to think about her future. Wasn't that why she was here on Cape Ann? New beginning, eligible new men to conquer, all the social engagements to attend once she was Mrs. Somebody?

Nora thought about Evan. She would have to fix this evening's obvious blunder, she admitted. She gulped the rest of her champagne, putting her glass down on the closest table. She searched for her keys and looked up ... smiling and ready to deliver the explanation for her departure.

"Hey, where are you going?" Christian asked, noticing Nora's sudden eagerness to leave. It was obvious he wasn't someone accustomed to being rejected, thought Nora, as she heard the annoyance in his voice. He pouted slightly. Nora found her keys and plucked them from the depths of her purse with a newfound fury.

She placed her hand on Christian's arm and leaned in closely, giving him a reassuring smile. "I'm sorry," Nora responded. "I've been running around so much lately, and I'm a little tired." She paused. But I promise we'll do it another time."

Christian smiled back, seemingly willing to let her go for now. Nora added, "And, I had forgotten how busy work's going to be tomorrow. We should both rest up." Nora's hand slid down Christian's arm. Her hand held his, as she planted a light kiss on his cheek.

"I am rested up. And ... " He looked her up and down admiringly, "Who needs sleep?"

Nora tried to ignore his suggestive tone. She smiled politely. "Thanks so much for the champagne. And the company." She hesitated then rose onto her tiptoes, giving Christian a warm, lingering kiss before turning toward the parking area. She waved flirtatiously, taking long, slow strides so that he could admire her legs as she exited. Once she was out of sight, she almost broke into a sprint, knowing she had to get back as soon as possible in order to do some much-needed damage control.

*   *   *

Nora drove quickly as she reviewed her new plan. She turned onto Rocky Neck and then onto a side street, searching for a parking spot and realizing it was starting to get dark. She parked, unobserved, bumping to a halt under a large elm tree before shutting the oversized door and making her way back to the cottage.

She entered through the white-picket gate, thinking about how she would have to work quickly. Nora imagined where Evan would be right now. Though he had arranged to get some time off tonight, he had probably gone right back to work after the concert fiasco. If that were the case, he might already be engrossed in work, unwilling to accept her invitation and be interrupted. She would need to call him right away.

Chapter 5

Nora dialed the private office number at the Rocky Neck Grille.

"Office," she heard Evan reply tersely.

She grimaced, noting the annoyed tone in his voice. She sat upright, mentally preparing herself for what might happen. "Evan?" Her voice sounded tentative and a bit shaky.

"Yes?" He replied, not immediately recognizing her voice.

"It's Nora."

Concerned by her tone, Evan replied, "What's wrong … is everything okay?"

"I, I'm fine. Would you come over for a glass of Chardonnay?" Nora knew that although Evan didn't drink much, he was a sucker for a good glass of the grapes. "I just got a bottle of Toasted Head, and I would really love your company tonight."

Evan remained silent for a moment, wondering why Nora wasn't with Christian. He didn't want to sound interested, he reminded himself. But how could he turn down such a sincere-sounding invitation? Nora sounded so vulnerable, he thought. It was almost as if she needed him. And no woman had ever really made him feel needed, or wanted, for that matter.

"Well, it's pretty busy here," he replied. His tone told Nora all she needed to know.

"Please. Just come over for a little while." Nora tried to turn on the charm as much as she dared without sounding desperate.

"Fine," Evan replied.

Nora smiled, knowing that though her victory might be small, at least it was a victory.

Evan reached into the second drawer of his desk and grabbed his toothpaste, toothbrush, and floss. As he practiced his perfect up-and-down brush stroke with his newly opened toothbrush, he thought about Nora. He admitted he was falling for her. He brushed again, then completed his meticulous flossing. Once he was finished, he tapped his toothbrush on the edge of the sink, then blotted it dry with a paper towel, dropping it into a fresh plastic case in his desk drawer. As he took out his personal size Altoid tin and replenished it from the larger version sitting on top of his desk, Evan made himself a promise. He was not going to overanalyze Nora's invitation, as he had with every date, dinner, or conversation he had ever had with the opposite sex. He made himself stop then took a deep breath, checking his reflection in the mirror behind the office door and casually running his fingers through his short, thick hair. He closed his office door, then strode past the hostess station, his demeanor confident.

"Back in a few hours," he muttered, trying to sound casual. Remy, the hostess on duty, shot him a surprised look. Evan was leaving right before the dinner rush, thought Remy. And that was very unusual for him. She hid her surprise, nodding politely.

Evan pulled up in front of Nora's cottage, popping an Altoid as he got out. He hadn't needed to ask her address. In such a small coastal community like Rocky Neck, not only did everyone know everyone else, but Evan had also mentally jotted down Nora's address from the day she had moved there.

He wanted to keep tabs on her because she was a new employee, he had reassured himself. But the truth was that he had driven by daily on his way to and from work, hoping to catch a glimpse of her as she went about her daily routine.

*   *   *

Evan pushed open the gate, eyeing Nora's cottage approvingly as he approached the front door. He had never been inside, but he knew he would love it as soon as he walked up the white shell path. The antique four-room cottage was fairy-tale like. Every window had a freshly painted dark green flower box. And in each window, a crisp white cotton lace curtain billowed softly and invitingly. It was the kind of cottage he had always dreamed of while growing up. Instead, for most of his childhood, he had lived in a large and impersonal monstrosity his mother had called their home. Upon a drive by or visit from casual friends or business acquaintances, the large, ominous looking white pillared mansion seemed impressive. But to Evan, it had always been a stark, hospital-clean smelling cavernous place, which for some reason had been cold and unsettling. Although the outside was pristine, the lawn perfectly manicured, and the topiaries his mother was fond of collecting perfectly groomed, it completely lacked warmth or personality, which sadly, described his mother to perfection as well.

Inside, as his mother had instructed the staff, all clutter and belongings were to be kept to an acceptable minimum. This included photos, memorabilia, and all things personal. The truth, Evan admitted in retrospect, was that there had never been that many family photos, for his mother had never taken the trouble to record his family's events, important occasions, and standard milestones. Instead, she had prided herself in maintaining the house, her efforts in keeping up appearances far exceeding her work at being a caring mother and wife.

Evan walked to Nora's front door. He lifted the gleaming starfish-shaped doorknocker. He rapped it politely three times then waited for the door to open. As the breeze billowed through a nearby window, he inhaled the scent of garlic, olive oil, and freshly baked bread, like the glorious scent in a small North End bakery as the door is opened to the public at sunrise. He listened to the faint hints of music streaming outside as he heard Nora's approaching footsteps. The door opened, and Evan heard the crooning of Edith Piaf, his favorite French singer.

Nora opened the heavy wooden door and stood inside the old-fashioned screen door. She smiled. Thank God, she thought. He decided to show up. For more than a few minutes, she wasn't sure if he would.

Evan smiled widely, forgetting his annoyance. He eyed her appreciatively, taking note that she had changed into a freshly pressed white sleeveless tank and matching short skirt. She looked so sweet and innocent, he realized. Almost angelic. Nora held open the door, motioning to Evan, "Come in … please."

He stepped inside, standing close to Nora in the small foyer. He grabbed her hands, ready to plant a polite hello kiss on her cheek.

As he did, he looked down as Nora extended her hand, holding one long-stemmed red rose. Evan tried to hide his look of pleasure and surprise.

One red rose, thought Evan, trying not to read too much into it. The symbol of true love. He wondered, for a moment, if she had chosen this color intentionally.

"This is for you," she whispered. She supplied no further explanation. Instead, she leaned in slowly, giving Evan a soft, lingering kiss on the cheek. As she pulled away, she placed each of her hands on his forearms and looked deeply into his eyes. "I thought you might appreciate a quiet dinner, just the two of us." She paused. "I love to cook."

Nora took two steps back into the petite, candle lit foyer. Evan stood closely, facing her, as he stared into her crystal blue eyes.

As if reading his mind, she explained. "This cottage. It's the kind of place I always wanted," Nora quietly explained. "It makes me feel comfortable. And safe."

Evan knew then that he could fall in love with Nora. And he suddenly felt an unexplained bond … as if she truly understood him. Nora grabbed Evan's hand and walked slowly as she led him through the kitchen and out onto the back deck. Though it was small, it was also perfect, Evan noted. Along the entire railing there were glossy dark green wooden flower boxes. And they were filled completely, brimming with greenery as well as a dazzling purple blue lavender. In one corner of the deck, there was a black wrought iron bistro table and two chairs.

Evan noticed that the chairs had been placed at an angle, their backs to the railing and set close to each other. On the opposite corner of the deck, aged terra cotta pots of various sizes were filled with an assortment of flowers, the larger ones overflowing with white daisies and Black-eyed Susans. Another grouping of glazed pots in varying sizes was also carefully arranged, all of them pleasantly plump with an assortment of fresh and mysterious herbs in different heights. As Edith Piaf crooned La Vie En Rose, Evan smiled at the bit of French countryside that Nora had lovingly nurtured, making her back deck a scene from a village in Provence. Too bad he had never been to France, he admitted. He had never been anywhere, for that matter. Not since his mother had put him to work in their restaurant's kitchen on his twelfth birthday.

Nora watched as Evan scanned her presentation. She smiled, pleased that her sense of taste had been appreciated. She had been careful in shopping for distinctive plates, silverware, wineglasses, linens and place mats throughout the year and during after-Christmas sales for three seasons. She knew that the right table setting always gave the right impression. And she had been so grateful that her sister had shipped these prized possessions.

Evan pointed toward the dinnerware, "I see you've been shopping at Williams-Sonoma. You have good taste." Evan was surprised that she had as much attention to detail as he did.

Nora answered carefully, "I know … I do have good taste." She smiled coyly, then motioned toward one of the chairs. "Have a seat. I've got a bottle of Toasted Head in the fridge. I'll be right back." Nora walked slowly toward the kitchen. As she stepped inside, she half-turned, wanting to make certain that Evan's gaze was still on her.

Nora carefully opened the refrigerator door, knowing that the light from inside would illuminate her silhouette through her thin white linen skirt. Evan watched Nora, his eyes scanning her shapely tanned legs and the high curve of her buttocks through the now slightly sheer fabric. His pulse quickened as he stared. Hours seemed to pass before Nora reached inside, leaning forward as she grabbed the wine.

Nora smiled, lingered slightly, and then turned as she closed the refrigerator door. She knew she had a captive audience and was certain at that moment that all was not lost. Christian had presented a small problem. But it wasn't something she couldn't handle. Thankfully, she and Evan were back on track. She walked out onto the deck and preceded to hand the bottle to him along with a corkscrew. Nora looked down at Evan's plate, eyeing the red rose that he had carefully placed on top of it.

"Should I put it in water?" Evan asked.

Nora smiled. "That's alright. I know where I can get more."

Evan tried to squelch his excitement. The last thing he wanted right now, he realized, was to let her know how much he wanted her.

Nora took her seat, watching him as he expertly uncorked the wine and poured each of them a generous glass. She waited for him to sit then turned her chair so that it was almost facing him, her right knee touching his thigh.

Evan seemed slightly nervous as he carefully placed the cork back in the bottle and settled it back into the nearby stand-up wine bucket.

Nora raised her glass, stared into it seriously, then made a toast, "Here's to being home ... and sharing a good glass of wine."

They raised their glasses, then each proceeded to take a long sip. Evan's hand was slightly unsteady, and Nora watched as he tried to put his glass down on the table without bumping into the carefully set dishes.

She turned toward him. "I wanted you to come here tonight so I could tell you how I'm feeling." Nora realized the words weren't coming out smoothly. "That is, what I mean is that I ..." Nora was surprised that she was genuinely flustered.

Evan smiled, obviously enjoying her moment of discomfort.

She smiled back, realizing that though she was a bit nervous, Evan had no idea that she was actually working on him. That she wanted him to fall for her.

Evan interrupted Nora, suddenly feeling uncomfortable and uncertain about her true feelings. He remembered how she and Christian had looked together at the concert. "I think you're a nice person, Nora. And I appreciate your friendship. Thanks for having me over."

Nora winced. That was not the reaction she had been going for.

Evan continued. "I know I shouldn't stick my nose into your business, but I think you should be careful about dating someone you work with."

Nora replied without thinking. "Oh ... okay. But if we dated, we could be discreet."

Evan continued, "It's not about being discreet ... I think it's more about the age difference."

Nora looked puzzled. "What do you mean? Because you're older than I am?

They stared at each other, suddenly realizing they were carrying on two different conversations.

Relieved, Evan added, his tone sounding lighter, "No, because Christian's too damn young for you."

Nora chuckled lightly, then gave Evan her most injured look. "Evan ... I'm not seeing Christian. I went alone to the concert. I ran into him there. As a matter of fact, he was with his parents. They were celebrating his mother's birthday."

Evan looked instantly relieved. "Oh."

She tried to explain her obvious blunder. "I thought you were talking about us."

Evan remained silent. Damn, she thought. He was going to be a little more of a challenge than she had anticipated. Nora continued, feeling slightly unsure of herself, "Evan, I wanted us to have a nice dinner together. I wanted to see you ... relax. And I just wanted to do something nice for you, especially since we're not going to have a lot of down time all summer. Nora held up her glass, looking intently into Evan's warm hazel eyes as they toasted.

"Here's to my first summer on Rocky Neck."

The music changed, and Evan realized that it was Norah Jones crooning "Come away with me." He looked down at the red rose, the only flower that a woman had ever given him. Then his eyes wandered, landing first on Nora's perfectly shaped ankles and calves. He let his gaze wander upward past her small waist, and farther north toward the curve of her breasts, finally sweeping up the soft turn of her neck. God, he thought, how he would love to place his lips on the soft, warm skin of her neck, burying his face and breathing deeply, allowing himself to become intoxicated with her scent. Evan swallowed, then forced himself to look up, his eyes meeting Nora's for a long moment.

He spoke, his husky, soft voice breaking the thick silence that lay between them. "What's for dinner?"

Nora stood slowly, still thinking about his hungry gaze. "Scampi ... a la Nora." Evan smiled.

"That's my version of Shrimp Scampi, but with a little punch," explained Nora.

Evan purposely lowered his tone as he watched her walk toward the door. "Scampi's one of my favorites. And I, um ... am looking forward to the Nora part." He grabbed his glass, suddenly embarrassed by his honest comment. He took several gulps of the wine, hoping he could cool himself down while Nora made the final preparations in the kitchen. He flushed, feeling the sudden rush of blood as it pulsed rapidly through his veins. He hoped he didn't look the way he felt right now--anguished and eager. All he wanted right now, he admitted, was to follow Nora into the kitchen, walk up to her, and kiss her. A braver man would have done it, admitted Evan. A man more sure of himself. Someone who didn't fear rejection.

Evan looked at his empty glass, hoping for further consolation. He grabbed the bottle, refilling his glass quickly as Nora worked in the kitchen. He thought about what she wanted. Up until now, he didn't have a clue. Was she trying to tell him she wanted to be friends? Or ... . did she want more? Friends. Evan winced. He wouldn't settle for that. He had to try. Especially since he hadn't felt this way about anyone before.

The screen door slammed and Evan's thoughts were suddenly interrupted. He looked up, watching her as she strolled out, a large ceramic plate in one hand, and a smaller bowl in the other. She set them down in the center of the table.

Nora spoke slowly, in a deliberate, sexy drawl. "I've cooked my special for you this evening. It's Shrimp Scampi, AKA Scampi a la Nora ... in a spicy garlic cream sauce with roasted fingerling potatoes along with tender asparagus wrapped in prosciutto and broiled to perfection." She smiled, noting Evan's praise as he surveyed the feast.

"I'm impressed," he replied as he took Nora's cue. He grabbed the serving pieces, serving her first, then himself.

As they ate their dinner, Nora decided to tell Evan just enough about herself to keep him intrigued. She put down her fork. "We didn't have a lot growing up. I never even had asparagus until after my mother left us." She waited a moment, then continued. "My first time was when my sister took me out to celebrate my eighteenth birthday. Just the two of us." She cleared her throat. "The way I see it, she's my only family. My mother and father both left us actually ... so Nancy and I took care of each other." She watched Evan's expression, one of caring and sympathy.

Evan spoke tenderly, "I ... I'm sorry. That must have been so hard for you." He reached over, placing his hand gently on Nora's.

"It was. But we both survived." She lifted her chin defiantly, her eyes suddenly misting over.

Evan held up his glass. "To a new and better life."

Nora lifted her glass. "Cheers." Then she added, taking a risk that she was telling too much, "Here's to getting what we want in life."

They both sat back, drinking their wine, each with his own thoughts, as the evening sky darkened to a midnight hue. The candlelight flickered silently between them.

Evan stood suddenly, breaking the mood by grabbing the plates and carrying them toward the kitchen. As he reached the sink, he ran the water, preparing for the cleanup ahead. Nora walked up slowly behind him. Evan felt her breath as she stepped behind him and leaned close to his ear. "Stop," she whispered. "Later." She planted a soft kiss on his cheek. Evan's reaction was immediate, as he felt her warmth pressing against him. He turned, ready to kiss her, only to watch her walk toward the corner hutch. Nora opened the cabinet, grabbing a bottle of Sandeman's Port along with two antique-looking glasses. She walked outside as Evan followed onto the deck, down the stairs, and around the side of the house toward the front yard. The narrow side path smelled of ferns and blue hydrangeas. He let Nora keep the lead as she guided him across the narrow side street toward the beckoning arbor. As they reached the antique gate, Nora waited for Evan to open it. He followed her down the slate path, the moss and occasional blades of grass punctuating the openings. The path ended and Evan looked out toward Rocky Neck harbor in all its glory. They made their way to the grasses' edge, the enormous boulders bordering the common path and framing the sharp drop to the rocky cove below.

Nora sat quietly, her legs hanging over the ledge. Evan took a place beside her, hesitating only for a second as he peered toward the pounding surf below. Nora held up the two glasses, a clear signal for Evan to pour their after-dinner cocktails.

Evan filled them, then took a large sip of the port from the tiny glass, almost emptying it immediately. The sharp scent of the salt air mixed with the fragrance of sea roses filled the heavy moist air surrounding them. They sat for a long moment, gazing at the stars as they started to dot the darkening sky. Nora looked over at Evan, her eyes brimming with tears.

"What's wrong?" Evan asked, as he put his arm around her, pulling her toward him.

Nora sighed deeply before speaking, "My mother loved the ocean. I always think of her when I see it," She explained.

Evan was touched, though he was disappointed that her obvious display of emotion had nothing to do with him. She was a woman with deep feelings, and maybe, some day, those feelings might be reserved for him. He forced himself to remain silent, not wanting to interrupt her thoughts.

Evan fought the impulse but finally looked at his watch. It was 8:40 p.m. His stomach lurched from the unexpected emotional highs and lows he had experienced tonight. He didn't want to be thinking about work, but he knew he had to at some point. Plus, he admitted, he needed to get back to his world.

Chapter 6

Nora tossed and turned that night, finally waking as she eagerly awaited the sunrise. She watched the clock religiously until it read 5:50 a.m. She then eagerly threw on a pair of form-fitting black yoga pants and matching hooded zip top. She would go for a walk around The Neck, she decided. The fresh air and exercise would be good for her. Maybe it would even clear her head. She had gone to bed, anxious and confused, wondering why she had dreamt of Evan. Nora stepped outside, breathing deeply of the early morning salt air. She headed down the hill, turning left toward the harbor. As she tried to organize her thoughts, her newfound feelings for Evan filled her mind. She resisted the romantic thoughts, focusing instead on the beauty of the morning. No one had any idea, realized Nora. That she could get up at the crack of dawn and find such beauty in nature. And that, yes, she was a romantic at heart. She looked toward the ocean, which seemed to be completely still, the reflection of the summer cottages of Rocky Neck perfectly mirrored in the dark blue salt water of the cove. In several places, mist rose from the water, as the early morning air collided with the cool ocean waters. The seagulls were quiet as they walked the water's edge, scanning the rocky shoreline for unsuspecting crabs that weren't aware of their casual descent.

Why did she suddenly have these feelings for Evan? And why was she almost unsure of herself around him? He shouldn't be that difficult to read. Nora thought he cared for her, too, as evidenced by the frequency with which she would catch him staring at her. But why was he making her work so hard? Why did he seem only slightly interested?

And why was he so guarded? Did he think she wasn't good enough for him? Though Nora never had even a fair amount of money, guys would normally chomp at the bit when she made herself as available as she had last night. Had she seemed too obvious, as she tried to get his interest? Or too desperate? She thought about last night. She had played the friendship card, and like all good men, Evan should have shown his interest in wanting to be more than friends with her. It usually worked, thought Nora. Why hadn't it this time around? Why hadn't he taken the bait? Nora zipped up her top, suddenly chilly. She picked up her pace as she tried to warm up.

As she reached the main strip, Nora walked past The Rowboat, her favorite restaurant on Rocky Neck. She glanced at the menu posted outside, impressed with the chef's new menu offerings. The Rowboat had an enviable loyal local following, and Nora knew why. In her opinion, everything about the restaurant had character. From the way the two owners dressed all the tables with handmade tablecloths, to the intimate corner seating area by the fireplace, it oozed warmth and charm. Whenever she dined there, she noticed that no one seemed to mind the long wait for a table. And once their dedicated patrons entered the bar area and ordered their first round of cocktails, all inconvenience was forgotten. The regulars were greeted by name, and no matter how busy the restaurant got, no one was ever made to feel rushed. The owners even offered up hand knit blankets when outside dining became chilly in the spring or fall evenings. Now that, Nora admitted, was a worthwhile dining experience.

Nora finished reading the specials, making a mental note of what was new on their menu. Maybe even the locals' palettes were becoming more sophisticated. Or maybe it was all the out-of-towners and Boston thirty-somethings offering bottomless wallets matched with limited vacation time.

Nora wanted to share all of this with Evan, knowing he would welcome news of a competitor's menu offerings. As Nora reached the dock in front of the restaurant, she quickly scanned the boats tied up at Evan's dock. To her surprise, "Living Dangerously", Evan's 42-foot sailboat, seemed to be occupied. The door to the main cabin was open, and a light was on down below. She also noticed two towels draped neatly over the lifelines on the port side. Again, Nora thought, evidence of someone's recent boarding. For a moment, she wasn't certain what to do. Evan never used his boat on the weekends, she rationalized, at least not since she had worked there. But maybe it had just been too cold.

Nora knew he would often board for a few hours after work. She would watch him from the restaurant's deck, pretending to be uninterested. Eventually, he would always go home, never seeming to stay overnight. What was he, or someone else, doing on the boat at 6:00 a.m.?

After hesitating for a moment, Nora decided that she needed to know who was on board. She quickly walked past the restaurant and onto the dock. As she approached, she started questioning her actions. Nora drew in her breath as she spotted Evan dressed only in a pair of tan shorts and walking up the stairs from the main cabin below. In his right hand was a steaming cup of coffee. He seemed to be concentrating intently. As he made his way onto the main deck and proceeded to the seat to the right of the wheel, he abruptly straightened up, realizing Nora was watching him. Evan stumbled, spilling most of his coffee onto the spotless deck.

"Oh … I'm so sorry." Nora was obviously embarrassed.

Evan said nothing. Nora looked down and was surprised that he wasn't instantly on his knees scrubbing the deck clean. Instead, he walked around the puddle, sitting down on the bench and shaking off his coffee-soaked hand.

Nora mistook his nervousness for annoyance. "Evan, I'm so sorry. I was up early and thought I'd take a walk. I was surprised to see someone on the boat and thought I'd check it out."

Nora hoped her explanation sounded sincere. She was surprised to see activity on the boat and wanted to check it out to make certain everything was okay. But why had she cared? It was a safe town. No one would be rummaging through Evan's belongings at this hour, or at any hour, for that matter.

Nora stepped back on the dock, suddenly embarrassed and ready to get the hell out of there.

Evan looked closely at her, silent as he studied her embarrassed expression.

Nora was flustered. But why, she asked herself? Because she hadn't expected to see him at this early hour? She prepared to flee, half turning as she planned her hasty exit.

Evan put down his coffee, walking over to the stairs on the dock. "Wait, where are you going? You haven't tried my famous coffee." He leaned forward, extending his strong hand. Nora took hold of it, pulling herself up over the lifeline and onto the boat. As she stepped onto the deck, she stood close to Evan.

"Why don't we go below? It's still pretty chilly out here," Evan explained in a relaxed voice.

The sun was just coming up, and the pale sky was streaked with bright pink hues. Nora carefully climbed backward down the ship's ladder after Evan and followed him into the dimly lit interior below. She looked around the cabin, admiring all of the thought-out details. Small lamps glowed with low wattage bulbs gently lighting the cabin's interior. The seat cushions were an expensive-looking tan print, and Nora noted that it was most likely a custom fabric. The shelves were neatly stacked with leather-bound books and nautical brass bookends, and there were antique looking wicker baskets carefully lining the shelves.

Evan held onto Nora's hand, leading her to the corner dining area.

Nora felt instantly at home as Evan waited on her. "Have a seat." He motioned as he walked over to the stove. "How about a cup of coffee?"

Nora nodded yes.

"It's French Roast," He added.

Nora watched him as he stood at the stove. She admired his athletic body, surprised that she had never noticed it before. Definitely a diamond in the rough, she delighted.

Evan turned and caught Nora's eye, suddenly seeming self-conscious.

Nora kept her eyes locked with his.

He walked over, standing near her for a moment. He then leaned closer, as if he were going to kiss her. Nora flushed, realizing he was reaching toward the shelf behind her, which contained an array of different colored coffee mugs. She looked down, embarrassed, as he leaned past her to grab a mug identical to his. He placed it gently in front of her then turned toward the galley stove.

Nora stared at the old-fashioned percolator that Evan was getting ready to grab from the stove. It reminded her of her childhood. It was one happy memory that she had, when her mother would make coffee in the morning, the coffee brewing wildly inside the clear glass cylinder atop its sturdy silver pot.

"I love your coffee pot," Nora remarked.

Evan smiled as he poured coffee into her cup. "Thanks." Believe it or not, it was my mother's, and when she got remarried and moved, I saved it from being thrown away."

Evan thought about that day. He hated that his mother had no passion for things old, no attachment to the past. She hadn't even blinked when she unceremoniously tossed all her old kitchen items into a variety of boxes, setting them out for the next day's trash.

Nora cupped her hands around the steaming mug.

Evan deposited the sugar bowl directly in front of her. "Cream?" He asked.

She nodded, stirring her coffee and savoring the rich scent. Nora tried to relax. She had done the flirting and dating thing so many times. Why was she so nervous? This was not going well, she thought. She shouldn't have walked down here and she hated being unprepared. She most definitely would have brushed her hair and left it down, as opposed to the tousled casual pony tail she was sporting. And though she looked perfectly acceptable, it wasn't what she would have chosen had she known she'd be seeing Evan. Nora continued to stir her coffee, trying to gather her thoughts.

She thought about last night. After their very platonic dinner, she couldn't exactly have thrown herself at him, she admitted. She wondered why he had stayed overnight. Her curiosity got the best of her. "What are you doing here?" Nora realized her question made her sound as if she cared. She took a fast gulp of the steaming hot coffee.

Evan walked over and grabbed a white cotton oxford that had been hanging on a hook near the doorway then put it on, leaving it unbuttoned. He felt self-conscious as Nora watched him. Why did he care, he asked himself? Last night, it seemed clear that she only wanted his friendship. He doubted she cared what he looked like without his shirt on. Without thinking, Evan sat down next to Nora. He thought about how alone he felt lately, even more so after leaving Nora's last night. He had come here because his boat was always his comfort--whether he was alone, lonely, or both.

Evan spoke quietly. "I couldn't sleep, so I came down here last night after finishing up at the restaurant." He waited a moment then continued. "I started doing a little work on the boat, and before I realized, it was late. So I stayed."

As they sat together, Nora realized she could smell the fresh detergent of his cotton shirt. Her thigh absently pressed against his and she felt comforted and aroused at the same time. She tried not to think about the fact that she hadn't had sex or made love with anyone since leaving Florida. She could feel herself getting flushed and unzipped her hooded jacket slightly.

Evan watched as the mounds of her firm breasts were revealed above the white cotton tank. He admired her openly, realizing they were both breathing heavily. He turned toward Nora, instinctively placing his hand gently on her right breast. To his surprise, Nora placed her hand over his, cupping his palm slightly and then sliding his fingers over her erect nipple. She closed her eyes, savoring the moment and leaning toward Evan, her lips parted invitingly.

No, Nora thought. This is not part of the plan. I haven't even showered. I have to stop. Evan's lips caressed Nora's. He gently stroked both her breasts as he unzipped her top completely. He then slid his right hand inside her tank, reveling in the pulsing warmth of her skin. Nora shivered with excitement. As Evan continued to kiss her. He parted her lips with his own, softly caressing her tongue with his. Nora was shocked by his passion, and by how much she was aroused. Her breasts tingled, and the inside of her thighs quickly became moist.

Nora wrapped her arms around Evan's shoulders and pressed herself closer to him. She knew that she would need to stop soon. Evan pressed eagerly toward her, then leaned back slightly, openly admiring Nora. He pulled at her tank, revealing both perfect breasts. As he continued to caress them, his kisses moved from her soft full mouth to her neck. Nora moaned softly. She needed to stop. Now. She half-heartedly pulled at her tank, which revealed her taut abdomen. Nora pushed herself away then stood up, trying to steady herself. Nora tried to compose herself as she pulled at her top, an obvious attempt to straighten it. Her gaze met Evan's, the look of disappointment evident in his eyes.

"Nora, I'm sorry. I thought ..." Evan couldn't finish his sentence. He couldn't look up. He stood. "I'll walk you out."

Nora remained silent, almost afraid to speak. If she did, then Evan would know that she cared more for him more than she imagined she could. She was angry with herself. Why did she let it go this far? They weren't even on a date. She wasn't going to make this some cheap summer romance. She had too much at stake.

As Nora composed herself and started up the ship's ladder, she admitted she didn't want to go. Nora placed one foot on the first step as she tried to sort her thoughts. Evan walked up from behind. He placed his arms on either side of hers. Nora closed her eyes for a moment and breathed in deeply. She knew she was at a crossroads. She knew she could control herself, if she really wanted to. But damn it. She didn't want to. To her surprise, she really wanted to be with Evan right now.

She turned around, so that her back was against the stairs, and for fear of being rejected, she closed her eyes, then placed her arms around Evan's neck, pulling him toward her. She felt his lips on hers as he returned her kiss. Nora parted her lips further as she allowed his soft and gentle tongue to caress hers. With her eyes closed, her senses were alive. She could smell Evan's sweet breath slightly tinged with sugar, coffee, and the scent of ivory soap on his mildly weathered skin. She could smell fresh lime, probably from after shave or shampoo, and the pungent smell of salt air and the earthy scent of the cabin. They kissed for what seemed like hours. Nora could feel their mingled perspiration and the growing dampness of her cotton tank.

They stopped kissing for a moment and Evan looked intensely into Nora's eyes. Right now, at least, he knew that she cared for him, whether she allowed herself to admit it or not. Evan placed both his hands on Nora's buttocks, lifting her slightly, as she wrapped her legs around his hips. She could feel his hardness as it rubbed against her through his shorts. Evan pressed closer, pushing eagerly against her womanhood. Their breaths quickened as they continued to kiss deeply. As Evan held onto Nora, he walked slowly backward toward the edge of the bench cushion. Nora kept her legs wrapped around his waist, and as they sat, she uncrossed them, leaning on her knees and pushing more deeply into him.

Nora had abandoned her sensibilities, knowing this wasn't her textbook approach. But right now, she didn't care. She was so aroused, and she was certain Evan was as well. She felt Evan's breath quicken as she rocked softly, arousing him even further. He watched Nora intently, his eyes gazing deeply into hers, his hands on her hips as he pulled her arched back toward him. They continued until their breaths were a frenzied single gasp. As they reached their peak, Evan held Nora closely, kissing the curve of her neck.

Nora leaned toward Evan, her lips parting as they felt their pleasure simultaneously. They held each other for a long moment and remained speechless. Nora felt his passion … and his tenderness. Evan kissed Nora again, gently at first, then more passionately. She was instantly aroused once more, disappointed as he pulled away. Nora didn't want the moment to end. She looked up, willing him to continue.

Evan looked intently at Nora. His voice was barely a whisper, "I have to warn you, I may not be what you expected."

Nora listened intently, wondering what else he would say. He leaned forward slightly, again whispering as if someone would hear him. "You know what they say. Still waters run deep."

For one of the few times in her life, Nora was without words. Not because she was surprised by passion, but rather because the passion had come from Evan, a completely unexpected source. At times, as she had already seen, he was so controlled, so calculated and orderly. And now, she had been witness to his passionate side. Nora stepped back from the cushioned bench, standing unsteadily.

She straightened her white tank, which by now was moist with perspiration. As she composed herself, Evan asked, "How about that cup of coffee? Your first one seemed to get cold."

Nora nodded, glad for his sensitivity.

Evan smiled as he stood directly in front of her.

He suddenly seemed confident. As Evan poured Nora's cup of coffee and placed it in the microwave to warm, he thought about what had just happened. He knew he could make Nora happy. And he wasn't going to let this opportunity pass him by.

He handed her the steaming cup and then led her upstairs onto the deck. They sat silently next to each other, watching the morning sky, which by now was a shocking bright blue.

Nora thought about what had just happened, and suddenly, she felt off balance. She hadn't expected to feel this way. She sat with Evan, and with her thoughts. She mused about the name of Evan's boat, which now seemed so appropriate. *Living Dangerously.* Indeed, she thought. They were both going to have to take some risks. For good or bad.

Chapter 7

Evan was elated. He had finally won at something personal in his life. Something he really wanted. And he felt good about it. Though they would have to be careful around the rest of the staff, he felt that he and Nora had a breakthrough, and now that they were being honest with each other, hopefully, they could start a relationship. Not that Evan knew exactly what that was. But he knew what he wanted, and if they continued as they had yesterday, they could have an amazing summer together … and maybe even more than that.

Evan pulled into the Rocky Neck Grille later than usual. It was 8:30 a.m., and on most days, he would have arrived by 7:00 a.m. That's alright, he thought to himself, he had a competent staff. Amazing what one romantic encounter could do for your disposition. Evan thought about how he had spent the rest of yesterday, after Nora left. He had fought the urge to ask her to spend it with him. He didn't want to make it look as if he didn't have any plans, which he didn't, of course, other than being at the restaurant for the dinner shift. But he mustered up all of his newfound self-confidence, placing a romantic kiss on Nora's forehead as he walked her onto the dock. He assured her he would call, and yes, he would love to have dinner with her again. It was hard for him to watch her leave, but he knew he had to try to play it cool. At least for now.

As Evan got out of his black Land Rover, which he parked in the back lot near the kitchen, he thought about when he should call Nora again. What did they say? Call the next day and that was too soon. Wait three days … and it was too long. Something like that. He wished he could ask someone, but he didn't have real friends right now. And he never really had, either. It was the curse of a restaurant family. Always working, always working late … it didn't leave much time for hanging out with anyone.

Evan strode through the back door and stopped in the kitchen where he spent a few minutes talking with Kevin Delaney, his new Chef who had just started this season. Evan had recruited him from The Gale, a popular fish and chips restaurant at the Gloucester Marina. The Gale was a hit with the tourists who dreamed of heaping fried portions, but it definitely lacked imagination and good taste. And the owner had a reputation for being miserable, which made it hard to keep employees longer than one season.

Evan noticed that Kevin seemed happy to let his creative juices flow. Hiring him was a gamble, he realized, since he was a local with a past and hadn't been professionally trained. But he had been working in restaurants since the age of sixteen … between fishing seasons and eventually full time, and he had paid his dues while working his way up. More than his skills, Evan admired his raw talent. He knew after his first meeting with Kevin that he had to have him at the restaurant. So, he had been generous with his first-year salary and days off after the peak season. Kevin's entrees, appetizers, and soups were becoming the talk of the town. Evan's favorite, a creamy Chilean Sea Bass and Scallop chowder, was already gaining fame on The Neck. And though they still had to oblige the fried seafood crowd, Evan knew they could eventually change that.

He looked over the menu, pleased with the additions. Though he loved to be the sole decision-maker, he agreed to give Kevin control of the menu, including the nightly specials. Thus far, Evan loved it, and he hoped Kevin's choices would continue to be good ones.

"This looks good." Evan perused the specials list. "Really good," he commented again, impressed with the holiday weekend menu offerings. He continued, "This weekend is going to be pretty crazy. It always is … for the Fourth of July. So at tomorrow morning's meeting, we'll go over the menu with the rest of the staff … who's on the VIP list, and any other questions or things you want to explain. Alright?"

Kevin nodded. Evan hoped his easygoing disposition would last through the season. He had seen one too many temperamental chefs once they made a name for themselves. "Sure, Evan," Kevin nodded reassuringly. "Not a problem. We've got extra hands on deck this weekend."

Evan noticed that he still talked like a fisherman. They nodded to each other and Evan made his way out of the kitchen and through the dining room, then down the hall toward his small office.

As Evan approached his office door, he put his key in the lock before realizing it had already been opened. He had employee records, the night's receipts, and the two cash register drawers, which were always counted the night before, ready for the next day's sales. He was certain he hadn't forgotten to lock up last night. He walked in, looking around cautiously as he did so. He heard the raspy smoker's voice. There, at her desk, sat his bookkeeper, Betty Alden, talking quietly into the telephone. Betty heard Evan approach and turned her head slightly. It was then that he noticed her red, puffy eyes. It looked as if she had been crying for most of the night. Evan said nothing, pulled out his desk chair, and sat down quietly.

"Yes", Betty said, "I can be there after the dinner shift tonight. All right. Yup. I'll look at the schedule too and see which train comes in closest to when I get off work. If I'm not there when you get in, walk over to the Dunkin' Donuts, have a coffee, and I'll pick you up when I can. Okay. I'll see ya tonight, honey."

Evan felt uncomfortable as Betty hung up the phone. He didn't know what to say.

Betty looked at Evan then explained, "Joe and I had a fight last night, and I came back here and slept on your sofa." She pointed to the blue slipcovered couch. It had been in Evan's playroom while he was growing up. It was a miniscule loveseat, not very large, and definitely not very comfortable.

Evan looked at Betty, "I'm so sorry. Is everything going to be okay?"

Betty's eyes welled up, "Oh, yeah, I'm sure. Just a little bit louder than the usual."

Evan knew that Betty's husband, a retired fisherman, didn't drink all the time, but when he did, he sure made it count. He could totally sympathize, since his mother had been an outrageous alcoholic throughout his teens, twenties, and thirties--until she had met her new knight in shining armor and had quit cold turkey.

"Betty, if there's anything I can do, please let me know." It seemed like such a feeble attempt at helping, but he knew all too well that there wasn't anything he or Betty could do. It had to be Joe's decision to stop drinking. That seemed unlikely, though, since all of Joe's friends did the same and thought it was normal to drink a six pack of beer and three shots every night. Down at the Port Side, that was called just getting started.

"Tommy's comin' for a visit," Betty sniffled. That'll help."

"Good," Evan replied, knowing in fact that it wasn't good. Tommy was just as bad as his father and had been in trouble for dealing drugs in the past. Evan decided to give Betty some space, realizing that her son was her solace right now, for better or for worse. Evan grabbed his cell phone, then turned and started out of the office. "I'm going to run a few errands. I'll be back in about an hour." He closed the door behind him, leaving Betty alone in the office. This would give her time to compose herself, he reasoned. Evan walked down to his boat and immediately started dialing Nora's number, his will suddenly depleted. It was now 9:10 a.m., and he knew she would be up, probably watering her flowers and having coffee on her back deck.

The phone rang four times before Evan heard Nora's message, "Hi, I'm not in to take your call right now. *Please* leave a message, and I'll call you back." Damn. Evan tried to think quickly. Did she have caller ID? Too late. He was going to have to leave a message.

"Hi Nora, it's Evan … I just wanted to check in and see what you were doing tonight after work. I thought we could go down to The Bradford and have an after-dinner drink. They have great espresso martinis. Give me a call on my cell: 339-5999. Thanks."

Evan closed his phone with a snap, proud of his attempt at coolness. He hadn't sounded too nervous, and he hoped Nora would say yes. It might be easier than having dinner, he thought. Especially since there might be some awkwardness after yesterday's unexpected encounter. Evan was instantly aroused, thinking about Nora in her white tank, her lips parted as she faced him. He felt his breath catch in his throat, his emotions almost overwhelming. He became aroused, thinking again about how beautiful and downright sexy Nora had looked.

He wouldn't call again, he thought. He would need to wait to hear from her. And hopefully, she would want to see him. Discreetly, of course, Evan reminded himself. He hoped Nora would understand the importance of being discreet. Especially since he was, after all, her employer.

Evan stood outside the restaurant for a moment then decided he would walk toward Nora's house. Maybe, he thought, he would catch a glimpse of her. His resolve was quickly dissipating. The resolve he had been so proud of just hours earlier. He started walking, as if on auto pilot. He hated his weakness. And right now, Nora was his major weakness.

Evan thought about her routine. Usually, she was out on her deck in the morning, having coffee and watering her plants. But if she had been home, then why hadn't she answered the phone? Maybe she was just in the shower, he reasoned. Evan drove by Nora's every morning, praying for a glimpse of her. Sometimes he would hear music. Other times, if he was extremely lucky, just when he was almost past the house, he would spot her, her hair loose and gleaming in the morning sunlight as she stood on the back deck admiring her flowers.

He walked briskly, his heart skipping a beat as he approached the street. What would he say if he saw her? His mind raced. He would tell her that Betty was in the office and needed some privacy because of a personal matter. And, he had decided to go for a walk since it was such a nice day … and he was going to get some ice cream … his favorite homemade cone with the lemon sherbet. Evan smiled, thinking about seeing Nora and inviting her for ice cream, her face scrubbed clean and all aglow as she took her first lick. He imagined the raspberry sherbet as she licked the cone. Except, why on earth would he be getting ice cream this early in the morning? Just then, Evan reached Nora's street. He panicked, wavering for a moment before forcing himself to walk up to the front of the house.

Evan stood motionless, suddenly not caring about making excuses to see her. He needed to see her. To smell and touch her. He opened the gate slowly, his attention now captured by the wildly billowing curtains. He scanned every window, realizing they were all open. Odd, thought Evan. It was still fairly early, and it was unusually cool this morning, probably only about 50 degrees. Why would all of the windows be open? It must be freezing in the house. Evan took the path around the side toward the deck. Not only was Nora nowhere to be found, but the back door was closed. He tried not to become suspicious, a feeling that he hated. God, thought Evan. Where is she? He fought to keep his thoughts in check. Maybe she had just gone to the store. Evan scanned the street for her car. He knew it was probably parked at least three streets away, in a less obvious spot. He had been amused by her vanity in wanting to hide the ugly duckling vehicle. Evan closed the gate behind him. He'd have to wait to hear from her. He was sure there was a good reason. He fought the thoughts struggling to surface … that Nora hadn't come home last night. Doubts entered Evan's mind. He made a quick loop around the neighborhood, not admitting to himself that he was looking for her car. He turned back toward the restaurant, picking up his pace as he tried to focus on the day's busy schedule.

Evan pictured Nora again in her white tank and tight fitting yoga pants, her hair pulled back casually. This time he felt a protective sensation unfamiliar to him. A strong desire to protect her, to hold her, and to take care of her. Maybe she was a little out of his league, he admitted, but he wasn't going to give up. Not yet, anyway. Evan entered the restaurant through the lounge. As he stepped into the bar area, he realized that Christian was standing at the counter cutting lemons and limes. What was he doing here? And why was he helping with the bartender's side work? Evan didn't picture Christian doing anything for anyone, unless there was something worthwhile enough for him.

He walked up to the bar and stood facing Christian. "Why are you doing that? He realized he sounded annoyed.

"Because he's a nice guy, that's why." Carly, one of the two full-time bartenders, chimed as she approached the bar with a bucket of ice.

You mean kid, thought Evan. He's a prima donna, just like his father, Evan thought. He wished he had been able to say the words aloud.

Christian answered for himself, obviously not intimidated by Evan, "Actually, I'm only a half hour early. I needed to share the car today, so I got a ride."

You mean your mother wouldn't let you borrow the car, thought Evan. "Of course," Evan replied. He smirked at Christian, hoping he noticed his sarcasm. Shit. Why did he let this kid bother him so much?

And what did he mean he was only half an hour early? Evan looked at his watch. 10:45 a.m. Lunch staff was required to come in between 11:15 and 11:30. How could that be, thought Evan? Did he really wander Rocky Neck for that long?

Evan replied, looking at his watch, "Right," not wanting to admit he had lost track of time while he was busy chasing down Nora. He felt embarrassed at his lack of self-control. He watched Christian for a moment, realizing that he probably wasn't helping Carly with his obvious lack of skills in citrus slicing. If he had been in a different state of mind, he would have admonished Christian for the poor job he was doing and would have shown him some proper technique. Where the hell did he learn to cut fruit anyway? Probably at home, where he practiced stocking the bar in their million-dollar mansion on the Back Shore, thought Evan.

He couldn't help himself. Evan picked up a mangled slice of lemon, looking at it for a long moment. He scanned the tray. No two pieces were the same size, some were twice as large as others were, and Christian had pressed down so carelessly that all of the lemon pieces had a smashed appearance. Evan dropped the lemon slice with an exaggerated motion. "Carly … you do your own side work from now on." He walked toward his office, not waiting for a reply.

As Evan reached his office door, his cell phone rang. He pulled it from his pocket, then looked down at the display to determine who was calling. Unavailable. Damn it. He hated when that happened. He liked being prepared. He thought about Nora, suddenly sure it was her calling him back. She would probably tell him she had just gotten in from grocery shopping or the dry cleaners.

"Hello?" His voice was impatient. Evan gripped the phone tightly as he heard the unexpected voice.

"Evan, what's going on? I called the office and Betty said she didn't know where you were. Isn't it almost the lunch rush?"

Evan's mother loved getting under his skin. She had an amazing knack for making him feel totally insecure. Every time he spoke to her, it was as if he was twelve again. He grimaced, trying to compose himself as he turned and made his way to the outside deck off the lounge. He opened one of the sliding glass doors and stepped out onto the deck facing the harbor as his mother continued her inquisition. Finally, he was allowed to speak.

"Mom, I had important things to do and Betty was tied up when I left. Everything is under control, as usual."

Evan heard the hesitation. "I don't know about that," she remarked sarcastically. "When *I* had the restaurant, I would never leave while deliveries were being made. And especially not right before lunch. What are you thinking? That's how you're going to get ripped off."

Evan fought the urge to reply sarcastically. Instead, he bit his tongue. He refused to let his mother know how she got under his skin.

She continued, "You should double-check your deliveries. You never know what those people may do."

By those *people*, his mother, AKA, the unpleasant Mrs. O'Neill, meant the staff. Evan had heard her accusations a thousand times. She trusted no one and had no faith in anyone's ability. And she was quite certain, as she had explained on many occasions, that human nature dictated that any one allowed the opportunity to steal, would. Though Evan was sometimes a cynic, he didn't subscribe to his mother's thinking. He truly believed in his staff, and in their innate honesty.

"Mother, please, that's none of your business," Evan whispered, his frustration showing for a brief moment.

He heard the other call as it beeped in, a welcome interruption to his mother's most recent attack. He pulled the phone away from his ear, and recognized Nora's cell number as it flashed on the screen. He had committed it to memory, as he had her home number. Evan spoke quickly, eager to get his mother off the phone. "I have to take this other call … it's important."

Evan switched to the other call, hanging up abruptly on his mother, something totally out of character for the good son, Evan. He felt a flash of regret, knowing there would be hell to pay later.

"This is Evan." He tried to sound professional yet casual … as if he didn't know who was on the other end. Evan remained on the deck, closing the sliding glass door behind him. Thank God, the lunch rush hadn't started yet. He wanted some privacy.

Nora tried to sound casual as she began to speak. "Hi, Evan, it's Nora. How are you?"

Evan answered politely, "I'm fine. What's going on?"

Nora replied, sounding a bit nervous, "I got your message. Tonight at The Bradford after work would be great. But we won't be done until late. Is that okay with you?" Nora knew that Evan didn't normally go out for cocktails at 11:30 at night, and he had probably never even had an espresso martini, as he had suggested.

"Sure, that'll be fine." He tried to sound cool. He changed the subject. "Hey, I'm in the middle of something. Are you home? Can I call you back?" He waited, hoping her answer would be yes.

Nora hesitated, "Actually, I'm running around doing a few things this morning, but I should be back home in about fifteen minutes. Then I'm heading into work."

"Right ... okay, then," he replied, wondering where she had been. "Why don't we just plan on it. How about if ... after you finish up tonight, you head home. I'll probably be fifteen minutes behind you ... I'll pick you up. At your place?"

"That sounds great," Nora replied.

Evan hesitated, "I'm sure we may run into other people from work ... which is fine. But how about if we play it casual ... like we just wanted to unwind after work?"

There was silence for a moment, and then Nora answered, unaffected by what Evan was trying to say. "Of course. I think that's a good idea. No one has to know ... our business."

Evan was relieved that Nora understood. "Great," he answered. "I'll see you when you get here."

Evan was flushed as he hung up the phone. He stood on the deck for a minute longer, trying to compose himself. Where had Nora been, and why didn't she just tell him if she had nothing to hide? Don't psyche yourself out, Evan reminded himself. You shouldn't make assumptions.

He walked back into the lounge, then crossed through the dining room. He passed the hostess station and pictured Nora and how she would look later tonight in the candlelit dining room. He was sure she would be beautiful.

The night went smoothly and the staff seemed to gel, Evan finally admitted at the end of the night. This was always a winning moment for a restaurant owner, especially on a holiday weekend. At the beginning of a season, you crossed your fingers and hoped that you had picked the right mix of reliability, experience, efficiency, and that star quality that always existed in one or two of the staff. And the staff seemed to be excellent so far. And as for star quality, this year, unfortunately for Evan, the star was going to be Christian. Evan had watched him expertly schmooze with the best of his patrons, women and men alike, while also priding himself on never spilling a cocktail or even a drop of the now-almost-famous "extra-large martinis" served at the Rocky Neck Grille. How, Evan asked himself, could a twenty-year-old who had only waited tables one season at an Irish pub be this good? Christian was definitely persuasive, realized Evan, and he added just the right amount of flirtatiousness and suggestiveness. Shit. He didn't like Christian at all … especially after watching him in action. But he knew the women did. And he wondered how Nora felt about him. Really felt about him.

Chapter 8

Evan looked at the clock for the thirtieth time and tried not to smile too widely as he realized he would be seeing Nora soon. She had left after finishing the dinner shift just ten minutes earlier. He had tried not to be overly friendly with her. She had looked gorgeous, as always, and she had worn a black sleeveless cocktail dress with a pearl choker necklace and stud earrings, her hair pulled back in a beautiful French twist. Evan sighed deeply, thinking about how overwhelmingly stunning she was to him. A vision, as his father would have referred to her and often referred to Audrey Hepburn in Breakfast at Tiffany's. Evan thought about his father, who had passed away almost ten years ago. Then his thoughts shifted to Nora, and the most minute details of her wardrobe, including the antique, pearl-trimmed combs that held back a few stray blond strands.

Evan looked at the clock. The entire staff had punched out, and he pulled the cash drawers from the two registers. He carried them into his office, anxious to count them and prepare the bank deposit for Betty's morning trip to the bank. As soon as he was finished, he grabbed his toothbrush, paste, and floss from his drawer, then made his way to the men's room. Though Evan would normally be dead tired at this time of night, he was as invigorated as a horny teenager, eagerly brushing and flossing to get ready for his date.

Evan checked his reflection in the mirror one more time. The black Banana Republic T-shirt with the tan chinos was a good choice, he admitted. He hoped it looked like he wasn't trying too hard. He wanted Nora so much, and he knew that it showed during their unexpected tryst on the boat. But Nora seemed to be enjoying this, too. Whatever it was. Evan didn't trust himself yet and swore that he wouldn't speculate or try to define this relationship until he saw Nora tonight.

As he drove to Nora's, he thought about whether or not he should ask her where she had been last night and this morning. No. Definitely not. He would not make the same mistakes he had made so many times before. This time he had to get it right. Evan pulled up directly in front of Nora's. He could hear her voice emanating from the back deck. He realized she was on the phone, so he made his way to the front door then knocked politely, half expecting that she wouldn't hear him. He waited and knocked a second time before he heard Nora's voice and her footsteps coming toward him.

"Coming ... I'll be right there." Nora stood at the front door, slightly breathless, phone in hand. "Sorry ... I was on the phone." Nora smiled then pushed the door open for Evan.

She turned toward the kitchen as Evan grabbed the screen door. "Let me just get my bag." He followed her into the kitchen then watched as she placed the phone back in its cradle and closed the back door. Nora seemed flustered. Evan couldn't help but hope that it was because she was excited to see him.

As Nora started walking past him, he impulsively leaned in toward her. He knew this wasn't in the least bit subtle, but he couldn't help himself.

"Nora", he whispered. "I missed you." Evan held her hips as he pressed softly into her. His lips parted as he kissed the nape of her neck. Nora closed her eyes, breathing deeply. Evan's lips were moist and warm, and he leaned in closer, kissing her slowly and deliberately, his thighs pressing against hers. Nora ran her hands along his muscular forearms then slid them down the small of his back. She continued, slipping her warm hands inside the back of his T-shirt and pulling him closer.

Evan's breath was heavy as he tried to control his arousal. He continued kissing her, first slowly, then faster and with more force. As he reached inside the hem of Nora's crisp periwinkle top, he slid his hand along her flat abdomen and up toward her eager awaiting breasts. He held his breath for a moment. Then he moved his fingers slowly back and forth over each breast. As he felt Nora's nipples tighten and become more erect, he thought about whether or not it would be wise to make love to her right now. He wanted to so badly, but he was unsure of Nora's feelings. Had their encounter just been a moment of weakness, or had it been something much more for both of them?

They were jolted out of their growing excitement as the phone rang, first once, then twice, then a third time. Evan stopped kissing Nora, pulling away slightly. "Are you going to answer that?"

Nora shook her head. "No. I'm not expecting any calls." She smiled devilishly. "I was only expecting you." She hesitated for a moment then grabbed Evan's hand, leading him up the narrow stairs to her bedroom. Evan thought about the phone call, wondering if it was the same person calling again.

Nora stood on the landing just outside her bedroom. She seemed unsure of herself, almost holding her breath as she thought about what they were doing. The light from the lamp on her nightstand illuminated the bedroom, casting a light orange glow on her soft skin.

She turned toward Evan, watching as he took a slow step toward her, his breath warm against her neck. Nora stepped back suddenly nervous but knowing she didn't want to stop. God, she thought. She desperately wanted Evan to make love to her. So much for playing it cool. Nora tried to compose herself, but she could only seem to whisper one word. "Evan," she breathed, her voice raspy. She grabbed his hand, cupping it inside hers as she looked into his eyes. "Evan, make love to me. I ... think that's what we both want."

Evan stroked Nora's hips with his strong hands, staring into her eyes for a long moment before taking her hand and walking her toward the bed. As they reached the nightstand, he stood behind her. He surveyed the long sweep of her neck then kissed it gently. She felt the immediate jolt of excitement. Evan leaned closer, his manhood a reminder of his eagerness as he pressed into her. The room was quiet, save for the sounds of their breathing. Nora turned, facing Evan for the first time since he had entered her bedroom. She placed her head on his chest, fearful that her eyes would disclose the emotion and passion he was invoking in her. He grabbed her chin lightly then tenderly kissed her moist full lips.

Evan hesitated for a second then let his hands pull gently at Nora's top, gliding it smoothly over her head. They stood in the softly lit room, each watching the other as they both slowly undressed. Nora reached behind her, smoothly undoing the clasp of her white silk bra. She slid the lace-adorned straps down over her shoulders as Evan watched. He reached forward, gently pulling out the two pearl combs that had been holding back Nora's hair in a smooth French Twist. He let the combs drop to the floor as he ran his eager hands through her thick, soft mane. His gaze swept Nora hungrily, first as he admired her perfectly round breasts, then down toward her taut stomach, and finally over her small hips and lean legs. Evan's breath quickened as she slowly unbuttoned her short linen skirt. As it fell to the floor, he held his breath. He focused on her white silk panties as they lay waiting for his touch.

Nora stood very still, watching Evan as he admired her. The hunger and passion in his eyes equaled hers. He grabbed at the hem of his T-shirt, pulling it over his head and dropping it casually to the floor. His lean chest and stomach called for her touch. Nora stepped toward him as he unbuckled his belt and pants, watching as they slid to the floor. The tingling sensation within her loins rose as she kissed him slowly, wrapping her arms around his now bare waist. Evan's passion grew as he pulled Nora closer. He kissed her with more force as each finished undressing the other. Nora felt herself lose control as they both abandoned their guard.

Evan continued kissing Nora passionately as he edged his way toward the bed. He slid his hand over the soft skin of Nora's belly, continuing downward, feeling the warmth as he spread her awaiting thighs. He heard her tender moan as she placed her arms around his neck, pulling herself up slightly. Evan's breathing quickened and became ragged as he felt himself slide deep inside her. They were frozen for a long moment, each taking in the unimaginable pleasure. Nora pressed closer, wrapping her legs around Evan's strong hips. He held Nora tightly as he lowered himself gently onto the bed on top of her.

As they resumed their intense kiss, their heavy breathing echoed in the silent room. Nora rocked her hips, teasing him, slowly at first, indulging in the pleasure she saw reflected in Evan's eyes. As their breathing became more labored, Evan matched Nora's rhythm. He indulged in the sensual feel as their moist warm skin made contact, their pace quickening and becoming more frenzied.

Nora stopped for a moment as she pushed Evan gently onto his back. She remained sitting up, watching him through half-open eyes, her pace suddenly quickening, her hips thrusting more forcefully. Evan reached up, softly cupping Nora's breasts. As she moaned, Evan teased her nipples, feeling the tautness between his eager fingers. Nora arched her back, her pleasure quickly edging toward its peak. She whispered in a raspy voice, "Yes ... Evan ... Yes."

Evan fought to control his passion. He wanted this to last forever ... and he wasn't ready for this dream to be over. He grabbed Nora's hips, stopping their motion as he waited in the hope of catching his breath. Nora opened her eyes.

"Wait", whispered Evan. She fought to slow her ragged breathing. She looked into Evan's eyes, knowing at that moment that she was falling in love with him.

He gazed back intently into Nora's eyes. He wanted to tell her how he felt. But he didn't dare. Instead, he rolled her onto her back, sliding her gently onto one of the pillows. He lay tenderly on top of Nora for a long moment, leaning on his elbows so that he could look into her eyes.

Evan felt the ocean breeze as it cooled his moist, searing skin. As he felt the welcome shiver, he was reminded of the windows that had stayed open all night. He willed himself not to question where Nora had been. Evan forced the thoughts from his mind as he watched her lean forward. She placed her slightly swollen lips gently on his. She kissed him, softly at first. Evan's tongue teased hers. When she could stand it no longer, Nora placed her hands on Evan's hips as she guided his excited member deep inside her once more. She felt his deliberately slow thrusting. Nora moaned softly, "Evan, please." She felt so close to him, and she wanted to tell him everything. His thrusts quickened as her body began to shake with her orgasm. He pushed deeper inside her, wanting to fill her, his breathing becoming more labored.

"Nora ..." Evan felt the enormous release as his body shook with pleasure. "Yes ... yes." Evan slowed his movements as he held Nora closely, not wanting this moment to be over.

They lay in each other's arms listening to the wind and sounds of the ocean, its miniscule waves touching lightly on the rocky shore.

"Nora," Evan whispered. He waited a moment, not hearing a reply, just light breathing. "Nora?"

"Sorry," Nora answered groggily. "I must have dozed off."

"I wasn't sure if you were awake." Evan looked at the alarm clock glowing on the dresser across the room. "It's almost one." He smiled. "I think we missed last call at The Bradford."

"It was worth it," Nora replied playfully.

Evan's tone seemed to become serious. "I … should be going."

Nora sat up slightly, surprised that Evan would want to leave. "Oh." She added, obviously disappointed. "Sure." Nora didn't like how this was going suddenly. She didn't want this to happen. Why were they trying so hard to play it cool, constantly second-guessing each other? They had just made passionate love, for God's sake. And now he was going to leave. Nora pulled Evan closer, realizing she would have to tell him soon how she felt. She whispered sincerely, "Stay."

Evan lay on his back and pulled Nora effortlessly onto him.

"What?" Evan teased. "Tell me what you want."

"I … " Nora's voice trailed. She was embarrassed, though she knew Evan was playing with her. They laughed softly, breaking the tension, as Nora started kissing his chest lightly and then moved toward his hard stomach. Her soft kisses became deliberate sensual licks as she realized how aroused they both were becoming again.

Nora thought about the evening's unexpected turn. Though the plan had gotten off course, she prayed that it would be all right. She couldn't deny that she really cared for Evan now. Not only had she been incredibly aroused by him tonight, but she was also certain she could fall in love with him. She was no longer in control. Not completely. And she knew she should be fearful of the unknown … and of the unexpected risk she was taking. But her fears quickly took a back seat to this passion … a passion Nora had never experienced. And to the pleasure that was fast overtaking her.

Chapter 9

Evan awoke to a wealth of fragrances as they wafted up the stairs from the kitchen. For a moment, he lay on his side, his eyes closed, thinking that he was dreaming about waking up in Nora's cottage after having made love to her. Evan smiled as he realized that it wasn't a dream. Unfortunately, panic set in as he sat up. He searched for the clock on the dresser. Evan secretly prayed that it was early enough so that he could spend the morning with Nora. 7:14 a.m. He didn't usually sleep this late, he thought. But then again, they hadn't gotten to sleep until after 2:30 a.m. Evan smiled again. He pulled himself away from thoughts of making love to Nora so that he could figure out his schedule for the day.

It was Saturday. Big kick-off to the summer. He thought about how crazy the restaurant would be, as it had been the last two years for the Fourth of July weekend. Okay, he reasoned. It isn't that late. If he went right to work from here and just stopped at the boat to shower and change, then he could stay with Nora until about 9:00 a.m. That left him almost two hours. Evan sat up, throwing his legs over the side of the bed. He looked around admiringly at how warm and inviting Nora had made the room. The sun shone through the lightly billowing lace panels onto the weathered wide pine floors, and even the hand made quilt on the bed coordinated perfectly with the antique tan striped wallpaper.

As he stood up, he anguished over what he should wear. If he got completely dressed, it would say to Nora that he was done and was ready to leave. But if he went downstairs in just his boxers, then it would almost seem disrespectful. Evan slipped on his pants, without the boxers or leather belt, and opted to leave his T-shirt on the floor for now. As he walked down the stairs, he caught a glimpse of himself in a small antique mirror. He tried to straighten his hair by running his fingers through it then headed straight into the downstairs bathroom, which was across the hall from the kitchen.

After he used the toilet and washed his hands, he quietly opened Nora's bathroom cabinet and searched for toothpaste. No toothbrush or toothpaste. Maybe she kept it somewhere else. Evan made do by gargling with some mouthwash he found instead. As he left the bathroom, he crossed into the doorway of the kitchen, where he saw Nora, her back to the door. Evan stood quietly for a moment, taking in the vision of Nora preparing him breakfast. This is how his life would be if he and Nora were married, he thought.

He slowly walked up to her as she stood in front of the stove. As he approached her, Nora put down the tongs she had been using to turn the French Toast and turned toward him. She smiled without hesitation and wrapped her arms around his waist. "Good morning," she said softly, kissing him gently on the lips. "Mmmmm, minty fresh", Nora crooned.

Evan was so relieved that it wasn't all just a dream and that Nora was obviously happy he had spent the night. "I hope you don't mind," he explained, "I wanted to brush my teeth and I didn't come prepared, so I used some of your mouth wash. I was looking for toothpaste, but I couldn't find any."

Nora had pulled away from Evan so that she could turn the French Toast.

"Oh, yeah, sorry. I took my toothbrush and toothpaste to work yesterday so I could have it for freshening up.

Evan replied instantly, "I know what you mean, I like to have mine at work, too."

He looked out toward the deck and noticed how beautifully the table was set. Black-eyed Susans filled a blue ceramic pitcher on the table, and a sunny yellow and blue tablecloth framed the periwinkle blue bowls, plates, and coffee mugs. Evan looked back toward Nora. She was amazingly gorgeous, her skin gleaming, her short white silk robe loosely tied and slightly revealing her tanned breasts. Her hair was up in a loose French twist, and her bare feet were slightly tanned and displayed her fresh pedicure. Evan noticed this was a more casual look for Nora, but it was one he instantly loved. It seemed so genuine, so natural.

"Wow," Evan whispered, his voice catching in his suddenly raspy throat. He seemed embarrassed as he admired her, realizing he had just verbalized his thoughts.

Nora seemed flattered, and she smiled.

Evan tried to recover, "I mean, everything smells so fantastic. What are you making?"

Nora placed the last of the French Toast onto a white platter and grabbed a ceramic bowl and matching mini ladle. The contents of the warm bowl were steaming and smelled of warmed blueberries in syrup. "French Toast a la Nora, of course."

Evan nodded his approval. "I'm a lucky man." He held out his hand, offering his assistance in bringing out the remaining serving plates. As he walked outside, he eyed the two glass pitchers, one filled with freshly squeezed orange juice, and the other filled with tomato juice. "Could I pour you some juice?" He asked.

"Yes, please, I'll take orange."

Evan poured Nora her juice then filled his own with the tomato. He breathed deeply as she poured them both coffee from a silver carafe. The fragrance was a deep French roast, akin to being in a country bakery in the early morning hours.

He grabbed his coffee mug and took a long sip then looked at Nora across the table, "I need to know something … " His words trailed, and suddenly Nora was concerned.

Evan continued, "Now that you've taken advantage of me … what are your intentions?"

Nora looked intently at Evan, trying to decide if he was serious. Just then, he smiled and put his hand on hers. She had never seen this side of him. He was self-assured and relaxed.

"What would you like my intentions to be?" Nora asked jokingly.

"Well, I'd like us to see each other," he replied. This time he sounded more serious than he had intended. There was a pause.

"Me, too," replied Nora. She was careful to try to keep it light. This was such a refreshing side of Evan, and she didn't want to ruin it. Not that she wanted him to take her lightly, either. But she felt she didn't have to worry about that with Evan. He would always take her seriously, and besides that, she was starting to believe that he was falling in love with her, as she was with him.

Evan enjoyed every bite of his breakfast. Once they were both finished, he took a long sip of his juice then looked up, "Do you have lemon or lime?"

"Sure, I have both. They're in the fridge."

Evan got up. "Can I get that for you?" He grabbed the plates and carried them into the house, depositing them into the sink. Then he opened the fridge, searching for the lemon and lime. He gave the interior a quick once over, then spotted the white ramekin. As he picked it up, pulling it toward him, he stared inside past the wrinkled plastic wrap. He uncovered it and stared at the crudely chopped and mashed pieces of lemon and lime.

Not like her, thought Evan. He carried the container outside and placed it on the table. As Evan seated himself, Nora looked down, spotting the ramekin and citrus slices inside. She pulled the dish toward her, quickly covering it and setting it aside.

"Evan, what time do you have to leave?"

"Well," he tried to think of the right answer. "It depends on what time it is now and what you had in mind."

Nora pushed her seat back and walked over to him quickly. She motioned Evan to push his chair back. As he did so, Nora slipped onto his lap. She proceeded to kiss him, teasing him. As she continued, she wrapped her arms around his neck, sliding one down his muscular chest. She could feel how aroused he had become in those few short moments.

Evan slid his hands over Nora's smooth robe, gently caressing her hips. He forced himself to stop kissing her. Then he pulled back slightly and took a deep breath.

"I think I should head over to the boat and get cleaned up for work."

"You can get cleaned up here," Nora replied. She stood up and grabbed Evan's hand. "Come on. Last night you told me what you wanted. Now, it's my turn."

Nora leaned forward and whispered, "Please."

Evan liked the slight pleading in Nora's voice and didn't intend to contradict her. As he followed her past the table, he quickly glanced down at the ramekin containing the lemon and lime slices. He would have to have his tomato juice a little later, he thought.

He followed Nora upstairs, expecting that she would be leading him into the bedroom. Instead, she walked to the far corner and into a small master bath. Evan hadn't been in this room of the house before. Up until now, he hadn't even known it existed. He scanned the bathroom, marveling at how different it was from the rest of the house. Everything was a shade of sage green or off white, and there were at least half a dozen white pillar candles placed carefully on shelves and on the long counter to the left of the sink.

Nora opened the glass door to the large walk-in shower and turned on the water. Immediately, the room started to steam up. She took off her robe and hung it on a hook beside the shower door. Evan held his breath as he marveled at how naturally beautiful she was. He followed her with his eyes as she slowly and deliberately walked around the room, lighting each of the candles.

The closed white plantation shutters on the bathroom's only window kept the room quite dark. As the steam continued to rise and gather, it created a soft billowing light. Nora faced Evan and watched as he unbuttoned his pants and allowed them to fall to the floor. She leaned in, kissing his lips. Then she stepped away, walked toward the shower and started adjusting the water temperature.

"Do you like it hot?" Nora asked teasingly.

Evan was immediately beside her, completely aroused by the steam, the heat, and by her brazenness.

"Yes, I do," he answered as Nora closed the glass door.

"Tell me what you want," Nora asked.

"You already know," replied Evan.

*   *   *

Nora tied her robe and left the bathroom, careful to close the door so that it would remain steamy and warm for Evan. As she entered the kitchen, she remembered the mashed citrus pieces that she needed to replace. She opened the refrigerator, seeing the empty bowl where she usually stored her lemons and limes. Damn him, thought Nora. Why didn't Christian tell me he used the last of them? She leaned on the counter, thinking about Christian for a brief moment as she grabbed a blank note pad and pen.

"That must be some list you're working on," Evan commented. Nora turned abruptly, apparently startled.

"Evan, I'm sorry, I was working on my grocery list."

Evan walked over to Nora, then stood in front of her.

"I need to go, but how about that tomato juice first?"

Nora inhaled the scent of Ivory soap. She smiled, openly admiring Evan, whose rugged masculinity suddenly seemed so apparent. She was surprised, she admitted to herself, at how attracted she was to him now. Nora followed Evan outside. The weather had changed considerably since yesterday, and it was now extremely warm, as evidenced by the condensation on the two glass pitchers as they moistened the cotton tablecloth.

"Can I pour you a fresh glass of juice? That one's probably warm," Nora noted.

Evan removed the plastic from the ramekin containing the lemon and lime slices and removed a large mashed lemon chunk. He held it up, amused, and looked at Nora.

"No, it's fine, I've got to be quick any way."

Nora sat down, watching Evan as he attempted to squeeze the mangled piece of lemon. He took one sip of his juice, realizing it was too warm. He put the glass down as he spoke, "Looks like you need some new knives. Were you trying to kill that citrus or just maim it?" Nora chuckled nervously. Evan stood and reached over to kiss Nora as she started to stand.

"Don't get up. I'll see you later. Oh … and don't forget we have an early meeting today," he stated in a soft voice. Evan turned and walked through the house, realizing it was getting late. He opened the screen door and let it slam behind him. As he got into his vehicle, he looked up, realizing that Nora was standing in the doorway, watching him. As he drove away, Evan sighed uneasily as he thought about Nora's sudden nervousness. He headed toward the boat, parked the SUV and sat for a moment. He replayed the morning's events, smiling until he thought about Christian cutting lemons and limes at his bar. Yes, he had been there, admitted Evan. Christian had been in Nora's house. He glanced at his watched then rushed toward the boat to get ready. Try not to jump to conclusions, he warned himself. Evan felt unsettled, knowing what he didn't want to admit. Christian, as self-serving as he appeared to be, would have been in Nora's house for one reason, and one reason only. His heart sank. The insecure feeling he had fought to control all his life was now stronger than ever. "Stupid," he mumbled to himself. His emotions turned to anger. He continued to prepare for work, ignoring the warning bells as they went off in his head. He chose a light blue Brooks Brothers oxford shirt and pleated tan cotton pants then took a long, critical look in the mirror closest to the doorway. It was going to be a big weekend, and he wanted to look the part of the confident business owner. His smart white and navy blue striped tie coordinated perfectly with his shirt and pants, and his dark brown leather loafers completed the look. He was ready. Evan took a deep breath, knowing that he couldn't take the time right now to think about her. She had lied to him, and for that, she would be sorry.

Chapter 10

Evan walked through the kitchen of the restaurant, taking comfort in the familiar sights and sounds. It was 9:02 a.m., and he had a lot to do before his first meeting at 11:00. He stopped and spoke with his Chef, Kevin, for a minute as vendors hurriedly came in and out through the back door with the weekend's deliveries.

"Just a reminder that after the meeting I'll have you talk to the wait staff about the new weekend specials. I'm also going to talk about who we're expecting as VIP's this weekend."

Kevin nodded, "No problem."

Evan was glad that he still seemed calm for his first big weekend. He nodded then proceeded toward his office. For the first time in his life, he thought about having a drink before lunch to soothe his frazzled nerves. No, he thought, he would not. He would never be like his mother. He could handle it, and he would manage his disappointment as he always had, with control and diplomacy. He wasn't going to let Nora know that he cared. Evan took a deep breath and forced himself to walk over to the mirror hanging on the back of his office door.

He stood in front of it, taking in his appearance. For one of the first times in his life, he saw himself, as he wanted to be seen by others, with a confidence and strength that he had always lacked. He was finally his own man, not a boy living in his mother's shadow.

As Betty walked in, Evan finished his review and sat at his desk. "Good morning," he replied.

She answered eagerly, "Good mornin'," in her thick smoker's voice. Evan knew he had been avoiding Betty lately, but he didn't want to get involved in her personal problems. Besides, he reminded himself, she was the strongest person he knew, and like his mother, she seemed to be able to handle anything life threw her way.

Evan excused himself and walked through the restaurant and into the lounge. As his cell phone rang, he realized he hadn't checked his messages since late yesterday afternoon. He answered, not checking the caller ID. "Yes?" Evan felt his newfound confidence wane as he heard his mother's shrieking voice on the other end.

"Evan, where have you been?"

He knew that he didn't want to deal with one of his mother's abusive interrogations today. It was unpleasant enough when he was having a good day. But not today. Evan held the phone away from his ear as his mother rambled on.

"Why haven't you been answering your cell phone?" She continued. "Do you know that the Wells family wants to come in for dinner tonight at 7:30? They need to be assured they'll be getting the best table."

Apparently, Mrs. Eugenia Wells had called her last night while they were out and had left an urgent message that she and her husband were expecting important friends in town for the weekend and needed the best table for dinner. Tonight. Of course, thought Evan. "Mother, I've been having trouble with my phone, and I haven't been able to access my calls for the last day and a half." Evan was proud of himself for thinking on his feet with his mother, for once in his life.

The distinguished Mrs. O'Neill was speechless. "Okay, well then. Could you just be sure to fit them in, please? The best table, at 7:30 tonight, for four. Oh, and don't have their son, Christian, wait on them. That would be embarrassing, of course."

Evan's mind wandered for a moment as he fantasized about humiliating Christian. But he couldn't do that. It wouldn't be professional.

"Yes, mother," Evan answered in a very annoyed voice. I'll take care of it. I need to go. Bye."

Mrs. O'Neill stared at the phone for a moment and thought about Evan. Why was he acting so strangely? This was not like him at all. Perhaps it was because he had hired all those crazy out-of-towners. And he was probably stressed because they were stealing from him. Evan's mother began dialing the Wells residence in order to assure them that their table was reserved. Thank God for other people like her, she thought. The others were all just tourists and barbarians.

Evan sighed and wrote a note to himself regarding the Wells party. Although they were already overbooked, he knew that he could make it work, as he always did. He wanted to put this reservation in the book immediately.

As he walked toward the hostess station, he saw Nora and Remy standing together at the podium carefully going over the reservations for the evening. He knew this would be a long day for everyone. Saturday of Fourth of July weekend always was. Most of his staff would be working a double shift today, but he would reward all of them with a great end-of-summer party as he had for the last two years since becoming the new owner of the restaurant. That was something his mother just never understood. Good shifts, good compensation, and a good environment meant good employees … for the most part.

Evan felt himself getting nervous as he approached. As he reached them, Nora looked up, smiling widely. Evan thought about Christian. He tried to veil his disgust, not wanting Nora to know how strongly he felt about her. He watched her smile, wondering if she had smiled at Christian like that before sleeping with him.

"Ladies," he asked. "Could you put this VIP in the book for tonight at 7:30, please? We're booked, but if we need to have someone else wait, let's just comp them with a round of cocktails, ok? Oh, and, make sure you don't seat them in Christian's section. They're his parents."

Remy rolled her eyes as Evan walked away. "Okay," replied Nora. "I'll take care of it."

Nora wanted to tell Evan she had had a great time last night, but not only was Remy standing beside her, but Evan seemed annoyed and all business. She placed the bright orange post-it note directly into the book aligned with the 7:30 reservation space. She was sure she and Remy could juggle tonight's schedule. They would just have to smile alot, and get their customers drinking early. Nora closed the reservation book then headed toward the lounge in order to grab a glass of water before the meeting started. As she approached the bar, she could see Christian leaning over it, pouring a ginger ale for himself. He looked up, giving Nora a knowing grin.

Christian looked gorgeous, as usual, thought Nora. He had on his regulation white oxford, black pants, and black apron. But, damn, she admitted, he was definitely a Ralph Lauren model in the flesh. Christian's hair had lightened from his daily morning sails just off Good Harbor Beach, and his sunburn was just beginning to turn a deep golden brown. He had also started keeping a trimmed five o'clock shadow, making him look sexy and slightly dangerous, like the bad boy he knew he was and always wanted to be.

Normally, Evan would have commented about Christian's need to shave, but as much as he hated the look, he admitted that his customers, from the eager twenty-somethings to the seasoned retirees from the club, all adored his new look. Evan witnessed their school girl flirtations on a daily basis. And he also knew that Christian's admirers had been ordering twenty percent more in drinks than any of his other patrons, consistently, over the last two months since Christian had started. Evan sighed to himself, knowing that he would have to veil his dislike for him, especially since he was becoming such a valued employee. And a star waiter, especially to the ladies.

Christian turned to Nora and whispered in her ear. "Hey, my parents are going away on Sunday, and I'm throwing a party. Why don't you come over?"

Nora could feel Evan looking at her, and she immediately became flushed.

"Thanks, but I have to work Sunday."

"That's okay," he replied quickly. Come afterwards, it's going to start late."

Nora began to reply but stopped as she saw that the meeting was getting under way. She wanted to move in order to distance herself from Christian as well as Evan's scathing look, but the meeting was starting and all the seats were taken. Nora watched as Evan looked around the room and began to speak.

"Hey, everyone, it's going to be a long, crazy weekend, but I know we can work together and pull it off successfully."

Nora noticed that Evan seemed more confident than she had ever seen him. He certainly looked assured. She thought about last night and this morning. And she thought it had gone really well. Why did he seem so agitated?

Evan talked about the weekend and the expected VIP's, and then

Kevin talked about the specials. Nora's mind wandered. How was she going to tell Christian that he needed to back off? She was still angry with him for stopping by the night before last. And what infuriated her more is what had happened afterward. She needed to get control of herself.

If this all fell apart, she might have to face moving again, and she definitely didn't want that. She really liked it here. There was something about this town that felt like a real home, the kind of home Nora had always wanted and imagined. And then there was Evan. Nora admitted that she was falling in love with him. But she was afraid. She wanted the relationship to happen, but she didn't want to be in love. That would only lead to total loss of control and heartache. It was so much easier if you weren't in love, she reminded herself.

Nora looked up only to realize that the meeting had ended and everyone had left the room except for her and Evan. He was leaning over a table and quickly jotting down his notes. She stood, frozen, not knowing what to say. As she started to walk toward him, Remy entered the room.

Nora watched as Remy made her way toward Evan, her glistening dark brown hair shimmering in the sunlight and swinging over her shoulders as she walked. Though she looked younger, Nora estimated that Remy was in her early-to- mid thirties. Her stylish black eyeglasses accentuated her sexuality somehow, and her tasteful and expensive clothing accentuated her fit body.

Nora admired Remy's ensemble, which consisted of a slightly sheer short sleeve white linen top Nora had seen in the Banana Republic catalog. She had coordinated it, effortlessly of course, with fitted black Capri pants. And Nora openly envied her shoes, which were devastatingly high-heeled, low-cut black pumps which revealed the tops of her tanned, silken-looking feet. God, thought Nora, even her feet were perfect.

As Remy walked toward Evan, Nora thought about her. What was her deal, exactly? Nora had heard rumors, including that she had moved from San Francisco to avoid something or other. She hadn't paid too much attention until now. So the rest was a mystery, since Nora didn't try very hard to get to know other women. Not usually. Unless she needed something, that is. Nora had also heard that Remy lived somewhere downtown in a loft, but as far as she knew, Remy kept to herself and didn't really know anyone very well, except when she'd go out occasionally with the crew. She was always polite to the staff as well as the customers, but today Nora saw her first display of rage and frustration.

She thought about Remy's very obvious annoyance as Evan notified them of the special arrangements for Christian's parents. So, she doesn't like Christian. Still, that was nothing. Alot of people didn't like Christian. He has a lot going for him … and he is also arrogant, thought Nora. Not with her, Nora admitted, not really. Just some flirting. But she had heard the remarks. Money, lots of money, a mansion … and good looks. No wonder he was cocky. She knew she would be too, if by some miracle she were ever in his shoes. Nora should be so lucky.

She thought about Remy again as she waited for her to finish talking to Evan. She pondered the obvious question. Was Remy running away from an old boyfriend? Or a husband or soon-to-be ex-husband? Why had she left San Francisco? And how had she ended up on Rocky Neck? If Nora ever learned to trust women, she probably would choose Remy, who seemed to have a genuine air about her. And, in some ways, they seemed alot alike. But Nora trusted women even less than she trusted men. They would stab you in the back without a moment's notice. You don't need girlfriends, Nora reminded herself. And you definitely don't need to tell anyone your secrets. Nora was jolted back to reality as she heard Evan slam his fist down on the table in front of Remy. She was surprised and slightly alarmed.

"Remy, last time I checked," Evan yelled, "*I* was in charge. And I'm telling you, that we will find a place for the Wells reservation at 7:30."

Remy refused to back down. "That's fine in theory, but we've given away all of the *good tables*, and we'll never hear the end of it if the *Wells* party ends up sitting next to the hostess station or near the bathroom hallway."

Evan rubbed his hands together in an agitated manner as he spoke. "I appreciate your wanting to accommodate everyone, but the truth is that we can't. Let's move someone else if we have to. If someone has to wait too long tonight, they'll complain, and we'll deal with it when it comes up. It's Fourth of July weekend, for God's sake. People must realize that," he said, obviously frustrated.

Remy turned away abruptly and headed for the bathroom. Nora hesitated then started following her, reasoning that she should make sure Remy was going to be okay for her shift. But Nora did feel badly, she admitted as she rushed after her. Especially since Evan was definitely out of line and acting like an ass.

Nora walked into the bathroom and ran the water while she thought about what to say. As she turned off the faucet and pulled out a paper towel from the dispenser, she walked slowly up to the stall in which Remy was hiding. Luckily, the one next door was empty.

"Remy", Nora whispered softly, "It's Nora. I just wanted to make sure you were okay." Silence followed. No movement from the stall, either. Nora walked up to the door and leaned closer so that she wouldn't have to raise her voice. "Remy", she whispered again. Hey, I'm coming in."

Remy still didn't respond. As Nora slowly pushed open the door, she saw Remy, arms crossed and head down, leaning against the stall. Nora thought she was crying. She stepped inside, then closed the door and locked it behind her.

"Hey," Nora said as she leaned toward Remy. "Don't feel bad. Evan can definitely be a prick sometimes. Trust me, I don't think it was really directed at you."

As Remy looked up, she put her arms around Nora's neck. Nora stood, stiff and shocked, wondering what her reaction should be. Nora reluctantly put her arms around Remy, awkward in her efforts as she halfheartedly patted her back in an attempt to comfort her.

"Hey, it's alright, Nora assured her. "Evan will be fine. He just has alot going on. He'll feel better once Monday afternoon rolls around and the long weekend is over."

Remy held onto Nora and didn't say a word for a moment, then she replied. "It's not Evan," she explained. I've worked with my share of bastards in my lifetime, and believe me, he's not one of them."

Nora pulled away as she looked at Remy and tried to understand her. Remy continued to hold on as she unconsciously stroked Nora's hair with her right hand.

"It's that pain in the ass, Christian." Remy explained. "Why is it that, wherever I go, there's some privileged uptight-and-white asshole who expects to have everything handed to him?"

Nora looked at Remy with a look of surprise, not because Remy was wrong. In fact, Nora agreed with her, but more than that, it was because Remy never had a bad word to say about anyone. Why had Christian gotten under her skin?

Nora thought for a moment then replied. "Hey, that pain in the ass will be out of here soon. After the summer, we'll have the whole place to ourselves." Nora waited a moment, wondering if her attempt at humor was working. She added, "Christian's clueless sometimes. He's just used to girls throwing their legs up in the air as soon as they see him. He'll eventually marry some frigid society page bitch that'll get fat right after the big wedding. Don't worry, he'll get his."

Remy leaned back, smiling. She kissed Nora lightly on the cheek. Nora blushed and tried to pull away casually so that Remy wouldn't see her discomfort. As Remy opened the door and followed Nora out of the stall toward the sink area, she dabbed at her eyes and smoothed her hair. "Thanks. It's nice to know I have a friend here. You know I don't really know too many people yet, and it's been a little lonely. Would you want to have dinner some time?"

Nora didn't know quite how to reply. She wasn't accustomed to spending much time in the company of other women. "Sure," she answered. "We could do that. Now, let's get this weekend over with."

As they headed back into the lounge, Nora remarked, "God, we're going to need a cocktail by tonight."

Remy nodded, "No shit."

Nora was surprised. She liked Remy already.

Lunch went as well as could be expected, thought Evan. Considering there were three times as many hungry tourists as was the usual for a Saturday lunch shift during the summer. Somehow, though, it had worked out. The cocktails had flowed at the bar, and Carly, the head bartender, had lost count after she made what seemed to be her one hundredth Apple Martini. Kevin was happy with his Sous Chef and kitchen staff so far, and Evan finally allowed himself a deep breath.

Nora looked at her watch. 3:30 p.m. She hadn't had anything to eat since this morning, and she was hoping that Evan would show up soon to relieve her. He was going to let both her and Remy take off until 5:00 p.m. He would man the hostess station himself during their break. Nora reached down onto the shelf at the podium for her purse.

As she retrieved it and straightened up, she watched Evan as he walked toward her.

"Hi, what did you think of lunch? It seemed to go well, don't you think?" Nora asked.

Evan got very close and looked into her eyes. "Yes," he replied quickly. Let's just keep our fingers crossed for dinner," he added dryly. "You can go now. Why don't you and Remy come back at 5:00." Evan looked down at a menu, too busy to make any additional conversation.

Nora was annoyed. Why was he being so matter-of-fact with her? Was it because of that little episode with Remy this morning? What the hell was wrong with him? Normally, she got a much better reception after she slept with someone. Except that this time, it wasn't just sleeping with someone. It had definitely been more than that. Maybe he can't handle it, she thought. Nora tried to hide her agitation. She grabbed her purse and headed toward the bathroom so she could wash her hands and check her makeup before heading home.

As she pushed the door open, Remy was exiting, and they almost ran directly into each other. They smiled politely as Remy asked, "Hey, are you here to save me again?"

Nora was surprised by Remy's joking and level of familiarity with her, something she wasn't accustomed to. "Yeah," replied Nora, "Evan sent me in here to look for you."

They both smiled again and stood awkwardly in the doorway.

Remy spoke first. "Hey, Evan had said he was going to let us take off before dinner. Has he cut us yet?"

Nora answered. "Actually, he just told me we could go but that we should be back at 5:00."

Remy looked down at the floor. "Okay, that's great," She said in a disappointed voice. "Too bad I don't live closer. It's going to take me twenty minutes to get home and twenty minutes to get back with all the traffic. It's almost not worth it," Remy explained. "Maybe I'll just hang out here."

Nora knew that Remy was hinting about coming over, and if she were a guy or if Nora knew her better, then she would have felt more comfortable extending the invitation. Still, she couldn't just make her stay in the restaurant by herself. Evan would put her to work.

"Why don't you come over, and we can hang out on the back deck and soak up some sun for a little while?"

Remy smiled brightly and seemed appreciative. "Great." She followed Nora out of the bathroom, through the lounge, and into the sunny artist and tourist-filled street. They walked together past the newly painted artists' galleries.

"I live right down the street," Nora explained. As they walked by The Rowboat, they could see that the staff was preparing dinner. They peered through the open door and into the lounge area, longing to be inside. The gleaming bar, which looked as if it had been built hundreds of years ago in the days of hard-drinking and wealthy sea captains, was stocked with trays of fruit and garnishes ready for the evening. The overflowing stainless trays with their rectangular sections displayed over-sized pimento stuffed olives, carefully arranged lemon, lime and orange wedges, as well as maraschino cherries. There were hundreds of white cocktail napkins, perfectly stacked in neat rows at the edge of the bar and placed on the counter in front of each tufted and worn leather barstool. The shining stacks of heavy water glasses, along with frosted water pitchers filled to the brim, were positioned strategically at several stations along the bar.

The statuesque bartender, who wore a straight, perfectly combed ponytail and a green and white tropical print shirt, smiled as they lingered by the door.

Nora and Remy glanced at each other, both obviously having the same thought. Wouldn't it be nice to unwind and have a huge martini right about now? Remy grabbed Nora's wrist. "Let's go. Just one, I'm thirsty, and I'm buying," she led Nora inside, not giving her a chance to object.

Damn thought Nora. Tonight is going to be so busy, and I haven't even eaten lunch. She followed Remy without a protest like a schoolgirl being led off to smoke her first cigarette. They climbed onto the cool, soft leather seats of the overstuffed barstools. Instantly, Nora felt a calm spread through her.

Remy smiled at the bartender. "Hi, I'm Remy and this is Nora. We work at the Rocky Neck Grille and we're taking a quick … um, mental break."

Nora chimed in, "Before it gets crazy tonight."

The bartender smiled widely, knowing exactly what they meant. "Hi, ladies, my name is Todd. What can I get for you?"

Remy motioned to Nora to order. "I'll have a KJ." Nora loved Kendall Jackson Chardonnay.

To that, Remy turned quickly in her chair. "Oh, Nora, come on, you need to relax ... for tonight, and that sure as hell isn't going to do it."

Remy turned toward Todd. "We'll have two Absolut Apple Martinis, not too sweet, please."

Nora started to say something and Remy looked over. "Yes?"

Nora gave her a questioning look. "Nothing." She cleared her throat. "That'll work for me."

Todd expertly mixed and poured the drinks, placing the very chilled and extremely full martini glasses in front of them. Remy carefully raised her glass to make a toast, making sure not too spill any of the light green liquid. Nora raised her glass as well, concentrating as she brought it toward her eagerly awaiting lips.

"To us," toasted Remy. They both motioned as if to toast, then quickly started drinking. As they each took a long sip, they breathed deeply of the fresh salty air that was rolling in through the rows of French doors separating the dining room from the outside deck.

Nora put down her glass, noticing that Remy was staring at her intently. It was making her feel like a silly schoolgirl.

"Nora, I know you don't know me yet but I was wondering ..." Remy purposely let her voice trail, hoping she could muster some curiosity from Nora. "Have you ever thought about dating a woman?"

Nora normally could figure people out in advance, but this time she had not been on the ball. "Actually, No I haven't." It was better to be right up front, thought Nora. Especially if Remy was hitting on her. She hadn't even been friends with any lesbians, but she had heard that they were pretty much strong-minded and could be down right intimidating.

"Okay ... sorry," Remy replied. "I have a friend, and she's not dating any one right now, and I thought ..." She saw the surprised expression on Nora's face, quickly adding, "Sorry," I didn't think so. But you never know."

They both laughed nervously as Nora blurted out, "God, Remy, I thought you were hitting on me for a minute. And we don't even know each other yet." Nora could see that Todd was listening intently as he pretended to clean the already perfectly polished bar.

"No, of course not," Remy teased. She paused then added, "Besides … you're not my type."

Nora had taken another long sip, and she almost spat out her drink.

Remy waited for Nora to absorb her bombshell. "I'll bet I surprised you … "

Nora looked over, suddenly feeling almost bad that she may have offended Remy. "No, it's not that. It's just that I haven't ever really known any women that … "

Remy decided to put Nora at ease. "That speak their minds?

Nora was grateful for Remy's compassion. "Yeah. That's it."

Remy looked up at Todd and held up her almost-empty glass until she caught his attention. "We'll have another round, please."

Nora didn't seem to mind. They remained for their last hour of freedom before heading back to work.

Chapter 11

Lucy Callahan had been to this spot every morning at 5:00 a.m. Every morning for the last four and a half years. She prepared for the stifling reality of working at the United States Post Office in Gloucester by making herself a strong cup of Green Mountain Nantucket Blend coffee and depositing it into her mug by 4:45 a.m. Then she would drive up to the street side of Good Harbor Beach, park her red Ford pickup truck, and walk the boardwalk-like ramp onto the beach where she would spend exactly thirty minutes taking in the beauty of Gloucester that the tourists almost always missed. Sundays were the only mornings when it was a little more relaxed. Not only because she got to go in an hour later to work, but also because she got to work the sorting area, which meant no tourists and no contact with the rest of the world.

Lucy's routine was to take her thermal coffee mug, amble down the walkway until her sensible postal regulation shoes hit sand, then she would meander near the shore and watch the sun rise as the seagulls flirted with the early morning waves. Occasionally, she would see a romantic couple or someone with a dog walk by, but most often, she was alone, which was how she liked it. On this day, however, which happened to be Sunday of Fourth of July weekend, the tone had been different from the start. Lucy always liked Sundays better than the rest of her workweek. Not only did she not have to wait on annoying tourists as well as impatient locals, but also she got to daydream about her upcoming two days off and how she would spend them.

Lucy had pulled up in anticipation of the morning's relaxing walk only to find a beaten up Volkswagen Jetta sitting right in front of the entrance to the beach. As she walked around the car, she intentionally tried to shoot the driver an annoyed look. As she did so, she couldn't help but notice that the male driver appeared extremely disheveled and the girl next to him appeared to be sleeping or passed out. Lucy vowed that she wouldn't let this annoying site mar her peaceful walk on the beach. She made her way around the nuisance and proceeded to breathe deeply as she walked down the long boardwalk-like path onto the beach. She stopped, as she always did, at the strong intersection between the rough-hewn boards and amazingly soft, cool sand.

As Lucy stepped onto the glistening grains, she looked up at the glowing pregnant sunrise. It was going to be an amazing day, weather wise, thought Lucy. The old adage she had been taught as a child swam through her mind playfully. "Red sky at night, sailors delight, red sky in the morning, sailors take warning." She eyed the sky, which was a robust bright orange, and she knew that it would be even more beautiful in a few moments. She wondered if the forecast would be right. Lucy looked at her watch. 5:15 a.m. She had about another half-hour, she thought. Then it would be back to the grind. Soon, she would be standing and sorting for hours, and her time would no longer be her own.

She rolled up her regulation navy blue cotton chinos so the cuffs wouldn't fill with sand then proceeded down to the shoreline as the boisterous seagulls called to her.

Lucy walked past the lifeguard chair and continued toward the small morning waves about 50 feet away. Out of the corner of her eye, she saw the large dark object as it flapped in the early-morning breeze. She was startled by the unusual shape and started to turn her head toward it so she could stare more closely. As she did so, Lucy cursed. Fuck those tourists, she thought. Why do they bring disgusting bags of garbage and then leave them on the beach? As she continued to walk toward the large flapping object, she thought about why some people had such disrespect for nature. It's the way they're raised, she thought. Jake and I would never leave trash on the beach. She thought about the annual camping trips that her parents had taken them on while growing up, and for a moment she smiled.

The shocking site was a stark contrast to the thoughts Lucy had just had of happy family vacations. She stood directly in front of the large mass, then bent over slightly to get a better look. It was as if she needed a moment so that her brain could accept what she was actually looking at. What she thought was a garbage bag was in fact a moth-eaten gray blanket, and peering out from the blanket was a perfectly tanned ankle and an expensive-looking brown leather shoe. She could see that the exposed ankle looked as if it were twisted in an unnatural direction and the shoe was half off.

Lucy stood up suddenly and stiffened as she allowed herself to realize that the mass underneath the blanket was a body. She hoped it wasn't a dead body. Lucy looked around. No one. She knew she shouldn't touch it but wanted to know if the person was alive. "Hello," she said loudly. "Hello?"

Lucy reached out reluctantly with her right foot and pushed on the mass with the toe of her shoe. It felt stiff and unmoving under her foot. She stumbled backwards, realizing that whoever it had been was probably dead. Dead. In his perfect leather shoes. She started running quickly toward her truck. Maybe that Volkswagen was still there and she could have them go for help. Stupid, she thought. If they had gone onto the beach, they either saw the body and didn't want to get involved or they had something to do with it. Neither was good. Lucy thought about the driver, his appearance extremely disheveled as if he had been in a fight.

She reached the street. The Volkswagen was gone. Her hands shook as she picked up her cell phone and dialed the police station. In her hurry to get back to the truck, she had spilled coffee all over her right hand, and she felt the stickiness as she held the phone to her ear. The operator answered in a matter-of-fact tone.

"Gloucester Police Department, your call is being recorded, how may I help you?"

Lucy gulped as she said the words. "Hi, this is Lucy Callahan, could I talk to my brother Jake? Jake Callahan?" Lucy sighed as she heard her brother's familiar and comforting voice. "Jake. Hey, it's Lucy." Lucy continued without letting her brother interrupt her. "I've, I've been out at Good Harbor, and you need to come right away. There's a guy on the beach. I think he's dead."

Lucy sat in her truck as she waited for the police to arrive. It had been a slow night for the force in Gloucester, Jake had explained. After he and his partner had shown up in their unmarked car, another four police cars appeared, all of them screeching to a halt dramatically as they pulled up to the entrance.

Jake got out of the passenger side and ran over to Lucy's truck. She got out and hugged her brother. "I think he's dead. He's over there by that lifeguard chair." Lucy pointed in the direction of the body.

Chapter 12

Nora lifted her head slowly, trying to focus. She lay on her stomach, not certain where she was until she surveyed the room. As she turned slightly to the left, she saw the familiar landscape of her bedside table. Phew, thought Nora. She was home. She sat up, slowly and painfully sliding her legs over the side of the bed as she strained to make out the time on her clock. 8:12 a.m. The pounding in her head almost overcame her. She stood slowly, feeling instantly off balance and lightheaded. She looked down nervously, trying to piece together last night's events. Relief overcame her as she looked down. She was still wearing her pale pink silk bra and matching panties. That was definitely a good sign. At least she hadn't slept with anyone. Thank God for small miracles. She eyed her knees curiously, noting that they were both scraped. One of the them bared a large splotch of dried blood.

She made her way to the toilet, sitting down slightly off center as she realized she was still feeling the effects of last night's drinking. Damn it, she thought. What the hell had happened? Nora held her head in her hands. The evening's events were unfolding slowly. She thought about the powerful martinis she'd had for lunch. She had gotten instantly buzzed, a lethal combination of too little food and too many cocktails. She remembered running home with Remy for a quick minute to freshen up and get rid of her alcohol breath.

Oh, that's right remembered Nora, I did have lunch. She thought about the handful of cashews she had swallowed just before she and Remy headed back to the restaurant for their evening shift.

They had practically sprinted on their way back, and as they entered the restaurant, both out of breath, they ran into Evan, who was standing impatiently at the hostess station, menus clenched in hand. Nora looked at the clock on the wall directly above him. It was 5:05 p.m. Slightly late. And for Evan, they may as well have been two hours late. Nora watched as he looked up at the clock, mumbling under his breath as they made their grand entrance. As if handing off his baton in a sprint, Evan started walking away as soon as they reached him. He spoke over his shoulder, "Time to get to work. And pay attention, please."

Nora and Remy exchanged a relieved look. At least he hadn't freaked out, thought Remy.

The rest of the night had been filled with the usual busy restaurant dilemmas of too many mouths to feed and not enough tables. But they had gotten through it all amazingly well. Nora suddenly remembered the Wells' reservation. And the drama. She stifled a laugh, enjoying the thought that the really rich got really drunk sometimes, too.

The evening's reservations and seatings had started out perfectly. The Wells party of four had arrived exactly at 7:30 p.m. And, by some divine intervention, exactly at that moment, the perfect table in the perfect section had miraculously opened up. Evan had smiled in relief as he personally seated them, in view of everyone, directly in front of a window in what Evan called the VIP section. The view was perfect, and it would be a perfect evening. He had breathed a sigh of relief. Until all hell broke loose.

Mrs. Eugenia Wells, once seated, had opened her rather large mouth. Nora had looked up, through the crowded restaurant, to see what appeared to be an argument between the waitress, Heidi, and Mrs. Wells. Before Nora could react, Heidi had turned away abruptly, walking briskly toward the hostess station.

"Heidi, what's wrong?" Nora panicked as she saw the tears well up in Heidi's eyes.

"That cow told me she didn't want me waiting on her because she doesn't like my sister," Heidi spit out loudly.

"She said that?" Nora asked incredulously.

"Well," Heidi went on as she imitated Mrs. Wells, "Aren't you that Cooper girl who has that sister with the illegitimate child?" Heidi imitated loudly. "Who even talks like that?" screeched Heidi. "That's what she said. She had the nerve to say that. Don't worry, I didn't tell her what I thought of her. I just said excuse me. But I'm not waiting on her!"

Nora responded immediately. "I'll handle this. Why don't you take a quick breather in the lounge … and get yourself a coke or something to drink. Okay? I'll be back in a minute after I straighten this out."

Christian had seen the exchange and quickly walked over to Nora at the hostess station. "What's going on with my folks?" he asked in an annoyed tone.

Nora answered as she started walking toward the table. "Nothing, I'll take care of it." As she reached them, Nora realized that Mrs. Wells was quite intoxicated. And Mr. Wells and the other couple were red faced, obviously embarrassed. Nora looked directly at Mrs. Wells.

"Hello, I'm Nora, the hostess. Is there a problem?" She looked around at each of them. Nora noticed that Mrs. Wells was struggling to focus on her as she answered.

"No, Nora, there is no probb-lem, I just want a drink, but that girl, who was rather unfffleasant, didn't seem to waaant to get me one. I eeeven tried to maaake small thalk with hhher," she slurred.

Nora looked at Mr. Wells. "Excuse me, Mr. Wells, could I speak with you for a moment at the hostess station, please?" She kept her eye contact on Mr. Wells as she waited for him to stand up.

Mr. Wells shot up quickly and followed Nora. As they reached the hostess station, he whispered. "Sorry, my wife has been having a hard time of it, and she shouldn't have had that martini at home, especially while she's on medication. I'm sure you understand. We'll just order dinner and it'll be fine."

Nora looked back toward the table. She thought that the distinguished Mrs. Wells had either had a lot more than one martini, or a lot more than one pill of whatever she was taking. She looked up at Mr. Wells and smiled knowingly, "Of course." She continued, "Mr. Wells, I am certain Mrs. Wells is just a bit under the weather, and we'll even be glad to make arrangements to get another waitperson, but I'm afraid we'll only be able to offer Mrs. Wells a non-alcoholic beverage. Will that be all right?" Nora wished Evan was nearby. She would have preferred that he handle this.

Mr. Wells turned on his heel, waiving Nora off impatiently. As she stood at the hostess station trying to locate Evan, she watched the distinguished Mrs. Wells and the other couple as they walked hurriedly past her and out the door without any further explanation. Mr. Wells followed, but stopped briefly, handing Nora a folded twenty. "That's for the waitress", he muttered. I'm sorry we can't stay, but we're going to take Mrs. Wells home."

Nora smiled, "I'm so sorry to hear that." She signaled Heidi from the lounge, as Evan approached, a look of panic on his face.

"What happened?" He asked, obviously distraught that they had somehow been offended.

Nora leaned in closely, whispering, "Mrs. Wells ... wasn't feeling well."

Evan made eye contact with her, "Oh, too bad." He gave Nora a knowing look, as if he had seen Mrs. Wells in that condition before.

The rest of the night had run smoothly, and then the entire exhausted and very thirsty crew, including Evan, had gone down to the Port Side to let off some steam and drink with the locals. Nora didn't remember much, but she did recall Evan's nasty behavior toward her as they all entered the Port Side. Even Betty had gone, at Evan's insistence. Betty seemed to be having a really tough time of it lately, and since her husband was away for the weekend visiting his sister in New Jersey, Evan thought it would be a good time to get her out to relax for a few hours.

Before leaving the Rocky Neck Grille, the staff had all gathered in the lounge, and Christian had started the trouble by ordering a round of shots of tequila for all the wait staff. As they finished their first round, Evan had walked in. Silence ensued as he looked around. He realized at that moment, that if he didn't allow them to let loose for a little while, they would do it anyway and would rebel by getting out of control. That meant that most of them would show up in a sorry state tomorrow, and Evan couldn't afford to have that happen on Sunday of Fourth of July weekend. He had thought about it for a quick moment, then had jumped in.

"I know you all had a long night, so how about if I take you all out for drinks, so long as you agree to call it a night by 1:00?"

The staff had become more jovial as they ordered one more shot. Evan panicked then thought about what the alternatives really were. He looked at the staff as he prepared to drink his first shot of tequila with them. "Here's to a great staff. Let's head out of here and down to the Port Side. Cheers!"

He had never seen drinks guzzled with such voracity. He knew how they felt. Happy to celebrate and let go of their frustrations. He also knew that it wasn't about working so hard. Rather, it was more about waiting on the idle rich and the hard-to-please tourists, all the while having to bite your tongue and pretend it didn't matter.

Evan started his Range Rover and waited in the parking lot for Carly, Remy, Nora, Kevin, and Christian, all who had volunteered to ride with him to the Port Side. As he watched the back doors open and his staff pile in, he thought about why he was really doing this. Because I want to keep an eye on them, he thought. They piled in, and Kevin slid into the passenger seat beside Evan, leaving the other four to squeeze into the back. As they did so, Nora was the last to enter. As she climbed in, Christian had practically picked her up, depositing her onto his own lap. Nora laughed nervously, causing Evan to clench his teeth as he watched her in the rear view mirror, her arms wrapped around Christian's neck. Evan was shocked, remaining speechless as they reached the bar. He sat in silence as the back doors opened forcefully and his thirsty staff piled out.

As he stepped out of the car, he heard Nora tell Christian, "I'll meet you inside."

She watched as Evan slammed his door closed, his frustration apparent. "That was quite a little show. I didn't realize you and Christian had gotten so cozy." Evan had enjoyed two shots of tequila, the obvious reason for his not holding back, Nora realized.

She stood motionless and shocked, as if someone had thrown cold water in her face. "What did I do, exactly? I didn't do anything wrong!" Nora remembered the words she had uttered. "Evan, I … I love you."

Evan seemed unimpressed. He looked at Nora in disgust. "Close your door so I can set the alarm, Nora. You never know what kind of lowlifes could be around here."

Nora slammed the door and walked away, tears filling her eyes. How could he treat her this way, she thought? What had she done to deserve this from Evan? As she reached the entrance to the dark and smoky bar, she heard Christian's call.

"Hey, Nora, over, here, sweetheart." Nora had been so upset. She followed his voice and made her way to his side at the bar. As she walked up beside him, she stumbled. Christian had reached out his long arms quickly, catching Nora and hugging her. As he did so, he whispered in her ear, "Hey, sweetheart, let me get you a cocktail."

Nora clung to Christian, as the rest of the evening became a huge blur. She remembered drinking her third tequila, after which she slightly recalled kissing Christian on the dance floor as the jukebox wailed out a Van Morrison tune. She struggled to remember the remains of the night. Shit. She could have been naked, for all she knew. Where had Evan gone? And how had she gotten home?

Nora stood at the mirror, eyeing her disheveled appearance. She splashed cold water on her face in an attempt to wake herself up. She thought about how busy work would be today and tonight and how she would have to make it through in this state ... extremely hung over. In a feeble attempt to wash off the mistakes of the previous night, she stepped into a too-hot shower. She scrubbed her skin almost raw, fearing the answers to the questions she had been asking.

It had all gone so wrong, thought Nora. What was she going to do now? She was sure she had embarrassed herself, not only in front of Evan, but also in front of every one else she worked with. God. This was her worst nightmare. She pictured herself, drunk and falling over, making a huge ass of herself. She blushed, thinking about facing her coworkers ... and Evan.

She thought about Christian, realizing he definitely was no gentleman. And she was sure he hadn't behaved like one last night either. To her dismay, Nora recalled his very public groping, fearing what her reaction had been. Had she given into him, in front of her coworkers, right there on the dance floor? For the first time in years, Nora said a prayer. She wanted to fix all that had gone wrong. And most of all, she wanted Evan in her life, as she had never wanted anyone before. She remembered how distraught and sad she had been last night as he had dismissed her, practically telling her that she meant nothing to him.

Nora sobbed in frustration, knowing that she might not be able to repair last night's damage. Especially if she had somehow embarrassed Evan by engaging in public displays of affection with Christian. Why hadn't she been more careful? Nora was overcome, sobbing loudly as she dried herself off in an attempt to get ready for work.

Nora listened, frozen, as the phone rang. On its third ring, she admitted she wasn't ready to talk to anyone just yet. She had to piece together last night's events. She ran to the toilet as she lost her fight to hold back throwing up. She let go of her towel, dropping to her knees as she added insult to injury by retching forcefully. God, how she hated Tequila. As the sweat broke on her brow, Nora tried to formulate a game plan. Should she play it cool, as if it was no big deal that she got so drunk, assuming that everyone else had as well? She remembered her friend, Tiffany's, advice in high school, "Admit to nothing. That way, other people who see you acting like an ass will chalk it up to the fact that they were drunk too. And if you admit to nothing," she insisted, "Then they won't be sure if what they saw was real … or not."

Nora sighed, feeling sad and extremely isolated. She knew she was all alone and that no one else really cared enough if she embarrassed herself. She was going to have to hold her chin up through this by herself. She thought about why she had come to Rocky Neck. To find a husband, she answered without thinking. No, realized Nora. It shouldn't be to find a husband. It should be about finding herself. And standing on her own two feet.

Nora dried her face then mentally planned her outfit, as trivial as it might seem. She was going into a battle of sorts today, so she'd have to look super confident to make up for how she was feeling. Nora finished buttoning her white silk blouse and took one last look in the mirror. She looked good … surprisingly. Considering how she had felt when she woke up. As she put on her shoes, the phone rang again. This time there were four rings then a hang up. She checked her reflection for a long moment, finally smiling with satisfaction. For a quick second, she thought about the calls. Her three-quarter sleeve white silk blouse contrasted perfectly with her fitted knee-length black linen skirt. She wore her hair in a low ponytail, and the large pearl earrings drew attention to her strong jawbone and sexy neck.

Nora composed herself and was ready for a fight. If Evan didn't want her, she admitted to herself, did she really care what the restaurant staff thought? She had done worse things in her past life … with less notice. She took one last glance in the small foyer mirror then unbuttoned one additional button of her blouse. War, she thought, means being ready to fight. She had decided that she was done with trying to romance anyone. She would earn and spend her own money, eventually buying her own nice house and her own nice car. She was done with having to rely on her good looks to get what she wanted. After all, the looks would give out eventually, and then where would she be?

She made her way downstairs, poured herself some juice and grabbed her purse. The phone started ringing again. This was the third time someone had called, Nora realized. She felt anxious as she picked up the phone. "Hello? Nora?" The voice sounded familiar but strained.

"Evan," Nora replied nervously. "What's wrong?"

He answered in a hesitant tone. "Nora, listen to me, please. This is important. Did Christian take you home last night?"

Nora felt a chill and knew immediately that something was wrong. She answered, "No. I mean ... I'm not ... Why, Evan?"

Evan knew at that moment that Nora was in trouble. "Christian is dead."

Nora was silent, her shock evident to Evan. "What do you mean? That's ... impossible. I mean ... how can that be? What happened?" Nora heard herself say the words, not yet believing what Evan had just told her.

"It's true. I got the call about ten minutes ago from the Gloucester Police. They wanted to confirm that he ... was an employee of mine. They found him over on Good Harbor Beach early this morning. They're not sure what happened, but they asked me questions and want me to call the whole staff in for a meeting right away."

Nora struggled to speak, her words suddenly catching in her dry throat.

"Nora ... they're interested in talking to anyone who saw him last night. They're going to want to know how everybody got home ... and who saw Christian last."

Nora felt as if Evan was trying to warn her. God, Nora thought, as she started sobbing uncontrollably, she didn't even *know* how she got home, much less what she had done with Christian. For all she knew, she could have slept with him. As she thought of the police's discovery, the notion of sleeping with Christian almost made her ill. She had to fight to control herself so she wouldn't get sick.

"Evan," sobbed Nora uncontrollably, "I don't know what to do." She barely got the words out. She felt her throat constricting and, for a brief second, she thought that maybe if something happened to her, then she wouldn't have to deal with this. Nora felt the panic. In all her years of partying, she had never had her memory completely wiped out this way.

Nora continued to sob as Evan tried to talk to her. "Nora, listen to me. Do exactly what I'm telling you. Put a key under the potted plant by the back door, then lock the front and back doors, and make sure the curtains are closed, and then go upstairs to your room. Don't answer the phone. And wait for me. I'm going to be over as soon as I can."

Nora continued to sob, tiny whimpering sobs that told Evan she was close to losing all control.

"Nora," Evan asked sternly, "Can you do this? Do you understand how important this is?"

"Yes," she whispered. "I'll be here."

Evan sighed heavily as he hung up the phone. He didn't know what Nora's involvement was, but he feared the worst. Christian was dead. And most of the staff had probably seen that they had practically been a couple last night. God, thought Evan. He knew that the police would be here soon. He walked out of his office and through the kitchen. He quickened his pace past Kevin, who was in the walk-in refrigerator with his back to the door, trying not to draw too much attention to himself.

Kevin turned toward him. "I'll be back in a little while," Evan muttered, stopping in his tracks as he saw Kevin's battered face. His left eyelid was black and blue, and his lip was obviously swollen.

"What happened to *you?*" He tried to sound casual so as not to alert Kevin just yet.

Kevin answered casually, "That's a crazy place. After you left, some dude got pissed because he didn't like the music I was playing on that old juke box."

Evan looked Kevin in the eye. He noted that his body language and eye contact seemed to say that he was telling the truth. Or he was just a good liar. Maybe he had gotten into a fight with Christian. He was sure the police would be curious about it, too.

He started toward the door again, "Too bad. Looks like the guy played dirty." Evan eyed the scratches just below his eye. "You should put some ice on that." He didn't wait for Kevin's reply and was out the door thinking about Nora. He knew he was taking a huge risk by helping her, especially since she would most likely be a suspect.

Evan walked as fast as he could. As he approached her gate, he saw that it was slightly ajar, as if someone had already been there. He looked around then quickly made his way around the side of the house and onto the back deck. He picked up one side of the large terra cotta pots filled with lavender and slid his hand under the heavy bottom dish as felt the cold of the key against the moist wood of the deck. Evan grabbed it, dropping the heavy pot with a thump.

He carefully put the key in the back door, let himself in quietly, then closed and locked the door behind him. The house was dark and lifeless with all of the curtains and shades closed. He started walking upstairs. As the first step creaked loudly, he called out.

"Nora?" He waited. "Nora, I'm coming up." He raced up the stairs and stopped on the landing. The shades were closed upstairs as well, and Evan could detect the stale air that smelled slightly of alcohol. He was nervous that Nora hadn't answered. "Nora. Where are you?" Evan approached the bed and finally made out the shape of Nora's limp form sitting on the floor. She was slightly hunched over, hugging her knees, and sobbing quietly. Evan reached her and leaned down on one knee. "Hey. Are you okay?"

There was silence for a moment. Then Evan heard the gut-wrenching sobs that Nora could no longer control. "Sure, " Nora replied sarcastically. "I'm doing great. She started, as if to explain, then whispered, "I'm doing just fine." Nora pulled away as Evan tried to touch her tear-soaked cheeks.

"What happened?" Evan asked in a low tone.

"I don't know. I don't know." Nora continued to sob as she tried to shield her face from Evan's. "I know I would never do anything to him. But I don't know how I got here. And I don't mean that I have an idea but I'm not sure." She finally looked up, "I mean ... I don't have a clue, and I don't remember anything. After the third tequila. After I danced with Christian. I *don't* remember. What *happened* to him? Did the police tell you?"

Nora looked up as she wiped her tears and waited for him to answer.

Evan wanted to believe her. Nora seemed to be telling the truth.

"The police didn't say. They just called to tell me and to confirm that Christian had worked for me." Evan was silent for a long moment. "Nora," he whispered. It was so strange to be in this room again, this time under such different circumstances, he thought. Evan knew it was selfish but he had to know how she felt about him. He leaned forward and brushed the tears from her face. "By the way, I remember what you said last night … And … I love you too," he whispered. Evan kissed her gently. Nora felt his passion and pressed herself closer to him as their kiss lingered.

She started to push him away. "I … think I need to figure this out on my own." She stared at him, hoping he understood her sudden need for independence. "I'm going to wash my face and get myself together. Whatever happens today …" Nora couldn't complete the sentence, knowing that she would be questioned and might very well be a suspect.

Evan shook his head. "You don't know what you're getting yourself into. The police are going to be brutal. They're going to ask alot of questions. You need to come up with a plan."

Nora shook her head as if to defy Evan. "No. I can't remember everything that happened yet, but I'm sure I didn't do anything wrong. And I'm not going to act as if I did. Nora prayed for the strength and conviction that her voice courageously implied. She was so scared, and had it been light in the room, Evan would have seen her hands trembling. Nora wiped her cheeks as she held back more tears. She stood up, straightened her skirt and blouse then clicked on the lamp on her nightstand. She looked directly at Evan. "I'll be at work in about twenty minutes. You should get back there before anyone starts wondering where you are."

He started walking toward the stairs. "Evan," Nora almost pleaded, "You know I didn't do anything wrong, don't you?" Evan kept his back to Nora as he hesitated for a moment.

"I know. I know that you wouldn't intentionally hurt anyone." With that, he sped down the stairs. Evan turned the key in the back door lock then returned it to it's hiding spot. He thought about whether or not Nora was telling the whole truth. And if she was guilty.

Nora heard Evan's retreating footsteps and felt a sudden panic envelop her. She ran back into the bathroom and started running the water. As she splashed the cool liquid onto her face, she thought about what might happen today. She forced herself to mentally prepare for the fact that she would probably be taken down to the station to be questioned. She knew that someone would tell the police that she had been very drunk last night and had been dancing with Christian. It could be even worse than that, Nora suddenly realized. Nora reapplied her makeup then forced herself to leave the house.

Chapter 13

The bright sunshine and bright blue sky were such a shock. It's as if everything should have been gray today, thought Nora. She walked slowly down the path and turned onto Rocky Neck Avenue toward the restaurant.

As Nora walked, she thought about whom she could call for help. Her mind quickly ticked through the options. Her sister ... and maybe Evan. Not much of a list. Nora's decision was made at that moment. She would defend herself and go it alone. She was probably never going to make it as Evan's mother had ... marrying into all that money. And she suddenly realized that wasn't what she wanted. Nora had *never* wanted that. Not really. But she'd never had the self-confidence or resolve to make it on her own. Well, given the situation, she was going to have to rely on herself. Time would tell if she could make it.

Nora stood up straighter as she approached the entrance to the Rocky Neck Grille and spotted the police cars and arriving camera crews. God, give me the strength, asked Nora. She would need it today as she had never needed it in her life. As she pushed the door open to the lounge, she saw Evan speaking with a police detective. She continued walking toward the bar and waited to be stopped. Once she reached the bar, she saw that two detectives were eagerly heading toward her. Nora knew what she had to do. She looked up at the officers and glanced at each of them before speaking. "Hi, I'm Nora." She tried to look surprised. "What's going on?"

The younger-looking detective, who had bright blond hair and blue eyes, wore a blue and white striped oxford and tan chinos. The other, taller officer, seemed older, and he wore a Life is Good T-shirt and jeans. They both seemed like ordinary guys, and their demeanor and casual looks were unexpected. The blond spoke first, "Excuse me, miss, you are?" His voice trailed off in a question as he waited for Nora to complete the sentence.

Nora lifted her chin and straightened her back. "Nora Mason. I'm the hostess here. One of them. Can I ask what's going on?"

Blond answered, "Miss, this is regarding Christian Wells. He was found dead on Good Harbor Beach early this morning. We need to ask you a few questions."

Nora almost lost her composure as she thought about what her reaction should be. "Oh my God. What happened?" She felt frightened, knowing that they were scrutinizing her as she spoke. She looked appropriately upset, which she was, as tears welled up in her eyes. She tried not to look toward Evan, who she could see out of the corner of her eye.

Blond jumped in eagerly, "Oh, I'm sorry, I'm Detective Callahan, Jake Callahan. And this is Detective Parsons. We're sorry to have to deliver the news. It seems he was a friend of yours."

"Friend?" Nora asked. She thought about Detective Parsons for a moment. He seemed like the serious type. His first name was probably Norman or Eugene or something like that. A name that he never abbreviated. She tried to sum up Detective Callahan for a quick minute. He seemed like a nice guy and probably would be easy on her. It doesn't matter, thought Nora. I haven't done anything wrong, and I don't have to sweet talk these guys. It'll work out. I have to have faith in other people for once in my life. It'll be okay.

"Yes," answered Detective Callahan. "You worked together ... and you seem very upset."

Nora looked at each of the detectives and then spoke softly. "I'm so sorry to hear about Christian. I didn't know him very well, but he was a nice guy. I'll be glad to answer any questions." Nora looked around and noticed that everyone else, including Evan, had backed away from the three of them and were talking in small groups or pretending to go about their business.

Jake Callahan spoke again, "When did you see Christian Wells last?" He stood with a small notebook and pen in hand.

Nora answered slowly. "We all went out last night after work. We had some drinks here and then down at the Port Side." Nora tried not to let the panic show on her face as she waited for the inevitable next question.

The other detective took his turn questioning Nora but did not have a notebook. Detective Parsons asked the next round of questions in a more serious tone, "You were seen dancing with Christian Wells and then the two of you went outside together. Did you leave with the subject?" Detective Parson's voice seemed to pierce the room as the question hung in the air.

Nora knew she would only have this one moment to give the right answer. She looked into her interviewer's eyes and squared her shoulders as she prepared to answer.

"I followed them outside then Nora and I walked to my place. I have a loft downtown." Remy spoke confidently and smoothly as she walked toward them from behind. "Nora and I left Christian there at the front door. He was drunk and was getting out of hand. So, I rescued her. She came back to my place and stayed over. I gave her a ride home about 6:00 this morning. I knew we were going to have a busy day at work today." Remy answered with such conviction that Nora wanted to believe her.

The two detectives looked at Nora. "Yes," Nora answered in a low voice. "We left Christian outside, and I went to Remy's place. And she took me home this morning." She nodded toward Remy and tried not to let the detectives see that she was holding her breath.

Remy broke in casually as she looked at each of the two detectives. Nora could smell Remy's Calvin Klein perfume as she leaned in toward them. "I'm sorry," Remy replied solemnly, "I haven't introduced myself. I'm Remy Fournier, the other hostess. I hope you don't mind. But I heard you talking. It's terrible what happened to Christian. He was a good guy."

Nora listened to Remy's replies and suddenly felt uneasy. She had never been in a situation where she didn't know what to believe about her own whereabouts. She felt as if she were watching a drama unfold, not knowing who the bad guys were.

*   *   *

The rounds of questioning had subsided by 11:00, and Evan had then held a staff meeting. The mood was somber as he asked everyone to keep Christian's family in their thoughts and prayers. Nora had found this unusual, since Evan wasn't a religious man. On the other hand, she mused, how often was it that you had to tell your staff that one of your waiters had died unexpectedly. Evan had made it seem to the staff that the police hadn't determined the cause of death, but that it looked like an accident.

Nora was certain that Evan was trying to calm everyone down so they could get through the busiest day of the year without falling apart. As she walked over to the hostess station to drop off her purse, she saw Kevin approaching. She stood frozen and watched him, noting his bruised face and lip. He glared at her, almost oblivious to his appearance, as he grabbed a menu and pretended to read it.

"Nora," Kevin asked in a strained tone, "Did Evan explain all the specials to you? I know today's meeting wasn't the usual." She prepared to recite them as Kevin leaned toward her. His whisper sent chills through her body. "You're a lucky girl, you know that?" He stared at her coldly, then dropped the menu and walked toward the kitchen.

Nora was shaken and tried not to show it. She realized that Kevin was trying to intimidate her. She thought about the possible reasons. Maybe he had seen her leave with Christian. Or maybe he had witnessed something else that she couldn't remember. Whatever was going on, she realized that Kevin didn't want to share it with the police. Otherwise, he'd be over at the bar talking to them right now, she thought. She paced nervously behind the hostess station. She needed answers. Nora fought to take several deep breaths as she watched Remy walk toward her. She watched as Remy scribbled a note on a cocktail napkin she had carried over from the bar. Remy looked around, making certain that no one was watching her. She finished writing, "Here you go, Nora."

Nora glanced down at the cocktail napkin. There were no complete sentences, just the following:

Cocktails

My place after work

Important

155 Water Street, Unit No. 5

281.7715 if you can't make it

Otherwise, don't call.

Nora noticed that below the phone number, Remy had scribbled, "We need to talk."

Nora looked around casually as she folded the napkin and stuffed it in a pocket inside her purse. What had she gotten herself into? And what would she have to do to keep off the detective's radar? She prayed, for the second time in her life, that God would give her the strength to make it through the day … and night.

As she thought about what she would need to do to survive the day's onslaught of tourists, Nora realized that the police were formulating their suspicions into a concrete accusation, and for now it seemed to center around Kevin Delaney. As Kevin had tried to meet with his Sous Chef and kitchen staff after their regular meeting, Nora noticed that both Detectives Callahan and Parsons seemed to be rough on Kevin. They hadn't even spared him the embarrassment of questioning him in front of the kitchen staff. They had immediately wandered into the prep area and had fired off personal questions as Kevin's staff prepared for the biggest day of the year. It was loud enough that she could hear most if it out by the hostess station.

"I told you guys," Kevin insisted, "I didn't have too much to do with Christian last night. He was drunk out of his mind for most of the night. He was really annihilated. A couple of times he took out a bottle and took a couple pills or something. At one point, he went outside with Nora. End of story. I got these bruises because some guy didn't like the tunes I picked out. And after Christian took off outside and I got into the fight with that dude, I walked Carly home to my place and we got some pizza next door on the way."

Detective Parsons resisted backing down. "So, Kevin, you and Christian didn't speak again after he went outside?"

Nora had walked up to the utility closet just outside the doorway of the kitchen. She listened intently. "No, Detective … What did you say your name was?"

"Parsons. Detective Parsons."

Kevin continued. "No, Detective Parsons, I didn't see Christian again. I was having a good time and dancing with Carly when Christian went outside. With Nora. You should ask her about it. They never came back."

Jake continued and seemed annoyed at Kevin's lack of respect for them and the seriousness of the situation. He spoke in a stern voice. "We were informed of that. Let's stick to what you were doing. How was it that you knew they went outside if you were busy, or dancing or whatever you were doing?"

Jake stared sternly at Kevin as he waited for his reply.

Kevin replied loudly, not caring if the rest of the staff overhead him. "I told you, man. I told you that already. It's not a big place, and I was facing the bar and saw them go outside." Kevin's voice sounded frustrated and slightly strained.

Detective Callahan closed up his notebook and walked around the stainless steel prep table. He stared at Kevin. "You'll be available if we have questions?"

Kevin nodded over his shoulder then went back to prepping his lobster and crabs for the night. His sarcastic reply was heard throughout the kitchen, "I can't help it if that stupid rich kid got himself killed. You should think about who his friends were." Kevin continued separating the crabs as the detectives finally decided to retreat, giving him a break for the moment.

*   *   *

Nora stared at her watch a thousand times until her shift was finally over. When it was, she grabbed her purse, freshened up in the bathroom, then exited through the lounge. She made her way down toward The Rowboat where a cab was already waiting. As she stepped inside, she whispered, "Port Side, please."

The cab driver looked in the rear view mirror. It wasn't every day that a cutie like this went to party at the Port Side. They drove in silence, and Nora sat up in anticipation as the cab approached the front door. She got out and waited for the cab to drive away, then looked toward the door from where the loud music and laughter emanated. Nora closed her eyes, trying desperately to remember what had happened. It was only last night, but for all that she remembered, it may as well have been years. Nothing came to her. It was as if her mind had been erased.

Chapter 14

Nora started heading down Main Street and counted the five blocks before pulling out the napkin from her purse. She tried to hold it up to the streetlight that was directly overhead. Damn, she thought. It was dark tonight. Where the hell was this loft, anyway? She didn't really know the addresses downtown, and Water Street could be just about anywhere in Gloucester. Nora looked up suddenly and saw the sign directly to her left. Water Street Gym. She surveyed the building. This might be it, she reasoned. She pulled on the heavy glass door, surprised that it was unlocked, then walked through the lobby toward the elevator. As she approached the elevator doors, she noticed the directory listing the businesses on the first two floors. No other listings.

She must live above them, thought Nora as she pressed the up arrow and waited for the door to open completely before stepping inside. She pressed the number five then looked up at the convex mirror and stared at her distorted reflection. Had she gone to Good Harbor with Christian? She stared at the mirror as if her answers were there. And what would Remy tell her tonight? That she had humiliated herself and had been caught in the act with Christian outside? That she had witnessed something involving his death? Did Remy want money or something else in order to lie for her? Nora braced herself for the most horrible possibilities.

As the elevator opened, Nora walked down the hall, her body almost completely numb. She looked at the cocktail napkin again. The number was penned neatly. Unit Number 5. She stepped up to the door. Here it is, thought Nora. Let's get this over with. She could hear the music inside and recognized it immediately. It was Barry White belting out his infamous words, *"Let's get it on … Let's get it on."*

Nora looked again at the door to make sure she had the right apartment. As she pressed the buzzer, she mouthed the words, forgetting for a moment that she was standing in front of a female co-worker's condo in the hopes of being offered friendship and a corroborating story.

The door opened quickly and revealed Remy standing in tight-fitting white yoga pants and a white cotton camisole top with thin spaghetti straps. She was barefoot and held two filled-to-the-brim wineglasses in her right hand.

Nora gulped. "Hi, Remy. I got your message." Her voice trailed as she noted the sharp comparison between how uptight and serious she must look and how casually elegant and composed Remy appeared to be.

Remy smiled and pulled the door open so that Nora could step inside. "I'm glad you're here." She held the door and motioned Nora inside as the music enveloped them. "Could I interest you in a glass of Kendall Jackson?"

Nora grabbed one of the glasses then looked around admiringly. "Wow." She tried not to sound too impressed, though she was. "Nice place." Nora instantly realized, as she peered around the room that Remy came from money. Lots of money. The art hanging on the walls hadn't just been purchased. If so, then Evan was paying Remy alot more than he was paying her, she mused. She walked toward the amber colored leather couch and slid onto one of the soft cool cushions. She watched as Remy made her way toward her, sitting down close beside her. Remy turned, facing Nora and looking into her eyes. Nora noticed Remy's slightly unfocused look. She wasn't sloppy drunk, but she had already been enjoying a few cocktails.

"I'm glad you like it." Remy looked around, "Most of this, except for the couch, the dining room table, and my bed, is from my parent's property."

Nora took a huge gulp then replied, "You mean, estate, don't you? I know I sure as hell didn't come from a property with paintings and furniture like this."

Remy smiled, slightly tight-lipped, then continued. "Yeah, I guess you could say that. My family is pretty much like Christian's. As a matter of fact, I have an obnoxious younger brother almost exactly like he is." Remy hastily corrected herself. "Sorry. I mean, like Christian was. Silver spoon and all that."

Nora looked puzzled. "But ..." Her voice trailed.

"But I hated Christian. I know," Remy cut in. "He was an ass. He was a spoiled rotten player-in-training and a total mama's boy. He got everything he wanted ... I know. The difference between my brother, Martin, and me is that ... he and I both happen to like *girls.*"

Nora remained silent, knowing that Remy would tell her more, especially now that she had been drinking for at least a little while.

Remy continued, "Unfortunately, as soon as I came out to my parents, they more or less disowned me. And did you catch the clever way we were named? Remy and Martin? My parents see their bar more than they ever see either of us ... even my perfect brother, Martin."

Nora sighed. "I'm sorry." She didn't feel the need to tell Remy about her sordid family or lack thereof.

Remy added, "Yeah, I'm sorry, too. But it just goes to show you ... what happened to Christian was sad, but I'm not that surprised. You can't go through life being such a prima donna and pissing off people left and right without getting at least one person mad enough to want to kill you."

Nora's shock was evident on her face. "You think it was ... premeditated?"

"Maybe ... or maybe not. But I wouldn't be surprised if it *was* intentional. You didn't know him that well. I mean ... neither did I. But I heard alot of stories being passed around the restaurant about Christian."

Remy downed the rest of her glass and moved slightly closer to Nora. "Hey, I'm sorry, I don't want you to think I'm a jerk. After all, we're both working girls just trying to make a living and get what we want, right?"

Nora noticed that Remy was no longer coy or guarded. And she had learned more about her in the last few minutes than she had known for the last few months. Nora thought about what Remy had just said. Did Remy think that she had something to do with Christian's death? Did she know more? Or was she testing the waters, trying to get Nora to admit to something? And what did Remy want from her exactly, now that she had volunteered an alibi for her? Shit, thought Nora, now she really wished that Remy hadn't done that.

Nora took a deep breath and downed the rest of her glass of KJ. She held it out so that Remy would refill it. She would need a little time to warm up Remy. Then she would find out. As Remy got up and walked over to the granite countertop of her kitchen's center island, Nora spoke, "Hey, by the way, how much is Evan paying you that you can afford this place?" Remy smiled, "Yeah, right. I wish I were getting a half-decent paycheck. This is all SF money."

Nora looked confused. Remy walked back over with their refilled glasses. "San Francisco. Family money. I used most of what I had left from my trust fund. The sad truth is, I spent most of it trying to impress the wrong people." She stopped for a moment to see what Nora's reaction would be. Nora listened intently. "And now I'm wiping down menus with lemon water for a living. If my friends could see me now," Remy mused sarcastically.

Nora instantly felt she wanted to defend Evan and his meticulousness for some reason. But she didn't. She didn't want Remy to know yet that she cared for him. She wanted to find out her agenda first. She watched as Remy slid closer to her. Nora wanted to lean back, to keep her personal space, but she fought the urge so as not to offend Remy. Instead, she leaned in slightly. "I need to ask you something." Remy nodded and swayed slightly as the alcohol started to take its toll.

"Why did you tell the police I stayed over last night?" Nora made eye contact then waited for a reply.

"Because you would have been screwed if you told the police you didn't remember anything. Which is my guess, by seeing the shape you were in. Am I right?"

Nora nodded, afraid to speak. Remy continued, "Besides, I know you didn't do it. Christian gave you a couple of pills, which you took, by the way. I think it was Xanax."

Nora looked horrified.

"Don't worry, I was the blocker at the bar. I don't think anybody else saw you. At least not when you did that. He kept bragging that he borrowed them from his mother. And that he could get anything he wanted from his father."

This time, Nora interjected, "What do you mean, from his father?"

Remy leaned closer, whispering in an exaggerated tone, "His father, the distinguished Dr. Wells, is a shrink."

"So his father … ?

"Apparently. Christian had a big mouth and that was what he was saying … and the rumor at work is that he did a little dealing of his own."

Nora sat up straighter as she asked the dreaded question in a barely audible whisper, "So …What else happened?"

Remy replied in a reassuring tone. "Don't worry. Xanax doesn't make you want to kill somebody. Not usually, anyway."

Nora felt as if Remy were almost taunting her.

"No really. The worst that could have happened is that you would have passed out. After you took the pills, I heard you tell Christian you weren't feeling well. That you were going to be sick and you needed some air." Remy stopped as Nora waited tensely.

"But after you were gone a while, I got nervous. So, I went outside to check on you. That's where I found the two of you."

Nora tried to remain calm as she asked, "Remy … what were we doing? Did anybody see us?"

"Yeah, a lot of people saw you. But nobody we know. Everybody going into the bar had to pass by you. It wasn't awful … don't worry. But he *was* all over you. Nothing they haven't seen before, I'm sure. He practically had you pinned against the wall. I couldn't hear what you were saying, you were kind of … mumbling. But then you pushed him." Remy took another long sip. "You probably told him to fuck off. I was going to say something because he was being so obnoxious, but then you just walked away and crossed the street. I was practically yelling your name, but you just kept walking. You were headed toward Rocky Neck.

Nora took a deep breath and exhaled loudly. She looked up at Remy. "Where did you go. Did you leave then, too?"

Nora thought she saw Remy hesitate for a moment, "Yeah. I did. I left Christian standing outside. He was really a mess. I walked home, but I was worried. So after I got home, I waited about forty-five minutes and then tried calling your house. Your voice mail kept picking up. I actually drove over early this morning, but you never answered the door."

Remy waited a moment before asking. "You went right home last night … right? You didn't go to the beach with him or anything crazy like that? He didn't follow you and pick you up or anything like that, right?"

Nora straightened as she answered honestly. "Remy." She stopped and rubbed at her forehead as if willing herself to recall the scene. "I know I'd never try to do anything to Christian." Nora waited a long moment before continuing. "And I was home this morning. I must have been in the shower when you came by." Nora instinctively didn't tell Remy that Evan had come to the house.

Remy's look told Nora that she wanted to ask more questions but was hesitant. Nora turned to Remy, holding up another half-empty glass. "I think I need a lot more." Remy grabbed the glass by the stem, intentionally holding on to where Nora's fingers were.

"It's going to be ok. I know you didn't do it. We just have to stick to the story."

Nora burst into tears as Remy grabbed the glass from her. She tried to hold back the tears, suddenly overcome with panic. "There's only one problem. Kevin knows something. He came up to the hostess station this morning and pretty much let me know that."

Remy replied in a high-pitched whisper, "What did he say to you exactly?"

Nora choked on her sobs as she answered. "He walked up to the hostess station, asked if I knew what the specials were, and then he leaned in and said something sarcastic like, *You're a lucky girl.* Or something like that. He knows Remy. He knows." Nora's voice was high and strained.

Remy shook her head back and forth with conviction. "No, he doesn't know. Trust me. The only person that knows is Christian, and he's sure as hell not going to tell anybody. When I came outside, a few people had just gone in, but no one else was out there. Kevin was inside dancing. The whole thing happened so fast. Then you left in one direction, and I left in the other. And it was so dark." Remy hesitated for a moment, "Kevin just doesn't want the suspicion on him."

"Are you sure?"

Remy let her words sink in. "Yes. Come on, Nora, look at him. He has bruises and looks beaten up. No one believes his story. I know *I* don't. Did you know that Kevin deals on the side, too? A few times, I've been in the kitchen at the end of the night when I've heard his phone ringing. Then he goes outside. Trust me, the police are going to look at him first."

Nora wanted so badly to believe that Remy cared about her and wanted to help her. She asked the question aloud that had been bothering her, "Was Evan standing next to you the whole night?"

"Yeah, he was. He was at the bar standing right next to me. He was watching you a lot. But it was really loud. I could hear you, but I doubt he could. I saw him watch you and Christian go outside. He didn't look too happy. And when I told him I was going to check on you, he looked pissed."

Remy sat down next to Nora and leaned in closely, "Don't worry, I'll help you. I'll take care of it."

Nora thought about what Remy meant by that but couldn't stand to ask. As if on cue, the music on Remy's CD player switched, and a sultry *I Only Have Eyes for You* started playing. The lighting was soft, and she could smell the fresh ocean breeze billowing in through the set of French doors leading from the small waterfront balcony off the kitchen.

"Remy, do you know why I came to Rocky Neck?" Nora looked toward Remy to make sure she had a captive audience before she started. "I came here to get away from a bad situation. But, unfortunately, I've gone from the frying pan and into the fucking fire. She shook her head back and forth in disbelief. Nora hesitated, wondering if she should confide in Remy. She didn't want anyone to know, she was ashamed, but she needed a friend. Nora sobbed quietly, then tried to wipe the tears streaming down her face.

Remy felt Nora's pain and anguish. "What is it? Really, I know you don't know me, but I promise, you can tell me anything. No one else will know."

Nora wanted to believe her. She had never felt so alone. Instead of cultivating friendships these last ten years, she had wasted her time trying to date and marry the right man. Obviously, that hadn't worked out so far.

Nora cleared her throat. "Remy, I got involved with my boss and …" She hesitated. I mean, what happened is …"

She suddenly became angry as she spat out the words, "I was accused of something. I didn't do it … but it looks like I did … " Nora tried to compose herself. She placed her empty glass on the coffee table and tried to wipe her face dry with her hands.

Remy finally spoke, "Look, whatever it is … you can tell me when you're ready. But it's not as if you killed somebody or anything … right?

Nora finally laughed, "Of course not. But I took off unexpectedly after he fired me … and he might still try to find me. To repay the debt.

"So you think he's looking for you?"

Nora stiffened. "It got pretty ugly … and yes, he might come looking for me."

Remy continued. "I'm sure he was just really pissed." Then she added, in a teasing voice. "I know *I* wouldn't have wanted you to go." She touched Nora's cheek.

"I don't want to talk about it any more." Nora responded as she pulled away.

"Okay. I'll take you home. We both need some rest. We're going to need it for tomorrow. Remy seemed annoyed. "Thank God, it's finally Monday. This has been some fucking weekend."

Remy grabbed her keys from the sterling bowl on the kitchen counter and reached over to turn up the lights. Nora wiped her face one final time. "Thanks. I'll be fine. I just need a little time to get it together. I don't think I got much sleep last night." Nora thought back to waking in her pink underwear. Please God, she thought, I can't handle anything else right now. Please let this be all right. "Remy, are you alright to drive?"

Remy answered quickly. "Oh, my God, yes. You don't know me. I can handle my liquor. Years of practice growing up in the Remy-Martin Household," she commented in a sarcastic tone. "My brother and I were trained at an early age. My parents just kept re-stocking that bar without ever even noticing how much we drained it."

Nora had a nagging thought for a moment but tried to dismiss it. God, stop being so suspicious of everyone. She's going to be a friend.

She straightened her hair and looked in the antique mirror to the right of the door as she and Remy prepared to go down to the parking area. As she peered at her reflection, she noticed that Remy was walking up behind her.

"Pretty," Remy remarked.

Nora looked in the mirror at Remy, "Thanks again for everything. You're a real friend. And God knows I could use one about now."

Remy placed her hand gently on Nora's shoulder and guided her out the door. "No worries."

As they drove the two miles back to Rocky Neck, they each contemplated their situations. Remy knew that Nora wasn't interested in her. Not that way. And she wasn't going to beg. And as for everything else, including Christian's death and Nora's ex, she knew it would eventually work out. Growing up on the set of Mommy Dearest had trained Remy for the worst. Except for that little breakdown in the bathroom the other day. It had been a shock seeing Christian looking and behaving just like her ungrateful, pain-in-ass brother. And it had made her think about San Francisco. She had been so sad to leave. But she had recovered. If Nora only knew, thought Remy. If she only knew what her life had been like up until three months ago, it would make Nora's life seem like a picnic.

Remy pulled up in front of Nora's. It was 12:45 a.m. Nora opened the door.

"Just remember," Remy replied, "The cops always know less than they seem to know, and they ask questions over and over just to see if you're telling the truth. So, just keep the answers short if they come around again, which I'm sure they will. I'm going to do the same. You and I left Christian outside, alone, and we walked to my place. You stayed over, and I drove you home in the morning." Remy looked up at Nora to make sure she was paying attention. "Now get some sleep."

Nora watched Remy as she drove away. She saw a side of Remy she didn't know existed. Determined. And fearless. She started feeling better. Then she thought about how their made-up story had become the truth in Remy's mind. She definitely told a good story. And with such conviction.

Nora put her key in the door and let herself in. There was a light on at the top of the stairs. She knew she hadn't left one on, since she hadn't been home since this morning. She dropped her purse and key chain on the front foyer table and stood for a moment. She tried to think about what she should do and then jumped at the voice that came from the darkness.

Chapter 15

"I've been worried about you. Where have you been?" Nora held her breath for a moment as she threw herself into Evan's arms. He smelled of soap and his breath was slightly tinged with alcohol.

Nora lost her sense of composure, "You scared the hell out of me, but I'm so glad you're here." She held Evan tightly while she thought about the fact that he had probably been watching for her and had seen Remy pull away.

"I love you." Evan held her as he uttered the words.

Nora thought about what Evan had just said. "I love you, too." Nora was so relieved. "I'm in love with you." She stifled a sob and held onto Evan for a long moment. It was the first time she had ever said the words and really meant them.

Evan looked at Nora earnestly. "Where were you?"

"Remy said she needed to unwind after such a rough day, so I had a few glasses of wine at her place, then she drove me home." Nora wanted to be completely honest, as she never had been in her life, but she didn't want Evan to get involved if it could be avoided. She would tell him everything, she thought, even about Florida, but not right now. But her plan with Remy would stay between them. She didn't want Evan to get sucked in. Nora hoped she was doing the right thing. "I don't want to talk," she whispered. She looked up at Evan again. Will you stay with me tonight? Please?"

Evan nodded yes. "I brought over a bottle of champagne, and I opened it a little while ago. Let's get into bed and have a glass."

Nora thought of the irony of the situation. She and Evan were going to celebrate the beginning of their relationship, while Christian's family prepared to mourn the end of his life. She felt such deep sadness. The tears came to her eyes, spilling down her cheeks uncontrollably.

Evan saw the anguished look on Nora's face. "I know what happened was horrible, but we didn't have anything to do with it. I thought about it alot today. I know you're too smart to have gotten involved with Christian, and I'm sure you didn't have anything to do with what happened to him. They're probably going to determine it was an accident. He probably just lost his balance and *fell* off that lifeguard chair."

Nora leaned in and kissed Evan gently. This is what she always wanted, she thought. Someone who really loved her for who she was. She was sure Evan would understand when she finally came clean and told him the truth. Soon. She would tell him soon.

She wanted to reassure Evan. "I didn't have anything to do with what happened to Christian."

Nora held her breath while she prayed that she was telling Evan the truth. There's nothing we can do to control or change the past, reasoned Nora. But we can definitely control the future. She knew they both wanted this relationship, and she wasn't going to jeopardize it.

Evan spoke softly as he held Nora. "I wanted to ask you about last night." Nora tried not to stiffen.

Evan continued, "So you went home with Remy last night?"

Nora was so tired and couldn't seem to think. She wanted a hot shower and a warm bed, hopefully with Evan beside her.

"Yes. I walked home with Remy, and she brought me home early this morning."

Evan looked surprised. "How early this morning? I thought you couldn't remember what happened?"

Nora felt herself getting flushed. She didn't want to lie. But she knew she had to protect him right now.

"She dropped me off a little while before you called. I didn't remember much, but as the day went on, it started coming together, especially when Remy helped me to fill in the blanks. I'm embarrassed. I don't normally drink that much."

"Well, that makes sense, because I saw you leave with Christian and then Remy said she was going to check on you. She went outside and I didn't see her again."

"Yeah," Nora answered, wanting to change the subject, "When did *you* leave?"

Evan grabbed Nora's hand and started walking her upstairs. He spoke over his shoulder. "Oh, I left a little while after you and drove right home. Almost everybody was gone by then. Betty ran into a friend who offered her a ride home, and Kevin lives around the corner, so he said he'd give Carly a ride. I got out of there and went to bed."

As they got to the top of the stairs, Evan stopped. "Nora, the first time … on my boat …" He looked into her eyes and waited for her to acknowledge their first passionate moment. "That's when I knew."

Nora kissed him softly. "Me, too."

Evan started walking toward the champagne, "Let's have a glass … then maybe we can take a really hot shower together."

Nora smiled. She watched him pour their glasses of champagne. As he did so, she noticed the condensation on the napkin he had placed under the bottle. She wondered how long he had been here, in her house, waiting for her.

Standing by the window, she felt the cool salty air as the curtains billowed with a sudden gust. She closed her eyes as she held the glass just under her nose. The champagne bubbles danced toward the surface and made tiny popping sounds as they burst. Nora opened her eyes as she felt another gust of cool ocean air. She stopped dead in her tracks, blanching as she realized someone was watching her. There, under the street light in front of the house, was a dark figure. A chill ran down her spine as she almost dropped her glass. She leaned forward, frantically searching the street below.

"Nora, what's wrong?" Evan asked in a surprised tone.

Nora was silent, as she stood crouched at the window. Her eyes darted back and forth. She stared into the darkness across the street, trying to focus in the direction of the oversized maple tree where she had seen the figure.

What is it?" Evan asked as he stood behind her, mimicking Nora as he stared in the same direction.

"I … I just saw somebody standing under that tree." Nora said as she pointed. "There. There was someone right there."

Evan strained to look toward the darkness, then scanned the entire street, left to right. He examined each spot slowly. "I don't see anything," he replied as he backed away from the window.

"I'm sure I saw somebody. I'm not being paranoid," she replied defensively.

Evan stared at her, almost annoyed that she had broken their moment. "Why would anyone be watching you? If anybody would be watched right now it's Kevin. I'm going to keep him working at the restaurant, but honestly, I think it's just a matter of time."

Nora looked at Evan with a surprised look on her face. "You mean, you think if someone was out there it would be the cops? You think they're watching Kevin? He's a suspect?"

"Well, you know they don't come right out and say that. But it sounded that way by their questioning today. Plus Kevin was in a brawl with somebody, and everyone knows that he and Christian didn't get along."

"I didn't know that," whispered Nora.

"Yeah, it seems that your friend had alot of enemies." Evan reached in front of Nora and closed the window and the shade, then grabbed Nora's hips and turned her toward him.

"He wasn't my friend." Nora's tone was defensive.

"Whatever." Evan started to say something then stopped. "You need to relax. The worst should be over after tomorrow."

Evan tried to hold Nora. She stood stiff as a board.

"How about if we have dinner tomorrow tonight? An early dinner. It'll be busy for lunch, and then all the visitors to Rocky Neck are going to head back home. How about if we meet about 6:00?" Evan moved very close.

Nora could smell the sweetness of the champagne on his breath as he kissed her ear and then held his mouth to her forehead. "Why don't you meet me on the boat after work? We can cut out about 5:00, then you can go home and get changed. Remy and Betty can handle it. It's going to be slow."

Nora nodded.

"We'll have dinner on the boat and stay over. Then we can go for a sail the next morning. Maybe even catch the sunrise … if we're up." Evan kissed Nora's neck as he tried to ease her obvious tension.

She kept her eyes closed, trying to imagine that she and Evan were on a faraway island. Soft warm breezes tinged with coconut fragrance billowed in through their beachfront cottage windows. She could almost smell the warm salt air. She could taste the slushy sweet fruit of her cocktail. She could feel the hot sun on her heated skin. She began to relax.

"That sounds so nice right about now."

Nora held onto Evan and tried not to think about who had been watching her. Could it be Remy? Or Kevin? Or maybe it was one of the detectives. She felt the panic rise again in her throat, and she could hear the relentless pounding in her head. This had been the longest day of her life. She just wanted this nightmare to be over.

Nora pulled back slightly and looked into Evan's eyes. "Let's take a hot shower and go to bed. I want to sleep next to you." She put her head on Evan's shoulder. He kissed her lips tenderly then followed her into the bathroom.

Chapter 16

Nora awoke to the sounds of the ocean beating against her closed shades. She could feel the summer heat even at this early hour. She had been awakened at 3:30 by what she swore were footsteps outside, and she hadn't been able to get back to sleep. Her heart was in her throat, and she kept trying to swallow to clear it. Evan, on the other hand, was sound asleep. In light of the fact that he had just lost a member of his wait staff to a possible murder, he was being a rock, thought Nora.

She tried not to move as she thought about what the day might bring. Nora felt the panic as it started to overtake her. She was starting to feel herself become totally unglued. Is this how her mother had felt before she had abandoned them? As if she had no choice but to leave? She tried to shift her thoughts away from Florida, which only made her think more about why she had left. What if Tom had decided to come looking for her? What if Remy started coming on to her in exchange for her alibi? What if Kevin told the police he knew she and Remy were lying about going home together?

Nora felt she would be sick. She sat up suddenly, then looked over at Evan. He was still sleeping like a baby. It must be the 500 thread count cotton sheets, Nora thought. Of course he appreciated them. Evan loved nice things, sometimes even more than she did. Nora stood up, trying to walk softly toward the window so as not to wake him. She raised the shade and pushed up the creaking window, then looked out instinctively in order to see if anyone was still there. No one. God, maybe she was going crazy. Nora climbed back into bed and fell asleep from pure exhaustion. When she woke up again, startled that she had overslept, it was 8:14 a.m. She breathed a sigh of relief. Plenty of time for coffee and maybe even a walk along the shore. She needed something to help her relax. She grabbed her robe, then straightened her hair in the dresser mirror. We're probably all going to be questioned again today about Christian's death, she admitted. She still couldn't accept that it might be a murder. And she still couldn't believe that Christian was dead.

Evan stirred. He sat up slowly, watching Nora as she straightened her hair.

"Are you okay?"

"Yes," Nora answered. "I'm fine."

Evan stood up and walked over to her. He slipped the robe off her shoulders. They were both naked as the orange morning sun tinged their skin with warm golden sunlight.

"Nora," Evan whispered as he stood facing her, "Come back to bed."

He grabbed Nora's hand. As they reached the bed, Evan leaned into Nora, pushing her onto the mattress. He lay gently on top of her, watching her as she spoke, "Would you believe in me no matter what I told you?" There was silence as Evan looked at her in surprise.

"Yes. I would. Why, is there something you need to tell me?" He asked.

Nora hesitated. "I … guess I just needed to know that you love me for who I am."

"I love you for who you are."

Nora needed to feel the physical comfort of being next to Evan. She moved on top of him and pressed herself against his body until she could feel his mounting excitement. Evan grabbed Nora's buttocks and moved her body slowly until he could feel that he was inside her. Their mutual passion was evident as Evan started to make love to her. They both felt a welcome and quick release, and they held onto each other for a long moment afterward. Nora pulled away reluctantly and forced herself to walk toward the bathroom and into the shower. She enjoyed the sensation of the steaming hot water as it poured over her tired shoulders. She half-waited for Evan to join her, hoping that he would.

As she wrapped a towel around herself and walked toward the closet, she felt Evan watching her from bed. "I'll jump in the shower in a few minutes. Is that alright? Now that … we're dating?"

Nora was glad that he had finally said the words. "Of course." She smiled, happy that they were together now but feeling slightly off balance about Evan being in her home, alone, with all of her things.

She got dressed, grabbed a quick glass of orange juice, and then headed toward the door.

"Don't forget," Evan instructed as he started toward the shower. "If they show up to ask you more questions before I get there, don't worry. Just make sure you keep it brief and just tell them what you told them yesterday. Sometimes they try to make you nervous by asking the same questions over and over. And don't volunteer information they don't ask you for."

It was the second time she had heard this advice, thought Nora. She walked out the door toward the restaurant. As she did, preoccupied now with getting to work, she never suspected or noticed her admirer watching her from across the street. She stopped for a moment and checked her watch, deciding against going for a walk. Not today. Today, she just needed to make it through.

As Nora walked inside, she looked over her shoulder. She needed to stop being paranoid, she thought to herself. She reached the hostess station and went to place her purse on the lower shelf. As she did, Nora realized that Remy had already placed her bag in the spot that Nora usually used.

She tried to ignore this small lack of consideration on Remy's part, but for some reason, it really annoyed her. She bit her lip and instead squeezed her purse onto the upper shelf next to a row of menus. As she straightened up, she heard the phone ring. She looked at her watch. 10:15 a.m. Nora was surprised that customers would be calling this early. Before and after lunch and dinner, the phone was answered in the bar, and though it was early, Nora heard Carly pick up the phone.

Nora checked her nails and then heard the unmistakable buzz at the hostess station. The phone system was old, but it worked. And as Evan pointed out, it had old-fashioned charm. Nora walked over and pressed the flashing intercom button on the front panel.

"This is Nora," she answered politely.

"Nora," Carly asked, do you know somebody named Nina Martin?"

Nora blanched, as if feeling the pain of a sharp knife stabbing into her chest. She tried to answer but strained to catch her breath instead.

"Why?" Nora asked in a shaky tone.

"Because this guy is calling for the second time this morning, and he's insisting that this person works here. Can you take it?"

"Sure. I'll take care of it." Nora was certain this was how a slow death felt as someone was being suffocated. She couldn't breath and was sure she would be in the Gloucester City morgue by morning. Nora looked around, and luckily, since she had come in early, there weren't alot of staff milling around yet, and no one was within earshot.

She picked up the heavy black handset and tried to hold it casually to her ear. "Hello, reservations, how can I help you?"

The caller answered with a slight Southern drawl and a rough tone. "Well, I knew you'd turn up. I've been looking for you for a little while."

Nora could hear the familiar sound of inhaling as she pictured him with a large Cuban cigar.

"Now I can finally come up to see ya." The caller cleared his throat. "You miss me, too, babe?"

Nora tried to steady her trembling lips and continued, "I'm sorry, sir, unless you need to make a dinner reservation for this evening, I'm afraid I can't help you."

"No, I don't need a reservation, sweetheart."

Nora tried to force her shaking voice to be still. "I'm sorry, sir, the person you're looking for isn't here. I think you have the wrong number."

"Yeah. Right." The caller laughed softly then hung up.

Nora was certain everyone could hear the menacing voice on the phone and the relentless pounding in her ears. She was frozen and couldn't seem to place the phone back on the handset. She finally looked around after what seemed an eternity to make sure no one was watching her.

Nora hung up the phone with an unsteady hand then self-consciously straightened her hair and tried to wipe the beads of sweat from her forehead.

She looked up and saw Remy walking toward her. Nora welcomed her support and needed to tell her what had just happened.

Remy stood close to Nora. She doesn't know that my fucking world is falling apart, thought Nora. Remy looked at Nora admiringly then whispered loudly. "Wow, I love what you have on. You look beautiful."

Nora blushed instantly. She composed herself and replied. "Thanks." She looked around then whispered to Remy. "I need to talk to you about my … former boss."

Remy interrupted before Nora could explain. She flipped her hair back with a quick over-the-shoulder move and smiled brightly. "Oh, I'm on top of it. I was going to look into it for you."

Nora's voice trembled as she answered. "Yeah, well, I think he beat you to it. Remy gave Nora a puzzled look.

"He found me." Nora knew she wouldn't cry. She was too frozen with terror.

Remy asked immediately, "What's wrong?"

"He … he just called here. I told him he had the wrong number, but he knew it was me. How did he know where to find me?" Nora didn't realize she had raised her voice.

Carly looked up from the bar in the lounge.

Nora admitted now what she had known all along. The fundamental truth was that no one could be trusted, no matter how much he or she pretended to care. This seemed like too much of a coincidence. She just happened to bare her soul to Remy last night, and this happened today? Damn her. She was going to have a talk later tonight with little Miss San Francisco.

Nora's head was pounding. She didn't think things could get worse. Until, of course Jake Callahan showed up. The charming *Detective* Jake Callahan. Nora had been helping to set up the tables and was in the process of carrying out and setting up the water glasses. They were unexpectedly short-handed without Christian. Nora went to the bar to get another tray. She was concentrating walking with the two tiers of glasses as they chattered on the tray in front of her. As she started to pass the hostess station, Nora spotted them. Jake Callahan looked rested and relaxed in his short sleeve blue and white checked Ralph Lauren cotton shirt and dark blue Levi's. Detective Parsons, on the other hand, looked disheveled in his heavy black jeans and a wrinkled gray T-shirt.

Nora guessed that they would be scheduling another round of

questioning, and she knew instantly who would be playing good cop and who would be playing bad cop. The staff braced for the inevitable and waited to see who they would summon first. What the hell, thought, Nora, what are they going to do, torture us on a daily basis? Why didn't they ask all of the questions yesterday?

She was so tired and prayed that she would make it through the day without declaring herself the culprit just so that she could get a good night's sleep. As she started giving herself another pep talk, she heard the welcome sound of Evan's voice.

He had entered the restaurant through the kitchen, then walked through the dining room and into the lounge. As he approached the two detectives, he spoke a bit loudly so the entire staff could hear.

"Detectives."

Evan nodded to each of them and shook their hands as if they were there to discuss a lucrative business deal.

"How can I help you this morning? I'm surprised to see you. I thought we had all cooperated and answered your questions yesterday."

The staff seemed to slow as they purposely lingered within earshot. Everyone was nearby except for Kevin and his Sous Chef, who were both in the kitchen busily prepping for lunch and dinner, and Betty, who was in the office getting the drawers for the registers.

Detective Parsons spoke first. "We're going to need to continue the investigation process. We have a few more questions." He stood with his arms crossed and deliberately looked around as if to make the staff nervous. Nora wondered if this was another of their not-so-subtle tactics they had learned at Detective School.

Detective Callahan looked uncomfortable and jumped in. "We actually got some additional info, so we need to ask a few more questions."

Nora noticed they were both careful not to say too much.

Evan got ready to interrupt but Jake spoke first. "We know you have a business to run, but if we can get this out of the way, then we won't have to take anyone downtown. We know you need them all here for work today, right?"

Evan nodded and didn't doubt that Jake was trying to be considerate. The other guy, though, was what his mother had always called "one of those shifty assholes." Evan's mother had always seen them as power hungry and more than willing to abuse their positions, as evidenced by the countless times they would show up unannounced one minute past closing in the hopes of catching the bartenders serving alcohol.

Evan answered politely, obviously not wanting to make any enemies. "Sure, I understand. But could we use my office?"

Jake nodded. "Sure. Why don't we head in there?" He looked at his notebook then looked back up. "Can we start with Nora?"

Chapter 17

Nora heard her name and felt as if a thousand porcupine quills had been shot all over her body. She felt sharp pain everywhere, including her chest, and after her name was called, her vision started to blur as she felt the room beginning to sway beneath her feet. She held onto the hostess station podium and waited for the detectives to walk out toward her.

"No," Evan corrected. "Actually, could you start with Betty, our Bookkeeper? She's already in the office and should be finished up by now. That way, she won't have to leave. Why don't I go tell her you're coming in."

Nora steadied herself. She knew that Evan had just rescued her, and she was so grateful. It was inevitable that she would be questioned, but at least she could try to mentally prepare herself. And maybe, if Remy went first, she could find out what they were going to ask. Nora had never relied on anyone as she was now doing, and she hoped that she wasn't making a mistake.

Evan walked into his office and saw that Betty was on the phone. The drawers were ready to go. He went to grab them. As he did so, Betty hung up and turned toward him.

"What's goin' on?"

"The detectives are back, and they want to ask each person more questions. I said yes because otherwise they're going to make you go down to the station. They're coming in here in a minute, and they're going to start with you, if that's ok. If you don't want to answer, that's fine, too. It's your decision.

Betty nodded stiffly. She sat in her chair and waited for the knock on the door.

It was a sudden, hard knock, and it made both Evan and Betty jump. An abrupt opening of the door followed it, and then the two detectives stood in the doorway blocking the sunlight.

"Betty, do you have time for a few questions?"

"Yeah, sure, why not?" Betty coughed loudly and tried to clear her throat as Evan left and they closed the door behind him.

"For the record, Betty, you stated you ran into a friend while you were out on the night in question, is that correct?" Jake tried not to sound too threatening as he questioned Betty. He always felt bad, especially when he was questioning older women; they seemed so fragile.

Both detectives practically jumped out of their chairs as Betty replied. "I don't know what the fuck yer getting at, but I'm a good employee, I haven't done anything wrong, and I got a ride home with one of my husband's friends. I told you my husband is out of town, and his friend made sure I got home ship shape. So whatever you're driving at, I had nothin' to do with it."

The detectives took a deep breath, and finally, after a few moments, Jake spoke. "Betty, I'm sorry for the trouble, we just had to ask if you went down to Good Harbor Beach at all, and we needed to know if you had seen a black Volkswagen Jetta that night either at the Port Side or at the scene."

There was a silence. Both detectives braced for yet another harsh answer from Betty. But she retreated suddenly. "I'm sorry. But this has been a tough time for us all, and we just want it to be over. By the way, do you know when the funeral's gonna be? Oh, and no, I don't know who drives what around here."

Detective Parsons answered this time, though he did so cautiously. "Thank you, Betty, that's it for now. We don't think we'll need to ask you any more questions. And, no, we don't know about the funeral arrangements, but I'm sure it'll be in tonight's or tomorrow's paper."

Jake walked Betty to the door and went out into the lounge to get the next person for questioning. He looked at his notepad then looked around the room. "I need Kevin next, please."

Evan answered immediately, "He's in the kitchen, I'll go and get him."

Evan walked into the kitchen where Kevin was prepping for lunch. "Kevin, the detectives were hoping to have a word." Kevin looked up and put down the knife he was using.

"Kevin, if you go in there and get it over with, then you won't have to go down to the station. They're meeting people one at a time in my office, so you'll have a little privacy, too. So if you just go in and get it over with, you can be done. They said they got some more information, and they need to ask a few more questions." Evan's voice lingered as he tried to seem more casual than he felt.

"These guys are a fuckin' pain in the ass." Kevin pulled off his gloves and started to walk around the steel prep table then headed toward the office.

Evan exhaled, hoping this would be the last visit from the police.

Kevin got to the office and pushed the door open. "You wanted to see me?" He made eye contact with Jake then with Detective Parsons. They motioned Kevin to close the door and then pointed to Betty's chair. "Take a seat, Kevin."

Jake flipped through his notebook, as the room was completely silent. Kevin lit a cigarette. Evan had always been very clear that there was no smoking allowed in his office. Kevin seemed not to care as he took a deep drag.

"What do you need to know, detectives? You know we're wrapping up our holiday weekend and lunch is going to be real busy today, right? So, I've got to be going soon. What do you need to know?"

Jake looked up and stared Kevin in the eye. "We heard that there was a car at the scene right before the body was found. It was a black Volkswagen Jetta. We also happen to know that's what you drive. So we need to know if you went to Good Harbor Beach that night."

Kevin stood up and took another drag of his cigarette. He looked at Jake and answered with conviction. "Nope. I wasn't a friend of Christian's, and I didn't go to Good Harbor. There are alot of Volkswagens in town. And it could a been dark blue or another color that looked like black in the dark."

Jake replied, "It was early morning. And a black Jetta with a couple in it was spotted just outside the entrance right before Christian's body was found."

Kevin shook his head and waved with his cigarette in hand. "No,

Detective, it wasn't me. I don't have alot of free time with work and all, and believe me, when I do have time and I go out ... I never spent it hanging with that freak."

"What do you mean?" asked Detective Parsons.

"I mean, not only was the kid a pain in the ass, but he was stealin' his mother's pills and sellin' em all over Gloucester. You'd think he had enough cash, but I guess not."

Both detectives looked at Kevin suspiciously. It was a known fact to the police that Kevin had dealt drugs when he was younger, so he hadn't flown under the radar. And now he was trying to point the finger at someone who couldn't defend himself.

Jake asked the next question. "What do you know?"

"Well, if you didn't know it, Christian was into trading and selling Xanex for all sorts of favors. He was giving them out at the Port Side Saturday night. Ask anybody at the bar."

Jake nodded and made some notes. He looked up and motioned toward the door. "Thanks. You can go."

Both detectives exchanged glances after Kevin closed the door behind him.

"What do you think about that?" Jake asked.

Detective Parsons answered, "He tried to fake us out with the it-could-have-been-another-dark-car objection. And the pills ... it's the first I heard of it. But let's find out from the Coroner's Office if they found any bottles of pills or if they found any evidence of Christian taking them. I think we would have heard something like that by now. They would have at least found them on him."

Detective Parsons looked at Jake. "Who's next?"

Jake looked at his notebook. "Why don't you go and get Carly. By the way, she seems pretty cozy with Kevin."

Detective Parsons went out to the lounge and pointed to Carly behind the bar. He seemed intimidating as he waved her over. "Carly. You're next."

Carly nearly dropped the glass she was drying as she put it down and walked around the bar toward the office. She followed the detective and walked into the office behind him. She stood frozen until they motioned her to sit at Betty's desk.

Carly placed her arms on both wooden arms of the chair as if to brace herself. "Detectives, I'll be glad to cooperate in any way I can."

Jake and Detective Parsons nodded. "Carly, could you tell me again, how did you get home Saturday night?" Jake stared at Carly and waited for a reply.

She cleared her throat and looked down as she answered. "I got a ride home from Kevin. We didn't have a car; so when we left, we walked over and got a slice of pizza at Delmonico's, then we walked around the corner to Kevin's. I went inside with him for a little while, then he took me home."

"What time did you say that was?" Jake tried to sound casual.

"It was late. I told you last time I didn't really pay attention to the time, but it was probably about 1:30 in the morning."

"And where did you go after you got in the car with Kevin?"

"I told you. He drove me home. I live over by the Stop and Shop."

"You mean the one near Good Harbor?"

"Yeah, that's it. But he took me right home."

"Okay. Thanks, Carly."

Carly breathed a sigh of relief as she started to stand up.

"Oh, Carly, one more thing, what kind of car did Kevin drive you home in?" Jake looked at his notebook as if the answer wasn't important.

"His car. I haven't been in it before, but I've seen him drive it. I'm not sure what kind it is, though."

"Thanks alot. You're all set." Jake stood up and walked Carly out the door.

Jake closed the door behind Carly. "You know they're tight. She wants to defend that loser, but you can tell she's scared. There's hope there. She was kinda shaky. From Lucy's description, it sure as hell sounds like them. What do you think about the time difference?"

Detective Parsons didn't hesitate. He answered in a low voice. "I think they're both lyin' sacks of shit and they had somethin' to do with it. Maybe they were partyin' at the beach with Christian. Maybe they got into a fight about the pills. Or maybe he was so shitfaced he just fell off the lifeguard chair but they're too afraid to say they were there." He looked at his watch and stood up. "I have to be somewhere in about a half hour. Can you handle the rest of 'em and we'll meet up at the station later?"

Jake shook his head. "No problem. I only have three more. If you get back first, how about checkin' in and finding out about the pills and if Christian had any on him."

"Yup. " Detective Parsons left and Jake looked at his notebook again and made a few notes. He stood up and started walking toward the door. Just then, it opened and Remy stepped inside.

"Hello, Detective," she said demurely. I guessed that I'd probably be next so I thought I'd save you the trip. Is that alright?"

Jake could smell her perfume as she walked by him. He closed his eyes for a moment and thought that it smelled like lavender. He took a deep breath and tried to mentally prepare himself for her questioning.

"It's Remy, right?" Jake smiled widely as he realized how sexy she was. "Wow, they don't grow them like you in Gloucester."

Remy smiled, obviously amused by the effect she was having on Jake.

"Ok, let's see. You were out Saturday night at the Port Side, is that right?" Remy nodded and crossed her legs so that her short skirt hiked up slightly and highlighted her toned calf and thigh muscles.

"You stayed for a while then took Nora home, is that right?" Remy nodded again. "Okay then, could you tell me about what time you left with her and any details that you think might be helpful."

Jake sat back. Remy was amused that he was trying to look casual. She knew instantly what kind of man he was. Pretty women had always been his downfall. And he probably had at least one or two ex wives already. She watched as he tried to look at a spot past her on the floor so as not to stare at her legs. She was glad she had worn something a little extra sexy today. Her short black-and-white polka dot silk skirt was perfectly fitted, as was her white linen blouse. She had unbuttoned the blouse's third pearl button so that the lace of her white silk bra peeked out when she leaned forward. The coordinating white silk scarf that she wore as a headband framed her glowing chiseled features. The ends of the scarf trailed seductively down her back and showed from beneath her glossy hair.

Remy leaned farther forward in her chair so that her bra showed. She looked intently at Jake as she answered. "Sure, detective. We all went together in a group. Christian was really drunk and he followed Nora outside after she said she needed air. A few minutes later, as I said before, I went outside to check on her. I was worried. And I walked outside and saw Christian all over Nora. She sort of pushed him away, and just then I walked up and told her we should leave." Remy ended abruptly as if she didn't want to say any more.

Jake took that as his cue. "And that's when you walked Nora to your place and she stayed over?"

"Yes. Yes, that's right. I walked her to my place and she stayed over. Then I gave her a ride in the morning."

Jake stopped for a moment. "Okay. So what time did you leave with Nora?"

"About 11:30, I think."

"Was there any evidence that Christian or anyone else was doing drugs that night?"

Remy hesitated for a moment. "I don't know about anyone else, but I did seen Christian take out a pill bottle, and I saw him take at least a couple during the night."

"What were they?"

"I'm not sure, and I don't do any of that stuff. My poison is martinis, actually. But he was obnoxious and bragging that it was some of his mother's stash.

Jake nodded. "I see. Well, thanks." Jake paused for a moment. "Oh … one last thing. What kind of car do you drive?"

Remy answered immediately." A white Saab. Convertible." I brought it with me from San Francisco."

"Okay. Thanks again. You can go." He gave Remy his most charming smile as he stood up and walked her to the door.

He looked at his watch then walked out to the hostess station where both Remy and Nora were standing. "Nora, could you have Evan come in, and then you'll be last."

"Sure. I think he's in the kitchen, Nora said. She fought to keep her voice from giving her away. "I'll get him for you."

"Evan. It's your turn, Nora said quietly as she walked into the kitchen. He smiled at her then walked toward the office. He closed the door behind him, waiting for Jake to start.

Jake motioned toward the chair. "Have a seat."

Evan felt the irony of the situation. It was his office, and a police officer was sitting in it directing *him*. "I have alot to do, and the lunch rush is going to start any minute," Evan explained as he remained standing. "If you don't mind, I'll stand."

Jake looked at his notebook, "I wanted to confirm a few things. What time did you say you left Saturday night?"

"I left about 12:00 ... or 12:15."

"And who did you say was still there?"

Evan hoped he was imagining the detective's skepticism.

Kevin, Carly, and Betty were still there. Remy and Nora had just left ... and Christian was outside ... or so I thought."

"How did you know that Remy and Nora had left? I thought Nora left with Christian."

Evan was amused and knew he was too smart for this game. "No. What I said is that Nora and Remy left. I didn't know it at the time, I found out today from Nora that she stayed at Remy's and that Remy gave her a ride home."

"Oh. And what happened to Christian?" This time, Evan was certain he heard the doubting tone in Jake's voice.

Evan tried not to sound agitated as he replied, "I saw Christian go outside. He followed Nora. Then Remy went outside after her. None of them came back in. As it turns out, Nora went to Remy's place, and no one seems to have seen Christian leave. But he must have left. Because when I got out there, he was gone."

"What condition would you say Christian was in?"

"I wasn't standing near him for most of the night. I couldn't hear everything he was saying, but I heard bits and pieces. He was really loud and pretty drunk."

"Did you see him take or offer pills to any one?"

"No."

"What condition were Remy and Nora in?"

Evan thought carefully for a moment before answering. He had to be somewhat honest. He knew that Jake was going to ask everyone this same question. "Nora seemed to have had a few drinks, then she danced with Christian. I think, more than anything, she wasn't feeling very well from the drinks, so she went outside to get some air, then called it a night

"Okay, thanks. You can go. Evan, about your car, do you drive anything other than your black Land Rover?"

Evan tried not to look surprised that Jake knew what kind of car he drove. "No. I don't."

"Okay, thanks. You're all set. Oh, and could you please send in Nora?"

Evan nodded and walked briskly out of the office and closed the door behind him. He walked up to the hostess station, where Nora was standing by herself. She looked sweet and innocent in her sleeveless linen one-piece dress. Her hair was pulled back in a perfectly brushed low ponytail, and she wore a shiny, nude gloss on her full lips. Her cheeks were flushed and slightly tan. Evan looked around then leaned in toward her. "He's going to ask you to tell him the same story. He wanted to know if Christian was doing drugs. I told him the truth. That I don't know. Then he asked me about my car and if I drove anything other than my Land Rover. Don't be nervous. You're up. He's waiting for you."

Nora tried to stride casually as she knocked then entered the office. Jake motioned to the chair. Nora sat down and fought the urge to start shaking her right foot, as she often did when she was nervous. She licked her lips and tried to swallow. She wanted some water but didn't dare for fear that the glass would shake in her hand.

"Hey, Nora, how are you?" Jake smiled, admiring her.

Nora noticed that he was studying his notebook as if he were searching it for something specific.

"Let's see, why don't you tell me again how you got home Saturday night."

Nora braced herself and took a deep breath before speaking. She cleared her throat then began. "I had a few drinks, then I danced with Christian. I didn't feel very well, so I went outside. He followed me out, and then Remy came outside. She offered to walk me to her place, so I left with her. I stayed at her place, and she drove me home in the morning." Nora realized she was speaking too fast and fought to sound more casual. "We left Christian at the door. He was pretty drunk. And … that's it."

Nora looked up to see Jake's arms crossed. She was surprised that he wasn't writing.

"Did you see any evidence of drug use?"

"Christian said he borrowed some Xanax from his mother. I didn't actually see him or anyone else take them."

"Okay. And what kind of car do you drive? Do you have a car?"

Nora tried to sound casual. "Yeah, I have a big old … a gray Cutlass, but I don't drive it that much."

Jake was staring at Nora again. She turned red and stood up suddenly. "Jake, is something wrong?" She knew this was the worst thing she could say, but she couldn't help herself.

"Nora, I'm sorry, but I think you and I both know why I'm here. Don't we?"

Jake tried to make eye contact with her.

Nora thought about what he was saying and realized she might be sick, right here in Evan's office.

Jake continued. "I mean, we should be honest about what's going on."

Nora didn't answer for a moment. Her mind was racing, and she was wondering if she should tell Jake that she was going to get a lawyer and therefore couldn't answer any more questions. But who would have told him, she asked herself?

As Nora started walking toward the door, she put her arm out, reaching for the knob. Jake put out his arm and grabbed hers.

"Hey, I didn't mean to embarrass you. I mean, I know this isn't regular detective procedure, but … " His voice trailed for a moment.

Nora stopped in her tracks as she started to recognize the tone in Jake's voice. The tone she had heard so many times from the men she dated.

"What I'm trying to say, even though this might not be the best time … I'd like to ask you out, and I was hoping I could take you to dinner. Maybe Friday night?"

Nora practically burst into tears as she realized that she wasn't going to be arrested or taken down to the station, or anything even remotely resembling that. She impulsively hugged Jake, and she was so relieved that she forgot for a moment that she was off the market and no longer available. I can't risk pissing him off, thought Nora. God. What the hell should I do?

She gave Jake a light kiss on the cheek and squeezed his arm.

She would have to explain to Evan later. She was sure he would understand.

"I work Friday nights, but maybe we can meet for drinks after work. That is, if you don't mind a late night."

"That would be great. I don't mind at all," Jake answered eagerly.

"Great, how about 11:00 o'clock at The Bradford Cafe? Call me at home if it doesn't work for you." She didn't doubt that Detective Jake would be able to get her number if he needed to.

"Done. I'll see you there." Jake smiled even more widely.

Nora walked to the door. Before she started opening it, she turned.

"Oh, by the way, maybe we should sort of keep this to ourselves for a little while."

Jake was touched that Nora was thinking about their professionalism and his career. "Yeah. Good idea."

Nora took a deep breath for the first time since Saturday night. She walked over to the hostess station smiling. Remy and Evan were both there, concerned looks draped on their worried faces.

Nora looked at each of them. "Everything is fine. Detective Callahan was very understanding and kind."

Nora grabbed menus and purposely began talking to the approaching couple. "Lunch for two? Outside on the deck, perhaps? It's a beautiful day."

Nora was pleased. She didn't need Evan and Remy's help any longer after all. She would work it out. And Evan loved her … and he would understand it if she needed to meet Jake. She would tell Evan. By Friday.

Chapter 18

Nora made it through the day almost forgetting that she and Evan were going to get out off work early, have dinner, then stay on the boat. She hadn't packed anything and would need a good half hour at the house before meeting him.

Right on schedule, at about 4:45, Evan came by the hostess station and looked at the reservation book. He spoke as he reviewed it. "What do we have going on tonight?"

Remy answered. "It's going to be pretty quiet. We only have a few reservations. The bar seems busy, but not the dining room. I think most people are in for the night."

Evan looked at his watch then at Nora. "Nora, why don't you take off at 5:00. Remy can handle it. I don't need you both here for the dinner shift. And I'm going to put Betty in charge while I do a few things tonight. Remy, you can reach me on my cell if you really need me. Betty has the number. Good night."

Remy looked surprised but relieved that it was quiet. Nora would be leaving in fifteen minutes. "Nora, I'm going to get some water. I'll be right back."

Nora nodded and tried not to smile. She was fairly certain Remy didn't realize she and Evan were going to be leaving together. She grabbed her purse from the hostess station as Remy returned with her water, then she headed toward the bathroom, and the usual stop at the end of her shift so she could wash up and check her makeup. There was a spring in Nora's step as she walked down the hall. As she reached the bathroom door and started to open it, she realized that the light switch had been turned off, and she held the door open as she fumbled on the wall for the outlet. Once she found it, she turned the light on and walked inside.

Nora's gasp was so loud she was certain it had been heard in the lounge. Her only saving grace was that the fan was unbearably loud. She stood, frozen, staring at the mirror. She read the chilling words that had been scrawled in large letters. She approached the mirror, then touched one of the bright red letters. It smudged as she pressed down with her forefinger. Lipstick. It was red lipstick.

Nora mouthed the words staring back at her. *Clever bitch!* She leaned on the sink, then ran cold water, splashing it on her flushed face. It could be for any female she worked with, she reasoned. Nora went through the list. Betty. Carly. Remy. What if it had been intended for one of them? Deep down, Nora knew the truth. It had been meant for her. She knew it in her heart. Nora backed away from the sink with water still dripping from her face. She wasn't going to tell anyone until she could figure out who could have done this. Fucker. She wasn't going to be frightened so easily.

Nora's strength and resolve grew as she thought about all of the bad situations she had been through and survived throughout her life. So what, she thought, this one wasn't so bad. She could overcome it. And she knew she was smarter than most. She wasn't going to be frightened like a poor scared rabbit. Nora looked around on the floor and near the sink for cleaning supplies. All she could see was extra toilet paper and a can of Lysol spray. The cleaning people brought the cleaners with them, she thought. She continued to look around for something with which to wipe off the lipstick.

Nora started pulling on the paper towels and collected a half dozen of them in her hand. She ran the hot water until it was steaming. She locked the door, then ran back to the sink. If customers needed to use the bathroom, they'd have to wait. Nora squirted the paper towels with a large mound of hand soap then ran them under the hot water again. It would be messy, but it should do the trick.

She put the foamy hot paper towels on the mirror and started scrubbing furiously at the letters. She jumped as she heard the loud knock on the door.

"Hello. Hello. Is somebody in there?"

Nora gave the letters one last furious scrub. "Just a minute." The pounding continued. "Just a minute."

She ran to the door and unlocked it, peering out slowly as she did.

"Hey, what's going on in here?" Remy tried to look inside past Nora.

God, thought Nora. Maybe *she* did this. Maybe she's trying to scare me. But why?

Nora still held the soaking paper towels that were by now covered with the smeared bright red lipstick. She looked up at Remy and answered quickly. "I'm … glad you're here. Some chick wrote on the mirror in lipstick, and I locked the door so none of our customers would see it."

Remy looked at Nora for a moment before replying. "Oh, God, that's pathetic. What did it say?"

Nora tried to think of something believable. She couldn't assume Remy had done this

"It was pretty rude. Apparently some guy named Ron has a large body part." Nora cleared her throat and seemed to redden.

"Damn tourists." Remy turned off the water and looked at the mirror. She stared at the remaining red streaks and the letters they still formed. She turned away from the mirror.

Shit, thought Nora. If I can see that, then Remy can, too.

Remy pretended not to notice, "I'm going to get some cleaner from the kitchen. Lock the door behind me so no one else comes in." Remy made eye contact with Nora for a brief moment before leaving. "Don't worry. We'll get rid of it."

Nora wasn't sure if she should be relieved or suspicious of Remy. Damn, she thought. Why does she keep coming to my rescue?

The loud knock on the door startled Nora. She practically leapt toward it and turned the lock. As she opened the door, she came face to face with her worst fear. Nora stared, speechless, into the cold gray-blue eyes.

"Hey, honey, I'm glad I found ya. They told me at the bar that you had left for the night. Lucky, lucky me."

Nora closed her eyes for a moment and prayed that this wasn't happening. In front of her stood the end of her dreams and the beginning of her nightmare. And this nightmare had come all the way from Florida.

Tom Almeida had obviously dressed to impress. His perfectly pressed and starched white oxford shirt bore his monogrammed initials on his left sleeve, and his brown leather belt matched his gleaming new topsider loafers. Even his slightly faded Levi jeans had been carefully ironed.

Nora finally spoke. "What are you doing here? Vacation?"

"Sweetie, vacations are for lazy people. I'm here on a mission to find somebody."

"Any body I know?" Nora winced as she waited for the sarcastic reply.

"Yeah, but seems she changed her name. Know anybody by the name of ... let's see ... it was something cute but not too original using the same initials as her real name. Oh yeah, I got it ... Nora Mason. Know anybody by that name?"

"Look ... it's a really bad time. Please tell me why you're here. And how long you'll be in town. Maybe we could meet and talk in a few days.

Tom's face reddened as he prepared to reply, but Nora spoke first. "Look, I know you came looking for me, and I know you threatened to ... " Nora's eyes welled up with tears. Today had brought almost more than even she could handle. "Could you just give me a break? Please?"

Nora's pleading tone didn't seem to affect on her former lover. She felt the nauseous feeling rise in her throat. She swallowed and waited for Tom to speak as they both stood awkwardly in the bathroom doorway. Remy came up behind them, the cleaner in hand.

Remy sensed the tenseness as she started to walk between them.

"Excuse me, I need to get through." She pushed her way between them and stood behind Nora as she held her post in the doorway.

Remy waved and placed her hand protectively on Nora's shoulder. "Hi, I'm Remy. Nora, honey, you haven't introduced us." Nora detected the knowing tone in Remy's singsong voice.

"I'm Tom. An old friend of ... Nora's." Tom nodded his head slightly, as if any more of a greeting would be too much of an unnecessary effort. He looked back and forth between the two women.

As Remy spoke again, she casually rubbed Nora's shoulder in a demonstrative attempt to comfort her. "Nora's told me all about you. That she used to work for you and that you were a good guy." Remy's tone sounded convincing, even to Nora.

"We'd love to have dinner with you while you're in town." Remy looked around then leaned in and whispered to Tom, as if to let him know it was strictly confidential. "No one knows that we're ... a couple. But since you're her old friend ... Isn't that right, sweetheart?" Remy looked at Nora with an adoring look in her eyes.

Nora didn't know whether to laugh or cry. My God, she thought, what have I done? Moving up here has turned my life even more upside down. She composed herself and played her part, not feeling she had a choice. "That's right."

Both Nora and Remy looked earnestly at Tom and waited for a reply. "You two?" Tom waved his fat forefinger back and forth then pulled a cigar out of his pocket. "Well, we have alot to talk about, don't we Nora? We need to catch up on things. And I can tell you what's going on with your family."

Tom had touched a raw nerve and that was his intention. Nora spoke immediately. "What do you mean? What's wrong with my family?" Nora hated that he could push her buttons in a matter of seconds

"Nothin's wrong with 'em. Not really. But we'll catch up on all that after tonight. I'm goin' apartment hunting. I thought I'd stick around for a little while. Kinda like an extended working vacation. You know what I mean?"

Nora tried not to sound upset. She had almost forgotten that she was meeting Evan in a little while. She couldn't cancel on him. She couldn't afford to have anyone else upset with her. She thought about the person watching her last night and wondered if it had been Tom. Just add one more person to the list, thought Nora. This was getting complicated.

"How long are you staying?" The words came out of Remy's mouth faster than Nora could say them.

"Depends how long Nora wants me to stick around." With that he dug into his right pant's pocket and pulled out the torn piece of newspaper with the circled ad. He held it up and read it aloud in an exaggerated tone.

"Gloucester, Mass. Rocky Neck. New one bedroom with fireplace, deck with water view, washer/dryer. No pets. $1500/month. Seasonal Rental. 978.555.7887. Is that a nice area … Rocky Neck?"

Nora couldn't tell if he was acting stupid or not. "Yes, that's a nice area. That's this whole area you're in right now. This whole neck that sticks out along the water. You didn't know that?" Nora practically spat out the words as her anger rose and her face flushed. How dare he come here and try to intimidate her.

"Oh, that's great, darlin', no I didn't know that. Tell me somethin', do you live around here, too? If you do, we'll be neighbors." He smiled a wide smile that was neither warm nor genuine. His perfectly capped, too-white teeth glistened in the late afternoon sun that was streaming through the lounge's sliding glass doors.

"Well, it's been great meeting you, Tom. We have to get back to work." Remy stared at Tom, and for the first time since Nora had known him, she detected a hesitation in his step. He turned and started walking away.

"I'll be in touch with you two little sweethearts." He spoke over his shoulder as he waved and walked toward the bar.

Remy slammed the bathroom door and quickly turned the lock. She leaned against the door. "Charming."

Nora's fists were clenched and Remy could see the taut muscles standing out in her neck. "God. Why me?"

Remy put the cleaner on the floor and walked up to Nora. She held her gently by both hands. Nora slowly picked up her head and straightened her back. Remy's lips were an inch from Nora's. They were almost the same height, and Remy stared intensely into her eyes. Nora inhaled the fresh citrusy tang of Remy's perfume.

As if reading her mind, Remy answered, "It's my favorite. I found it in San Francisco. It's Votivo Soku Lime. Body Mist."

Nora could smell Remy's sweet breath. It was tinged with a slight scent of Altoids. "Thanks for bailing me out again. You seem to be doing that alot."

Remy backed away slightly and then leaned down to pick up the cleaner. "No problem. You need to get going. I heard you have a hot date with Evan." She looked up and searched Nora's eyes for a response.

Nora reddened unexpectedly, not knowing why she suddenly felt bad; it was as if she was betraying Remy, especially after all of her help.

"Are you sure? I feel bad leaving you with this mess."

"Don't worry about it. Go. Or you're going to be late, and I don't want Evan to hold me responsible. I can't afford to get my ass fired. I asked Betty to watch the hostess station for a few minutes. I told her I had to clean up after some tourist. Now go." She waved her hands.

Nora walked to the door. "Do you think I have to worry about Tom?" The earnest tone in Nora's voice practically begged Remy to lie to her.

"Honey, he's probably whipped, just like most of the guys you've wrapped around your little finger. Even though he seemed to scare the hell out of you for whatever reason. But you need to think about who you want, not who wants you. Because, deep down, you can eventually have anything you really want. It doesn't matter how much money you start out with."

Nora knew Remy's statement was directed at both of them. She still wasn't sure what Remy's story was, but she was sure that she had been through some rough times, too. One of these days, Nora promised herself, they would have a heart-to-heart, the way other women seemed to.

Nora started to open the door. "Hey, I'm off tomorrow, so I'll see you Wednesday." By the way, since we're *secretly* a couple, would you be my date when I have to meet Tom? I have a feeling I'll have to see him sooner than later."

"Sure." Remy's tone turned serious for a moment as she resumed her scrubbing. "In a perfect world, we *would* have made a great couple, you know." Remy said the words without looking up.

"Remy, whoever gets you will really be lucky. I mean it." With that, Nora walked out and raced home.

Chapter 19

As Nora got to the front door, she could hear the phone ringing. She hurriedly unlocked the door and ran into the kitchen. She was starting to dread that phone. "Hello?"

"Hey, I thought you stood me up. Where have you been?" Evan's voice sounded unexpectedly stern.

"I'm sorry. Some tourist wrote all over the mirror in one of the bathrooms, and Remy and I took a while to clean it up, then I ran into an old … acquaintance …" Nora's voice trailed as she was interrupted by Evan.

"Which bathroom?"

"The one off the lounge. It's fine, it was just lipstick."

"And, yes, I've just met your old friend … Tom. He's right here having a beer with me. What a small world. Why don't you hurry over before he leaves and you can catch up."

Nora lowered her voice. "Evan, is he right there?"

"Yes. Yes, that's great," answered Evan.

"Listen to me, he's not really a friend. I'll explain later, but we don't need to spend alot of time with him."

"Okay, I'll see you in a little while." Evan hung up suddenly.

Nora opened the refrigerator and scrambled to find an open bottle of wine. She found an old bottle of white zinfandel someone had given her, which she loathed and only used for cooking. She frantically yanked out the cork then took a long swig from the bottle. She swallowed, grimacing, then took another deep gulp. Nora thought about Tom and the unkind words that could describe him. She leaned back on the closed refrigerator door and enjoyed the instant rush from drinking the wine on an empty stomach.

As Nora placed it back in the refrigerator, she noticed the shriveled pieces of lemon and lime in the white ramekin. Since the recent string of events, Nora had let her normally perfect housekeeping routine slip. She hadn't been grocery shopping, and even her usually stocked staples hadn't been restored. Nora picked up the small dish that held the unrevivable citrus. She had a flash of the night Christian had stopped by. Nora broke out in a cold sweat as her mind wandered to that evening.

There had been nothing shy or timid about Christian's demeanor. Nora had just come downstairs after taking a hot shower. It was about 10:00 p.m., and she had been wearing a freshly washed white cotton robe, the belt tied loosely around her waist. Nora had gone into the kitchen to get a glass of wine, and as she walked through the doorway, she was immediately startled to see Christian standing over a cutting board he had placed on the kitchen table. On it were two lemons and two limes. He pretended to concentrate on cutting the fruit as Nora admired his lustrous, tan body. He was unannounced, unexpected, and practically naked.

"Do you want lemon or lime with your martini?"

Nora was frozen, as if she were in a dream. She stood motionless, quietly observing him in his almost-nude glory. He had pulled off his navy short-sleeve Ralph Lauren polo shirt and had thrown it on the table. He wore only a pair of well-fitting tan shorts, a brown leather belt, and he had taken off his shoes. His perfectly toned washboard stomach gleamed softly in the dim kitchen light. Nora found him incredibly hard to resist.

As she approached the kitchen table, Christian watched her, waiting for her to get within an inch of him. As she reached him, he dropped the knife he had been using and wrapped both of his strong arms around her waist. He leaned close to Nora, kissing her passionately, his tongue playfully teasing hers until she moaned uncontrollably, her pleasure evident.

"I've got something for you, Christian whispered. "But first, let's have a drink."

Nora knew then that her body and mind would not be her own

unless she could somehow resist him. She was being so controlled by Christian's animal magnetism that she couldn't stop herself. They both tried to play it cool, but he was the first to pull away. Nora watched as he strolled to the refrigerator and opened the door to the freezer. He grabbed the bottle of Absolut Vodka, holding it up for Nora to observe.

"I see you brought a belated housewarming gift," Nora had teased.

"No. That's not what it's for."

Nora tried to remain calm, not wanting Christian to know how affected she was by him.

He held up two martini glasses.

"Hey, where'd you get those?" Nora questioned suspiciously.

"I poked around while I was waiting for you to get out of the shower."

Nora wondered exactly how much poking around he had done. She watched as he expertly poured the vodka into the glasses then squeezed a piece of lemon and lime into each drink before discarding the citrus pieces into the sink.

"You suck at cutting fruit."

"Yeah, well, I've always had someone else to do it for me."

"That's pathetic."

Christian stirred the drinks and smiled brightly. He apparently was unaffected by Nora's attempt at an insult. "Yes, but don't you feel bad for me?"

"No." Nora grabbed her drink and smiled back. She was nervous when she thought about what might happen tonight. "Did you know that I'm sort of dating Evan?"

Christian seemed unaffected. "You can do better."

Nora had to admire his confidence. "Really? And who would be better? Would that be you? Is that what you're thinking?"

Christian smirked and leaned forward. He kissed Nora softly on the lips then held up his martini. "You tell me."

He deliberately waited a moment. "Here's to getting liquored up on smashed fruit martinis. Or … Martinis a la Christian."

"That's usually my line … I mean … the *a la* part."

Christian took a deep sip. He searched the pockets of his shorts and pulled out a crumpled pack that contained about a half dozen cigarettes. Newport Lights, Nora noted.

"There's no smoking in the house." She took a deep gulp of her drink and waited for his reply.

"Then let's go outside." The night was starting to cool considerably and it was clear and very dark. Nora pulled out a chair and sat down, and Christian sat down close beside her.

As Nora's eyes adjusted, she could see that Christian's head was turned. He seemed to be admiring her.

"Sweetheart, you're hot. I've been dying to ask you out."

Nora felt as nervous as a schoolgirl out on a first date with a boy she liked. She crossed her arms as the wind started to pick up. "I can see that you're shy, too."

Before Nora could think about what she was doing, Christian was out of his chair and pulling Nora up onto the tips of her toes. "I'll warm you up."

He held her forcefully and kissed her with the perfect amount of roughness and passion. Nora had wrapped her arms around Christian's neck and continued to return his strong and sensual kisses. She could feel the wetness between her legs as she became aroused, and as Christian wrapped his arms tighter around her waist, she could feel his hardness between them.

"Let's go inside," said Christian. "It's getting cold."

"I think you should go."

Christian ignored what Nora had just said. He knew what she wanted. He grabbed their two drinks and headed for the kitchen.

As he reached the kitchen table, he put down what was left of them and grabbed Nora's hand. He led her up the stairs.

When they got to the top, he pressed Nora against the wall and grabbed her hips toward him. Again, he leaned down and started kissing her, this time leaving a soft, wet trail down her velvety, perfectly sculpted neck.

"Stop, Christian … Stop."

Nora was surprised by the agitated tone of her own voice.

"Don't you want this? He asked, searching Nora's eyes for confirmation. "I think you do."

"I know, but I … I can't. I'm sorry. You need to go."

Nora felt that she needed to apologize. She hadn't meant for it to get this far. She thought about why she was reacting this way. It's not as if Evan's declared his love, she thought. Why was she passing up this opportunity? They could have had a really great time, she had later reminisced. But she had said no.

"Could I stay over any way? It's late, and I'm pretty buzzed."

Nora thought that it might be worse to have Christian wandering the streets of Rocky Neck at this hour.

"Okay. If you promise to behave, I'll even have another drink with you." Nora suddenly felt in control and knew she would be okay.

"Cool. I'll go make us another one," Christian replied confidently.

Nora was sure that somewhere in the back of his twenty-year-old mind, he had the hope that she would get drunk and succumb to his advances.

"I'll come down, replied Nora. The last thing she wanted was for Christian to be spilling their martinis all over her handmade comforter.

Nora followed Christian downstairs. She walked into the living room and made her way over to the stereo. She thumbed through her carefully arranged CD's and then chose some music while he made them another drink. Nora knew that she didn't really want one, but that ploy had been one successful way of usually getting men to think about something other than sex. More alcohol. This would somehow lead, the male species always assumed, to sex.

Nora sat on the couch and pulled her knees beneath her while she waited for Christian to bring in their cocktails. Her eyes began to close as she heard the first song. It was one of her favorite Simon and Garfunkel tunes. She felt herself floating as the words asked, *"Are you going to Scarborough Fair?"* Nora was so tired. She closed her eyes for just a moment, afraid she wouldn't be able to fight off the fatigue.

"Nora, wake up. It's 6:20. Nora felt her body being shaken. "Nora." She opened her eyes and saw Christian standing over her. Suddenly, she bolted upright. The blanket she had draped over her slid to the floor as she stood.

"Oh, God, I fell asleep." Nora looked around and tried to get her bearings.

"Yeah. I couldn't wake you up last night … you were gone," replied Christian. "So we both slept on the couch."

Nora grabbed the blanket from the floor and covered her shoulders. "It's freezing in here."

"I know. It got cold last night." Christian looked at Nora. "How about a ride home? I share a car with my mother, and I told her I was all set last night."

"Shit, Christian, that means they'll see me drop you off."

"Right." Christian rolled his eyes. "My mother never wakes up from her Sherry and whatever before twelve … unless I drag her out of bed. Or my dad does. And he's probably already out on the golf course."

"Oh." Nora wondered about the kind of life that Christian really had. Maybe it wasn't as glamorous as it seemed. She ran into the guest bathroom and threw on a pair of yoga pants and the hooded zip top that had been hanging on the back of the door. As she grabbed her keys from the table in the front foyer, she thought about the situation. The sooner she could get him home, the less likely it would be that someone would see them.

"Let's go."

They walked the two blocks to Nora's car. "Why don't you park near the house?" He asked almost innocently.

Nora wondered if he was in fact being innocent or just a smart-ass. "Because I'm embarrassed. It's a crappy car, and *my* parents didn't buy me a BMW."

The sarcasm seemed to be wasted on Christian as he got in and slammed the mammoth door with a loud thud, "Whatever. I don't have a BMW."

"Yeah, but you have everything else."

Christian looked at Nora earnestly. "Not really. There are alot of things I want that I don't have."

Nora drove through Rocky Neck then turned right onto East Main Street as she headed over toward the exclusive Back Shore. She felt she had done the right thing last night. I must be losing it, she thought. I could have had a really good time with Christian. She pictured his muscular tan chest as he stood at her kitchen table last night.

"Take a right here."

Christian's words suddenly interrupted her thoughts. Thank God.

She was starting to regret her decision, Nora admitted. They drove through the gates and pulled halfway through the circular drive.

"Nice little place you have."

"It belongs to the rents. Believe me, it's their house one hundred percent. I'm just here for the summer. I'm practically the hired help. They probably can't wait for me to leave."

He got out of the car, held up his hand, and waved slightly. "Wish me luck. I have to try to get my mother up so she can give me a ride to work." His voice was tinged with sarcasm.

"Good luck." Nora waved quickly and pulled away, hoping she wouldn't see anyone she knew on her way back home.

Chapter 20

Nora made her way down the stairs toward the front door, her overnight bag in hand. She sped up her pace, thinking about Evan and how long he had been waiting for her tonight. She didn't want him spending too much time with Tom. This was going to be a great date that she and Evan were going to have, and in spite of all that had happened, she wasn't going to be the one to ruin the mood.

Nora felt instantly uneasy as she locked the front door and thought about what Tom might say to Evan. She couldn't even begin to guess what stories Tom would be telling him about their life together in Fort Lauderdale. She wondered if he believed that she and Remy were lovers. She doubted it. His ego would never allow him to believe it, even if it had been true.

Nora ran down the path and closed the gate behind her. If she could lose Tom, she knew everything would be great. She and Evan really needed this time off together.

She walked briskly toward the dock. She sighed as she took in the view. It was going to be another amazing sunset on Rocky Neck. The kind of sunset that inspired the artists who lived here. Nora walked down the ramp and stood almost directly in front of Evan's boat, watching the two figures as they talked. She could already tell that Evan was being polite and that he was ready for Tom to leave. She watched Tom and saw the unmistakable determination in the way he stood with his legs spread slightly and stiffly braced, as if he were preparing for an attack.

Both men looked toward her. Nora thought about the skirt she was wearing and about the fact that it was going to make for an awkward entrance onto the boat. One of them was bound to see her underwear, she thought. Hopefully, it would be Evan.

As Nora walked onto the dock and up the two steps, she quickly and gracefully swung each of her legs over the top lifeline then deposited her bag onto the deck. She could see out of the corner of her eye that Tom was getting ready to speak.

She straightened and walked up quickly to Evan. "Hi, sorry I'm late. I had a few things to do before I left work, and then I got tied up at home for a little while."

Evan reached his arm behind Nora and wrapped it around her waist. "That's alright. I got the chance to meet Tom." The conversation was interrupted as Evan's cell phone rang. "Yes?" he said in an annoyed tone.

Nora knew immediately that it was his mother. That impatient tone seemed to be reserved for her, especially lately. Nora continued to watch Evan, pretending not to notice as Tom tried to make eye contact with her.

"Yes, mother. Yes. I gave him the key and filled him in on all the details. He's all set. Mother, I have to go. He's still here and I need to wrap up. Bye."

Evan flipped his cell phone closed with an annoyed gesture.

"What's going on?" Nora asked.

Evan turned so that he was facing both of them. "Tom called one of the ads in the paper, and it turns out it's a building my mother owns and just had renovated. So, he's going to be moving in tonight. My mother called and asked me to give him a key. I keep copies of all the keys in case there's an emergency."

Nora's shocked look said it all. "Where's the apartment?"

Evan gestured with his hand to a building that was half a block away. "Right next to Sam's Ice Cream. That red building near the dock."

Tom spoke in his annoying drawl. "Nora, you're gonna have to come over and check it out. It's one sweet place. And Evan here told me his mother said I could stay as long as I want, since it's already July and they just finished it up."

He waited a moment and then continued to speak in his annoying drawl. "Evan told me I was real lucky to get it. There's nothin' available once the summer starts. And I met Betty, too, she's real nice."

"Yeah, you're pretty lucky." Nora tried not to sneer as she replied sarcastically. "What do you mean, you met Betty … why did you meet Betty?" Nora looked from Tom to Evan and back again.

"Betty is my Aunt, and she lives on the first floor. My mother rents it to her and her husband. They've been there for years. That's not one of the apartments that got renovated, though."

"You mean, Betty's related to you?" Nora was surprised and thrown off guard.

"Yes. She's my mother's sister. She's my Aunt Betty."

Nora thought about how close they seemed. "Well, that explains it."

"That explains what?" He asked.

Nora didn't realize she had verbalized her thoughts. "Nothing."

Tom looked back and forth between Evan and Nora. He chugged the rest of his Bud Light and held the bottle up for emphasis that it was empty in the hope that Evan would offer him another.

Nora knew she would have to intervene. She looked at Evan first, then at Tom. "Tom, I hope you don't mind, but Evan and I had planned to have dinner, and it's getting late."

She looked at her watch for emphasis. It was 7:40 p.m., and she had no idea if she and Evan were having dinner or just drinks.

Tom flushed as he was reminded he was the odd man out.

"No problem. I'm sure we'll have a chance to spend some time together. I need to head out so I can pick up a few things for my new place, anyway."

Nora didn't need to be reminded. "Great. Thanks for stopping by."

She walked him to where the stairs were on the dock and stood close by so that he couldn't linger any longer than he already had.

She couldn't bring herself to mutter the usual niceties. Her eyes said it all. Tom forced a smile.

Evan watched the exchange and purposely didn't make additional conversation so as not to encourage Tom unnecessarily. He was surprised at how unaffected he was by Tom's apparent interest in Nora. He couldn't wait for them to have dinner and share the night. He was prepared to romance her, and he knew she would love it.

Tom climbed out of the boat and waved briefly as he walked away. Nora breathed a sigh of relief. The irony of the situation hadn't escaped her. They had just entertained an ex-lover of hers on her new lover's boat.

Nora walked over to Evan and hugged him tightly.

"Would you like a glass of champagne? Evan asked. "I have some downstairs."

Nora nodded. "Do you want me to go down and get it?"

"Why don't we go down together. We can get settled, I can give you the official tour that includes the *sleeping* quarters, and we can have a cocktail and a bite to eat."

Evan carried Nora's bag and led her downstairs. As she got to the landing, she gasped. White votive candles were lit throughout the cabin, a large bouquet of white roses had been placed carefully in a vase on the table, and a gleaming silver champagne bucket was filled with several bottles of champagne. Nora spotted the familiar orange foil that told her it was her favorite, Veuve Clicquot.

Nora smiled. No one had ever done anything like this for her before. She got misty-eyed, grateful for Evan and their new relationship. She had done the right thing by turning Christian down.

She watched as Evan carefully popped the cork and poured the glasses nearly to the rim before setting the bottle back in the champagne bucket.

Nora took the glass as Evan offered it to her and watched the tiny bubbles as they traveled to the surface, guiltily remembering the concert in the park with Christian and the champagne toast they had shared.

Evan held up his glass and made a toast. "To finding love on Rocky Neck."

"I'm definitely a lucky girl," Nora replied.

He took a long sip, put down his glass, then took Nora's from her and placed it beside his.

They stood, holding onto each other, and Nora felt the comfort she had always longed for and the connection she was certain Evan felt, too. The evening wind was warm and soft, and Nora's hair billowed softly around her face as Evan leaned forward and pressed his lips to hers.

Nora closed her eyes and felt the warmth of soft lips on hers. He pressed earnestly, parting her lips with his and moving his tongue smoothly against Nora's. Their passion quickly mounted.

Nora shivered and slowly threw her head back as Evan alternated between tracing a path down her neck with his tongue and nibbling softly at both of her earlobes.

"Evan, I love you." Nora gasped as Evan's kisses sent shivers down her spine.

Evan's lips traveled back to Nora's. He stopped for a moment, his breath husky, as he leaned toward Nora's shoulder. He whispered in her ear, "And I want to make love to you."

Nora stopped, disappointed that he hadn't said the words. Evan continued, "Let's enjoy our night … and the champagne. Maybe we can even have some dinner.

Nora waited a minute then replied. "I'd love that."

Evan walked over to one of the shelves along the far wall and turned on the stereo. He pushed the CD button then turned toward Nora.

"It's Joao Gilberto. Girl from Ipanema." Evan walked over to the galley counter where he ceremoniously lifted a white linen napkin that had been covering a large square ceramic plate.

"For you … some of your favorites."

Nora smiled as she looked at the array.

"I made a light dinner for us." He pointed to the plates on the counter. "This is duck liver pâté with crackers with cracked black pepper and cornichons. This is crostini with sun-dried tomatoes and parmiaggiano reggiano, and here we have grilled shrimp with pesto.

Nora eyed the display, approving wholeheartedly.

"Oh, and for dessert, I have a surprise." Evan smiled widely as he enjoyed the look on Nora's face.

"You're the dessert? Or … you know I love dessert and want to get lucky?"

Evan's tone turned serious as he stared intently at Nora. "I am lucky. For the first time ever." He held Nora's eyes with his for a long moment.

"Do you want to eat down here or up on deck?"

"Down here. It's more private." Nora replied, as she took another long sip.

"I know what you mean. She does happen to be docked pretty close to the restaurant. There are plenty of curious eyes."

Nora replied teasingly, "Oh I don't care. I'm not embarrassed. I thought you would be, actually."

"I'm over it. What happened to Christian sort of put things in perspective. I'm not going to worry so much any more. I just want to take care of myself … and us."

Nora thought about what Evan had said. He was right.

He smiled, "Let's go have our dinner al fresco."

"Hey, I didn't get the full tour you promised me," Nora commented.

Evan chuckled and Nora watched as his smile completely lit up his sparkling green eyes. "I'll give you the tour later." He held up a quilt he had brought up with him from down below. "I thought if we were out here for a while we might need this."

Evan sat next to Nora and opened up the quilt. They laughed, drank champagne, and enjoyed the incredible meal. Evan emptied the bottle as he filled each of their glasses for the third time. He placed it upside down in the bucket and gave Nora a small grin. "There's more downstairs when we want it."

They took a break from their appetizers and proceeded to lean back onto the cotton cushions at the stern just behind the large gleaming wooden wheel. Evan placed his arm around Nora as she moved closer. He breathed deeply as he looked at the night sky. They remained quiet, taking in the beauty as the midnight blue darkened to black. The sound of the lapping water against the boat lulled them into a dream-like state. They could hear the muffled voices of people walking along the main street and the conversation and occasional laughter coming from the deck outside the nearby restaurants, including Rocky Neck Grille.

Since the boat was two stories below the restaurant's deck, they felt invisible as they enjoyed the sights and sounds of a festive summer evening.

Evan spoke first and broke the silence "Can I take your glass?" Nora took the last sip and handed it to him, who placed it on the small wooden table nearby.

"Would you … ?" Before Evan had finished his sentence, he had grabbed Nora's waist and had rolled her onto him. He sat back on the soft cushions facing her. His arms were wrapped around hers, holding her close.

"Do you want to go inside?" Nora whispered.

"No. I don't." Evan answered. "Do you?"

"What do *you* think?" Nora wrapped the blanket around her shoulders so that it covered both of them. She hiked up her skirt along her thighs, feeling Evan's strong legs under hers. As she wrapped her arms around his neck and moved closer, he wrapped his arms tightly around Nora's waist.

They continued kissing, their passion tumbling towards the point of no return. Nora leaned against Evan, their bodies pressed eagerly against one another's.

"God, Evan, what you do to me … "

His every sense was ignited as he held Nora's face in his hands, his eager tongue stroking hers. He placed his hand gently on the nape of her neck, allowing his fingers to feel the silky texture of her thick, soft hair.

"Nora, stay with me."

Nora looked at him in surprise. "Yes, of course."

Evan spoke even more softly, "No, that's not what I mean. Not just for tonight."

Nora didn't want to misinterpret. She didn't want to scare Evan away. They had finally gotten this far, in spite of Christian and Tom and who ever else didn't want to see them together.

"What are you saying?"

"I think you know." With that, Evan pressed his hungry lips to hers. He wanted to ravage her, be inside her, physically as well as emotionally. He pulled her body as close to as he could, smelling the soft fragrance of her perfume, the pungent scent of her shampoo, and the slightly salty scent of the evening air. Evan would always remember this one moment in time. He was finally where he wanted to be.

Nora could feel Evan's passion and kissed him back just as hungrily. She felt as if they were one being and no one else was on Rocky Neck at that moment. Her senses were exploding. She could smell the faint traces of Evan's cologne, the sweet fragrance of his soap, and the starch of his cotton button-down shirt. Nora didn't want to let go. She could stay here forever, she admitted.

Evan pulled away slightly as he spoke, "I don't want to share you with anyone else. Let's go down below. I'll give you the rest of the tour."

He led Nora downstairs and closed the cabin door. Tonight would be a night to remember. A true start to their life together as a couple.

Chapter 21

Nora awoke to the smell of freshly brewed coffee tinged with cinnamon. She looked out the small porthole window and could see that it was daylight. As she sat up and looked for a clock, she heard sounds coming from the galley.

"Are you ready for coffee?" Evan asked as he leaned his head into the sleeping cabin.

Nora was amazed that she had barely stirred yet Evan had known she was awake.

"Yes, definitely. What time is it? I think we missed the sunrise."

"It's 8:30. I was up early. Cloudy and raining today, so don't worry, you didn't miss it. I'll get your coffee."

"No, actually, I'm getting up." Nora climbed out of the bunk.

"How did you sleep?" Evan asked as he made Nora her coffee and she slid onto the bench at the table.

"I slept great. I've never slept on a boat before. It was like being rocked to sleep. Oh, and the before-sleeping part wasn't so bad, either." Nora felt slightly awkward telling Evan how much she had loved being with him last night. For the first time in her life, she hadn't felt the need to analyze her every word and action. She could be herself with Evan.

"I … me, too," he agreed. Evan handed her the steaming cup then grabbed his white T-shirt that had been on the table. He slipped it on as Nora looked on, admiring him.

"I meant to ask you something," Evan said more seriously as he slid next to Nora. "How well did you know Tom when you were in Fort Lauderdale? He seems to be … interested in you.

Nora thought about how much she should tell Evan right now. She wanted so desperately to be completely honest, but she didn't want to ruin the moment.

"I worked for him. He was my boss."

Evan stared at Nora for a moment. "So what's he doing here?"

It was as if she was in Fort Lauderdale all over again. She was panicked and wanting to run away. She hadn't prepared for this for some reason. Usually, she would have had prepared for something like this. She admonished herself, then looked into her coffee mug as she answered. "I think he wants me back."

Evan tried to understand what Nora was saying. "To work for him again? Doesn't he know you're happy here?"

He looked into Nora's eyes and suddenly realized what she hadn't told him. What he had feared most but didn't want to admit. He flushed as he realized how foolish he had been.

"I'm an idiot. You were involved with him?" Evan stared at Nora in disbelief.

"I didn't mean to … get involved. I mean, he was my boss, and one thing led to another. Then, even after I realized that I didn't want to go out with him … I felt strange about telling him. If you don't know it yet, you will soon. He's tough." Nora felt defensive in trying to explain the situation.

Evan's body stiffened with every word that Nora said. It was as if she were hitting him over the head with a hammer. He jammed his fists into the pockets of his shorts.

"You seem to have an affinity for dating your bosses. So, what are you saying? Maybe I'm just not quick enough to get it. That if you felt that way about me, I mean, if you didn't want to see me … you'd be too afraid to say anything and you'd just use me? To keep your job?"

"That *IS NOT* what I said," Nora answered back in frustration. "That was a completely different situation. He was … disgusting. You can't compare that to us."

Nora realized that she was digging an even bigger hole for herself.

"So, what you're really saying, is that he was disgusting, but you went out with him anyway? What does that say about *YOU*, Nora?"

"Look, I wanted to be completely honest about this, so I just told you the truth. Last night we were doing a little more than *talking*, so I didn't have a chance to tell you. Ask me anything, I'll tell you whatever you want to know." Her voice trailed as she turned away from him.

"We had a wonderful time last night. Why do we … you … have to ruin it?" Nora's eyes welled up with tears, more from the frustration of not being able to make him understand and convey to Evan how much she cared. She wanted to scream out that he could trust her. Damn, thought Nora. I'm finally totally honest about things, and it backfires.

Her frustration became defensiveness as she saw the angry look on Evan's face. She realized that he was not going to back down or try to understand. He had too much baggage, thought Nora. Just as she had. But it was just different baggage than hers.

"While we're on the subject of being honest … why didn't you tell me that Betty's your aunt? I've heard you whispering all those times in the office. What is she? Some kind of plant to watch everybody for you?" As Nora said the words, she realized she had gone too far. Not his family, she thought, she'd never win if she started criticizing his family.

"My sweet aunt is none of your damn business."

Evan walked to the stairs and started to make his way outside. It was pouring rain, and as he opened the cabin door, the cold drops pelted his T-shirt and splattered around him loudly onto the floor of the galley. "This date is officially over. I'll walk you home if you like."

*　　　*　　　*

Nora walked with her head down as the icy drops landed on her thin cotton jacket. The hostile wind tugged at her skirt and blew her hair in a thousand directions. She clenched her bag and started taking bigger steps as she approached the hill where her street met Rocky Neck Avenue. She stopped for a moment to zip up her jacket and wipe her rain-battered face.

Nora wanted desperately to cry, to let out her sadness and frustration, but all the events of this past week had dried her up emotionally. Her heart sank when she thought about the hurt and anger she had seen on Evan's face, a look that said she had betrayed him. But why, she asked herself? Why didn't he understand that this was something that had happened in the past and had nothing to do with the two of them?

Nora approached her gate, started to push it open, then watched helplessly as the wind ripped it from her hand and blew it back violently until it almost snapped off its hinges. She tried to close it behind her before realizing that the hinges had bent.

As she fumbled for her keys at the front door, she dropped her bag. She bent down to pick it up as the unexpected voice sent a chill through her already soaked body.

"You want a hand with that?"

Nora shook her head back and forth, praying that she could get in before he was any closer.

"We need to talk," the voice explained. Nora immediately recognized it as Kevin's.

She jiggled the key in the lock and finally felt it turn. She wondered if she could get inside without him. "There's nothing for us to talk about."

"Oh, yes, there is," he replied sarcastically.

Nora pushed the door open and ran inside. She turned, leaning with all of her weight onto the door as she tried to close it while he tried to force it open. Her trembling fingers fought to turn the lock. On her third try, she was finally successful. She leaned against the door, then slid to the floor, her body completely exhausted.

Nora felt one final heavy pound of his fist, "You fucking bitch."

The footsteps faded. Nora sat in the dark hallway for what seemed like hours before mustering the strength to force her trembling legs up from the floor. She awoke the following morning, hoping that it had all been a bad dream. She had slept fully dressed with all of the lights on, and for the first time since she had arrived here, she was frightened, not feeling at home and not certain of who she could trust.

Nora had stayed in the house that entire day. She had reasoned that it was because of the unexpected summer storm they were having. As the rain pelted her windows, she sat on the couch, contemplating how she was going to put herself back together. Christian was dead. Evan hated her. Tom had come back to claim her. Kevin wanted to frighten her. And Remy wanted to love her. It was too much to take in all at once. Her life was a full-on soap opera, just as her name had promised.

*   *   *

The next morning, Nora thought about what she needed to do. In any tough situation, she had always felt more confident when she dressed for the part. So, that's what she would do. She headed determinedly into her closet and pushed back her regular summer attire. She extended her arms out until her hands reached the back of the closet. She touched the garments, one by one, recalling when she had purchased each piece. She finally chose a black silk Chanel skirt and coordinating sleeveless blouse. With it, she paired a high-heeled perfectly pointed pair of Prada shoes--buttery soft black leather with angelic leather lace bows at the toe. The illusion was complete.

In addition, she wore a black silk headband that held back her silky blond hair and accentuated her strong chin. She would need a strong chin, thought Nora, especially today. She thought about what day it was. Wednesday. Friday was her date with Jake. Jake the Detective. She had been worried about telling Evan about it. But now it was a moot point. It didn't matter what he thought, she realized. Not now. Not since he had asked her to leave his boat. She thought for a moment about how and why she invoked such strong emotions in men. She thought about the anger in Tom's eyes ... almost the same look she had seen in Evan's.

Forget dating, thought Nora. She had enough of dating for now. She was going to go it alone. She thought about how she had drowned her sorrows in too much Chardonnay yesterday, as she had thought about how no man ever seemed to love her. They liked her all right. And they always wanted to sleep with her. But, until Evan, or so she had thought, she had never known the love that a man could have for her. Nora sobbed unexpectedly. She had always wanted the dream man. But it never seemed to work out. And she was getting so tired. This new venture had seemed like her chance for a new life ... and a new man.

She stood, frozen for a moment, as she saw the answer bright as day. She would have to go it alone. And she might never find Mr. Right. Nora was shocked by the revelation. And even more shocked by the fact that it no longer frightened her.

*   *   *

Nora reached the restaurant and purposely used the lounge entrance. She had arrived exactly on time to ensure that all of the staff was present in case Kevin got out of hand. She headed directly toward the kitchen.

Out of the corner of her eye, she could see Evan coming out of his office. She gulped and prayed that she could pull this off. Nora approached the large gleaming stainless steel table where Kevin was prepping for lunch. Her heart was pounding so loudly that she could barely hear herself think. She waited for him to look up before she spoke.

"If you don't stop harassing me, I'm going to have to tell them everything." Nora planted her feet and waited for Kevin's caustic reply.

"What are you talking about?" Kevin's eyes locked with Nora's.

"You know what I'm talking about. And if you ever harass me again, I'm going to have to file a complaint with the police." Nora's lips trembled slightly before she bit down on them in order to keep them steady.

"Crazy bitch," he whispered under his breath. "Leave me alone. I have work to do."

"I thought it was "clever bitch?" By the way, nice touch with the lipstick thing." Kevin pretended to look confused. Nora's voice grew louder as her frustration began to overwhelm her.

"There are a lot of people smarter than you. I'd try to remember that." She turned quickly and walked toward the hostess station. She did not intend to let Kevin know how intimidated she was. At least she had done something. She couldn't just stand by and let him stalk her.

"What was that all about?" Remy stood over her, ready to hear the answer.

Nora straightened as she placed her bag behind the podium. "I'll tell you later. I think he's been following me."

"Why?"

Nora looked around before answering in a barely audible whisper. "He thinks I had something to do with ... Christian. And he's pissed off that he looks more guilty than I do."

"Watch out for him. He's not the most stable."

"Unfortunately, I know." Nora nodded her head in agreement.

Remy changed her tone, "You need a break tonight. We both do. It's Wednesday, and you know what that means ... pool night at The Bull."

Nora welcomed the invitation. She hadn't normally joined the staff and hadn't realized that Remy had been out with the crew regularly. She had been with them once to Bull Tavern to play pool, and it had been the most fun she'd had since landing here. She had loved going to the old renovated mill building downtown. The appetizers and entertainment had been great, and there were plenty of foolish, innocent men willing to try to beat her at pool. Nora loved the fact that her looks tended to take guys off guard, and they were always convinced, especially after three Sam Adam's with a tequila chaser, that they would beat her. Nora would warn them. But they never believed her ... until she beat and embarrassed them.

"Meet me at 9:00. My place. Then we'll walk over." Remy whispered as she wiped down the lunch menus.

"What if we're not finished by then? We might still be really busy for dinner."

"You didn't hear?" There's a small private service for Christian tonight. And out of respect, Evan's closing at 9:00 tonight. Besides, it shouldn't be that busy."

Nora had to ask. "So no one was invited? No friends or co-workers?"

"Nope. I heard Christian's family only wants to have a small who's who list."

Remy looked over at Nora. "So ... are you in?"

"Yes," Nora answered. Are you sure it wouldn't be easier if we just met there?"

"No. I don't really like to walk into bars alone. Meet me at my place. And let's not invite the rest of the crew. I think we should lay low, at least a little, until the dust settles. Know what I mean?" Remy's eyes widened as she looked around.

"Yes. I do." Nora wondered if she should ask Remy her opinion about going out with Jake Friday night. Maybe it was a bad idea. She'd ask her later.

"Oh, hey, how was your date with Evan?" Remy asked casually.

"It started out okay. But then it got really bad."

"I'm sorry. What happened?"

"Let's just say that I don't think we'll get to the point of understanding each other. It's not going to work out." Nora listened to her own explanation, forcing herself to listen to her own advice, for once in her life. "I don't think we'll be going out again."

Remy saw the sadness in Nora's eyes, knowing she was trying to play it cool.

Chapter 22

Remy and Nora were dressed for the night out. Their clothing happened to be almost identical, snug hip hugging faded jeans and cotton ribbed turtlenecks. Remy's cotton turtleneck was black and Nora's was a light blue. They were identical purchases from the Gap.

Remy had laughed as she opened the door to greet Nora. "Wow. We're twin Gloucester pool hustlers. The guys are gonna love us."

Nora laughed, too. The local guys would be all over them tonight. Especially since their look differed from that of the local girls. She stepped into Remy's loft, handing her the bottle of Kendall Jackson Chardonnay. "How about a glass to loosen up our pool-hustling wrists before we head out?"

"Absolutely. Come on in." Remy waved Nora in and headed over to the kitchen to open the bottle.

"Hey, have a seat. We have plenty of time to go out," Remy commented as she stared at the antique looking metal clock on the wall above the stove.

"Nice. Not from Wal-Mart, I'm guessing?"

Remy watched Nora as she assessed it. "It's an antique from my Grandmother Martin in San Francisco. Good guess." She poured their gallon-size glasses of Chardonnay then handed one of them to Nora as she walked over to her at the island counter.

Remy held up her glass, "To putting Christian's mystery to rest … and to finding out what the hell happened."

"I know what happened." Nora chose her words carefully.

"What? How do you know?" Remy asked in a high-pitched voice.

"Evan told me. He told me that Christian fell off one of the life guard chairs on Good Harbor Beach."

Remy walked up to Nora, staring intently at her as she approached. "What do you mean?"

Nora's mind raced, as she realized that Remy didn't know. She spoke in a cautious voice. "Evan said … that it wasn't anybody's fault but Christian fell off the lifeguard chair." Nora realized what she had just relayed to Remy.

"How did Evan know that?"

Nora's face flushed as she answered. "Maybe the detectives told him?"

"They wouldn't do that." Remy's eyes widened as she looked to Nora for a response.

"I don't know the details. Maybe I got the story wrong. I'm sure there's an explanation."

Nora wondered how many cocktails it would take to relax tonight and forget about Christian … and Evan. She took several large gulps of her wine then proudly held up the empty glass. "Let's go." She turned to Remy intently. "Please don't tell anyone what I told you. Give me a chance to ask Evan about it. Okay?" Nora thought about what she had just said. Would Evan have given her the same chance?

Remy shrugged, willing to move on to other subjects, "Time to play some pool with the boys." She grabbed Nora's arm and headed out the door.

Nora inhaled the fresh saltiness of the downtown ocean air as she and Remy walked to The Bull. The parking lot was full, and before they even reached the front door, she could hear a blaring local rendition of Rod Stewart's "Hot Legs." They walked into the gray smokiness and made their way through the throngs of locals to the enormous L-shaped stainless steel bar. Both looked around casually and assessed the situation. Nora was surprised that Remy didn't mind hanging out with the local guys. Or guys in general for that matter. She was definitely surprised by Remy's willingness to adapt to any situation.

"Loser at twelve o'clock. Don't make eye contact. We'll be stuck with him all night." Remy's gaze remained focused on Nora as she checked out the situation out of the corner of her eye then continued her report. "Shit. Your Florida friend is at three o'clock."

Nora's eyes widened. Immediately, she made unexpected direct eye contact with Tom. "Remy, I can't handle any more excitement this week. Let's go."

"No, that's the worst thing you could do. Stand up to him, or he'll know you're intimidated and things will only get worse as he puts the full court press on you."

Nora nodded.

Remy continued, "Hey, wait a minute ... maybe you *are* intimidated."

"Shut up. That loser does not intimidate me. I can handle ... anything."

"Let's get a cocktail and see who we have to play with tonight then."

Remy grabbed Nora's hand and pulled her through the crowds of twenty-five to seventy-five year olds. That's what Nora loved about Gloucester. Anyone could blend in, rich or poor, young or old.

Remy's determination and charm got them their drinks served with breakneck speed. In less than two minutes, they were enjoying their Dark and Stormy's.

Nora grabbed her glass and took a long sip of the spicy rum drink tinged with lime.

"I asked for extra lime. Good isn't it?" Remy asked.

"Not my usual, but yes, it is. How'd you know that I'd like these?"

"There are a lot of things I think you'd like if you tried them." Remy said lightly. She had been leaning close so that Nora could hear her through the music and boisterous talking. She smiled and locked eyes with Nora for a long moment.

"Yeah, well, I've lived a sheltered life," Nora replied sarcastically.

"Right. I'll bet." Remy laughed and tried to search out Tom out of the corner of her eye. "I think creepy is gone."

"That doesn't make me feel any better. I think we should get it over with and just have dinner with him soon and find out what he's really up to." Nora looked down at her almost-finished drink. "I'm going to need another one of these. My turn." She turned toward the bar. "Do we have a tab?"

Remy smirked and raised her brows. "What do you think? Of

course. Don't offer to pay. Hopefully he'll just keep putting them on our tab and forget about a few."

Nora nodded and headed for the bar. Same bar tactics I've used, thought Nora.

*   *   *

Remy awoke to the hawking sounds of seagulls as they flew by hurriedly in search of their morning meal. She could hear the water running in the kitchen sink and suddenly remembered that she wasn't alone. She stood up and walked to the doorway of her room, stretching languorously before heading into the kitchen and over to the island counter.

"Coffee smells great. I need to wake up. Can you just pour it over my head?"

Remy watched as Nora got ready to reply, her full sensual lips parting slowly as if in slow motion. Damn, thought Remy. She looked so gorgeous ... even first thing in the morning. She watched as Nora reached into the cabinet for the blue ceramic mugs and pushed the hair away from her face as she poured their coffees. Her tousled blond strands were spread around her shoulders, begging to be touched. Remy noticed that Nora had gotten some sun, her nose and cheeks a child's favorite shade of rosy pink. Probably from seating tables on the outside deck all weekend, thought Remy. And Nora's hair was beginning to show bright golden highlights. Remy's glance moved down toward the tawny light golden brown of her chest and shoulders.

"Cream and sugar?" Nora asked.

Remy was shaken from her daydream. Her eyes shot up and met Nora's, the bright cornflower blue eyes that she had found mesmerizing since the first time they had met.

She cleared her throat, "Please. The sugar is in that cabinet," Remy pointed to the left of the sink as she made her way over to the refrigerator for the half and half. She placed it on the counter then took note of the white thin-strapped yoga top and matching boy shorts she had let Nora borrow last night.

"Definitely looks better on you than it does on me," Remy noted.

"Thanks. I'm sure it looks good on you, too." Nora stirred the cream into her coffee and then tossed two plump white sugar cubes.

"No, trust me, it looks better on you."

"Thanks for not letting me drive," Nora replied as she blushed and continued to stir. "Your couch is really comfortable. And it was nice listening to the ocean and birds." Nora stopped speaking as she saw the unexpected look on Remy's face.

"Hey. Are you okay?"

Remy's eyes had filled with tears. "I have no idea why I'm so emotional lately." She wiped at her unexpected tears. "I don't want to be like this. Especially in front of you."

"Did I do or say something … wrong?" Nora asked.

"No, I'm fine. It's just been a rough week, and I think I'm missing San Francisco a little, too." Remy wiped at her eyes again and sat up straight on the wooden bar stool. "And I'm a little lonely."

Nora remained silent.

"Don't get me wrong. I like this hanging out thing. It's just that in San Francisco, the dating pool is definitely a lot bigger for me, if you know what I mean. And being out last night with all those local guys just made me think about it. I … haven't dated since Hannah and I broke up." Remy shrugged slightly and took a sip of her coffee.

"I'm sorry. I hadn't thought about that." Nora lied. Suddenly, Remy's past had a name attached to it. Hannah. Last night, after a few too many drinks, she'd considered the possibility … for a split second. She tried to picture being with Remy. Then reality set in as she admitted it wasn't an option for her. She knew she would have to be blunt.

"Are you okay that we're just friends. And that I like guys?" Nora felt awkward and a bit childish as she asked the question.

"Sure. I'm fine with it," Remy lied. "I like guys, too. I just don't want to sleep with them." She summoned up a slight smile as she took another sip of her coffee. "I'm going for a walk on the beach. Do you want to come along?"

Nora put her mug in the sink as she answered, "Thanks, but I need to get back. I think I need a little down time before work."

She watched as Remy walked toward the bedroom. Her thin white short-sleeve T-shirt hugged her closely and fell just to her hips, her pale pink low-cut cut bikinis accentuating her tan buttocks and strong thighs. Nora cleared her throat, surprised to be surveying Remy this way. She walked over to the couch and started getting dressed. She thought about last night. She couldn't avoid one-on-one talks forever. She was going to have to tell Remy what really happened with Tom in Florida.

*   *   *

Nora entered her kitchen then glanced at the answering machine. She hit the play button as she made a pot of coffee.

The machine blared its impersonal message, "You have fourteen new messages." Nora's stomach knotted suddenly. "Tuesday, July fifth, 11:14 p.m." Beeeeep. Someone had hung up. No message. "Tuesday, July fifth, 11:45 p.m." Beeeeeep. "Wednesday, July sixth 12:12 a.m." Nora felt panic as she plodded through the remaining messages. All hang-ups. Her mind darted wildly as she thought about who had tried to call her that many times. Maybe it had been Evan and he wanted to get back together. Maybe it was Tom, and he was jealous after seeing her out last night. Maybe it had been Kevin, trying to track her down. Or maybe it had been Jake. No, he wouldn't have called so many times. Not before having a first date.

Nora listened to the gurgling of the coffeepot until it finished brewing. Then she made her way upstairs with her steaming mug. She slipped on a cool, clean robe and put on the television in a low whisper in an attempt to smooth her jangled nerves. She got into bed and tried to breathe deeply. It was Thursday and Evan would be at the restaurant all day. Should she confront him about the calls? And how should she handle the fact that Evan somehow knew that Christian had supposedly fallen off the lifeguard chair? Should she ask him about it?

She thought about Kevin and remembered the last time he had shown up at the house, pounding on the door like a madman. Maybe she should try to talk to him today, thought Nora. Then there was Tom. But that didn't seem to be his style. He was too up front and obnoxious for that. But he had seen them last night at The Bull. Maybe he had wanted to know what time she had gotten in and if she had been with someone. But it just didn't fit. He would have left a message, too.

Nora tried to ignore her pounding headache and decided that a hot shower would help. As she made her way toward the bathroom, she rubbed at her temples, willing the pounding to stop. She opened the cabinet, searching for the Ibuprofen. Shit. Where was it? She remembered the extra bottle she always kept in the kitchen.

Nora crept down the stairs and headed toward the kitchen in order to find some relief. She opened the refrigerator and grabbed the orange juice, then opened the kitchen cabinet. She stared inside, trying to focus as her eyes searched the various bottles. Vitamin C. Multi Vitamins. Echinacea. She reached inside, eager to find the Ibuprofen. She pushed aside several bottles, peering toward the back of the cabinet. There. Thank God. She grabbed the bottle, and as she did, Nora gasped as she eyed what had been placed behind it. The goose bumps quickly spread along her arms and down her entire body. Nora stood, frozen, not willing to believe what was staring back at her. The small orange bottle had a pharmacy label she hadn't seen before. Gloucester Pharmacy. Eugenia Wells. Take as directed. May cause drowsiness. Take with Food. She kept staring at the label. Xanax.

Nora's mind flashed to the night at the Port Side. This was it, Nora remembered. The bottle that Christian had pulled from his pocket on more than one occasion. His mother's pills. And they were here. In her kitchen cabinet.

Nora's hands trembled as she stood holding the bottle. She walked over to the phone. She knew who she needed to call. It was time for her to tell the truth. She stepped back unexpectedly as the sharp ring broke through the thick morning air. Nora's breath quickened and her heart pounded loudly in her chest as she held her hand over the phone.

"Hello?" There was silence. "Hello?" Again, silence, but this time Nora could hear the static. "Hello?" She listened intently, trying to discern any background noise before the caller hung up. Her mind raced. How long had these pills been in her cabinet? And what was she going to do with them? She hesitated for a moment then dialed the number.

"Gloucester Police Department, your call is being recorded. Lieutenant Samson."

Nora hesitated for a moment. "Yes, hello, may I speak with Detective Callahan, please?"

"I'm sorry, ma'am, but he's not expected until 11:00 o'clock. Can someone else help you?"

"No. No one else can help me. It's personal business. I'll call back. Thanks."

Nora stood against the kitchen counter, frozen. Her pounding head reminded her that she had not yet taken the Ibuprofen. She would speak to Jake, she thought. She didn't really know him, but she didn't know who else to call. She doubted Remy could get her out of this one. And Evan wasn't speaking to her. She would tell Jake the truth. Nora tried to reassure herself. You have nothing to worry about. You didn't do anything wrong. Just tell the truth. Nora placed the bottle in her purse then took four Ibuprofen, praying that she was making the right decision.

Chapter 23

Nora stared back at her reflection. Her hair was perfectly blown dry, stick straight then slightly curled at the ends. She parted it on the side, neatly tucking her long bangs behind her ears, and large single pearl earrings adorned her earlobes. She looked at her watch. 10:30 p.m. Time to meet Jake. She applied her perfume, first a light dab on both sides of her neck, then just a touch on her wrists. She made her final review. Her ivory silk sleeveless tank contrasted perfectly with her slightly faded tight-fitting low-rise Levi's. And her shoes, black patent sling back three-inch mules, were sexy and sophisticated. Nora reapplied her lipstick, an innocent shade of the palest pink, then carefully smoothed on a thin coat of clear lipgloss. She smiled widely for the first time in weeks. Perfect. She even forgot about Evan and the fact that he seemed to despise her.

Nora mentally reviewed the day's events, grimacing as she recalled her encounter with Evan first thing in the morning. He had been in the restaurant as she had arrived and had given her a hateful look as he passed her and walked toward his office. To her surprise, Betty had suddenly appeared by the hostess station.

"Where's Evan?" Nora tried to ask casually.

"Oh, he ain't feeling so well, so he's gonna take the rest of the day."

"I see." Nora could say nothing else.

Her shift was uneventful, except for Kevin's hostile manner whenever he saw her. Great, she thought, pretty soon there won't be anyone on Rocky Neck who doesn't either love me or hate me.

Nora had left the moment Betty started cutting the staff.

"His loss," thought Nora. She sighed heavily as she thought about the last time that Evan had made love to her.

She shook her head as if she were trying to fend off the feelings she knew she had for him. Why hadn't Tom ever made her feel this way? Her life would have been so much simpler. She thought about Tom and what he was up to, knowing he wasn't a man to wait around for long. He'd be making his move soon. Nora shuddered, as she remembered the last time Tom had tried to make love to her, her interest nonexistent as she fought to find excuses.

She jumped as she heard the honk of the cab's horn then promptly grabbed her keys and purse. No car tonight, thought Nora. Either Jake would be driving her home or he wouldn't, she mused. She suddenly felt a reckless abandon. What difference did it make? She had tried to change and be honest with Evan. And what good had that done? Honesty was overrated.

Nora stepped into the cab. "The Bradford, please. On Main Street."

She sat back and enjoyed the trip into town. As she got out and paid the driver, she looked toward the line outside. It was going to be a good night, thought Nora. She pressed through the impatient future patrons, finally reaching the front door. She tried to ignore the angry and frustrated stares directed at her from several women standing in the motionless line.

She smiled widely as she approached the doorman. "I'm meeting my boyfriend here. He should already be inside." Nora stood straighter so that her breasts pressed seductively against the fabric of her thin ivory-colored blouse.

The doorman smiled and stepped back slightly so that Nora could push through the crowd. As she reached the inside doorway, she spotted Jake immediately. He was standing with his back to her, his wide muscular back and sandy brown hair unmistakable.

"Hey, come here often?" Nora had purposefully placed her hand on his large shoulder. She felt him react to her touch as he turned toward her. His freckled, tan skin showcased his gleaming white smile, and his sunny blond-brown short hair looked perfectly casual. His caramel-color eyes twinkled playfully, and he wore a navy blazer that accentuated his trim waist and hard, rolling chest. Underneath, the jacket, he wore a plain white T-shirt. His Levi jeans were a bit more fitted than Nora would have expected for a conservative police officer, and his shoes were tan suede topsiders. Nora was pleasantly surprised. Her pulse quickened as she thought for a moment about what kind of lover he might be.

Jake kissed Nora's cheek lightly and placed his arm around her waist as he pulled her toward him. "I'm so glad you're here." He smiled again and waited for Nora's reply.

"Me, too."

Jake admired her. "I wasn't sure if you'd show up. You look really beautiful."

Nora relaxed slightly as she reveled in the compliment. "Thank you. You don't look so bad, yourself." Then she added playfully, "You're actually better looking than I remembered."

He smiled again. "That's good, right?"

"Oh, yeah. Definitely." Nora was enjoying the light banter. It was nice not to have the self-doubt and difficult discussions that seemed to be the norm with Evan lately.

"What would you like to drink?" Jake found a spot at the bar and claimed it instantly.

Nora replied firmly. "Dark and Stormy. Extra lime." She answered instinctively as she thought about Remy for a split second. What was it about her that she liked so much? She didn't usually bother with other women.

Jake's voice brought her back to the present. "That sounds, good." Jake stood at the bar and waited for the bartender, who walked over immediately.

One of the perks of being a cop in a small town, thought Nora.

"Two Dark and Stormy's. Extra lime. Oh, and two Quervo Golds-- straight up." Nora watched as the bartender went to make their drinks. She pressed closer to Jake and found his hand. "Are we both extra thirsty tonight?" Nora had heard that the police officers in Gloucester were a rambunctious group.

Jake nodded. He surveyed Nora, much as a police officer would do, without even realizing his eyes were roving over her entire body. He leaned toward her and kissed her lips lightly. "I get really thirsty sometimes. As a matter of fact, sometimes I'm almost insatiable. Know what I mean?"

Nora pursed her lips into a sexy pout and closed her eyes slightly in a sexy gesture. "Yes, I do. Believe me."

Jake grabbed the two shots of tequila from the bar first and handed one to Nora, as if challenging her. "I took a wild guess … but is this too strong for you?"

Nora quickly took the glass, held it up for a moment, as did Jake, and gulped it down in one fell swoop. "It's been a rough week. It feels great to unwind. She exchanged the glass for a piece of lime and sucked on it with pursed lips.

Jake handed the Dark and Stormy to Nora. He seemed to choose his words carefully before speaking. "I know it's been a tough week. You don't take it personally, do you? I mean, Harry and I are just doing our jobs."

Harry. The other detective actually had a first name, thought Nora. "No, I understand." It's not every day something … like that happens in Gloucester. Nora's words were stilted as she realized that he was analyzing her carefully as she spoke.

Jake raised his glass as he changed the subject. "Here's to getting back to normal. And to us. To … getting to know each other."

Nora felt a slight triumph. She raised her glass then took a deep sip. As she did, her elbow was pushed from behind as part of her drink sloshed onto the floor. She turned around abruptly, annoyed by the carelessness of the person behind her. "Excuse me!" Her voice caught in her throat as she stared up in disbelief.

"Sorry. It's so crowded in here." Beside her, standing too close for comfort, was Evan. "Great place to meet for a date, don't you think?" Evan asked the question as he stared at Nora then turned his eyes to Jake.

"Detective." Evan extended his hand and shook Jake's before starting to walk away.

Nora's gaze followed Evan as he walked past them. She watched as he took a seat almost directly across the bar from her. Nora had never seen him look so confident. And she had never seen the woman he was with, either. God, thought Nora. She could be my stand-in. Nora surveyed the woman competitively, as had always been her natural instinct. Size Four. Blond Hair. Not natural, but good color. Expensive looking highlights. Tan. Too even to be from the beach. Probably tans at least once a week. Shoulder length, perfectly dried straight thick hair. Hmmm, thought Nora. Evan will enjoy running his hands through that. Great clothes. Not from the mall. Definitely designer. Age? Nora choked as she admitted that she was probably no older than twenty-five. On a bad day.

"I didn't know he was seeing Katrina." Jake innocently made the observation as he stared admiringly at Evan's date. All men are pigs, thought Nora. She tried not to be agitated or to let it show. Her successful night out was slowly turning to shit. She forced the corners of her mouth to turn into an insincere smile. "She's cute. I wonder what time she has to be home by."

Nora's sarcasm went unnoticed. "Oh, Katrina's just getting started. Actually, she has a lot of late nights. She plays in a local band called The Kittens." Jake turned toward Nora. "It's an all-girl band ... have you heard of them?"

"No. But that's great." Nora was silent for a moment before her sarcasm oozed unexpectedly. "That little top she has on ... It's nice. Guess they didn't have it in her size, though." She was angry, and it was evident to Jake as well.

"Why do you care? You're not seeing him, are you?"

"No, of course not. And, no, I don't care. It's just that, I like Evan. And I don't want to see him taken advantage of. He's sort of ... innocent with women. And she seems old for her age."

"He's probably not that innocent. Isn't he forty something?"

"Yes, early forties. But that's not old. Why? How old are you?" Nora became anxious as she waited for the answer.

"I'm thirty two. Why, how old are you?"

"The same. I'm thirty-two too. What's your birthday?" Nora was grateful to be off the subject of Evan.

"March eighth." Jake turned toward Nora eagerly. "What's yours?"

"March seventh. Wow. What are the odds?" Nora's mind was taken off the failing evening. Her hope was renewed.

"Oh, no." Jake said in an exaggerated sad tone.

"What? What's wrong?"

"I'm dating an older woman." Jake laughed as he grabbed Nora by the waist and kissed her lightly.

Nora could feel Evan's direct stare.

"Oh, and I don't think you have to worry about Kat. She's the sweetest person. And so are her parents. She even helps out her mom with teaching Sunday School, she's into volunteering. All sorts of stuff like that."

Nora wanted to throw up. If Jake was a cop and was that innocent about Katrina, Nora couldn't imagine how quickly Evan would be sucked in.

Nora grabbed the lapel of Jake's blazer with her free hand and pulled him toward her. As she got onto her toes, she closed her eyes until their lips met. Not bad. He might be fun to go out with for a while. Especially since Evan seemed to have totally lost interest in her. How could Evan have proclaimed to love her, and here he was, just a few days later, dating someone who could almost be his daughter? Her anger and frustration made her flush unexpectedly.

Nora remembered the pills. She had planned to talk to Jake about them as soon as they met tonight. But she hadn't found the right moment. Especially since they had no privacy.

Nora would tell him tonight when he took her home. She had to.

*　　　*　　　*

Jake pulled up in front of Nora's cottage. He looked over and smiled. She looked so beautiful and peaceful. He knew that she had worked all week through the drama of interviews from the police. And she had worked a full shift today before meeting him out. He got out of the car and walked around to the passenger side, then opened the door of his red Mustang convertible. As he reached down to pick Nora up, he saw her bag on the seat. He swung her into his arms, and then reached in with his right hand to scoop it up. As he grabbed her bag by one handle, the contents spilled onto the well-worn black leather seat.

"Shit." Jake left the bag and carried Nora to the door. "Nora," he whispered in her ear. He climbed the two steps, placing her down gently on the landing as she awoke.

Nora clung to his shoulders, "Do you want to come in?"

"Thanks. I'd love to. But why don't we do it another time. I know how tired you are." Jake kissed Nora gently on the forehead. "Your bag is still in the car. I'll be right back."

Nora stood on the landing, waiting for her prince charming.

Jake reached her purse and quickly scooped it up. As he did, he realized several items had rolled onto the seat. Even in the darkness, he could make out the shadowy objects. He leaned over toward them, instinctively focusing on the obvious shape of the bottle of pills with the prescription label. He squinted so that he could make it out. Mrs. Eugenia Wells. Xanax. He retracted his hand within his jacket's sleeve, then carefully picked up the bottle and deposited it into the inside pocket of his jacket. He picked up the other two items, a tube of lipstick and a tin of Altoids, and placed them back into Nora's purse. His training as a police officer told him what he didn't want to admit.

Nora smiled and hugged Jake. He smelled of lotion.

Jake looked into Nora's eyes. "I had a good time. I'd like to see you again."

"Me, too."

Jake made his way down the path as Nora put her key in the lock. She was surprised that he hadn't wanted to come in. "Men." Nora mumbled.

Jake sat and watched Nora, knowing now what he hadn't wanted to admit. He stuck his hand into the inside pocket of his jacket, making sure the bottle was secure. He started up his car, thinking about what his next move would be.

Chapter 24

Nora awoke to the ringing of the phone. She bolted upright and ran downstairs as quickly as her legs could take her. "Hello?"

"I think it's time you tell the truth. I'm not going to keep following you around until you feel guilty enough to spill. Do it now or I'll do it for you." The cold chill in the caller's voice told Nora that he was serious. And he hadn't even tried to disguise his voice.

Nora pressed *69. She needed to face him. Today. And she needed to know where he was. The phone rang five times before he answered. "Yeah?" The voice was gruff and angry-sounding.

"Listen … Kevin. I have a problem." There was silence on the other end as Nora tried to choose her words. "I don't remember all of it. If I did … I would tell the police."

"Well, you better think hard. Soon. I'm not gonna be blamed for this. Me and Carly were nice enough to get you outa there that night. We coulda left you. But we didn't. So you better think about it and try to remember the rest."

"Okay." Nora hung up the phone. She was desperate for answers, and this latest twist only made the events of that evening seem cloudier. She stood at the kitchen sink splashing cold water on her face. She needed help. Remembering that she hadn't told Jake about the pills, Nora walked hurriedly to the front hall to retrieve them.

Her right hand shook as she plunged it deeply into her bag. Nora started taking out the contents, one item at a time. Her mind raced to last night. Maybe they had fallen out. Would Jake have taken them? No. He was such a gentleman. He wouldn't have rummaged through her bag. Or would he have? He was a detective, which by the nature of the profession made him more suspicious than most. For the first time since Christian's death, Nora was truly afraid. For all she knew, she could be blamed somehow and maybe even go to prison. And the odds weren't heading in her favor, especially since Kevin was breathing down her neck. Nora thought about the pills. Ultimately, they tied her to Christian. And they had somehow ended up in her possession. Nine tenths of the law, thought Nora. Maybe she should leave. Before it got any worse.

*   *   *

Nora poured herself a glass of orange juice and paced nervously back and forth on her back deck. The beauty of the summer morning was lost on her. She didn't care that her hair was a tangled mess and that she only wore a thigh-length teddy outside. She leaned on the deck's railing, breathing deeply. The heavy sweet fragrance of lavender and heather reminded her of the summer still ahead. The summer she had hoped for, sweet, romantic, and uncomplicated. She thought back to that night again. She had been leaning on the bar, and she remembered how ill she had felt. A feeling which had been present since they had gotten to the Port Side. Nora remembered the pills, and how many times she had turned them down. According to Remy, she had finally succumbed and taken them. She never took anything like that. Why had she acquiesced?

She gasped, horrified, as she remembered Christian's hot heavy breath on her face. She had gone outside to get some air. And suddenly, there he was, pressing her against the wall, his movements rough and almost brutal. Nora had tried to push him away. But she had felt so small, so weak. And he had been amused, laughing loudly at her, ridiculing her.

Nora tried to play back the rest of the night's events. Damn it! She didn't remember walking to Remy's place with her. An image started to form of someone talking beside her. She had tried to listen while her heavy head swayed against the leather headrest. Her eyes had been closed, and Nora had summoned every muscle in her body in order to sit upright. She remembered seeing the blurred figure of Remy beside her as she drove. She had kept talking.

Nora remembered the cool late night air as it had swirled around her. She had taken several deep breaths as she had struggled to regain total consciousness. Remy had sounded annoyed, and then Nora had heard Christian's unmistakable voice coming from the back seat.

"Thanks for picking us up. I thought I was gonna have to chase the bitch all the way back to Rocky Neck." Nora realized, even through her haze, that he was talking about her.

Remy's tone had become agitated, "You privileged fucking brat. Nora's more than you could ever hope to have. And way more than you could ever handle."

Christian's sarcasm had been evident, "Yeah, whatever, sweetheart. But at least *I* got to do her."

"I doubt it."

Silence had then filled the car as Nora kept her eyes closed. She had fought to stay awake. Why had Christian been in the car with them? Nora held her stomach as her body crumpled to the warm wood floor of the deck. She wrapped her arms around her knees and sobbed quietly, trying to recall the rest of the night. Nothing.

*   *   *

Nora got to work exactly on time. She walked through the lounge where she spotted Evan at the bar. She placed her purse at the hostess station, purposely avoiding eye contact with Remy, who was on the phone. Nora walked toward the kitchen, searching for Kevin, who she found standing alone in the walk-in refrigerator. She walked in behind him, her back straight.

"Give me another day or two." Nora waited for a reply. "Look. It'll be better if it comes from me. And I just need another day or two."

"Whatever." Kevin remained with his back toward Nora. He walked farther into the refrigerator as she walked away.

She made her way back into the bar area. Before she could lose her nerve, she spoke, "Evan. I need to talk to you."

He kept looking at the clipboard in front of him.

"I need to talk to you right now, please." Nora raised her voice slightly.

"Not here." Evan motioned with his chin. "In my office. Betty's off today. Let's go."

185

Nora walked ahead of him. She hadn't planned what she was going to say. He closed the door as she turned to face him.

"Evan. I know we're not seeing each other right now ..." She was interrupted by his sharp tone.

"You mean *any* more. We're not seeing each other *any more.*"

"Right." Nora stood at Betty's chair and leaned on it with her hands for support.

"I ... feel I can trust you." She tried to find the right words. There were none to describe how scared and alone she was.

"I think I'm really in trouble. I need your help so I don't ... end up ..."

She tipped her head back slightly so that the welled up tears wouldn't stream down her face. Nora wanted his help. Not his pity. She stared at Evan through brimming eyes.

"I found Christian's pills in my kitchen, and I tried telling Jake about them ... "

"You mean last night, while you were on your date?" Evan stiffened as he waited for Nora's reply. The somber look on his face didn't reveal whether or not he cared.

"Yes, while I was on my date. I was going to tell you about that, too. He asked me out the day of the questioning. Here in the office. And I was surprised and too nervous to say no. I was going to tell you that night on the boat. But then we got into that fight."

The silence filled the office and hung awkwardly like a thick impermeable fog. Nora felt no warmth or sympathy from Evan.

"Who don't you say no to?" There was just silence as Evan planted the hurtful dig.

"Forget it. I'll figure it out myself." Nora's tone became defiant. "I can never trust anyone. Forget it!"

"*You* can't trust anyone? Are you serious? Nora, haven't you figured out that you have to be trustworthy *first?* You have to *earn* people's trust? You can't just expect it. Especially when you're constantly *lying.*"

"What?"

"You heard me. Lying about yourself. About your life. About who you're sleeping with." Evan's voice trailed off for a moment. "And about where you were that night."

Evan stepped closer toward Nora. "*I'm* not the one constantly covering up one bad lie with another one."

He leaned in closely for effect. "For all I know, *you* had something to do with his death."

Nora's face reddened. "How *dare* you! I'm not the one who knew how Christian died. How did you know he *fell* off a lifeguard chair?"

Evan stared blankly for a moment before recovering. "Actually, that was someone else's idea. It was … "

Nora interrupted without letting Evan finish. "Don't try to defend yourself *now.*" I may not be perfect, but at least I'm trying to change *my* life. I don't see you trying to make any changes to *yours, Evan!* You're going to become a little old man … whispering in corners with Betty, doing the same thing day in and day out, and still trying to live up to your mother's expectations. You're always going to let her make you feel inferior. Oh, you didn't think I knew about how she treats you? Everybody knows! So don't judge *me.*" Nora couldn't make herself stop. She knew she would regret her words.

"You're … pathetic."

She wanted to take back the words. She saw his look. First, anger. Then, shock. And, finally, hurt. And it didn't make her feel any better. If anything, Nora instantly felt worse. She knew instinctively, as she watched him, that Evan was the one person who truly cared for her.

"Get out. Get out right now. Evan stared at her intently. "You're fired."

Nora was speechless.

"And don't *ever* step foot in my restaurant again. As an employee *or* as a customer. I am done. Get out."

Evan's tight jaw twitched violently. "Come back and see Remy tomorrow after twelve. She'll have your final check."

She stood, frozen for a moment. Nora hadn't thought that Evan would ever do this to her. She had almost forgotten he was her boss, not just her now-past lover. She walked out of the office, numb, as she tried to square her shoulders and make her way unnoticed to the hostess station. The restaurant was unusually still, as the staff went about their duties, none of them making eye contact as they pretended they hadn't heard the raised voices through the flimsy office door.

Remy tried to catch her eye. "Hey. What's going on? Are you alright?"

Nora grabbed her purse. "No. I'm not alright. Evan just fired me."

"Shit." Remy looked toward the office door as it swung open. "Call me tonight. After I get home."

Nora was so confused. She didn't know whom to trust. She remembered the story they had concocted about her whereabouts that night. She was so uncertain … noting how easily Remy seemed to be able to lie without it bothering her. Nora decided she didn't want to share anything with her right now. Not until she figured things out.

Evan walked out of the office and stared at Nora.

She stared back at him as she put her purse on her shoulder. "I'm getting my bag."

Nora walked through the lounge outside and was bombarded by the bright morning sunlight. She immediately felt overdressed, as she stood on the outside deck closest to the street, unaware of the tears that streamed down her face as tourists openly stared.

*　　　　　*　　　　　*

"You really look awful. You wanna get a drink?"

Nora was too tired to care that anyone was seeing her like this. She continued to stare at the harbor, willing herself to be on a remote island in the caribbean, alone. She had never wanted to be alone before. She closed her eyes.

"No. Thanks, though." She felt the tears of frustration well up in her eyes again. She had to stop crying. The years of being strong and seemingly emotionless had caught up with her.

Tom walked up to the edge of the dock and sat down, his manner clumsy. Nora had taken off her pumps and had placed them next to her purse. He picked up one of her dainty high heels. "You always looked good in shoes like this. They show off your great legs."

Nora had no reply. She stared toward the harbor as Tom placed the shoe back next to its match. She finally spoke. "What are you doing here?"

"I was taking a walk around the docks and the water. It's really nice. Not at all like Florida. A lot more rocky." He surveyed Nora. "What are *you* doin' here? Aren't you supposed to be workin' for your boyfriend right about now?"

"He's not me boyfriend." Nora remembered the scene outside the bathroom when Tom had met Remy. "Besides, there's Remy, remember?"

"Yeah, right." Tom chuckled. "I know you, and I don't buy it. Nice try, though."

Nora ignored Tom's last statement. "He fired me."

"I figured something like that."

"I know what you're thinking. It would be the perfect time to just ruin me completely by telling Evan about us and Florida and what happened."

"No. I wasn't thinking that."

"So just go ahead. I told him we had been a couple, anyway. So, just go tell him the rest. I deserve to be humiliated. Payback and all."

They were both silent as they watched the boats in the harbor bobbing and swaying in the gentle waves and light morning breeze.

Nora continued, relentless in her attempt to goad him on. "That's why you're here, isn't it?" She turned toward him.

"No. That's not why I'm here. I mean, hell yeah, at first I was so goddamned pissed, and I couldn't wait to find you. To teach you a lesson … make you pay." Tom made eye contact with Nora. "But I changed my mind."

"Why? Why wouldn't you tell everybody? I know *I* probably would." Her voice trailed.

"No you wouldn't." Tom sounded disappointed by Nora's apparent anger.

"Plus … I sort of miss you. That's really why I'm here." Tom lowered his voice. "And besides … I thought we did alright together."

Nora closed her eyes, thinking about how damned she was right now. If she didn't go back to him, he would probably change his mind and tell everyone. But she didn't want to go back. Not to him. And not to that life. And the way she had been.

"I need to think, Tom. I'm sorry. I can't make any promises. Even if that means … " Her voice trailed.

"Look. I may be a hardass, but I'm a man of my word. Even if you decide you *don't* want me. But that would be hard to believe. Considerin' what a great catch I am and all." Tom grabbed Nora's shoes as he stood. He held out his hand to her. "Come on, let's go for a drive. Let's get you outa here for a little while."

Nora grabbed Tom's hand, grateful for the first time that she had told a man exactly how she felt. In the late morning sunlight, he almost looked handsome, thought Nora. He wasn't such a bad person after all. He was just looking for someone. Just like everyone else out there.

"Okay." Nora grabbed her purse and decided to walk barefoot. She was almost amused at the sight of Tom, a tall, burly Portuguese man, attempting to be gentle as he carried her heels.

"Don't you want to know why I got fired?" Nora asked.

"You can tell me some other time." Tom proceeded ahead of Nora, paving the way from the docks to the main street.

"It's not what you think." Nora waited for a reaction. She continued her attempt to explain. "I had an argument with him and … "

Tom held up a hand. "It's really not important. My car's up here."

∗   ∗   ∗

Nora removed the rhinestone hair clip that held back her bangs and shook her head as if to release all of her stress and buried demons. She looked at the clock on the dashboard. 11:45 a.m. It was already humid and unusually hot, but she was reveling in the warm air as it enveloped them. They circled the rotary that emptied onto the main road heading out of Gloucester.

Nora had always loved convertibles, and she especially admired Tom's. The black antique Mercedes looked as if it belonged on a movie set, with its red leather interior and burred wood detailing. The aged fuzzy dice hung proudly from the rear view mirror. Nora smiled. She had always loathed them, thinking they were tasteless. But now, they seemed to fit. Like Tom, they were unexpected, the way he had behaved today, thought Nora. He had shown a compassion and empathy she had never seen. Maybe, she admitted, because she had never allowed him to see how vulnerable she could be. He had finally seen her human side.

"Where are you taking me?" Nora yelled as the loud gusts of wind crossed from the harbor and over the two-lane highway and through the car.

"I've been doin' a lot of exploring. I found this great seafood place. It's in Essex."

"Do they have cocktails at this great seafood place?"

"Of course. They have great drinks. And their seafood platter isn't bad, either."

Nora had forgotten how self-assured Tom had always been. Though he could be gruff and downright tacky at times, Nora admired that he was a self-made man. He had been on his own since he had landed on U.S. soil at the age of fifteen. By age sixteen, he was selling T-shirts to all the Fort Lauderdale tourists from an old milk truck he had painted. And by the time he was twenty, he had rented his first storefront. His tacky T-shirt empire, as Nora had secretly thought of it, had grown from there. Now, at about age fifty, he was on his way to retirement and an abundance of wealth. Something to be proud of, thought Nora. Though she wasn't certain of his age, as this was his one obvious vanity.

"So how much older than I are you exactly?"

Tom shook his head. "None of your business."

Nora reached over and patted his arm. "Thank you."

"No thank you's necessary. You can just sleep with me later."

Nora was silent for a moment, a little uneasy with their new banter. "No. Nice try though."

They both laughed a bit nervously as Tom wound his way through the narrow streets of Essex. Nora started to relax. She didn't remember the last time she had a Saturday off. It almost felt like vacation. She forced herself not to think about why she was off today.

Nora looked toward the storefronts as she admired the scenic town. The road had straightened as the colonials and aged barns became quaint shops converted from antique churches and tiny cottages. Tom slowed to about five miles per hour as the in-town traffic became heavier, and Nora's excitement was childlike as she admired the extraordinary array of antiques and collectibles spilling from tiny cottage doorways and along rambling old porches. "Could we walk around and look at some antiques after lunch?"

"Sure. Let's get a drink and some lunch first. You buyin'?"

Nora's shocked look amused Tom.

"I'm kiddin'. It's my treat. Even if it's not a real date." Tom moved his arm along the seat and stroked Nora's hair. Normally, Nora would have been annoyed that he might be affecting her hairstyle. But right now, she found it unusually comforting.

*　　　　*　　　　*

"Could we have that table just inside the sliding glass door?" Leave it to Tom, Nora thought, to be telling the hostess exactly where he wanted to sit.

"Yes, sir. But did you want to sit outside on the porch?" She asked as she grabbed two menus.

"Porch, no thanks. I get blazing sun all year. Besides. That's not a porch. A porch is covered. That's a deck, and by the looks of the angle of that sun, it's going to be about 100 degrees out there in about a half hour."

Nora flushed as the hostess started walking them toward a table without saying a word.

Tom held out Nora's chair and then made his way to his own. He had seated her so that she had a view of the flats of the Essex River. Nora sighed deeply, relaxing for the first time in what seemed an eternity.

"This is beautiful." Nora opened her menu as she watched the seagulls coasting overhead. On the banks of the river, the sparkling white herons walked languidly, as if soaking their tired feet. The air smelled of salt and a mustiness that was slightly reminiscent of clams Nora used to dig for with her family when she was very young.

"Could I interest you in something from the bar?" The young, fresh-faced girl looked barely old enough to be asking that question.

"Yes. I'm goin' to have a Sam Adams bottle, do you have that?" Tom waited for her nod. And the lady will have a … what is that you were drinkin' the other night?"

Nora sat up straight as she remembered having seen Tom at The Bull. "It was a Dark and Stormy. But no thanks, I'll have a Kendall Jackson Chardonnay if you have it."

"Yes, we do. I'll be right back."

"Honey, why don't you make that a bottle. I might have a glass, too."

Nora suddenly felt suspicious of Tom. "If you're trying to get me drunk, no amount of alcohol is going to do it today. I think I'm just numb."

"Oh, stop feelin' sorry for yourself for once."

"You have no idea the shit I'm in."

"You can tell me later. But not over lunch. Let's just enjoy this." Tom's convincing tone made Nora want to do as he asked.

"Alright then. But it's just going to be there when I get back."

"Well ... we all have our crap to deal with. Now get over it, or I'm gonna go eat by myself at the bar."

"Fine."

Nora held up the menu to shield herself from Tom's view.

They ordered their lunch and caught up on what Tom had been doing. Nora was grateful to have the focus on him, not on her. He had sold all but the original shop, he explained, and now he was looking around for a place to retire. He was thinking about The Keys. Some place where he could be relaxed, casual, and just himself. Nora was surprised that she was actually enjoying this.

By the time they had finished lunch and walked around the antique stores, to others they seemed to be just another happy couple out for a Saturday afternoon. Nora made herself a promise. She wouldn't worry for the rest of the day. Just for today. She would get a good night's sleep and then sit down in the morning and come up with a game plan.

*   *   *

The afternoon sun shone brightly as they made their way back into Gloucester. Nora fought back the panic as they drove through town and headed toward Rocky Neck. They made the inevitable turn onto Rocky Neck Avenue. Nora had to calm herself.

"Get a good night's sleep, and if you decide you still wanna talk about it in the mornin', call me. On my cell. It's still the same number." Tom looked at Nora, trying to reassure her. He walked her to the door.

"Thanks for salvaging this day for me. It started out as a nightmare." Nora hugged him and reached into her purse for her keys.

"No problem. How long do I have to act like this before you want to go back with me?" There was no reply. He smiled as he gave her a polite hug and headed to his car.

Chapter 25

Nora dropped her purse on the front hall table and made her way upstairs. All she wanted right now was a steaming hot shower. She let her clothes fall onto the floor as she quickly got undressed, not caring, as she usually did, to hang them immediately on their appropriate hangers. She made her way into the bathroom, lit a candle, dimmed the bathroom light, and reached into the shower to adjust the water. As she did so, she heard the knocking on the door. Not the brutal knocking that had been Kevin's the other day. No, this sounded much more civilized. Had Tom returned, immediately regretting being the perfect gentleman? She knew it. He couldn't be that way for long. Nora left the water running, thinking she would get rid of Tom as fast as possible. She grabbed her robe, threw it on, and tied it quickly as she ran down the stairs.

She opened the door widely. "Tom, you've given up on your gentlemanly ways already?"

She blushed as she stood in the open doorway. There stood Jake, staring back and embarrassed.

"Sorry," he replied.

Nora clutched at her robe, stepping back from the open doorway as she let him in. "Oh, my God. I'm so sorry. I just got dropped off, and I thought he had forgotten something." Nora motioned and stepped further inside. "Come in."

Jake had both hands stuffed awkwardly into his pockets as he walked through the doorway. "I'm sorry to just stop by, but I went to the restaurant and Evan told me you were …"

"Fired?"

Jake nodded, waiting for an explanation.

Nora flushed wildly. "It's true. We had a major difference of opinion about something." She remembered the missing pills. Maybe that's why he was here. Oh, my God. She wasn't even dressed. Would he make her go down to the station? She spoke without looking up. "I think I know why you're here."

"We need to talk. Just the two of us." Jake's tone was serious.

Nora looked up sensing that Jake wanted to confide in her.

"Okay. Why don't we go into the living room?" Jake followed her in.

"I'll be right back, I'm just going to run upstairs for a minute."

Nora walked slowly up the stairs. She blew out the candle and turned off the shower. In her past life, she would have seduced Jake, knowing that at least it would have bided her some time. But she was tired of using people. And she didn't want to do that now. Nora pulled on a pair of black yoga pants and a hip-length T-shirt. She walked barefoot down the stairs and took a seat beside him.

She sat with her arms in her lap, ready to deal with whatever he was going to tell her. "Go ahead. I'm listening." Her heart was pounding so loudly she felt she would hardly be able to hear him.

"I don't know how else to say this. But you have to give me your word that what we talk about right now won't ever be repeated." Jake stared intently at Nora.

"Yes. I give you my word."

"I want you to know how serious this is. I could lose my job. And you could end up …" He didn't complete the sentence.

"I know. I promise."

Jake looked around, as if he were making certain that no one else was listening. "I found them in your purse and I need to know how you got them."

"How did you find them … and where are they now?"

"When I dropped you off, I went to pick up your purse, and they fell out." Nora gave Jake a doubtful look.

"Honest. And I have them. I didn't turn them in."

Nora leaned forward, her eyes focused on Jake's. "Thank you." Nora spoke mechanically, wondering the entire while if Jake was just going to be another man who would disappoint her. Her thoughts darted back and forth between certainty that he was trustworthy and certainty that he wasn't. She decided she wasn't ready to believe in him completely. Not yet, anyway. She stared into his eyes and tried to look nervous.

"I went home with Remy, just as we told you. But I didn't feel great when I was at the Port Side. I think Christian might have drugged me. I didn't feel myself, and I was really nauseous and felt like passing out. Maybe he put the pills in my bag when we were at the bar."

Jake nodded, as he surveyed Nora carefully. "When did you find them?"

"I went to get Ibuprofen from my kitchen cabinet. I keep an extra bottle there. And behind the Ibuprofen, I found them."

"Did you put them there?" Jake queried. "Maybe after you found them in your purse?"

"I don't know. But after I pulled them from the cabinet, I tried to call you at the station. You were off until eleven. And I didn't want to tell anybody else. So I brought them out with me on our date. I was going to tell you. But I got nervous because it was crowded at the restaurant." Nora clenched her hands together and looked intently at Jake. The tears streamed freely down her cheeks.

"Jake, I swear, I don't know how they got there." Nora sobbed openly. "But it's going to look like I was involved or had something to do with Christian's death."

"I know. That's why I want to help."

"How? What the hell do I do now?"

Jake reached into his jacket pocket and pulled out a ziploc bag containing the bottle. "If you try to cover it up, it's bound to catch up to you." Jake opened the bag and dumped out the pill container onto the coffee table.

"I'm going to call my partner. I'm going to tell him that you found these pills and that you called me, and that you want to tell us everything you know." Jake crossed his hands and stared intently at Nora.

"What if they think I had something to do with Christian's death?"

"Nora, murderers never take that kind of chance. You would have gotten rid of the pills a long time ago if you were guilty. What you need to do is tell them what you know, and act like the innocent person that you are."

Nora thought about Remy. Why had she lied about taking Christian home? Nora couldn't tell Jake. Not until she figured things out for herself. She stood up and paced in front of the coffee table.

"Are you sure this is the right thing to do? What if it backfires, and I end up in jail?"

"That's why *I'm* here. And I'm hoping there'll be a second date. And not from jail."

"That's not funny."

Jake turned to Nora, his voice now somber. "It's better if we stay honest through this process. So. If it ever comes up as to whether or not out we've been dating, just tell the truth … that we went out once. And that it was very casual, but that we're friends, which is why you called me. You felt you could trust me, and the Gloucester Police. And tell them you found the pills in your purse and that you hadn't noticed them right away. They were in a zipper or something. That way, it'll look like he was trying to hide them and stuck them in your bag while you were out that night."

Jake looked at his watch. "Let's get this over with. Where's your phone?" He looked around the room.

"In the kitchen." Nora walked slowly toward the kitchen as if she were walking off to her execution. She thought about what she would have to do to put this behind her. Unfortunately, she would have to lie … the one thing she promised herself she wouldn't do again.

*   *   *

Once Jake's partner arrived, the questioning continued for a half-hour as Jake looked on. He had played the role of the caring police officer perfectly without seeming too interested in Nora. Detective Parsons was thorough without being brutal. Nora sobbed throughout the process. The detectives drove off, satisfied with their inquisition. Nora walked upstairs, too tired for her shower. She crawled into bed and fell into a deep, exhausted sleep.

Chapter 26

Nora walked along the sand, picking up sea glass at regular intervals. She marveled at the crystal bright blues and emerald green pieces that beckoned to her from the thick, grainy sand. She felt as if she were six years old again. She breathed deeply as she thought about yesterday's meeting with the police. She felt relief and an inner peace she hadn't felt since landing on Rocky Neck.

She reveled in the newness of her freedom and the unusual but pleasant feeling of not being on a rigid schedule. Normally by now, she would be getting ready to go to work. Nora looked up and watched the growing numbers gathering on the beach, all hoping to make the next six hours in the sun last a lifetime. She walked over to her neatly spread towel and sat on the edge. She kept her sand-covered feet far enough from the edge so as not to desecrate the now-warm cotton of her new towel. Nora buried her feet carelessly in the sand, feeling suddenly giddy and child-like. She scanned the horizon, watching the sailboats as they glided by so effortlessly.

Nora fought the urge then glanced at the date on her watch. July 10th. All the thoughts she had been staving off came flooding back. God, had Christian's death only been one week ago? She had waited anxiously but hadn't heard any more from the police. It seemed, so she thought, that they had been satisfied with her story. Kevin, on the other hand, would be looking for her soon. Nora tried to fight off the frustration as she again tried to recall the events of that night. She thought about Remy. And the fact that she hadn't told her about Christian being in the car with them that night. Was Remy trying to protect her? Or would she throw her to the wolves eventually? What had happened? And why had she blocked it from her mind? She had to know. So, she would proceed with her plan, beginning tonight.

*   *   *

Nora slid on the white just-above-the-knee linen skirt and held her breath while she zipped it. It was slightly uncomfortable, but it would be worth it. She glanced at her rosy-bronze skin against the black of her antique silk blouse and smiled approvingly. Nora slid on her pointed black 3" slingbacks then surveyed her legs as she spread an additional dollop of the lavender lotion along each of her tanned shins and calves. She glanced at her watch. 9:45 p.m. It was time. She spread the pale pink lipstick on her full lips and checked her reflection again. As she heard the car horn, she headed out the door. The familiar black and white checked logo of the Gloucester Cab rolled to a stop in front of her gate.

Nora stepped in carefully, her narrow skirt only allowing smaller steps. "McMurtree's, please." Nora didn't need to give the driver the address of the most popular in-town destination for tourists as well as locals. Nora over-tipped the driver as she got out of the cab. She slammed the door then leaned over provocatively toward the driver. "If I need a cab tonight at closing time, should I call and ask for you directly?"

"Sure. My name's Joe. So long as I'm workin', call any time." He handed her a card and smiled a wide smile that betrayed too many fistfights and years of a tough life on the open sea.

Nora purposely swayed as she walked away before heading inside the crowded restaurant and toward the bar.

"Can I help you?" The flustered hostess spoke too loudly as she tried not to appear overwhelmed.

"Yes. I'm meeting someone here. Just for drinks. Her name is Remy. She said she'd call if she was going to be late." Nora tried to look over the hostesses' clipboard.

"No. I don't have anybody by that name on my list. But we don't normally take messages for people not having dinner." Nora ignored the tone of the hostess.

"Actually, we're regular customers. It's just that tonight we're not having dinner. But we *are* having drinks. That still makes us customers, doesn't it?" Nora challenged the inexperienced hostess, her tone stern.

As the hostess started to answer, Remy appeared behind her. She wore a short fitted light blue sleeveless dress that accentuated her dark hair. Nora reached forward and hugged her then kissed her lightly on the cheek. "You look gorgeous." Nora proclaimed.

Remy smiled brightly. "Thanks. You look gorgeous yourself."

"I don't know about that. Since Evan canned my ass, I've been a mess."

"Well, it's done wonders for you. I've never seen you look better." Remy scrutinized Nora then smiled and fell silent.

"Do you want to get a drink?" Nora asked innocently.

"Is the Pope Catholic?" Remy followed Nora through the throngs of people until they landed behind two tall men talking about stocks.

Nora smiled brightly as she squeezed between them. "Could you boys excuse me? I'm just trying to get to the bar." Remy watched Nora as she charmed the two innocents.

"Sure, honey, any time!" The taller man surveyed them both. "You two with anybody tonight?"

Nora grabbed Remy's hand. "Yes. As a matter of fact." She purposely waited, then answered, "Each other."

Remy chuckled slightly as she waved to the two over-eager, open-mouthed men. She whispered to Nora, "What are you trying to do, get on my good side?"

"Yeah. Is it working?" They both smiled and turned toward the bar, feeling the stares of their new admirers.

Remy followed Nora with her fresh cocktail out onto the deck. The fishing boats interrupted the dark midnight blue skyline, and an occasional boat puttered by as it illuminated the charcoal waters with its running lights. Nora backed into a corner farthest from the music, and Remy slid in close beside her. They both remained silent as they assessed the crowd.

The locals, as evidenced by their casual chino shorts and well-worn cotton shirts, were a boisterous crew. The couples that seemed to be on dates were a bit more reserved, as the men sported expensive Tommy Bahama shirts and coordinating dress pants, and the women strutted in their new silk dresses. And some of the out-of-towners familiar with Gloucester tried to emulate the local artists by wearing their just-purchased straw hats and expensive but carefully- rumpled linen separates.

Nora took a long, languorous sip of her Dark and Stormy. She looked over at Remy, who was doing the same. "I'm hooked." She purposely let her words hang in the heavy July air.

Remy smirked. "Excuse me?"

"You got me hooked. On Dark and Stormy's." Nora smiled and took another sip.

"Tease."

"I know. But I'm good at it, aren't I?" Nora knew she had to pull out all the stops tonight. Her goal was to befriend Remy … whatever it took.

"Very good." Remy fidgeted with her glass as if she were nervous. "Nora, what are we doing? Is this just a friendly drink? Because I might be wrong, but that looks like a *serious* date outfit you're wearing."

Leave it to Remy to put it out there, thought Nora. She would have to reel her in a bit more slowly. And less obviously.

"I'm sorry. Am I being too obvious?"

Remy shrugged and chose not to answer Nora's question.

"I just thought … now that I've had a change of plans, what the hell? I need to … " Nora flushed and downed the rest of her drink then shook the ice nervously against her empty glass.

Remy reached out and touched her hand. "Sorry. I didn't mean to get so defensive. I'm really glad you called."

Nora moved closer and whispered carefully. "I can't make any promises. But I'm happy that we're here … and that we're friends.

Remy licked her midnight red lips. "Me too." She cleared her throat and lightened her tone. "And, hey, if nothing else, at least I got to see you in that outfit." They both laughed and ordered another round from the waitress who stared at them curiously.

*   *   *

Nora and Remy stood in the cool sand and stared out at the blackness of the harbor. They were each carrying their shoes and walked closely as they made their way to the water's edge. The soft blare of a nearby foghorn broke the now-cool evening air with rhythmic bursts.

Remy turned slightly and leaned closer to Nora, her face almost touching her shoulder. "I know a lot of women who would love to be me right about now."

Nora smiled. The welcome buzz from the three drinks she had imbibed had her feeling relaxed and less self-conscious. She swayed slightly in the pliant sand.

"I had a great time. But I have to admit. I don't know how to act with you." Nora felt her words slip out a bit too easily.

"You mean with *me*, or with another girl?"

Nora tried to answer but was suddenly at a loss.

Remy dropped her shoes and grabbed Nora's hands. "Act yourself. That's what I …" Remy second-guessed what she was going to say. "I mean, that's what any one would love about you. You have a great personality."

Nora could see Remy's smile. "Great personality? Is that actually a compliment?"

"You've probably figured out by now that I care about you and that I promise to look out for you. You know that, right?"

"I know. And I know you care about me. And obviously, I do too. I mean … "

Remy gently placed her arm around Nora. "Come on, let's go over to my place and get the car. I'll take you home."

Nora followed Remy. As they made their way along the beach toward Remy's loft, she thought about her botched evening. Her surefire plan hadn't been so surefire after all, and she hadn't found a way of making Remy confide in her. About the night of the murder or about Christian. The only thing she had succeeded in doing was make herself seem sexually confused. She would have to continue seeing Remy, she decided, not only because she liked her as a friend, but for research, of course. And nothing more.

*   *   *

Nora instinctively sat up as she awoke, not certain for a moment of where she was. She looked at the clock, wondering how much time she would have before she had to get ready. The soft clanging of the nearby church bells made her realize she had never paid attention to them before. She hugged her legs and stared at the dusky orange sunlight streaming through the windows. The breeze was stiff and refreshing, unusual for a July morning, and Nora watched the curtains as they danced wildly and chased each other with every new burst of fresh air.

For the first time since her sixteenth birthday, she didn't have a job to go to. No clock to punch. No employer to fear or avoid or sleep with. The large digital numbers on the outdated-looking clock jumped as she stared at them. 7:24. Nora listened as a family of birds chirped loudly in a nearby tree. Seagulls joined the revelry as their cries punctuated the morning air. She watched through the window, mesmerized, as she was soothed by the tranquility of the early morning. Nora was always rushing somewhere, she realized. To meet someone, to do something that at the time seemed so urgent. Now, she realized, it was all so unimportant. And there was only one thing that was truly important right now. And that was to get her life back on track.

She thought about her important task at hand. She would need to find out what role she had played in Christian's death. She was reminded of the unkind words Evan had spoken to her. Unfortunately, she admitted, he was right. She needed to change her life. She needed to learn to be honest with people. And with herself. But she also needed to learn to trust. She had used, and been used by others, so many times. How could she learn to trust if she doubted other people's intentions? Nora lay back and thought about last night. Remy had dropped her off, kissing her cheek and casually thanking her. But as Nora had gotten out of the car, Remy had asked her if she wanted to have a lunch and shopping date with her. Nora had been surprised until Remy had explained that Evan had given her the day off in appreciation of all her hard work.

Nora had suddenly felt jealous, but had quickly said yes. She had walked back to her front door, feeling unsure of herself and off balance. Had she embarrassed herself? Maybe she didn't have what it took when it came to flirting with the same sex, she realized. If she had made last night's moves on a member of the opposite sex, the night would definitely have gone differently. Not that she was going to sleep with Remy, of course. But she wanted to get close to her. And she sensed Remy wasn't letting her just yet.

Nora swung her legs over the side of the bed and made her way downstairs to make a pot of coffee. She wasn't meeting Remy until twelve. She had plenty of time to think about her plan … and to make herself irresistible.

Chapter 27

Nora heard the loud rat-tat-tat on the screen door just as her phone also began to ring. She answered it as she walked toward the front door, realizing that Remy was right on time. "Hello?"

She swung the door open widely as she heard the unexpected voice on the other end of the phone.

"Hi. It's Jake."

Nora stumbled slightly as she stood in the doorway. Her mind took a moment, as she stared at Evan standing on the other side of the screen door. He wore a serious look, a crisp cotton shirt, and he held an envelope in his hand.

"Hi!" Nora proclaimed in an almost too-eager voice.

"Hi, yourself," Jake replied. Obviously, he didn't realize that she had company, and that Evan was standing on the other side of the door.

Nora answered Jake awkwardly, "Could you hold on a second? Someone's at the door."

She realized how that sounded to Evan. He would be annoyed, she was sure. Nora held the phone to her shoulder and waved Evan in. "I'll be right back. Come in."

Nora walked toward the kitchen. "Hey, how are you?" She was polite but eager to get Jake off the phone.

"Great. Especially since I have the day off. I was wondering if you wanted to do something."

Nora was silent for a minute. "Sorry. I already have plans with Remy. And I think she's really looking forward to it." Nora was surprised she didn't feel regret over keeping plans with a woman while turning down a bona fide date.

"I understand," Jake assured her. "It was kind of short notice. But I was supposed to work and ended up with the day off."

"I have an idea," Nora replied. "We're going shopping and then to lunch. Give me a call in about an hour or so. If Remy's okay with it, the three of us can have lunch. What do you think?"

"Great."

"I'm not sure where we're going, but I'll let you know if she wants to meet."

"Cool." Jake cleared his throat. "By the way, there hasn't been anything new on that other situation. So, that's good. You're sticking around right?"

Nora didn't have to think about it. She didn't want to start over again. She *did* want to stay if she could.

"Yes. I want to. I've given myself the weekend off, then I'm going to start looking for a job."

Nora thought about her rent. It would be due in two and a half weeks. "Maybe I'll find something at one of the galleries." She thought about Evan waiting in her living room. "I've got to go."

"Okay, talk to you in about an hour."

Nora placed the phone back in its cradle. She adjusted her short white linen skirt and started walking toward the living room. She spotted the envelope on the coffee table and looked around then quickly walked to the door. Down at the end of the path was Evan, his back to her as he made a quick retreat.

"Evan!" Nora called loudly. He kept walking. Either he was choosing not to answer, or he didn't hear Nora. She stood watching him, hating the sadness she felt as she watched him retreat. She walked into the living room and picked up the envelope. It was a plain business size, the kind he used in his office. She stared at her name, which was printed carefully on the outside. Nora admired the perfect block letters. She held it, deciding to wait until she was alone and had some time to deal with whatever was inside. The quick slam of the screen door brought her back to reality.

"Hello ... Nora?" The footsteps made their way toward her. "Hey, are you ready?"

Nora hastily folded the envelope and held it in her hand as Remy entered the doorway. "Hi. Let me just get my purse and we'll go." Nora started walking past Remy then gave her a quick peck on the cheek. Nora breathed in the scent of Remy's perfume, which smelled of sweet summer flowers.

She stuffed the envelope into her purse then grabbed her keys. "I'm ready for a great Sunday." She smiled as Remy followed her to the door.

"Me, too. It's nice being a tourist for a change." They both walked eagerly into the dazzling afternoon sunshine.

Nora thought about all of the possibilities this glorious day held. She and Remy would bond over shopping and lunch. Jake was a potential prospect, no harm in that. Evan had surprised her by stopping and dropped off a potential love letter. And even Tom had surprised her. Almost perfect, thought Nora.

Thoughts of Kevin interrupted her thoughts of contentment. She forced herself to shake them off as she walked closer to Remy. They made their way toward the Gallery District. Remy led Nora toward the more-established galleries, as evidenced by their voluptuous gardens and well-appointed window-dressings. Some of the artists chose dark red velvet curtains and serious-looking tassel tiebacks. Others, wishing to appear younger and more hip, chose crisp white linen shades or no window dressings at all in their airy, bright-white cottage galleries.

Remy stopped and grabbed a brochure from a wicker basket outside one of them. She opened it and started reading aloud as Nora basked in the day's growing warmth.

"Listen to this. This is your art history lesson for the day, okay? She gave Nora a flirtatious smile then continued. "Great American painters Fitz Hugh Lane, Winslow Homer, Milton Avery, John Sloan and many others painted in Gloucester. From the world-renowned to those who paint simply for the love of it, it is more than the scenery that attracts artists here. It is said the light of Gloucester is different than that found anywhere else. The Rocky Neck Art Colony in East Gloucester is the oldest continuously operating art colony in America."

Remy turned toward Nora. "Impressive. Did you know that?"

Nora stepped closer, then grabbed the brochure from Remy's hand, "Can I see that?"

"What's wrong? You look like you've seen a ghost or something."

Nora stared at the brochure, then looked up at Remy. "I'm fine.

She looked back down at the familiar images. It was identical to the brochure she had found that fateful day in Florida. The entire reason she had come to Rocky Neck was held in her hand. The irony and coincidence suddenly struck her, and Nora tried to imagine the odds that someone had picked up this same brochure and had traveled her same path, eventually leading her here in search of a new and better life. Nora accepted what she had never believed before as fate. She slid the brochure into her purse and squared her shoulders confidently.

She leaned toward Remy. "I'm doing fine." She peered toward the entryway of the gallery and the gleaming wide-plank floor and desk beyond. "Let's go admire some art we can't afford." She grabbed Remy by the wrist and walked inside.

Nora felt tiny as she stood in front of the enormous oil painting. The frame was heavy and ornate, decorated with heavily gilded oak leaves. The gold paint that had carefully been applied to the wood frame years ago had come off in spots, giving it an aged, antique look. The painting was hung in an obvious place of honor, taking up almost one entire wall. She had spotted it immediately upon entering. Nora estimated that it measured about four feet tall and at least seven feet across. And it was mesmerizing. She was drawn to it and openly stared at the painting.

On the horizon, there were three large schooners. The distance was great enough that Nora imagined the boats were hours from shore. The dark murky ocean was choppy and a dark blue black, which was tinged with gray-white peaks. And on the shore, in the lower right hand corner, was a petite woman, wearing a long white dress peeking out from a navy wool coat. As the wind whipped the shore, she appeared to be trying to hold back her long blond hair. And the unmistakable expression on her face was one of elation. As if she had been waiting for her lover for many years, and the anticipation of his arrival had prevented her from waiting inside, even during the growing storm.

On a small gold plaque, centered along the bottom of the frame, Nora read the carefully engraved words: *Sweet Homecoming*. She continued staring at every detail of the painting, not realizing that Remy was now standing beside her.

"Amazing, isn't it?" Remy admired the painting as well. "And says it all, don't you think?" She turned toward Nora.

Nora became misty eyed. The painting had touched her on so many levels.

The hoarse male voice suddenly broke the silence. "I painted that last winter."

Nora detected a French accent.

"It's my favorite work, as I can see it is yours. Would Madame like a price list? It would include the price of this one, which I've only recently decided to make available. I had a difficult time letting go of her."

Nora flushed as he spoke to her. She was sure she couldn't afford the frame, much less the work of art. She looked to Remy for an appropriate reply.

"Yes, please, we *are* interested. Perhaps my girlfriend and I can discuss it over lunch." Remy held Nora's arm for a long moment.

"My name is Jean Michelle, and I am the artist as well as gallery owner. Here is a list of my current works available to the public." He handed the brochure and attached price list to Remy. Nora realized, by Remy's affectionate display, that Jean Michele assumed they were a couple. She watched as Remy made her way over to his enormous antique pine table, which he used to conduct his sales transactions.

She extended her hand confidently, "Remy Fournier."

"Thank you Monsieur Michelle. We will be back to you later this afternoon. Hopefully with good news."

"Oui." Jean Michelle reached out and kissed Remy's hand. "Enchante."

Nora stepped out of the darkened gallery into the crowded street. She tapped her foot impatiently as she waited for Remy to walk up behind her. "I can't even imagine how much that painting cost. Are you crazy?"

Remy laughed at Nora's innocence. "Nora, any one is allowed to look. Besides, they're accustomed to lots of people looking before they buy. It's just not that kind of every-day purchase. You have to think it over. Make sure it's right for you."

"Sure, with most paintings, I'd understand that. But that one must have been the most expensive in there." Nora let her voice trail, wondering if Remy would tell her how much it was.

"Yes. It definitely is." Remy started walking and Nora followed behind. "Why don't we grab some cocktails and a little lunch?" Remy asked. She looked at Nora and smiled.

"I noticed you said cocktails first. Did you purposely mention them in order of importance?" Nora was amused.

"Yes, I did. Cocktails, first. Lunch, second."

"What about shopping? Aren't we going to go into some of the shops?"

"Later. I'm so thirsty." Remy teased.

"Where are you taking me?"

"The Rowboat, of course. Come on. Let's go before the tourists take all of the seats. I either want a little table on the deck, so long as it's not full sun, or we can grab a seat at the bar." Remy sped up her walk as Nora followed behind.

"You're high maintenance," Nora commented. As she thought about how much she was enjoying the day, a muffled ringing emanated from her purse. Jake. She didn't want to change the mood now by inviting him.

"Are you going to get that?" Remy stopped just short of the path to The Rowboat and waited for Nora's reply.

"No. I'm not." They smiled at each other. "I'm having a great time. But don't scare the hell out of me by trying to forge a check for a million-dollar piece of art."

Nora started walking ahead of Remy toward the entrance, speaking over her shoulder, "Do I need to remind you that I wouldn't have anyone to hang out with if they put you in jail for writing bad checks?"

Remy stopped as they started to enter the restaurant. She turned toward Nora. "It doesn't cost quite that much. And actually, I could swing it if I really wanted to."

"What are you talking about?" Nora's tone rose slightly, her curiosity piqued.

"Come on." Remy grabbed Nora's arm and led her inside, "I'll explain over a cocktails."

Nora sat back in her chair and tilted her face toward the bright summer sun. She heard the footsteps approach and she sat up, eager to order their drinks, "Can I get you something from the bar?"

Carly held her tray awkwardly, as if she had never waitressed before.

"Hi, Carly. I didn't know you worked here." Nora felt awkward without Remy as a buffer. She hoped she'd return from the bathroom soon.

"Yeah, well, Evan hired a second bartender for the rest of the summer, and I needed extra shifts, so here I am."

"Oh."

"And Kevin and I broke up. He used to help me out sometimes. So now I need the money."

Nora realized Carly seemed embarrassed, as if she had revealed too much unexpectedly. She suddenly felt for Carly. She knew what it was like to struggle. " I'm sorry. I guess I didn't really even know that you'd been dating."

"Yeah. But we kept it quiet. That's how Kevin liked it."

There was an awkward silence.

"Anyway, can I get you something to drink?" Carly looked at the other chair.

Nora saw the look and responded instantly. "Oh. Yes. I'm having lunch with Remy as a matter of fact. She wanted to cheer me up."

"Oh, yeah. Sorry about that." Carly replied.

"It's okay." Nora didn't feel the need to tell Carly the details. "We'll take two Dark and Stormy's, extra lime. And we'll wait a little while to order. Thanks."

She sat back and stared toward the harbor. "Oh, Carly ... " She watched as Carly turned back toward her. Nora lowered her voice. "Could you make the first round we order doubles?"

Carly shot her a knowing glance. "Sure."

Nora watched as Remy walked back from the bathroom, a skip in her step. She sat down, looking around eagerly for the waitress.

Nora knew what she was thinking. "Don't worry, I've got it all under control. The cocktails are on their way."

Nora wondered what Remy's reaction would be when she saw Carly. She closed her eyes and let the sun beat down onto her already-rosy cheeks. She was enjoying its intensity. Her skin was tingling, from the sun as well as anticipation. She thought about lunch and the possibilities.

Chapter 28

Nora walked through the cool shady bar area back toward the deck. The sunshine was still so startlingly bright that she could not make out the figure of the person standing at their table. She walked toward them, feeling the slight unsteadiness after consuming her two Dark and Stormy's. As she reached Remy's chair, she was instantly disappointed as she recognized Jake. She worried that his presence would break the bond she had felt between her and Remy.

"Hi. How are you?" Nora knew her voice betrayed her lack of excitement.

Jake leaned in and gave Nora a perfunctory kiss on the cheek. "I'm great. How are you?" He remained standing at the table. Nora realized how obvious he was in trying to get an invitation to join them. She wondered how he had found them so quickly.

"What are you doing here?" Nora asked as she tried to make eye contact with Remy.

"I got the day off unexpectedly. And I wanted to treat myself. So, I'm sitting at the bar and having lunch. How about you two?" Jake looked back and forth between them.

Remy spoke first. "I brought Nora out as a treat. And we've been having a girl's day."

"Oh, I'm sorry. I didn't mean to interrupt. I just wanted to say hello." Jake seemed genuinely concerned that he had interrupted their conversation.

"No. Please feel free to join us." Remy's tone was perfectly half-hearted. And Nora knew Jake would pick up on that. Hopefully.

"Oh … thanks, but I already ordered. And I know the bartender. So I'm gonna catch up with him over a few beers. But maybe next time. Maybe we can all get together. Shoot some pool or go over to McMurtree's and hang on the deck."

Nora felt an instant pang of uneasiness. It was no coincidence that he had just mentioned all the places she and Remy had been recently. Did he want them to know he had been keeping close tabs on their whereabouts?

Nora answered eagerly, anxious for Jake to leave. "Yes. Let's definitely do that soon." She sat down and smiled, not seeing the expression on his face with the sun shining directly behind him.

"Great. You girls have a great time. And don't drink too many Dark and Stormy's." Again, thought Nora. He wants me to know he's been watching me. Or was it Remy he had his eye on? Maybe both of them, Nora realized. And, it probably wasn't just business related. Like most men, he was probably fascinated by their friendship, imagining all sorts of scenarios.

Remy waited until Jake was safely seated back at the bar. "He's definitely got your number." Remy sat back and analyzed Nora.

"You know how it is," Nora whispered. "You go out with them once, and they want more." She decided not to tell Remy about the pills, and how Jake had offered to help her. She wouldn't tell her yet. Not until she knew the whole truth.

Remy leaned forward. "Sweetheart. You should be careful. You've got too many pokers in the fire. Someone could get hurt. Or worse … pissed off."

Nora wavered as she prepared to answer. Was Remy trying to help her? Or warn her? Was she talking about Evan, Tom or Jake? Or about herself?

"I know," Nora conceded. "I didn't mean to. He asked me out and I felt a little weird saying no." Nora looked at Remy, waiting for a reaction. Remy sat back, saying nothing. Nora continued, "He's a nice guy, actually."

"You don't have to convince me. But I'm not the one he wants to date … or whatever. And that's your decision to make."

Nora saw this as the perfect time. "Remy, I know you're my friend.

And I've never really had a close woman friend before. Can we be honest?"

"Sure. What's up?"

Nora licked her lips, suddenly nervous. The sun was making its slow descent, and she was glad that it would finally be cooling off. She was flushed. From the sun, from the drinks, and from nerves. "I just want to feel we can talk about things. Maybe not here ... " Nora's voice trailed. She suddenly felt tongue tied and slightly flustered.

"I *am* your friend. Ask me anything. I don't care." Remy said as she looked around to assess the proximity of the other diners.

"Okay." Nora was surprised by Remy's response. "Well, let's start with your family. I thought you were broke. Am I going to have to be the pathetic poor friend now?"

"Yes." They both laughed, releasing some of the tension. Remy waited, obviously enjoying the reaction from Nora.

"Tell me, damn it!"

"You remember the clock on my wall?"

"The red one?" Nora remembered it, and all of her other furnishings, very well.

"Yes. The one my Grandmother Martin gave me." Remy continued. "Well, we've been in touch, and I think she feels bad for me. She writes beautiful letters to me practically every month. She said she misses me. Well, anyway. She's giving me a little of her own money, which is where it all comes from anyway."

Nora waited. She wanted details.

Remy went on. "She's set up a new trust fund for me. But I had to promise to be less foolish this time. No spending crazy amounts of money on girlfriends."

"Shit. Does that mean you're not going to buy me that painting?"

"No ... sorry. I think my grandmother would notice."

Nora held up her glass. "A toast. To your new-found old wealth." Nora thought about Remy's revelation. For once, she was actually happy for another woman. A woman who she felt was also her friend. Someone she was going to trust with her secrets. And hopefully, Remy would feel she could trust her, too.

*　　　*　　　*

Remy climbed the narrow ladder and pushed open the skylight. As she reached the last rung, Nora heard a click and the turning of a knob. Suddenly, the darkened stairway was bathed with the colors of the sunset. Remy climbed out onto the small rooftop deck then held her hand out for Nora. As Nora climbed the last rung unsteadily, she grabbed onto Remy's extended hand, grasping it tightly. She reached the landing and climbed over the edge of the old skylight. As the full horizon came into view, Nora gasped in awe. She stood motionless, taking in the breathtaking view.

The setting sun was a deep orange ball, and as it made its slow descent, it began to meet the ocean. The sky was bathed in every imaginable shade of orange and red, and the passing boats were distant on the horizon as seagulls skimmed by gracefully. Nora walked to the edge of the deck and held on carefully to the old railing. She tried not to think about the fact that they were six stories up.

Remy stepped up beside her. Nora saw the champagne glass out of the corner of her eye as Remy held it out toward her. "Are you still thirsty?" Remy held a chilled bottle of champagne in the other hand.

Nora looked toward the bottle, surprised by the label. "Remy Fournier, I have two questions for you. Where did that come from? And, most importantly, is this some of the frivolous spending your grandmother is worried about?" Nora held out her glass, waiting anxiously for Remy to open the bottle of Dom Perignon.

"A. I snuck that up here while you were in the bathroom and B. Yes, this is probably going to be seen as frivolous spending. But if I don't do it all the time, I can slide it by. Trust me. But don't call my grandmother and tell her."

"What's the occasion," Nora asked as she watched Remy pop the cork.

"We needed to celebrate my new-found old status, of course. Plus, just think how much we saved by not shopping this afternoon."

Nora took a long sip, reveling in the dry, sweet-tart flavor. They held up their glasses as Remy toasted. "To friendship on Rocky Neck."

Nora thought about the similar toast she had had with Evan. She hoped this one would hold true. By now the sky had turned a deep purple blue, and the bright white slice of moon was flanked by hundreds of brightly twinkling stars. The wind had picked up, and Nora wrapped her arms around herself.

"Do you want to go inside?" Remy asked, standing close enough so that their forearms were now touching.

"No. I love it out here. It's so beautiful." Nora's tone got serious. "Remy, there's something I have to ask you. And as my friend, I'm going to ask you to be completely honest with me." Nora kept looking straight ahead as Remy turned toward her in anticipation.

"What's wrong. What is it?"

"Do you promise?" Nora asked again.

"Yes, I promise."

Nora hesitated as she tried to find the right words. "That night Christian died. You said you took me home." Nora waited.

"Yes, I did say that."

"But I'm confused. We came up with that because I couldn't remember what happened." Nora turned toward Remy and made eye contact.

"You … you didn't come home with me, actually. But I did give you a ride. It happened a little differently than what we told the police." Remy seemed to be gathering her thoughts before she continued. "You were stressed and didn't remember. And we didn't have much time with the police doing their questioning right away." Nora noticed she was trying to keep her voice from shaking.

"I know you want to protect me. But what happened?"

Remy sighed deeply and downed the remaining champagne in her glass. "You started walking home. I kept calling but you kept walking. So I went home, got my car and then picked you up. You were half way to Rocky Neck."

"That's it?" Nora asked.

"Yes." Remy seemed to stumble.

"Remy, I remembered part of what happened. I remember being in the passenger seat and feeling really sick." She paused. "And I remember that Christian was in the car."

Remy shot Nora an anxious look then grabbed the bottle of champagne and started climbing down the ladder.

Nora watched as Remy struggled on the steep steps. "Wait. I want to talk to you." Nora leaned into the stairwell. She watched, helplessly, as Remy missed a step and swayed uncontrollably. She heard her scream followed by the subsequent sickening thud.

"Remy!" Nora climbed down the ladder, not remembering the descent as she made her way toward her crumpled body.

"Remy!" She knelt beside Remy and lifted her eyelids. Remy groaned loudly. Nora breathed a sigh of relief as she got up and ran to the first available door. She started pounding wildly. "Help. Please." Nora sobbed. "Someone please call an ambulance! There's been an accident!"

Chapter 29

Nora sat in the stiff plastic orange chair of the Gloucester Hospital Emergency Room. She looked at the old-fashioned school clock on the wall. She had been waiting almost two hours since they had wheeled Remy in. She took a sip of the almost-cold coffee and tried to tune out the noise of the Emergency Room as sirens periodically blared and phones rang. She thought about what she must look like and grabbed a compact from her purse. Her eyes were red and puffy, and there were stray marks from mascara under both of them. Nora rubbed at the tender skin in an attempt to remove the mascara. Then she grabbed her clear gloss and applied a thin coat. She looked up as she heard the footsteps approach.

"Nora Mason?" The tall middle-aged doctor stared at her, his eyes serious.

Nora stood up, anxious to hear the results. "Yes?"

"Your friend will be fine. She's resting. She has a bad sprain in her ankle and wrist and plenty of bruises, but miraculously, there were no broken bones."

"Thank God," Nora sighed with relief.

"She also suffered a slight concussion. I'm going to recommend plenty of bed rest and Motrin." He looked at Nora and waited for a response.

"Thank you doctor. When can we leave?"

He looked at his watch. "About thirty minutes or so. When we're ready to release her, a nurse will bring her out."

"Great. Thank you."

The doctor continued. "She's authorized you to take her home."

Nora thought about the fact that Remy had ridden in the ambulance as she had frantically grabbed a taxi. She looked up at the doctor. "I need to call a cab. "But, yes, I'll take her home."

The doctor nodded and made his way to the desk. Nora sat down, tears welling up in her eyes as she felt the incredible sense of relief overcome her. She knew it had been an accident and that Remy would be fine. But it could have been so much worse. Nora shuddered as her mind suddenly reverted to the night of Christian's death. She felt herself go instantly pale.

My God … Christian! She remembered. The screams echoed in her head as Christian plunged to the ground from the lifeguard chair. She had climbed down, frantic to get to him. And she had sensed as soon as she looked at his face, that he was dead. His legs were twisted abnormally, as if he were a rag doll. He lay motionless, his hair perfect and his eyes closed … as if he were sleeping.

Nora put her head in her hands, desperate to remember the rest. How had he fallen? And why hadn't she just called the police?

Nora thought about her new life, as she had known it up until now, certain that this revelation would change it forever. She was never going to have the love she had always searched for. Or the life she had so desperately tried to improve. It was going to be over soon. She thought about Remy. Had she been trying to protect her? Had she seen what had happened? Nora shook uncontrollably, trying not to think about the fact that she was probably the one who had ended Christian's life. She remembered how angry she had been with him, his sweat-dampened body pinning her against the outside wall of the Port Side. She remembered his ruthlessness and his cruel whispers as he had mercilessly groped at her over and over.

And she remembered her tears of frustration as onlookers walked inside without helping her. How small she had felt as she tried to resist his advances. Nora sobbed openly, as she again felt the frustration and fear of that evening. Christian's cruel and belittling words had echoed in her head. She recalled how she had wanted to hurt him. How she had wanted him to feel the pain and humiliation she had felt. Nora hugged her knees as she sobbed, admitting finally that her world was falling apart.

*   *   *

"Hey, miss, you all right?" The voice was gentle and caring. Nora looked up and wiped her eyes. "Did you call for a cab?"

"Yes. Yes, I did. But my friend hasn't come out yet. I need to take her home." Nora's voice was barely audible.

"Well, I'll tell you what. It's not too busy right now. How about I wait outside and you come out when you're ready?" He nodded his head and started to walk away.

"Wait. What about … ?" Nora's voice was interrupted.

"Don't worry, so long as you come out in the next fifteen or twenty minutes, the meter won't be running."

Nora was grateful for this small kindness, from a man who didn't know her and shouldn't care. "Thank you." Her voice broke as she wiped her eyes again and made her way to the desk.

She waited for the heavyset nurse to look up from her clipboard. "Yes. Hello. I'm waiting for Remy Fournier. Could you tell me how much longer, please? I have a cab waiting."

The nurse grimaced, obviously annoyed. "It should be soon. We'll let you know."

Nora didn't have the strength to argue. As she turned to make her way back to her chair, the two wide metal doors swung open. Remy was pale, her hair pulled back off her face into a makeshift ponytail. Her head bobbed slightly, and her eyes were partially closed, as if she were very drowsy. The nurse pushing the wheel chair followed Remy's pointed finger.

"Over there. That's my friend."

The nurse approached. "We have to keep her in the chair until we get to your vehicle." She looked toward the two exits. "Which way?"

Nora flushed. "Oh. Actually, I called a cab. It should be right outside."

The nurse motioned with her hand. "Go ahead. I'll follow you."

*   *   *

"155 Water Street, please." Nora had remembered the address. She thought back to the first time she had been there with Remy. If only she knew then. She stopped herself. It didn't matter. The truth would

219

have to come out. She turned toward Remy, who was leaning on her. "How are you holding up?"

"I'm okay."

Nora scrutinized Remy's pale face. "You don't look so great."

"Yeah, well I bet I look better than I feel. My head is pounding."

"Okay. No more talking. Close your eyes for the rest of the ride."

Nora's guilt was enormous. Ultimately, Remy's fall had been her fault. She lowered her voice. "Don't say anything. But I just want you to know how sorry I am." Nora paused. "For everything."

She felt Remy nod. Nora fell silent as she watched the driver navigate the quiet streets as he headed toward downtown.

∗   ∗   ∗

"Thank you." Nora paid and tipped the driver, hesitated, then gave him an extra five-dollar bill. "Thank you for everything. I appreciate it."

The cab driver held out the bill, obviously wanting to return it to Nora. "Thank you, Miss. But you were already very generous."

"But, you were so kind … and I appreciate it. Really."

The old gentleman looked Nora squarely in the eye, his pale blue eyes sparkling. "Young lady, my mother taught me one very important lesson that's always stayed with me. No act of kindness, no matter how small, is ever wasted." He smiled.

Nora steadied Remy as she closed the door. "Thank you. I'll remember that." She watched him drive away, the quote still hanging in the cool early dawn air.

She grabbed Remy's crutches with one hand and circled her waist with the other. "Just lean on me so you don't put too much pressure on your foot."

Remy did as she was directed. "Nora, I don't feel very well. I think I'm going to be sick."

Nora braced herself as she stopped. "You'll feel a lot better once we get inside and you lie down. Now close your eyes." Nora looked to make sure Remy's eyes were closed. "Take a deep breath." Remy inhaled and exhaled deeply. "Good."

"One more."

"Good. Now don't think about anything other than making it into that elevator. Okay?"

"Okay." Remy's stared straight ahead, her face still strained. She hobbled awkwardly as she leaned on Nora. Nora thought about her most recent revelations, glad for the opportunity to be distracted by playing nurse to Remy. As they reached the elevator, Nora pushed the fifth floor button and settled back, fighting the urge to check out her appearance in the mirror above. She thought about the long night, and how she must look right now. For once, Nora didn't care. Right now, she needed to take care of Remy. And then she would take care of herself. She still couldn't admit what she feared most. But she would make things right. No matter what the consequences.

*   *   *

Nora covered Remy with the light cotton quilt which she had partially kicked off during the night, then tiptoed out of the darkened bedroom and walked toward the kitchen. She looked up at Remy's Grandmother Martin's clock, remembering what Remy had told her. Nora was glad that Remy had a family, and that she would always be taken care of. She felt the slight pang of jealousy and sadness, knowing that she had no family, not really, who could look after her or who could help her. Nora tried to shake off the self-pity as she looked at the time. 6:17 a.m. She folded the blanket she had used that still lay on the couch from the night before. She'd had a fitful night's sleep, alternating between forcing herself to wake up to check on Remy, and having nightmares of being arrested, her hands cuffed as she was led away in a police car.

Nora grabbed the letter she had written and folded it in three. She propped it up inside the sterling bowl that held Remy's car keys. On the outside of the letter, she had carefully written: *Remy, Please Read. This is my confession, which I'll be giving to the police.*

She hesitated for a moment, then tiptoed over to Remy's bedroom doorway once more. She watched her as she slept then glanced at the nightstand to make certain everything Remy might need was within arm's reach. Tissues, a bottle of water and a glass, a large bottle of Ibuprofen, a small plastic container in case she wasn't feeling well, the TV remote, and the phone. Lastly, there was a note: *Call me if you need me. I've also left a letter you should read. It's in the kitchen. Thank you for being my friend. -Nora.*

Nora turned and walked hastily toward the door. Now that she had made a decision, she needed to move ahead. She unlocked the door and stepped into the hall. She thought about talking to Jake. Hopefully he was working today. It would make things easier for everyone. But first, she desperately needed a hot shower and a strong cup of coffee.

Chapter 30

Nora's strides were long and remarkably self-assured as she made her way back toward Rocky Neck. She had decided to walk. And why not? It was a gorgeous day, the sun was shining, and she was in no hurry to turn herself in. This might even be her last walk of freedom, she mused, somewhat dramatically. Still, somehow she felt at peace with her decision. There would be no more wondering, no dreading that the phone would ring or someone would be pounding on her door. She would come clean. Completely clean. She would tell them everything she remembered and would hope for the best. In this case, the best would be that, yes, she *had* pushed Christian but, *no,* she hadn't thought of the consequences while she was in her alcohol and drug-induced fog.

Nora looked at her watch. She had been walking for about thirty minutes. She thought about Remy. The night Christian died, Remy said she had gone home to get her car and then had come back for her. Nora calculated that it probably would have taken her about thirty minutes to get to where Nora now stood. She pictured herself, drunk and completely out of it, with Christian hot on her heels. Nora stopped for a moment to catch her breath. She took in the spectacular view of the cove directly across the harbor from her, noticing that she could see the restaurant from here.

She closed her eyes for a moment, trying to clear her head and calm herself so that she could continue. Her eyes suddenly widened as she gasped. She recalled Remy's conversation with Christian while they were in the car together. Remy's voice had been angry as she argued with Christian.

"You know, it's guys like you that ruin it for girls like me. You smug bastards. They always think they want to be with you. And you end up treating them like shit!"

Nora remembered the anger in Remy's voice.

Christian had replied smugly. "Sweetheart, you'd be lucky to have one night with me. Just get me to the fucking beach so I won't have to listen to your bitching." He had been different. A Christian that Nora had never expected.

"You fucking rich boys are all the same," Remy had added. "Just like my brother." There was silence for a moment before Nora heard it.

"I can't wait until you leave at the end of the season … unless I kill you before then, you pain in the ass."

"Whad you say?" Christian's words were labored and slurred.

"Nothing. Here we are. Now get out!" Remy had practically shouted.

Christian had climbed out of the back seat and over the door without opening it. Suddenly, Nora felt a hard tug on her arm as he tried to pull at her seemingly dead weight.

"Come on, Princess. We're heeeeeere."

Remy's voice screeched as it hung in the night air. "What the fuck are you doing? You leave her alone. The deal was that I'd give you a ride. I'm not leaving her with you. Besides, don't you think you fed her enough crap. She's barely conscious."

Before Remy could finish her sentence, Christian had opened the door. Nora felt herself being dragged out. As she was pulled onto the sidewalk, she lost her balance, landing on her knees for a long moment before regaining it and standing up.

"Come on, Nora. Let's go," Remy had insisted, her voice high-pitched and unsteady.

Christian's voice boomed through the night air. "Oh, no, you don't, lesbo. Goldilocks stays with me."

Remy's voice echoed her frustration. "Christian, what do you want? I drove you here. That's what you wanted, isn't it? I'm telling you right now, I'm not leaving Nora with you. Look at her. I think she's really sick!"

"Okay, okay." Christian slurred. "If you two ladies come up with me on the lifeguard chair for a little while, so you know, we can have a little … romantic date, then I promise you can go. Okay?"

"Five minutes. You have us for five minutes. Then we're leaving." Remy grabbed Nora's other hand and started walking toward the lifeguard chair.

Christian continued, "Yeah … *that's* what I'm talking about. You two won't regret it."

Nora remembered Remy's gentle hands as she had helped guide her up the rungs of the lifeguard chair. She had followed behind Nora in order to help her balance.

Remy continued as she walked up behind her. "This is insane, you crazy bastard. You're going to get us killed." With the last word, Remy had reached the top and seated herself next to Nora.

"Yeah, well it'll be worth it. Show time, laaaadies." Christian had landed with an awkward plunk as he reached the seat. He purposely sat between them, his large, groping hands fondling each of their thighs simultaneously. Nora remembered pushing Christian's hand away, at which time he had had abruptly stood, his feet balanced precariously on the edge of the top rung of the lifeguard chair, his open hand raised as if to strike her.

Through the deafening sound of the ocean, Nora heard Remy's voice, a tone deep and angry, which emanated from her depths.

"If you hurt her, I'll fucking kill you. You understand?"

Christian had looked at Remy, challenging her words. He turned and slapped Nora, his open hand landing squarely on her unsuspecting, upraised cheek. The rest had seemed to happen in slow motion. Nora had sat down, shocked and holding her face, as Remy stood. She shoved Christian forcefully. In a split second, without a word spoken, he had leaned backwards, out of sight for a moment, as he had plunged and landed in the sand below with a loud thud.

Nora remembered feeling instantly sober and awake as she had climbed down from the chair and stood over Christian's body. She stared, mesmerized by what she couldn't accept. She recalled Remy's pleading, as she stood staring at Christian for too long. She had finally looked over her shoulder to see Kevin running toward her, his feet heavy in the soft sand.

Kevin had stood beside Nora staring at the figure in disbelief.

"I didn't do it," Nora had replied. "I didn't ... " She had realized, even in her condition that proclaiming her innocence would only condemn Remy. She turned around, realizing that Remy had slid away into the darkness away from the gruesome scene. Nora slipped into silence, realizing that Kevin knew she was probably too drunk to connect her thoughts about what had just occurred.

"Nora, what the hell happened?"

"I ... don't know. I ... I don't feel well." Nora remembered standing, panicked, wondering what she should do.

"Come on. Let's get the hell out of here." He and Nora had run toward the edge of the beach, to his car. As she had climbed in behind his seat, she noticed Carly half-dozing in the passenger seat. She had lain down in the back, grateful to be gone from the scene and praying that it had been a bad dream. She fought to stay awake as her eyes began to close, the events and the alcohol and pills suddenly taking their toll. As Nora started to doze, she heard the trunk click open for a moment then slam shut again. What seemed like hours later, she finally heard Kevin get in and slam his door closed.

"Hey, where did you go?" She asked.

Kevin had waited a long moment before answering, "I wanted to have a little respect for the dead. So, I put a blanket on 'em. At least he'll be covered up."

"Do you think we should call the police?"

"And tell them what?" That we don't know what happened?" Kevin started the car. "Count me out, but you can stay if you want."

Nora was floating in and out of consciousness as the car idled for a few moments before pulling away.

"Shit. That chick was staring at me," Nora heard Kevin remark, not understanding what he was talking about.

Nora recalled the smell of exhaust as it hung in the thick salt air just before she passed out.

*   *   *

Nora concentrated on the task at hand as she finally reached Rocky Neck. She had been walking for almost an hour. She was suddenly exhausted. She stood in front of the door to her house as she fumbled in her purse. She continued her fruitless search, suddenly realizing she had left her keys at Remy's. She stood indecisive, almost too tired to think of a solution before remembering the spare key tucked under the clay pot out back. Nora recalled how she had initially left if for Evan the morning he had come over after Christian's death. She hoped it was still there.

Nora walked along the white seashell path toward the back deck. As she approached, she stared at her carefully-planted flowers and neatly-arranged clay planters. She missed her home. She wondered if she would ever be able to enjoy it again. In peace.

Nora reached underneath the clay pot as she lifted it slightly. She felt the cool metal of the key against the damp wood of the deck. She opened the door, returned the key to its hiding place then walked into the kitchen and instinctively pressed the button on her answering machine, "You have no new messages." Nora breathed a sigh of relief.

*   *   *

She sat at her wrought iron table, the one where she and Evan had had their first dinner together. The shower had definitely helped, for a brief moment, anyway. And the strong coffee, which she had always lived for, now seemed unsatisfying and almost bitter. She placed her mug on the table and closed her eyes, thinking back to early that morning. When she had left Remy at the loft, Nora had convinced herself that she, in fact, had been the one who had accidentally killed Christian. But now that she knew the truth, she felt sadness that it had in fact been Remy, the one person she thought she could trust. What should she do now? She couldn't turn her in. Though Remy hadn't been honest, she was the only person who had ever defended her ... or cared about her. Nora squeezed her eyes tightly as she begged someone, anyone, to give her answers.

Nora thought about the cab driver and the wisdom he had tried to impart. Kindness to others, she mused. How could she help Remy? And possibly herself, too? As she pondered the question, she heard the ringing of her cell phone.

"Nora?" The voice cut in and out.

"Hello?" Nora walked around the deck until she finally positioned herself so that she could hear the caller.

"Hey, it's Jake."

Nora thought about the call she had planned to make to him this morning, before her memory had returned.

"Hi," Nora replied in a monotone voice.

"How are you feeling? You sound like you're coming down with something."

Nora tried to smile as she answered, "Oh, I'm fine. I think I'm just a little run down. You know … " Nora purposely let the sentence trail.

"I hear ya. I think you need a night out. I mean, I understand how Remy wanted a girl's lunch and all, but I was hoping you and I could try to get together soon." There was an awkward silence for a moment. It was broken by the sound of her home phone ringing.

Jake responded immediately, "I'll let you go so you can get that. I'm gonna be in the area later. I'll stop by, and maybe we can plan a weekend or something."

"Okay." Nora grabbed her home phone.

"Nora? Oh, thank fucking God. You didn't call the police yet, did you?"

"No. No, I didn't." Nora didn't want to provide any further explanation. She wanted to talk to Remy in person.

"I'll be right over. Nora, please don't call anyone. I have to talk to you. I'm on my way."

Chapter 31

Nora stood in the kitchen as she refilled her coffee cup. She heard the knock on the front screen door and peered through the unlit kitchen toward it. It was overcast this morning, and the kitchen was dark. Nora stood, motionless, staring at Jake as he waited on the other side of the screen door, his shadow illuminated by the daylight behind him. He squinted, trying to see into the foyer.

"Nora? Anybody home?"

Nora realized that he couldn't see her at the end of the unlit hall. She stood, carefully observing him, her presence still unnoticed. She watched as he adjusted his shirt and ran his hands through his hair, an annoyed look on his face telling her what she already knew. For the first time since she had met him, Nora had to admit, she disliked him. Though at times his actions were those of someone who wanted to be helpful and caring, she realized his intentions were, ultimately, selfish and self-serving. Like most men, thought Nora. They were interested in one thing. Except for Evan. Evan was different. But unfortunately, he wasn't hers.

Nora surveyed Jake as he looked at his watch then tried to peer through the screen door again. This time, he cupped his hands around his eyes in an attempt to see past the screen into the house. She looked at the clock on the kitchen stove. Why, she wondered, had he shown up already? Had he been right outside? Nora remained still while he continued to stand in the doorway. Finally, he turned and walked away. She knew he'd be back. But maybe by then she and Remy could formulate a plan. And maybe Jake could help them without even knowing it.

Nora was jolted back to reality by the awkward sound approaching the front door. Step... clunk ... step ... clunk ... step ... clunk.

She listened, realizing that Remy was right outside, and ran to open the door. "Get inside. Jake was just here knocking. I didn't answer."

Remy stumbled slightly as she maneuvered her way into the living room. Nora closed and locked the door behind her then ran to the back door and checked that lock as well. Nora fought the feeling inside. As if she were a prisoner in her own home. She walked toward the couch then sat, watching Remy as she stood awkwardly.

"Where are your crutches?" Nora asked.

"I can't coordinate those damn things." Remy shifted back and forth from her left foot and then her right heel, which was wrapped tightly from her instep all the way up to her calf. "It's alright. It won't kill me."

Nora looked up in surprise at her bad choice of words.

"Shit. I mean ... " Remy struggled to find the right words. "Nora, thank you for waiting to talk to Jake." She paced clumsily in front of the coffee table that separated her from Nora. "I know you're really upset, and that you want to tell the truth." She sighed deeply. "I don't know how to say this ... but please remember that I care about you very much, and my intentions ...SHIT! I'm rambling." Remy wrung her hands.

Nora felt Remy's discomfort, yet she didn't know how to help her relieve it. She wondered what she would say. And if she would tell the truth.

"There's something I have to tell you. I never meant for this to happen. I swear I was trying to defend you. And I didn't think about what could happen. God, Nora. I would never do anything to hurt you. And I would never let you take the blame. Not for something *I* did."

Remy stood awkwardly, her voice trembling as she stared at Nora. "I did it. I killed Christian ... by accident." She looked up slowly, almost afraid to look into Nora's eyes.

Nora responded instantly. "It's okay. I know what happened. It *was* an accident. I know you didn't really mean for ... it to happen." Nora still couldn't say the words.

Remy was visibly shaken and trying to keep control. "How do you know?"

Nora stood and walked over to her. "I remembered. Almost everything. This morning, while I was walking home. I was walking the same route I walked that night. And I remembered." Nora's voice was almost a whisper.

Remy paced nervously. "I'm going to turn myself in. I can't let you take the blame." Her last statement was barely audible. "I swear to God. I never wanted this to happen." With that, Remy tried to choke back the tears. She stood, waiting for Nora's reply.

"I know. I know what you did for me."

Remy's tone was frustrated. "Well, what I did for you is going to get us both into deep shit. I have to tell them."

Nora stood motionless, thinking about how they were going to get out of this. "Why do either of us have to take the blame?" Nora said the words, raising her eyes to meet Remy's.

"What do you mean?"

"I'm not sure what I mean." Nora's tone changed suddenly. "But I'll tell you what I do know. Jake's been all over me all of a sudden."

Remy was alarmed. "Why. What does he know? If you knew everything this morning, why did you call him?"

"I didn't call him. But I think he's been keeping a close eye on me. He called first thing this morning. Then he showed up. I wanted to talk to you first, that's why I didn't go to the door."

"Shit."

"I think it's okay, actually. I don't think it's about Christian." Nora tried to give Remy a knowing look.

Remy looked puzzled.

"I think he's on the prowl and looking to … get laid. He said he wants to take me away for a weekend. He's doing the full court press."

Remy nodded. "Of course he is. Do you actually like him?"

"No. But he doesn't have to know that."

"What are you talking about?" Remy sounded frustrated. "I'm not following."

Remy continued. "Why don't I just tell them what happened and that it was an accident? That I didn't think he'd … " She tried to clear her throat.

"No. Absolutely not." Nora looked optimistic for the first time. "Remy, would you say you and I are smart?"

"Of course. Sometimes."

"No. Really. Smarter than most men?"

"Of course. That's a given. There are alot of idiots out there. You don't have to convince me of that."

"Well, a man got us into this shit, and a man is going to get us out."

"What do you have in mind?" Remy's eyes held a glimmer of hope.

"I don't know yet. We need to come up with a plan. But I'm thinking Jake is going to help us. Or, let's just say, we're going to help him."

Remy held her hands up in surrender. "I don't care what it is. It's got to be better than *my* plan."

Nora realized she hadn't told Remy about finding the pills in her kitchen. "You don't even know the half of it. I found Christian's bottle of Xanax … in my kitchen cabinet."

Remy didn't look shocked. "Why am I surprised? He was always up to something."

"We have some things to figure out." Nora shifted into high gear. She looked at her watch. "I'm going to make a call. Then let's get the hell out of here." Nora grabbed the phone from the kitchen.

He answered in two rings. "Hey. I was just *at* your place. Where were you?"

Nora put on her most coquettish voice. "Oh, it was you. Sorry about that. I was in the shower, and I thought I heard something, but by the time I got downstairs, no one was there. Too bad I missed you." She paused for a moment. "I thought you were going to come by *later*?"

"Yeah, I know. But I was in the neighborhood. I had to take care of some official business with your former boss."

Jake's power play didn't slip by Nora. He wanted to sound like the big man on campus. Nora fought the urge but couldn't resist. "Oh? Is everything okay?"

"Well, we've narrowed down the search in Christian's case, and I had to look around a little more."

Nora knew Jake wasn't at the station. If he had been, he wouldn't have been so careless with this information.

"Oh. You think you're close to solving it? The case?" Nora's tone rose slightly, and she had to fight to keep her voice calm.

"We're getting there."

"Good. Then, what's the saying? Justice will be served." Nora tried to sound sad and sincere.

Jake changed the subject to one Nora was sure he found more interesting. "Hey, enough about that. How about we get together? I was thinking that maybe we could go away. How about we go into Boston this week. Maybe stay over for a night?"

Under normal circumstances and with a different guy, Nora would have loved it. She tried to veil her lack of interest. "That sounds great. But I'm just starting to look for a new job this week. Could we have dinner instead? Maybe Wednesday night? Then we can play it by ear and see how it goes." Nora was hoping she wouldn't have to take that trip with him but wanted to keep Jake hopeful.

"Sounds good." Nora was amused by how thinly disguised his disappointment was.

"I have to go and get dressed." Nora hoped Jake was envisioning her. "I won't be around much for the next two days … you know, job hunting. She hoped this would explain her absence in case he was keeping tabs on her and didn't see her around.

"I'll pick you up at seven on Wednesday. I'll surprise you. I have a new place in mind." Jake's voice rose a notch with excitement.

Nora took a deep breath. "Great. I can't wait. I'll have a surprise for you, too." She purposely let the comment hang before she went on. "I'll wear something really special." She hung up immediately, hoping she had sounded enthusiastic but not overly eager.

Remy pursed her lips disapprovingly. "Wow. Award winning." She hobbled over to the couch and sat down clumsily.

"Thank you. I gave it my best." Nora walked toward the door. "I'm going to get dressed. Then you're taking me to your place. I'm staying over for the next few days. When we get there, you need to call Evan. Tell him you had an accident and you need to keep off your feet for a few days. And tell him about the concussion. He won't want you to go to work." Nora took another deep breath. "Hopefully, that'll give us enough time."

"What are we doing?" Remy asked curiously as Nora started up the stairs.

"I don't know yet. We'll figure it out." As an after thought, she stopped short and leaned over the rail. "And grab that new bottle of Cuervo from the cabinet. Bottom right hand side. To the left of the fridge." Nora bounded up the stairs, her mood suddenly hopeful for the first time in days.

*   *   *

Nora pulled into the parking garage a little faster than she had intended. The slight screech of the tires seemed loud and exaggerated inside the almost-empty concrete space.

Remy pointed toward one corner. "Over there. That's my space. And try not to park too close to the wall."

Nora opened her door and slammed it a bit too loudly. "Bossy, aren't we?"

"You like me that way. If I were a guy, I'd be all set." Remy said sarcastically.

"Wow, what happened to the apologetic tone of an hour ago? You've changed your tune already?" Nora half-teased.

"No. Of course not. But you know that's just my personality. It's when I stop being sarcastic and teasing that you should worry."

"Well, thanks for the warning." Nora smiled, knowing that Remy's defense mechanism was just that. She reached into the back seat and grabbed her purse, her overnight bag, and the bottle of tequila. She walked around to the passenger side to see if Remy needed help. Remy waved her off. "You've got your hands full. I can handle it."

They made their way to the elevator together, the second time within the last twenty-four hours. Remy remarked, "Hey, isn't this déjà vu all over again?"

"Yeah, don't remind me. Come on. Let's step it up. You need to call Evan."

*   *   *

Nora leaned back into the supple leather of Remy's couch. She stared at the unopened bottle of amber liquid. Ahh, she thought. The mother lode. She could relieve alot of stress with that one bottle. She took off her shoes, hesitated, and then placed her perfectly pedicured feet on top of Remy's antique pine coffee table.

Nora watched Remy as she hobbled from the bathroom and walked over to the kitchen counter. She picked up the phone. Before she could dial, Nora interrupted. "Oh, hey, did you find my keys?" Remy dialed the phone and picked up the keys from inside the sterling bowl on the counter. Nora walked over and grabbed them, then mouthed the words, "Thanks." She watched Remy as she waited for someone to answer the phone.

"Hi, Carly? How are you? It's Remy."

Nora watched as Remy listened for a moment before answering. "Yes, we should get together some time. Aha. Yeah … that sounds good. I'm … I've been better, actually. Is Evan there? Thanks." Remy bit her lip nervously while she waited for Evan to come to the phone. "Hi, Evan? It's Remy. I'm so sorry, but I had an accident yesterday, and I'm going to have to take the next few days off. I fell off a ladder … backwards. No, I'm okay. I went to the hospital. But I have a badly sprained ankle and wrist and a concussion." She listened intently. "Yes, I am. Yes. I will. I'll check in with you on Wednesday night."

Remy started putting down the phone, then pulled it back to her ear. "I'm sorry, what's that? Oh. Yes. I had lunch with her yesterday." Remy pointed toward Nora as she listened to Evan. "She's okay. Actually, she's going through a bit of a rough time right now."

Nora shook her head back and forth as she mouthed the words "No."

Remy pretended not to see her. She continued, "Yes. I think that's a good idea. You should call her. Okay, I'll check back." Remy hung up the phone, almost afraid to look up.

"Why did you say that?" Nora shrieked. I don't want him to feel bad for me!"

"He sounded very sincere. He said he's going to call you to make sure you're alright."

Nora played with her keys that were on the counter. "Whatever."

She suddenly remembered the letter he had dropped off. She had almost forgotten about it during last few night's tumultuous events. Nora walked over to coffee table, then reached into her purse and grabbed the envelope. She brought it over to the kitchen island.

"What's that?" Remy asked.

"A letter from Evan. He dropped it off right before you came over yesterday."

Remy put her hand over Nora's, stopping her from tearing it open. "Don't open it now. It might be really personal. You might want to be alone."

"It's alright. We don't have any secrets." Nora thought back to her life in Florida. Almost none, thought Nora. She would confide in Remy. Soon.

"Well, not on Rocky Neck, anyway." She purposely let her words trail.

Remy responded immediately. "Nora. We all have our shit. If something happened in Florida or between you and Tom, that's private. You screwed up. So what? I've screwed up plenty. You deal with it. Then you *move on*." Remy emphasized the last two words. "Don't be so hard on yourself." She looked intently into Nora's eyes. "Got it?"

"Got it." Nora looked at Remy curiously.

"Doesn't everybody go to a new place to start over?" Remy asked as she smiled.

Nora smiled in agreement. "Yeah." She folded the envelope in two, then walked over to Remy, hugging her for a long moment. "Thank you." There was a long pause. "I love you. You're a great friend." Nora surprised herself.

Remy's trademark sarcasm lightened the moment. "Yeah, sure. You'll be married to Evan in no time. Then I wont' have anyone to drink Dark and Stormy's with … or martinis … or Margaritas."

Nora released Remy. "I don't think you have to worry about that. It's never gonna happen." Then she added. "Besides, I may stay single just to help you out."

Remy gave Nora a curious look.

"*Somebody* needs to help you find a new girlfriend." They both smiled.

Remy's look was more serious. "Well we can help each other out. You know … you're not so bad yourself. Evan's a lucky guy."

"Why do you keep saying that? We're not even together."

Remy sighed. "I know. But I think you will be."

"I don't know. It was easier when I really didn't care ... you know?"

"Yes. I *do* know. I should have been on a flight back to San Francisco by now."

"What?" Nora asked, shocked.

"Well, I got up thinking about it, about getting out of town for a little while ... so I could decide if I wanted to stay here. But then I read your letter. In the past, I would have just taken off. But I didn't." Remy paused. "Shit, you should have seen my driving. I'm lucky I didn't get pulled over this morning on my way over." Remy looked at her swollen foot. "God, this is killing me. I need medication." With that, Remy pulled two large Margarita glasses and two shot glasses from the open shelf closest to the sink. "And inspiration." She looked at her Grandmother Martin's clock. It was 9:17 a.m. "Too early?" She asked Nora.

Nora walked toward Remy's fridge. "How does the saying go? Desperate times call for desperate measures?" She opened the door, then pulled out a bowl of limes. "Besides," Nora said as she looked back up at the clock, "It's twelve o'clock somewhere. Isn't your grandmother from Paris?" Remy nodded, amused. "It's *at least* twelve o'clock in Paris."

Chapter 32

The gray early morning had turned into brilliant sunshine as Nora and Remy sat at a comfortable ivory-colored, antique wicker table and two matching side chairs with coordinating seat cushions in a vintage red and tan floral fabric. They were both enjoying the view as they peered out from Remy's small deck. The two French doors were open wide, the long white curtains billowing in the morning breeze. Nora had turned their chairs so they were facing out directly toward the beach. The small table was between them, and on it was a half-empty pitcher of Margaritas, two still-unused shot glasses, and a small yellow note pad and pen, which had not been picked up since they sat down two hours earlier.

Nora took a long sip then licked some of the chunky salt from the rim. She sat back, put her glass down on the table beside her, and adjusted the white bikini top she had borrowed from Remy. She looked over toward Remy, who was wearing a black polka dot halter-top and coordinating boy short bottoms. She was leaning back slightly in her chair, her long tan legs bent at the knee, and she had placed both of her feet on a small tufted hassock she had grabbed from the living room. Under her right foot was an additional pillow to help keep her sprained ankle elevated.

She refilled their glasses as they sat quietly, each with her thoughts. They listened to Norah Jones crooning, "I'm just sitting heeere … waiting for you to come on home and turn me on … "

Nora broke the silence. "This was the first CD Evan and I ever listened to together. She continued. "I cooked him dinner. I remember thinking he wasn't that smart and that he might be pretty good marriage material. You know, because he has money." She took another long sip. "I've tried to make that one of my criteria … when I started looking for a husband. I tried the same thing in Florida. But I was never in love with Tom." Nora purposely stopped, waiting for Remy's reaction to her candid statement.

"And?" Remy asked.

"And, as it turns out, not only am I in love with Evan, but he's much smarter than I am. And he's kind, sweet, charming, thoughtful, a great kisser, *and* really amazing in bed. The irony is, that I wouldn't even care if he didn't have money."

"He's great in bed?" Remy asked, curiously.

Nora was amused that that was the first thing Remy wanted to know about. And she was surprised that she felt comfortable talking to her this way. "Yes. But does it bother you? I mean …"

"I think it's been more of an infatuation. I've been lonely. No offense. But I'm okay with the way things have turned out. We're friends. I don't have too many of those. It's good."

Nora replied sincerely, "I never had a lot of friends either."

Remy sat up, now curious to hear more about Evan. "I want to hear more about Evan … you know, the gory details."

"God, he's just … I don't know how to explain it. He's sensual. He has this deep, passionate side. And his body is gorgeous without his clothes on."

Remy looked at Nora in disbelief.

"No. I'm telling you. He's lean but muscular. Like a runner's body but not too thin. And he just knew what I wanted. It was amazing. And his kissing is amazing."

"I never would have guessed." Remy replied, still not completely convinced. She sat back again, looking at the shimmering sand.

"I was madly in love with Hannah." She waited to see if Nora wanted to hear her story.

"What happened?" Nora asked.

"We lived together for three years. She's an advertising exec. in San Francisco. I met her at a party. Very fit, very well dressed, very composed. Very everything. Except in love with me." She continued with her stats. "Thirty-five. My age. Always perfectly put together.

Short, sexy blonde hair. Like Meg Ryan's in … did you ever see the movie French Kiss?"

Nora smiled. "Yes. I love that movie." She thought about how Meg Ryan's character got the guy in the end and they lived on a vineyard in France happily ever after. If only real life was like the movies.

"Yeah. She looks like that," Remy replied.

Nora saw the look of longing on Remy's face. "Well, anyway. She moved in with me right away. And from that point on, I catered to her every fucking whim. She made a lot of money, but it seemed I was always the one taking care of her, taking her away … giving her anything she wanted."

"Where is she now?" Nora looked over at Remy, seeing her tears for the first time.

"In my condo with all the rest of my things."

"The rest of your things? You have more?"

"Yeah. I just brought a few staples with me," Remy replied.

"Right. Just a few staples." Nora rolled her eyes, thinking about her one good bag and the few boxes her sister had forwarded to her after she had gotten settled.

Remy continued. "And the best part is that she's in *my* place with *my* things … and she's seeing somebody."

Remy looked earnestly at Nora. She wiped her eyes roughly, angry that she was getting emotional. "His name is Matthew. Math-hew Bright-man." Remy exaggerated the syllables. "He's her boss. They make a charming couple."

Nora looked surprised.

Remy understood instantly and answered her question. "Yeah, well, Hannah was in the middle of a divorce when I met her. I didn't think she was ready, but she swore she wanted to be with me. But I guess she didn't. Or she did until somebody better came along."

Remy composed herself, not wanting to wallow in the misery she had felt her first entire month on Rocky Neck. "I just left. I still have a lot to straighten out."

"That sucks." Nora was careful not to say anything derogatory about Remy's ex. She could tell that she was still in love with her.

"I'm sorry. Obviously, you deserve better." Nora was sincere.

"I know. It truly sucks."

Nora and Remy sat back, silent and pensive, as they took in the beauty unfolding before them on the shore.

She changed the subject. "So, Sherlock. What the hell are we going to do about Christian?"

"I don't know yet. I think I need more inspiration." With that, Nora refilled their glasses.

*   *   *

Nora awoke suddenly, feeling the burning sensation from her just-acquired sunburn. She looked down at her legs, then pushed her right thumb into the tender flesh of her inner thigh.

"Well, I'm done." She looked over toward Remy.

The other chair was empty. Nora looked at her watch. 1:12 p.m. She must have dozed off. She sat up and tried to straighten her back, which was stiff from having fallen asleep in the not-too-comfortable chair. She turned and looked around, surveying the kitchen and living room. Remy was sprawled on the couch, speaking in hushed tones into the cordless handset of her phone.

Nora stood up and rubbed her stiff neck as she surveyed the beach then walked inside toward the kitchen barstools. Remy had brought in the almost-empty pitcher of Margaritas as well as the still unused shot glasses, which were all on the counter along with the bottle of Cuervo and the bowl of limes. The notebook had been scribbled on, and Nora turned it toward her.

Carly. 8:00 o'clock. 121 Washington Street. Third Floor.

Remy hung up as Nora was reading the pad. "Carly just called. She said she wanted to check in on me." She waited for Nora's reaction.

Nora walked over to her overnight bag and extruded a long-sleeve white T-shirt. As she pulled it over her head, she answered, "I don't buy it. All of a sudden, she's interested in hanging out with you?"

"I think she's lonely. You told me she said that Kevin broke up with her, right?"

"No, I said that she said they *weren't together any more*. Those were her exact words." Nora emphasized each syllable. "Why?"

Remy sat up, her eyes bright, "Maybe she needs a friend ... to talk to. Know what I mean?"

"Oh, I get it. I know what you're really thinking," Nora said as she pointed at Remy.

"What?" Remy asked defensively.

"That somehow, Carly has some deep dark secret or confession, or something like that. And that after one glass of Zinfandel, or whatever it is she drinks, she's going to tell you everything. Hey, maybe she thinks she killed Christian, even though she was passed out that night!" Nora's sarcasm was evident. Then, her eyes widened as she realized what she had just discovered.

"What? What is it?" Remy watched Nora, anxious to know what she was thinking.

"That night. I ran back to the car with Kevin. Carly was practically passed out. Like I was." Nora turned toward Remy. "Do you think she's been taking pills ... from Christian ... or Kevin?"

Remy paced. "I don't know."

Nora stood with her hands on her hips. "I changed my mind. Go have drinks with Carly. Without me. I think it's a good idea."

"What are you thinking?"

"Go have drinks with her." Nora said again.

"No, really ... what are you thinking?"

"I think there was a lot more going on between Kevin and Christian. Kevin was dealing. Someone was following me. I had all these hang ups on my phone. I thought I saw somebody outside my place one night. Then there was the bathroom mirror thing."

Nora looked at Remy and waited for a reaction.

"I wondered what that was all about." Remy admitted.

Nora continued, her speech quickening, "I thought Kevin was just hounding me because he wanted me to tell the police it wasn't him. Because he gave me a ride that night and he knew that there was somebody else up on the lifeguard chair." Nora looked at Remy reassuringly. "But he doesn't know who was up there."

Remy breathed a sigh of relief. "I didn't *think* he knew. I took off down the beach while he was still running up from his car. I had parked past the entrance, around the corner. But ... but when we got there, he wasn't there yet. He must have pulled up after us. So I'm pretty sure he never saw my car." Remy made eye contact with Nora. "I'm sorry I left you there. I tried to get you to come with me. But you just kept staring at Christian. And when I saw Kevin running toward us, I didn't know what else to do."

Nora continued. "He still doesn't know it's you. He's just been putting pressure on me to tell the police that it wasn't him."

Remy asked the question again, wanting to be reassured, "So he definitely doesn't know it was me?"

Nora shook her head. "No. When he ran up and saw me with Christian, he just kept asking what happened. And then we ran to his car." Nora tried to recount the details accurately. "I lay down on the back seat. I was so sick. Carly was almost passed out in the passenger seat. She didn't acknowledge me when I got in. Her eyes were closed. Then Kevin got in and sat for a little while smoking his cigarette. The car was running. I remember feeling so sick, like I was going to pass out, and waiting and waiting for him to take off, but he just sat there. Like he was thinking or something. Weird, considering Christian was lying on the beach. Wait. I remember hearing ..."

"What? Concentrate!"

"I am!" Nora shot Remy a frustrated look. "I remember hearing all this rustling ... like he was looking for something. And like ... a zipper or something ... opening and closing. As if he was looking for something."

Nora turned directly toward Remy and looked her in the eye. "He jumped out of the car. Then I heard the trunk slam a few minutes later. He slammed it shut and it was really loud. I thought he was going to get back in the car and we were finally going to leave. But he didn't come back for a while. Maybe five or ten minutes. I asked him what he was doing. He said something about respect for the dead or something. The last thing I remember, he was swearing, mumbling something then we finally drove away."

Remy's tone was serious. "He has that black backpack that he brings to work. He doesn't ever leave it. I've seen it on the floor behind one of the prep tables when he's working." Remy leaned on the island counter and looked closely at Nora. "Now what did you say about the trunk?"

Nora explained. "He went to the trunk. And when he finally came back, I asked him what he was doing. He said he wanted to show respect for the dead. That he had covered Christian. For when someone found him."

Remy shook her head back and forth. "Nora, you know Kevin a little bit, right?"

Nora nodded yes.

"Does he strike you as the kind of guy who would be so concerned about having respect for the dead?" That he would grab a blanket or whatever it was from his trunk to have respect for Christian?"

Nora answered with conviction. "Shit, no. You're right. He wouldn't care. He was *looking* for something. And he knew I was awake. Barely, but I was awake. And he must have gone back to get something from Christian. That Christian had on him. Something he was worried about someone finding."

Remy and Nora looked at each other, mouthing the words at almost the same time, "The pills."

Nora continued. "But that doesn't make sense. The label had Christian's mother's name on it. That wouldn't incriminate Kevin." Nora sighed deeply. "Shit. What was he looking for?"

Remy interrupted Nora. "It's almost time. We're going to have to figure this out later."

Nora nodded, still thinking. "So am I going to be in the picture tonight, or are the two of you going out alone?"

"I think you should stay here. Or drop us off." Remy gave Nora an apologetic look. "Sorry, I think it'll be better if I go alone. You can brainstorm while I'm out."

"Really?" Nora eyes widened slightly. "She doesn't really like me, does she?"

"No."

"Oh."

Remy tried to explain. "I was always really nice to her. You acted like she didn't exist."

"Whatever." Nora crossed her arms. "You're right. But I didn't mean to be like that. I've just never been good with other women."

Remy replied, "I know." She walked toward the fridge. "How about I make us some lunch?" She turned to the task of pulling out some items, including whole grain bread and some assorted cheeses.

"Oh, and by the way. It's not a date. Carly's definitely not my type."

Nora couldn't help herself. "Yeah, that's what you said about *me.*

Besides, it would help if she were … oh, I don't know … gay? You need to concentrate on fishing where the fish are, if you know what I mean."

"Whatever. I don't know if I'll meet anyone here anyway."

Nora's tone was defensive, "What do you mean? There are plenty of gay people here. I see them come into the restaurant and they walk around Rocky Neck all the time."

"And, how would you know?" Remy asked, surprised by Nora's statement.

"I know." Nora answered. "Plus, when I see couples holding hands, or with their arms around each other, it's a dead giveaway."

"Impressive. How you figured that out, I mean." Remy smiled.

Nora knew they couldn't ignore the task at hand. "Let's come up with the schedule for tonight. I'm going to drive you to Carly's at 8:00 o'clock. You'll talk, blah, blah, blah. So glad you called me. Blah, blah, blah. Decide where you're going for drinks. Then explain that I had to drive you because you can't drive." She looked at Remy seriously. "And then you listen to everything she says. Every word. You never know when the smallest thing might be useful." Nora thought about the fact that Remy had called in sick. "You just have to be sure not to run into Evan."

"Why don't I take her some place out of the way? Or where Evan wouldn't go?"

Nora nodded. "But let her come up with the place. Some place she's comfortable." She paused. "Then relax, put your feet up, and ply her with a whole bottle of tequila." Nora's tone was half-kidding.

Remy answered seriously. "Actually, that's a good idea."

"Oh, God." Nora shook her head then looked down at the notepad. She scanned the names that Remy had written down:

Evan Betty Kevin Carly Nora Remy.

"Suspects," replied Remy.

Nora looked at the pad. "You're kidding, right?" Nora asked incredulously.

Remy's look was completely serious. "No."

"But we're on here."

Remy answered, "We can't rule anybody out. At least that's how the police see it right now. Any one of us could have done it."

Remy and Nora stared at each other, knowing what the other was thinking.

Chapter 33

Nora finally got up from the couch and went over to wash the dishes that had been left from lunch. As Remy took a shower, she thought about where she should go while Remy and Carly were out tonight. She could always go home. Nora thought about how disconnected she felt from her home lately. It wasn't the haven it had once been. She thought about Evan and the letter he had written. She had been so eager to open it earlier. But now, she saw it as her only glimmer of hope. She wanted to believe he was in love with her and wanted her back. Nora would wait. She didn't want to be disappointed.

Her thoughts drifted to Carly and then to Kevin. She would have to talk to Kevin again soon. To pretend she was preparing to go to the police. Now that she really thought about it, she didn't think he would dare go to the authorities. He was just calling her bluff in order to get her to make a move.

Remy glided into the room as Nora wiped the last dish. Nora openly admired her. "Perfect. Not too snooty. A combination of resort wear and down and dirty drinking attire."

Remy smiled widely. "Why thank you. I did my best." Remy stood as Nora reviewed her ensemble. She was wearing very fitted cropped ivory linen pants and a black, short sleeve cotton T-shirt. "Wow. That looks great."

Remy turned exaggeratedly then pointed down toward her foot. "Is this a good look?"

Nora laughed. "Of course. Very coordinated." Remy had wrapped a black and white silk scarf around the lower half of her foot and ankle in order to cover the bandage. On the other foot, she had a strappy sandal.

*　　　　　*　　　　　*

"Are you sure this is going to work?" Remy asked as Nora drove toward Carly's apartment.

"No. I'm not. The whole thing might seem pathetic, actually, especially to Carly." Nora gave Remy a frustrated look.

Remy ignored her attempt at sarcasm. "Well. Here goes." She opened the passenger door of her Saab. The cars buzzed by her as she stepped out onto the sidewalk on Washington Street. As she placed her purse carefully on her shoulder then slammed the door; she faced Nora and repeated the plan in a low tone. "Okay. I go up and get her. I tell her I couldn't drive and you had stopped by to check on me. I explain you're outside waiting with the car, but not to worry. That you're going to drop us off and then leave so we can hang out. I wait to see what she says and let her pick where we go." She looked to Nora for approval.

Nora started to interrupt, then Remy remembered, "So long as it's not someplace Evan normally goes."

"Someone's been paying attention. Even after two tequila shots." Nora nodded approvingly. She grabbed the Altoids tin from her purse. "Here. Take a few."

Remy did as she was told, smiled, then licked her tongue over her teeth as she grinned widely. "Teeth check."

Nora nodded.

"Lipstick check."

Again, Nora nodded as she surveyed Remy's appearance. "Perfect." She looked at her watch. "Go."

Remy nodded and tried to seem casual as she felt eyes on her from the third floor window.

*　　　　　*　　　　　*

Nora looked at her watch again, realizing she had now been waiting twenty-two minutes. Her concern had grown, and she breathed a sigh of relief as she watched Remy and Carly make their way toward her from the front door. She planted a generic half-smile on her face.

247

Remy spoke first. "Sorry about that. But Carly and I were … talking. And then she took a phone call."

Nora detected the strain in Remy's voice. "Oh, no problem. Just think of me as your limo driver for the night."

She looked up at Carly, "Hi, it's nice to see you. How's it going?" Nora noticed Carly's slightly swollen eyes. She forced herself not to look at Remy.

Carly answered timidly, "I'm okay."

Remy had pushed the passenger seat forward, and Carly settled into the back seat. Nora watched as Remy positioned herself above the seat before getting in, plunking down, careful not to bump her foot. "God, this hurts more than ever," she announced.

Carly spoke from the back seat, "Do you wanna make it another night? I'd understand."

Remy answered quickly. "No way. As a matter of fact, I definitely need a cocktail to get rid of the pain." Remy turned sideways in her seat. "Where to, Carly? Your choice."

Carly looked first at Remy, then Nora. "How about the Port Side? It's my … well, it was our favorite place. Kevin used to love to go there. And I got to like it, too."

"Sure," Remy replied. "Port Side it is. But are you sure? Will it make you think too much about … I mean, I know it might be hard for you right now."

Carly answered in a surprisingly steady tone. "That's fine. I told Nora we broke up. "Anyway … everything makes me think about Kevin. What are you gonna do? I'm not gonna stop going there," she said defiantly.

Remy continued, "What if he's there?"

Carly replied immediately. "Oh. He won't be. He's working until at least ten."

"Okay. We're there," Remy replied enthusiastically.

*   *   *

Nora stared intently at the road, realizing she had just passed the Port Side. She pulled a sharp U-turn, setting off horns from agitated drivers as she straightened out Carly's Saab and pulled up to the door. "Here we are."

Remy shot Nora a look. "Hey, easy there Mario Andretti. I don't think my insurance covers stupidity."

Nora started to say something then bit her lip. "Sorry. Nothing like the way my car makes a turn." She looked toward Carly. "Everybody okay?"

Carly straightened her hair. "Oh, yeah. That was great." She smiled. It was the first expression of happiness she had ever seen from Carly since she had met her.

Remy looked quickly at Nora then started opening the door handle. She seemed hesitant. "Nora, I'll call you in a couple of hours. You have your cell?"

Remy stood outside the car door and pulled her seat forward so Carly could get out.

Carly spoke as she stood up. "Nora, why don't you come with us?"

Nora was surprised. "Oh, no that's okay. I know you'd planned to get together with Remy. Plus I have a few calls I really need to make. So, go have some drinks, relax, and forget your troubles. And just call me when you're ready. Just make sure you give me ten minutes to get back here."

Carly stood on the sidewalk, obviously eager to take Nora up on her offer and get inside to the smoky, familiar haven with Remy.

Nora took the cue and tried to lighten the moment. "And play a game of pool for me ... but don't hustle too many of the fishermen. They'll get pissed"

Carly waved, then yelled. "Thanks."

*   *   *

Nora pulled away, not certain in which direction she should head. For the first time in her life, she was disappointed in not being invited to hang out with other women. In the past, she wouldn't have given it a second thought.

It's fine, she reassured herself. Carly will feel more comfortable talking if it's just the two of them. She hoped that Remy would keep her eye on the ball. They were running short on time. And Carly might be able to help them. She dialed Remy's cell.

"Hello?" Remy answered, "Hold on."

Nora could hear the pulsing music in the background as Remy

yelled to Carly. "I'll be right back. I just have to take this call. Yes. Dark and Stormy, extra lime … and a shot of tequila."

Shit, thought Nora, she wanted her to be alert, not asleep.

"Yes?" Remy sounded surprised that she was calling.

"Hi. I know you can't talk. But I just wanted to remind you not to drink too much, so you can pay attention in case she wants to have a heart-to-heart. Oh … and try to sit someplace, maybe at the bar, so she can be more relaxed. And don't play pool. Otherwise, you're never going to get to talk."

"Oh, my God. Is that why you called? You're being a pain in the ass."

"Well … I just … "

"Don't worry, Sherlock. I can handle it. I'm just a little more subtle than you are. Plus, I've already made some progress. I'll fill you in later."

"What. What is it?"

"Later. Now, don't call me again."

"Fine." Nora was surprised at Remy's tone.

"No, really," whispered Remy. Nora could tell she had walked back into the main bar area. The music was blaring. "Thanks for your concern, though. I'll call you later."

Nora drove aimlessly down Main Street. The restaurants were all bustling with patrons, and the mood was jovial, as passersby laughed, couples walked hand-in-hand, and music streamed out from doorways with windows resembling portholes. Her heart sank as she thought about Evan. She still didn't know if she could bear to read his letter. She dialed her home number. "Hi, you've reached Nora … "

Nora interrupted the message, pressing the pound key and then her password. She realized she hadn't checked her messages since yesterday and hoped, without admitting it to herself, that Evan had called. "You have five new messages." Nora smiled and waited for the machine to start. She tried not to let her disappointment upset her. All of the messages had been hang-ups. Damn it. Had Evan been calling and hanging up? It just seemed so unlike him. Frustrated, she tossed her cell phone toward the passenger seat. It bounced onto the floor, landing out of sight.

She drove down to the end of Main Street then decided to head back toward McMurtree's. She had entertained going back home for a few hours, but now she really felt she would be lonely there. The house would feel sad and empty. And she didn't want to feel so alone right now.

Nora pulled up into the usually crowded parking lot. To her surprise, it was dark and vacant. "Shit." She looked toward the darkened interior of the restaurant, then at the sign on the door. It was closed. She always forgot they were closed on Monday nights. She sat for a moment, trying to come up with a new plan. Maybe she should go someplace else. But Remy and Carly might not be that much longer. And she didn't want to wander around town, looking for a place where she would feel comfortable going to … alone.

She remembered the bottle of tequila that Remy had stashed in the car. She had hastily poured two shots before they left the loft, then had insisted on bringing it with her. Just in case, Remy had explained. In case she needed more liquid courage before going up to see Carly. Nora had been surprised by how unusually nervous Remy had been. They had both been on edge, she admitted, until the tequila had worked its magic.

Nora reached down and extended her hand onto the passenger side floor. She found the brown bag and grabbed it. The sound of the empty shot glass clanked against the bottle inside the bag. As she started to straighten up, she saw the gleaming of her cell phone and grabbed it from the floor. She parked and walked through the restaurant's lot toward the beach. She reached the wide set of stairs just where the tar became sand, and she looked toward the wooden stairs leading onto the restaurants expansive outside deck. She hesitated for a moment, then started her ascent. They were closed, she reasoned. What harm would there be if she hung out up there for a little while? In the darkness, the moon illuminated her path as she made her way through the rows of vacant tables and chairs.

She walked to the darkest corner, then chose the table closest to the railing. Just in case, thought Nora. Though the restaurant was dark, if any of the staff was inside and decided to peer out, they probably wouldn't see her in the darkness. She made an attempt at wiping off the damp chair with her hand then took a seat. She was finally ready to unwind and enjoy the starlit night.

Nora gazed at the dark glistening ocean directly in front of her. The only sounds she could hear were the pounding waves against the sleepy shore. There were no birds and no other signs of life. The continuous crash of the waves, though powerful and almost intimidating, was surprisingly peaceful sounding. Nora slipped the Cuervo bottle from it's rumpled bag, filled her glass to the rim, and for a moment, felt like a lone patron in an empty bar. The wind whirred noisily along the deck as it danced through the closed patio umbrellas. She pulled at her cotton sweater, wrapped it more tightly around her, and stared into the moody evening sky as she listened to the booming waves crashing on the shore. She sat, motionless, appreciating the shoreline. Nora sat up as the distinct and unexpected ring of a cell phone startled her. She listened, knowing it wasn't her own and wondering who else was there with her.

"Yeah?" There was a pause. The gruff monotone voice was unmistakable. Nora gasped as she recognized it as Kevin's. "I can wait. How long you gonna be?" He turned sideways. In the moonlight, Nora stared at his profile. "I already told you. I don't know where he put it. I know. I've been lookin'. Believe me. And I don't think that bitch has it either. I checked. Yeah?" He listened for another long moment, then raised his voice. "Look, don't fucking threatin' me. We had a deal. Just give me a couple more days. Alright?" Nora seemed to be holding her breath. "Yeah, I'll be here."

Chapter 34

Nora sat up, realizing she suddenly felt nauseous. She and Kevin were both on this same dark shore. Alone. She craned her neck slightly, scanning the pitch black horizon. The moon was a mere slice, not shedding enough light for her to make out anything or anyone else just yet. She peered over the deck railing, desperately willing her eyes to adjust to the night sky. She slid her chair back slowly, careful not to make a sound, then hunched over until she was on her knees. She approached the railing and watched through the deck slats as Kevin stared toward the water. Beside him was a long black shadow. An inflatable boat of some kind, Nora guessed. She noted Kevin's rolled up pants, which bared his thin white ankles in the streaming moonlight. Had he just motored over from Rocky Neck? She watched as he cupped his hand around the flame of his lighter and then lit a cigarette. The fast-burning butt glowed fiercely as the wind caught it. Nora smelled the tobacco smoke almost immediately, realizing how close he really was.

She remained frozen, her heart beating in her throat, thankful she was downwind of him, making it less likely he might hear her stir. Her legs burned as she continued to kneel on the hard wood deck. She would have to get the hell out of here before Kevin met whoever he was waiting for, thought Nora. She looked up at her table. If he made his way over to the deck, he would definitely see her things. She wondered if she could successfully grab them and run unnoticed.

Nora thought about Remy's car. If the person Kevin was meeting arrived by boat, then she would be okay. But if he pulled into the parking lot, then Remy's Saab would definitely be seen, and recognized, if Kevin walked over to meet him. Nora felt the rising panic. Should she make a run for it? Or should she just grab her things from the tabletop and stay where she was until he finished whatever business he was conducting? If she stayed, then she could at least see what Kevin was up to. She thought about Carly's last comment before she had gotten out of the car … that Kevin would be at work until at least ten. It was probably only 9:00 now.

Nora thought more about what Kevin was doing here. Was this his weekly ritual after he got off work? On Mondays when McMurtree's was closed and the shoreline was dark without the hustle and bustle of the restaurant? Was this how he conducted his business … his drug deals? Nora's head pounded wildly. She knew she would have to make a decision soon. She prayed she would do the right thing. She didn't know just how dangerous Kevin was, but she knew she didn't want to find out.

Seconds dragged into minutes, and before Nora could be certain of her decision, she saw another figure as it emerged from the water onto the shore. The approaching stranger dragged a small dinghy.

Nora quietly slid the tequila bottle along with the glass, her purse, and her cell phone onto the wood deck. She tried not to think how much her knees throbbed, intent on listening to their conversation. She longed to take a sip from the bottle to soothe her nerves and her knees, but she didn't dare.

She watched as they shook hands.

Kevin spoke first. "Here." He looked around, then picked up a large bundle from his boat and handed it over. "The usual."

The stranger spoke next. "Yeah. Except for what you were supposed to get from Mr. BS. I knew he'd change his mind. You just better make sure you find it, or I want my money back. All of it. I shouldn't have given you nothin' in advance." The stranger coughed then spit loudly.

Kevin replied angrily, "I told you. He wasn't gonna give it to me without the cash up front."

The stranger's voice was stern, "I'm givin' you 'til Wednesday night. Meet me after work. If you can't find it, all bets are off. You understand what I mean by that? You made me look bad because of that son of a bitch. He lied to both of us. And I'm never gonna let somebody make me look that bad again. Not without payin' for it."

Kevin lit another cigarette. He remained speechless, continuously taking drags and pacing slightly. Nora watched the enormous glowing head of his cigarette.

The stranger reached down and pulled out what appeared to be a knapsack, opened it, then stuffed the package inside. "Adios."

As he got back into his boat, Nora watched Kevin follow him into the water, taking a few careful steps out from the shore then giving the boat a swift, hard push. She heard the small engine as it started, almost choked, then caught and sped up. As the sounds of the motor faded into the darkness, she heard the unmistakable ring of her cell phone. She stared at the blue glow of the screen then pounced on it, hanging up the call as quickly as she could. She looked around, hoping that Kevin hadn't heard it. As Nora turned off the phone, she looked around again, panicked at the thought that Kevin had found her out. She paled as she realized he was out of sight. She scanned the shoreline once more. As she did, she tried to take a deep breath. The unmistakable sound of footsteps in the sand grew louder. She braced herself, afraid of what Kevin would do, now that she had witnessed the transaction.

"Hey, are you all right?" Nora jumped, shocked by the unexpected and unfamiliar voice. She looked up from where she had been crouched for the last half hour. Standing directly in front of her was a smiling, handsome face sporting a goatee, a gray Army T-shirt, and a black knit hat. His jeans were perfectly faded, and he smiled widely, as if she were a long-lost friend.

"Shit," replied Nora. "You scared the hell out of me." She breathed a sigh of relief and stood up. She glanced around one more time. No sign of Kevin. Both he and his boat were gone. Nora wondered how he had left, unobserved. She looked at the person now standing directly in front of her.

"I'm sorry! I was expecting someone else." She laughed, delirious with relief.

"I'm just glad you're okay. I thought you were hurt or something." His voice trailed, obviously curious as to what Nora was doing out here, in the dark, huddled on the ground with a bottle of tequila.

"Yeah. Thanks. Thanks a lot. You have no idea." She laughed her nervous laugh.

He eagerly explained, "I was on my way into town and decided to come down to check out the waves. I'm walking over to The Bull. You want to join me or something?"

His politeness touched Nora. She surveyed him again. He was probably only about twenty-five … and he was asking her out for drinks. I guess I still have it, she thought, glad for the distraction.

She replied politely, "Thanks, but I have plans. I have to meet my friends at the Port Side."

He looked surprised. "See you around town, then." He extended his hand, "My name is Oliver. I'm here for the summer."

Nora tried to compose herself as she straightened her hair and picked up her things from the deck. She stepped carefully down the stairs, her legs unsteady, then headed toward the parking lot. Oliver followed her, staring for a moment at the bottle of tequila she carried.

"I like to drink alone." Nora chuckled nervously. Oliver smiled politely. As they reached the Saab, Nora took one last quick look toward the shoreline.

Oliver hesitated then slowly walked past her. "I'm going to head over." He pointed across the street toward The Bull. "I'll see ya round." He crossed the street, a spring in his step.

Chapter 35

Nora opened the door and crawled into the seat, suddenly feeling overwhelmed by what had almost happened. She was mentally and physically exhausted. Tears sprang to her eyes as she started up the Saab. She grabbed her cell phone, then turned it on, anxious to return Remy's call. She thought about Remy and Carly, who were either worried or pissed that she hadn't gotten back to them. Nora put the car into reverse and backed up slowly as she simultaneously dialed Remy's cell.

She answered on the first ring. "Hello?"

It was so loud, Nora could barely hear her. "Remy? It's Nora. Hey, can you hear … " Nora felt the sharp pain as her hand was crushed by a large, clammy fist and the phone was ripped from her fingers. She tried to turn and pull away as the attacker grabbed her from the side. She watched her phone as it was slammed shut and was tossed violently onto the floor of the front passenger seat. Nora jammed the car abruptly into first gear as her assailant stumbled. She screamed, knowing that given the chance, he would hurt her. He climbed into the back seat as she tried to reach the main road from the parking lot and grabbed her hair forcefully, pulling her head back. Nora felt the searing pain. She hit the brake, realizing she was losing her battle. Her breathing was heavy as she gasped, the pain like shards of glass in her chest.

Nora trembled uncontrollably as she tried to look over her shoulder. Her body stiffened as the fear overcame her. Kevin leaned over, his left arm choking her as she saw the gleaming steel of the fishing knife in his right hand. His fetid breath enveloped her as he leaned closer.

"Please. Please. What do you want?" Nora knew her voice was trembling.

"Were you watching me?"

Nora felt she was choking from his tightening arm. "No. No. I … I came here to be alone. I don't know what you're talking about."

"Yeah, right." He released his arm, causing Nora to jerk forward. Out of the corner of her eye, she could see that he still had the knife in his other hand. He held it just above her right ear, almost daring her to move.

"Maybe it's better this way. No more sneakin' around trying to look on my own …"

Kevin's words seemed slightly slurred. He continued, "I need to find somethin' … and you're gonna help me." He leaned even closer. Nora imagined his crazed expression as he pressed against her face. She could smell the alcohol and cigarettes on his breath.

She whispered in a pleading tone, "I don't know what you're talking about but, please … I'll help you. Just don't … "

"Don't what, sweet cheeks?" He let the words trail, his voice lecherous and taunting. "Just shut the fuck up and put the top up." His agitated tone alarmed Nora even more. She hesitated.

"Now!"

Nora heard the anger and frustration in Kevin's commands. She feared there would be no reasoning with him tonight. She would need to go along with him, not challenge him. She scanned the dashboard nervously, fumbling as she looked for the button that would put the top up.

Kevin screamed, "Now, damn it. Put the fuckin' top up now!"

Nora reacted, panicked at his tone. "I'm trying. Please. This is Remy's car. I don't know where everything is!"

Kevin seemed to calm down. As he did, thankfully, Nora found the button. She watched as the top came up. She tried not to choke as the overwhelming stench of alcohol and cigarettes enveloped the car. Kevin pulled out a pack of Marlboro's and proceeded to light one. She fought the impulse to plead with him. As they sat at the edge of McMurtree's parking lot, she thought about Oliver as she imagined him sitting at the Bull drinking his beer. She should have gone with him.

Kevin finally spoke as he took a deep drag of his cigarette. "We're gonna go on a little mission. Then I'm gonna take you someplace I'll bet you've never been." Nora knew he was determined to find what he had been looking for, with or without her. She shuddered, trying not to think what might become of her if she couldn't help him. And about the pills that she had found in her kitchen.

"Which way?" she finally asked, her tone defeated.

Kevin pointed with his cigarette. "Right."

She put it into gear as she heard Kevin sit back into the seat behind her. As Nora drove down Main Street, she tried to slow the car as they passed the Port Side, hoping for a miracle. If only Remy or Carly would spot them. But she knew deep down it was wishful thinking. They were probably inside having a great time, cursing her for not calling back, and after too-many drinks not really thinking that something could be wrong. Nora prayed for the first time in years. She prayed that Kevin would somehow be reasonable and that she would get out of this alive.

She headed toward Rocky Neck. "Are you going to tell me when to turn?" Nora asked anxiously.

"You know your way home, right?" Kevin whispered into her ear. Nora could only imagine what he looked like right now, his smile eerie, his lip curled, showing his graying, crooked teeth.

"Is that where we're going?" Nora asked, trying to remain calm.

Kevin snapped again, impatient and wanting to sound in control. "Listen, bitch. I'm in charge. I'll tell you what to do when it's time."

Nora was afraid to say anything more. As she approached the general store, The Last Stand, at the corner of Rocky Neck Avenue, she made a wide right turn.

She looked in her rear view mirror, hoping there would be some one behind her to notice them. There were no cars in sight. She drove slowly.

When they were four blocks away from her street, Kevin instructed her, "Here. Turn down here."

Nora knew the street was a dead end. She did as she was told, driving even more slowly as she waited for Kevin's next order.

He pointed to the last house on the street. "Park there. In front of that house."

Nora did so, then sat with the engine running, hoping that a neighbor would hear or see them.

He turned to her, as if reading her mind, "Turn off the fuckin' car. And then we're going over to your place. You better behave. Or believe me, you'll pay."

Nora heard a zipper and then a rustling of nylon from the backseat. It was the same sound she had heard when she was in the car with Kevin the night Christian had died. She got out of the car, stiff legged, and he pushed the seat up and jumped out. For a quick second, she thought of running. But even in his drunken state, she knew Kevin could tackle her quickly before attracting too much attention. She resigned herself to staying with him for now. As he started to close the door, Nora's eye caught the gleaming silver of her cell phone. It was still on the floor, along with the tequila bottle. Kevin's eyes followed hers.

"Wait just a second. We forgot somethin' important."

Nora was afraid he would grab her phone. At least if he forgot it, she would have a chance to grab and hide it later.

Kevin started to reach in then looked at Nora suspiciously. "Grab the bottle. We might need it. I'm getting thirsty."

Nora shuddered, thinking that was a comment she had used so many times in the past, but would probably never use again. She reached into the car, trying not to imagine Kevin's lecherous thoughts as she did so and quickly grabbed the bottle. He walked closely beside her as they made their way toward the house. Nora carried her purse and the tequila bottle, and she glanced over at Kevin as he carried his backpack slung carefully over his shoulder. She shivered involuntarily as she thought about the knife he had held up to her throat.

Nora's movements seemed exaggerated, as if she were walking in slow motion. This didn't seem real, she thought. It was as if she were watching herself through someone else's eyes. She heard the sounds of the foghorn and clanging buoys drifting up from the harbor. Kevin and Nora reached the path in front of her cottage as Nora pushed the gate open and started toward the front door. She felt the panic rise as she neared the steps and stuck her hand in her purse, realizing that her keys weren't in her bag. She had left them, again, on Remy's kitchen counter. She peered toward Kevin, afraid to explain her dilemma as she pretended to look for them. Kevin stared at her, impatient to get inside and off the street.

Finally, Nora got up the nerve to explain. "I forgot my keys."

She didn't want to say they were at Remy's. Kevin hadn't thought to ask why she had Remy's car. And Nora would stand a better chance of getting through this if he didn't know that Remy and Carly would be waiting for her, expecting her. She prayed they would at some point become alarmed and call the police.

Nora thought about the key under the clay pot and about Kevin. She surprised herself, thinking for a moment that getting his fingerprints wouldn't be a bad thing. She purposely dropped her purse on the ground before making an agonizing sound as she bent over to pick it up. "Ohhhhhhh." She held the small of her back for extra emphasis. "Oh, my God. My baaacccklk!" Nora was pale and appeared to be in pain.

"Shhhh." Kevin yelled. "What the hell is wrong with you? He paced back and forth as he watched her.

"I have a pinched nerve. And I guess I must have really agitated it tonight." She groaned, trying to sound convincing. "But I'll be fine."

Kevin raised his arm, and Nora realized he was going to break the window of her front door.

"No, wait. I think I still have a spare key out back."

Kevin was suspicious, grabbing her by the arm and dragging her toward the back path.

"Please … " Nora groaned. "That really hurts. I can't really straighten out that well."

Kevin continued to hold her tightly, leaving red indentations on her arm. As they approached the back deck, he released her, pulling the bottle of tequila from her hands. Nora watched as he pulled off the top and took a long sloppy swig. He held it out to her in a motion for her to drink as well. Nora wanted a drink desperately, but was repulsed that his mouth had just been on the bottle. She nodded. "No, thanks."

Kevin shoved it in her face. Nora closed her eyes, trying not to think about what she was doing. "Thanks." She choked as the warm liquid glided down her throat.

Kevin pushed her toward the door, motioning. "Go get it." He stood watching her.

"I, I really can't. Could you get it, please? I thinks it's under the first one." She pointed to the first pot, hoping he would impulsively reach over and grab it.

"Lazy bitch." He mumbled.

Nora tried to look thankful as he pushed over the clay pot and reached underneath it.

He grabbed the key then held it up in the moonlight. "That's not a very smart place to hide a key, is it … sweet cheeks?" I could a found that, if I'd been tryin." He laughed cruelly as he put the key in the lock with one hand, holding her arm roughly with the other. He looked her in the eye, leaning toward her for the full effect. "Maybe that's why the last time I was here nosin' around, I went through the basement door. He pointed toward the door that led to her dirt basement.

Nora gasped, thinking about the fact that he had been in her house … probably more than once, looking for whatever he was missing.

Kevin seemed amused as he turned the lock then pushed Nora into the darkness. "That's right. I've been here already. But maybe you can help me this time."

Nora heard the deadbolt turn as Kevin locked it from the inside. She was now a prisoner in her own home.

Chapter 36

The room was very dark, and Nora held her breath, not knowing exactly where he was standing or how close he was to her. She heard the flip of the light switch. God, he *had* been here before. He knew exactly where it was.

"Close all the shades. We're not gonna be here too long. But just in case." He followed Nora through the house, which was still dark except for the light spilling from the kitchen. He carried the old knapsack on his shoulder and followed her closely as she pulled all of the shades and curtains.

Nora finished and stood by the stairs. She wrung her hands nervously. "Now what?"

"You come across a bottle a pills? From Christian?"

Nora tried to think quickly. Why would he think she had them? Nora answered her own question. Because they had something to do with what Christian had promised to get for him. And because Kevin had seen Christian wave them around all night. And because he had gone back to look for them … on Christian's dead body. The thought was too gruesome for Nora to fully envision.

Kevin was growing impatient. "Answer me. I'm sick of this shit. My ass is gonna be in a sling if we don't find 'em."

Nora was hoping Kevin would keep talking. She wasn't convinced that one bottle of pills was all he was after. Nora knew there was definitely something more. Much more.

She braced herself for his anger then admitted the truth. "I found them last week. So I called the police and turned them in. I didn't know … how they got into my purse. But I had alot to drink. The police think Christian probably put them in my bag." Nora instinctively decided not to tell Kevin she had found them in her cabinet, and that maybe there were other clues there that she hadn't noticed.

"Fuck." Kevin swore loudly, pacing the floor of the hallway as Nora remained silent. His level of agitation alarmed her.

She thought about Christian putting the pills in her purse. If he had hid something else in there as well, wouldn't it have been large enough for Nora to notice it, even in her condition? And if she had taken whatever-it-was out, not remembering, wouldn't she have stumbled upon it by now? Nora realized now that Christian probably had second thoughts about turning it over to Kevin and had stuck it in Nora's purse instead for safekeeping. But if that were the case, then where the hell was it? And what was it?

She tried to remember if she had seen anything either in her purse or in the house that seemed out of the ordinary. No, thought Nora. Nothing. She tried to remember the whole conversation she had heard on the beach between Kevin and that other man. The stranger had said that he shouldn't have paid up front, and that Kevin had to find it by Wednesday. What would happen if he didn't? What would happen to Kevin *and* to her? Nora was suddenly perspiring. She felt as if she would pass out, and she started to sit on one of the steps leading up to the second floor.

Kevin grabbed her arm roughly and pulled her up. "Oh no you don't. We have work to do. He licked his chapped lips. "Where's that tequila?"

Nora pointed, speechless. He watched her as he backed into the kitchen and grabbed the bottle from the table then walked over, swaying slightly as he opened it. His mouthful was even more gruesome than the last, observed Nora, as she watched the brown liquid drip down his chin. He wiped it with his sleeve then handed her the bottle.

"Please. I can't drink anymore."

Kevin ignored her, shoving the bottle up close to her face.

Nora grabbed it, her hands shaking, and she started to take another sip. As she did so, she watched as Kevin took the backpack from his shoulder and unzipped the front pouch. He reached in carefully, then extracted the long double-edged knife. It gleamed in the semi-darkness.

Nora's heart was in her throat. She watched as he held up the knife, pretending to examine it. He was enjoying taunting her, making her fearful. More fearful than she had ever been in her life. She took a long sip of the tequila, then extended it toward Kevin. He put the knife back inside his backpack, zippered it, then placed it back on his shoulder. As he grabbed the bottle, Nora realized he wanted to be in control, to feel important, and to make her feel intimidated.

Kevin tried to focus on her. "You remember finding somethin' else?"

Nora shook her head. Her voice was hoarse, "No. I don't. I swear."

Kevin continued to stare at her, as if trying to decide if she were telling the truth. "If I find it, then that means you were lying."

Nora shook her head again, now more frightened. "I'm not lying. I swear to you, I'm not lying."

Kevin backed down slightly. "Well, I'm dead if I don't find it, so we better figure somethin' out."

Nora heard the desperation in his voice. She watched as he started toward the kitchen, motioning.

"Come on, sweetheart, let's see if your boyfriend, Mr. BS, left you a little present. I wanna look in your bag … and around the house. In case it slipped your mind or somethin'."

Nora realized he wouldn't believe her until he searched every inch of her beloved house. She followed Kevin toward her purse, dread setting in, realizing what was to come. She absently asked the question, hoping it would bide her some time. She turned toward him, making sure to sound sincere.

"He was never my boyfriend." She stopped for effect. "And why'd you call him Mr. BS? For bullshit?"

Kevin laughed aloud, apparently amused by her ignorance. "No, but that's a good one. I'll have to remember that and tell my friends." He laughed again, a demented, disingenuous laugh. His tone turned more serious. "It's for Mr. Back Shore. Cause his family lives on the high fuckin' falutin' Back Shore."

Nora stood facing Kevin across her kitchen table. Maybe she could get him to keep talking and drinking. She needed more time. Enough time so she could be saved. She tried to think about how long Remy would wait before being worried enough to call the police. Hopefully, not too long. She decided she couldn't think about what might happen, and her survival instincts kicked in. She looked at Kevin under the soft overhead light. It grotesquely illuminated his sweating face and damp hair.

He held out his hand toward Nora's face, as if on cue, and she tried not to cringe. He attempted a sexy voice, "You sure are good lookin'." He licked his dry lips. Nora gulped, forcing herself not to flinch as he slid his clammy hand down her cheek.

"Thank you." She gulped again, "You're not so bad yourself. And you're a very talented chef." Nora waited for Kevin's reaction, hoping that she had sounded convincing. She continued, "Hey, " she said in a slightly sultry voice. "You don't know everything." She waited for his response. She wanted to appear to be confiding in him.

"Not only was Christian not my boyfriend, I didn't even like him. Especially after that night." Nora hoped he would be interested enough to continue the conversation in his haze. Anything to delay his ransacking her house and then dragging her off to God knows where. She felt chilled to the bone.

Kevin reacted immediately. "That's not what I heard. Christian was always talking about banging ..." He stopped abruptly, suddenly embarrassed. "I mean, you're definitely too classy for him, even if he was a rich kid. But he used to say you two were ... hot and heavy."

Nora wasn't surprised. She had learned a lot about Christian since his death. A gentleman, he was not. She could only imagine what he had really said about her. Nora flushed as she recalled how cruel and insulting he had been with her that night outside the Port Side and on the beach. Where had he learned to treat women that way?

Nora continued confiding in Kevin, knowing it was a calculated risk. She stared at the floor as she spoke. "He attacked me that night." She looked up at Kevin. "I was really upset."

He grabbed his cigarettes and lighter from his back pocket, lighting a cigarette nervously, staring all the while at Nora. "That why your little buddy pushed him?"

Nora bristled, not knowing exactly which tack she should take. "No. That's not what happened at all. It was an accident. He fell."

Kevin laughed. "Yeah, right. You mean your little buddy didn't help him?"

Nora continued. "No. He lost his balance. And who knew it would kill him? It wasn't that high up. He … he just fell the wrong way. It was the luck of the draw."

There was a long silence as Nora watched Kevin take another swig from the bottle before offering it to her. She took a small sip, wanting to remain as alert as possible.

He took another long drag, then continued in a lowered tone. "All that dough didn't help him that much, did it? I mean, not when it really mattered." He paused again for effect, then continued, apparently uninhibited now. Nora looked at the bottle. It was more than half-empty.

Kevin smiled at Nora. She could see that he was trying to hold back, but the alcohol had loosened him up. He looked so eager to talk and to shock her, to brag to her, even.

He made eye contact again then continued. "Turned out, he got himself into a little trouble. Made some promises he didn't keep. He was playin' with the big boys. And he kept their money. That's why he got what was comin' to him." He paused again, coughing. "Guess all his old money and fuckin' blue blood didn't matter. Turned out his blood was red. Just like everybody else's." He smiled an evil smile.

Nora tried to hide her shock. What was Kevin telling her in his alcoholic stupor? That Christian hadn't died from the fall? And was that why he had gone back to the beach? She couldn't complete the thought in her mind. It was too much for her to imagine right now. Nora remembered the knife Kevin had held to her throat. The knife he probably always carried with him in that backpack. She must be delirious. He couldn't have. She gulped, trying not to think about the possibility or she would be sick.

Kevin motioned her to sit then pulled out his own chair unsteadily and plunked down before putting a fresh cigarette in his mouth. He grabbed Nora's purse, spilling the entire contents then throwing it onto the floor. He changed the subject from Christian to the task at hand.

"I don't know why I'm botherin'," he slurred, staring at the contents.

Nora stared at her things, all the items she always carried in her purse, except for her keys, which were at Remy's. She wondered what Christian had tried to hide … and where it had ended up.

Kevin was leaning forward, his form unsteady now. She braced herself then placed one of her hands on his. "Kevin … I swear … I didn't hide anything. Whatever Christian had that belonged to you, it must be somewhere else."

He reached over and planted a sloppy kiss on Nora's lips. She was so revolted, yet she forced herself to smile. A brief, trembling smile. She watched as he took another long drag. The kitchen was filled with smoke, and Nora focused on Kevin through the bluish haze. She was in hell.

He finally dropped his backpack onto the floor, tired of guarding it so closely. Again, Nora thought about the knife inside. She looked down. The bag had landed exactly between the two of them and one of the shoulder straps was lightly grazing her foot.

Kevin placed a hand on his forehead as he flicked his cigarette toward the sink. Nora watched as it flew through the air and landed squarely inside it. He had no respect for others and their things, thought Nora as she turned back toward him and tried to veil her disgust. She gathered her courage and grabbed hold of his hands, massaging them lightly as she spoke, "Kevin, are you okay?"

He looked up then pulled his hands away. "No more questions. Let's go upstairs. See what Christian left for you."

He stood up, suddenly wise to Nora's intentions. "I know what you're doin' … " His voice trailed, "You just be careful. Or the same thing could happen to you. Don't make me do that. I don't wanna do that. You're too pretty."

Nora watched Kevin's wide, drunken smile.

"Hey, maybe we can go out some time, huh?"

Nora felt sick. "Sure." She forced herself to look down at the floor so that he wouldn't see how repulsed she was. And realizing how much she should fear him. She was desperate to tell Remy, and she prayed she would be given the chance.

*　　　　*　　　　*

Nora awoke to the sound of the police radio. She heard the crunch of the shells on her path, as a person with heavy footsteps retreated toward the street. Her tears welled up then covered her cheeks. This had been her chance. Remy had probably called the police. But since she hadn't been gone very long, they probably did a routine drive by the house. It would appear as if no one was home. She thought about the shades and curtains that Kevin had made her close. They would have no idea. And she finally admitted she would have to escape on her own.

Nora thought about Remy's car. If the police did a routine drive around the two main streets of Rocky Neck, it would never be seen, hidden on that dead end street. She thought about screaming. No, that wouldn't work. She could already hear the slam of the car door and the swift sound of the retreating patrol car. What if this had been her one and only chance?

She glanced over at Kevin passed out on the couch beside her, his arms hanging, puppet-like, over the rolled arm. Thank God. She didn't think he'd ever have enough tequila. She looked toward the floor and saw the almost empty bottle lying on its side. She surveyed him again and tried moving her arm slightly. Kevin didn't budge. It would be safe for a little while, she reasoned.

From her position on the couch, Nora scanned the nightmare that was now her living room. Kevin had gone on a rampage, emptying every drawer, opening every cabinet, and rifling through every shelf, both upstairs and down. Nora was shocked that she wasn't more upset right now. She had gotten past that, she realized. She was strictly at the survival stage. Food, clothing, shelter. And safety. She wanted nothing more right now than to get away, to feel protected. And of course, to see Kevin behind bars for everything he had done.

Nora gulped then slid slowly to the floor from where she sat, landing on her knees without a sound. She would have to get rid of it, she decided. Her couch would always carry the stench of hard alcohol and cigarettes. And the memories of this night and all that Kevin had done.

Chapter 37

Nora remained crouched where she landed on the floor. She prayed that Kevin wouldn't stir. She looked up nervously, alarmed that he may have awoken. Kevin's eyes were closed tightly, and his thin frame seemed cadaver-like as it leaned awkwardly over the arm of the couch. Nora glanced at her watch. 1:57 a.m.

Finally, after reassuring herself that she had to make a move in order to get out of the house alive, Nora stood up. The floor creaked beneath her feet, and she froze every time the wide panel planks protested too loudly. After five agonizing minutes, Nora was finally at the back door, ready to escape. She assessed the deadbolt. Her heart sank. The key, thought Nora. Damn it, Kevin had locked the deadbolt from the inside with the key. Short of breaking the door down, she had no easy way out. Except for the window. The one directly behind the kitchen table leading to the deck. She would have to climb onto the table, through the window, then out onto the deck.

Nora crept to the table's edge, her heart beating wildly. She took off her shoes then climbed up, taking a deep breath and gathering whatever courage she had left as she slowly slid the window open. The loud creaking stopped her dead in her tracks. Shit. How was she going to pull this off without waking Kevin? Nora thought about what she would do once she had escaped as she searched the floor for Remy's car keys. They had been in her purse. The same purse that Kevin had dumped unceremoniously onto the table. She continued to scan the floor then climbed down and retrieved the keys from under it. This plan would have to be all or nothing. If she took her time, the window would scream loudly as it was being forced open. She would have to move as swiftly as possible. She'd jump back onto table, hoist the window up with one push, then she'd climb through and run like hell toward Remy's car.

Nora thought about the possibility of going to a nearby neighbors. No, she decided. Kevin would be able to get to her before anyone answered her. At least if she made it to the car, she could drive away as quickly as possible ... or at least lock the doors and call for help.

She said a short prayer she had recalled from childhood, then pushed as hard as she could. The window snapped up loudly. She then struggled with the stiff screen as she heard the pounding of her heart. Or were those Kevin's footsteps? The screen finally cooperated. She slid through the narrow opening then extended a leg down toward the floor of the deck. She lost her balance, tumbling forward before she felt the agonizing pain as Kevin dug his nails into the bones of her ankle.

Nora struggled, pulling at her leg and refusing to give in to him. She kicked wildly with all of her might, with all of her remaining strength. She felt Kevin's stiff fingers loosen their grip on her. She pulled herself free and landed on the deck with a thud.

"Fucking bastard. You fucking bastard!" Nora screamed the words as she scrambled to her feet. She watched as Kevin's fingers suddenly shot out of the window, extending toward her. She reached for the outside window frame and pushed down hard as she heard the sickening thump as his unsuspecting hands were crushed beneath the heavy wooden casing.

She turned, focused for a moment, then made her way down the steps onto the rough shells of the path. Nora ran, barefoot, as quickly as she could. As she reached the gate, she heard the unmistakable slam of the screen door. She knew Kevin was coming after her. She could hear the screams in her head but was too tired to release them. She remembered Kevin's knife. At this point, she realized he couldn't risk having her talk to the police.

Please, God, Nora prayed. Please give me another chance. Another chance to make my life what I've always wanted it to be. Right here on Rocky Neck.

She threw open the gate and continued running toward the street then hesitated for a split second. The restaurant. No one would be there by now. Rocky Neck was completely still. There wasn't a single person on the street. Making it to Remy's car would be a long shot. But the cell phone was there. If she could make it, then she could lock the doors and use it. She turned right, away from the restaurant, running down Rocky Neck Avenue in the direction of the car.

Nora felt the sharp rocks and occasional shell as she ran in her bare feet. She could only hear her own heavy breathing. Until Kevin started to close in on her. She could make out the pounding of his boots as he started to inch closer. She wanted to scream but knew she couldn't afford to waste her breath. She widened her strides, trying to run faster. She could see Kevin's extended hand out of the corner of her eye. Nora's breath became more ragged. The pain in her chest was becoming almost unbearable. She was concentrating on how fast she was going. She never saw the pothole. Until she felt the pain as the pothole engulfed her entire foot. Her twisted ankle felt as if it had been mercilessly torn off. Then her body made its rapid descent, as it flew uncontrollably toward the granite curb. The ground rose up to meet her, and she hoped she wouldn't be knocked out. She needed to stay conscious. The pain was like a sharp knife, stabbing at her now badly twisted ankle. She groaned, rolling onto her back, dazed and unable to move.

She immediately felt Kevin's weight as he landed on top of her, his arms spread to prevent her from getting up. Nora saw the backpack as it lay on the ground beside her just out of arm's reach. She struggled underneath him. The sickening feel of his clammy hands and arms on hers almost made her wretch. He stood up, still unsteady from having consumed an enormous quantity of tequila. As he did so, he grabbed Nora's arm, pinching it painfully and forcing her up onto her feet. She stood, and he yanked her toward him.

"You fuckin' bitch." His whisper was more frightening than any shouting could have been, thought Nora. He grabbed the backpack then started pulling her toward the dead end street where Remy's car was parked.

"My ankle ..." Nora whimpered.

Kevin reacted, "First it was your back, now your ankle. Shut up and get over it."

Nora limped awkwardly as he pulled her down the street. She was dazed. And she almost didn't feel the pain, though she glanced down and saw the dark blood and deep scrapes on both of her knees and right shin. She touched the lump that had already developed on the back of her head. Nora was so lightheaded, she had to will herself to continue. She would not pass out. Not after all she'd been through.

They finally reached the car, and Nora surveyed the nearby houses, hoping to see at least one light on. That's all she needed, she thought. Just one glimmer of hope. She scanned both sides of the street. Except for a few outdoor lights, there was no sign of life. The rest of the world seemed to be sleeping. Kevin pulled her toward the driver's side door, then looked at her expectantly. He yanked at her roughly, whispering, "The keys. Where the fuck are the keys?"

Nora was simultaneously relieved and afraid. She would have a little more time before he dragged her off to wherever to end her life. She spoke in an equally low tone. "I must have dropped them. I had them in my hand. They must be on the grass back there." Nora pointed toward the main road. At least there, she thought, she might have a chance. Once he drove her somewhere remote, she knew it would be over.

"Fuck!" Kevin half-screamed suddenly. "Why can't anythin' be easy."

He pulled at her arm, turning back toward the main road. Nora tried to think of a plan. She didn't remember seeing the keys when she stood up. Had she dropped them when she was running from the house? She remembered having them until she had fallen. The storm drain. Nora remembered the high curb on which she had landed. The keys had jerked from her hand. And by now, Nora assumed, they were probably resting in Gloucester's ancient sewer system. She braced herself for what Kevin would do once he found out.

Nora tried to limp more slowly as Kevin practically dragged her. She thought about her injuries, wondering if she was dying and didn't know it. Don't be dramatic, Nora berated herself. You can handle it. You can do this. You're much smarter than he is. And more sober.

They reached the spot, and Kevin started fumbling immediately through the long grass above the curb. The streetlight was old and blinked periodically, and Nora watched as he leaned closer and closer, desperate to find them. Nora started backing up, wondering if she could finally make a run for it. It would be hard with her ankle. But she would have to at least attempt it. She spied Kevin's backpack, as it hung precariously from his shoulder, then watched as he let it drop on the ground next to him. After a few minutes of searching unsuccessfully, he expanded his hunt by making a wide, exaggerated sweep with both of his long arms through the overgrown grass.

"Where the fuck are they?" He growled, looking up at her.

Nora waited until he looked back down before taking two small steps toward him. Then two more. And two more after that. She stood just above Kevin's hunched body, and for the first time since he had been holding her captive, she realized he was too preoccupied to care what she was doing. He had become too sure of himself. Too sure that she was afraid and wouldn't take action, thought Nora. Nora watched as he continued his search, unaware of her intentions. Then, quickly, she grabbed the handle of his backpack with one swift movement. As she did so, Kevin's arms flew toward her, furiously grabbing at her ankles finally pulling the injured one, causing her to stumble. Nora ignored the unbearable pain, focusing only on her task at hand. She caught herself before falling, hugged the backpack closer to her chest, and started running. She thanked God that her ankle held out and that it was probably only sprained.

Nora tried to glance sideways, surprised that Kevin hadn't already caught up to her. He seemed to be struggling, as if the alcohol had finally taken its toll. She slowed, watching him as he held his stomach, leaning forward as if he was going to vomit. He spit loudly, recovered, and started running slowly toward her. He had become bolder, assuming no one would hear him.

Nora heard his taunting as he yelled toward her, "What are ya gonna do? Get me with my own knife?" He laughed.

Nora knew she would never be able to use a weapon. At least she didn't think she was capable of it. But would she ever know, unless she was in a situation where she had to save herself? A situation like this one?

She limped slowly as she neared the restaurant. The lights that usually shone on the antique Rocky Neck Grill sign were on, as they always were, even after closing. Nora looked toward the lounge area. It was completely dark, as she had expected. And she knew Evan was very cautious in locking all of the doors. She stared through the glass doors into the lounge, eyeing the faint light coming from the hallway beyond. The hallway that led to Evan's private office. She burst into tears. Nora didn't want to get her hopes up. But she had to. She needed the hope right now, even if it turned out to be false. She reached the door of the lounge entrance, pounding furiously with her tightened fists and screaming as loudly as she possibly could.

"Please. Someone please help me. I'm being attacked."

She pounded on the glass for what seemed an eternity. Then she saw Kevin fast approaching. She gave the door one last desperate pounding.

"Please. Please help me. Someone, please!"

She screamed again, this time, as she never imagined she could. Nora looked around. It hadn't brought anyone. How was that possible? She leaned with her back to the door, her entire body shaking. She was defeated and too tired to run any more. Kevin reached the main path. He took a deep breath and started walking toward her. His look was confident. He knew he had beaten her. Nora reached behind her, absentmindedly trying the handle again. She shook at it, knowing it was locked, but in a last desperate attempt, trying it anyway. She pushed on the door with all of her weight. She heard the undeniable click of the door popping open. The latch must not have caught all the way, Nora realized. Whoever had locked it was tired or had left in a hurry and hadn't double-checked it. Thank God.

She pushed open the door then turned immediately to close it. She finally heard the latch as it caught and the door locked ... just as Kevin reached the door.

Nora backed away from the glass, terrified that he would be able to push it open as she just had. She clutched the backpack and continued to back away.

He pounded on the glass and shook the door handle violently. "You fuckin' bitch. Now you've done it. You're gonna regret this."

Nora could barely hear his threats through the pounding in her own ears. She leaned forward for a moment, hoping she wouldn't be sick. She turned and ran toward the phone behind the bar. As she reached the end of the bar and started walking behind it, she heard Kevin's muffled voice from outside.

"Get the fuck off me."

Someone was there. They had heard her. She wanted to see who it was but knew she had to call the police. She picked up the handset with trembling fingers and attempted to dial 9-1-1. She hung up and tried again, realizing she had pressed the wrong buttons. Nora forced herself to concentrate.

"Gloucester Police Department dispatch. This is Officer Kelly. Your call is being recorded. What is the nature of your emergency?"

"Please. I'm being attacked. I'm at the Rocky Neck Grille. Inside. He has a knife and he's dangerous. His name is Kevin Delaney."

Nora ignored the operator who was trying to ask her questions. "Please ... I need help." "He's trying to kill me. And he killed Christian Wells." Nora burst into tears, knowing she would have to explain to the police.

The operator continued, "Miss ... miss?"

Nora hung up the phone, too shaken to continue the conversation. She walked slowly toward the door, afraid to look yet knowing that she must. Kevin lay sprawled on the ground face down, his arms behind his back. Half-sitting on her attacker was Evan. He seemed totally in control as the successor, one knee on the ground, the other pressed forcefully into Kevin's back, holding him in place.

Nora ran outside, then leaned against the wall. She sobbed with relief.

Evan looked up. "You okay?"

She nodded yes as tears of relief streamed down her face. Her tears became sobs

Evan continued, "Have you called the police?"

Nora nodded again, unable to speak.

Evan pressed harder with his knee, making sure Kevin couldn't wriggle free. "I worked late and decided to stay on the boat." He hesitated. "I heard the screams just as I was going down below. But I wasn't sure who it was at first."

The police arrived at that moment, the blue and white lights brightening everything in the nearby-darkened harbor with an eerie flashing glow. Two officers grabbed Kevin, struggling with him as they put on the handcuffs and read him his rights.

Evan stood up and walked toward Nora as she collapsed in his arms. She wiped her face, not wanting to imagine how she looked right now.

Evan looked into her eyes, "You ... are beautiful. I love you."

Nora whispered, "I love you too," knowing that she couldn't imagine ever loving him more than she did at that moment.

An unmarked car arrived as they were escorted to a police car. Nora prepared herself to go down to the station with Evan. She would tell the police everything. She held Kevin's backpack, the knife still inside. This would be the evidence they would need in solving the case.

She stepped into the police car as she watched the doors of the unmarked car fly open. Jake stepped out and surveyed the situation. Then Remy and Carly climbed out of the back seat. Remy searched the crowd and spotted Nora then pushed through the growing crowd toward her. Police officers as well as half-awake curious neighbors stood by.

Jake reached Nora first, a genuine look of concern on his face, "I heard what happened. Do you want to come with me? I can give you a ride to the station."

Nora looked over at Evan. "Thanks, but I'm with him." She hoped Evan would appreciate what she was saying.

Jake replied. "I know. You always have been. I guess I'll have to make other plans."

Nora smiled again, grateful at his remark. "I think I will have to make other plans, too." She looked at Evan, hoping for a reply.

He finally spoke, looking at Jake. "She definitely has other plans."

Remy approached them, tears in her eyes. "Nora Mason. Don't you dare ever pull something like that again. You scared the fucking hell out of me."

Nora hugged her, grateful for a true friend.

Chapter 38

Nora dressed carefully, trying not to disturb the bandage on her right foot and shin. She had chosen to wear the white linen skirt and sleeveless blouse she had worn for Evan before. She thought back to everything that had happened. And what she now called fate that had brought her to Rocky Neck.

She thought about her first date with Evan. Deep down, she had known she was in love with him, even then. She thought about her first time out with Remy, and how she had come to value their friendship. And she thought about how much she had come to love her new home.

This past week hadn't been easy, thought Nora. After she had gone to the police station and was questioned by the police, she asked herself whether she really wanted to stay here. But as the days had gone by, she had come to know her one and only answer. Not only had she fallen in love with the people of Rocky Neck, she had also fallen in love with the place.

Rocky Neck … and all of its magic.

Nora applied her lipstick, thinking about Kevin. He was in jail now. The police had questioned Remy and Carly again, and then they had officially determined that Christian's fall had been an accident. He had in fact been alive when he had hit the ground.

But it was Kevin who had finished the gruesome task. He had killed Christian with a fatal stab to the heart. In cold blood, to avenge his reneging on a drug deal.

Nora had found out that the police, including Jake, knew it had been a stab wound that had killed Christian, not the fall. But they had kept it under wraps, knowing that their key suspect, Kevin, would eventually let down his guard … with his drug dealing as well as in continuing to cover up the murder.

Nora thought about the missing evidence. The police still hadn't found what Kevin had been looking for. And Nora wasn't certain exactly what that was, either. Had it been more pills that Christian had gotten a hold of? Maybe it had something to do with Christian's father, the infamous Dr. Wells, who happened to be a psychiatrist and no doubt had been over medicating his wife. And what had become of the money that Christian had taken for the deal-gone-bad? Nora couldn't help but wonder if those questions would ever be answered.

She was still deep in thought as Evan walked up behind her. He kissed her neck softly until she moaned with pleasure.

Nora whispered. "If you don't stop, we're going to be late for dinner." Nora smiled, shaking off her thoughts of Kevin and Christian. "I just put on my lipstick. See?"

Evan chuckled lightly, not showing any signs of stopping, "I know, very nice."

*   *   *

Nora dialed as soon as she and Evan had gotten into the car. "Sorry. We're running a little late. We'll be there in about fifteen minutes. Okay. I'll tell him."

She turned toward Evan. "Remy said that you have to share me with her tonight." She laughed as she said the words.

Evan raised his eyebrow and replied. "I was an only child. I was never taught to share."

She openly stared at him, thinking how handsome he looked in his jeans, white T-shirt, and tan cotton jacket. This diamond was no longer rough, she admitted proudly. Evan wound through the streets of Rocky Neck then made a quick left toward Remy's loft.

He looked over once he had navigated the sharpest turns. "What?" Evan kept looking back at her, waiting for a reply.

"Since we're already late … " Nora looked at her watch. "It's ten of five. We can still make it. Can we stop at the post office? I haven't been there in weeks for my mail."

Nora thought about her post office box and the day she had called to reserve it. The day before she had left Florida for Gloucester. She would probably always keep that box she thought. And it was her lucky number, twenty-four.

Evan nodded, "I'll pull up front. While you're there I'll run down to the corner for a bottle of wine."

He parked in a spot that had just opened across the street. "I'll meet you back at the car."

Nora ran up the old granite steps of the downtown Gloucester Post Office and grabbed the door, thankful to have made it before closing. She pulled her keys from her purse and walked toward her box. As she stood in front of it, she viewed the accumulated mail through the glass window. She picked through her keys until she found the familiar mailbox key with the round top. Nora stared at the keys for a moment, confused. There, on her key ring, next to her mail box key, was a second key ... identical to hers, except the teeth were slightly misaligned. She only had one mailbox key, she thought. Nora tried the inside key first, the one closest to her house key. Her box clicked open, and she took out her mail.

Nora walked over to a large wooden table, plunked down her envelopes, and assorted junk mail. She stared at the other key. Nora gasped as she thought of the possibility. Could this be? No. No way. She thought of Christian. And what Kevin had been looking for. Kevin had been looking for a package. Not something as small as a key.

Her hands shook as she stared at it. What should she do? Wasn't it a felony or something if you went through someone else's mail? Not if the owner of the box gave you the key, even if it was supposed to be temporary. It was as if Christian was giving her permission. Nora thought about Christian. She was sure he had planned to get it back from her without her even knowing it had existed. He had used her, and he had put her in danger to hide his secrets. Didn't she deserve to at least know what was in the box?

Nora knew Evan would be waiting outside. She turned and looked at the long line of impatient patrons. She wouldn't have time to wait. She hesitated then walked up to the counter alongside someone who was writing a check.

Nora interrupted innocently, "Excuse me, I'm sorry, but I'm supposed to pick up mail for someone's family. But I forgot the box number." The short hefty blond woman looked at her suspiciously. Nora held up the key. "I have the key right here. And I have ID if you need it. I have a box here, myself."

The woman looked at the clock, obviously annoyed that it was now 5:05 and she still had to be polite. She stepped toward Nora. "What's the name?" She said in a lowered voice.

Nora answered quietly, "Wells." She hoped she was right. If not, she would have some explaining to do. She continued, "The family asked ... "

The stocky woman held her hand up, signaling Nora to stop talking. "Just a minute." She came back a moment later. Nora prayed the woman wouldn't mention Christian's first name, as the other patrons waiting behind her would surely recognize it from the headlines and might be suspicious. "It's the lower ones. The bigger boxes. Number 192."

Nora nodded, then looked around hoping no one in line had heard her. She followed the numbers until she was in the farthest corner. Her eye went down to the lowest row. The boxes had solid gold-looking metal fronts. Nora had hoped for a window so she could see inside. She leaned forward ... ready to insert the key.

"Nora?" She straightened, suddenly feeling very guilty.

She watched Evan approach the entrance behind a line of waiting customers.

Nora flushed, "I'll meet you outside. I'll be right there."

Why hadn't she just told Evan? Because she wanted to see what was in the box. And she knew Evan would want her to turn the key over to the police. Immediately. Nora hesitated as she stared back at the large box. She didn't think Christian would be bold enough to mail himself ... what? Probably not drugs. Nora thought about the money that Kevin had talked about paying Christian. Money he probably wouldn't want to keep at home or wouldn't want questioned if he deposited it. Could he have? Would he have? Nora agonized, knowing what Evan would want her to do.

And what would Remy want me to do? Shit, thought Nora. She'd definitely want me to open it ... and keep it if it was legal. Nora sighed, obviously torn. She threw her keys into her purse and picked up the mail. She would have to think about it and wait for now.

Nora ran to the car. Evan looked at his watch, a look Nora had seen many times before.

"Sorry. I had to go through my mail and check out a couple of things."

"I guess I'd better get used to it." Evan smiled.

They reached the loft a few minutes later, and he pulled into a guest parking spot right next to Remy's Saab. They quickly made their way upstairs. As they got to her door, Evan kissed Nora gently on the lips. She tried not to think about what she had found. She didn't want Christian invading her thoughts. She wanted to focus on Evan tonight. Evan looked into Nora's eyes.

"Did you read what I left for you?"

Nora thought about Evan's letter. She still hadn't opened it, though she carried it with her always. "It's still in my purse. I guess I've been nervous about …"

Evan interrupted her, "About what it might say?"

"Yes."

Evan turned toward Nora, looking lovingly into her eyes. "It says that I want you to stay with me here on Rocky Neck, that I love you just the way you are. And that you're perfect … for *me.*"

Nora grabbed his hand. She whispered, "I know."

They heard the music as the door swung open, and there stood Remy, holding three glasses of champagne. The music of Jimmy Buffet drifted out into the hallway.

She held the glasses out until Evan took two, one of which he handed to Nora. Remy held the door open, gesturing them to come inside. As they stepped in, they looked around appreciatively, touched that Remy would go to such lengths for them. Vases overflowed with wildflowers in varying shades of blues and yellows, and dozens of tiny silver pots were filled with purple-blue lavender.

The kitchen island was covered with an array of appetizers in plates of all shades of blue, and Nora noticed the second bottle of champagne near the champagne bucket. The dining room table was decorated with a crisp white linen table cloth and glimmering white plates. And sterling silver candlesticks completed the perfect setting.

Nora walked into the living room hand-in-hand with Evan, taking it all in.

"Let's go out on the deck, I have a toast," Remy requested.

The French doors were open invitingly, and the sun was still bright in a flawless light blue sky. The three stood at the balcony taking in the shimmering ocean and sandy beachfront.

Nora spoke first. "I hope you don't mind, but I have a toast, too." She began her short speech, "To Kevin."

Remy looked at her, surprised.

Nora continued, "If it wasn't for him, we wouldn't all be here together."

They raised their glasses. Nora took a deep breath then continued. "And to this." She held up the key. Evan and Remy exchanged glances before looking back at Nora.

"I found it just a little while ago. It's a post office box key. Christian must have put it on my key chain."

Remy was the first to respond, "Oh my God."

Nora interrupted, "For safekeeping." Her eyes darted back and forth between Remy and Evan, who remained speechless.

"I didn't look inside," Nora confirmed. "I wanted your opinion."

They nodded, finally realizing why the police hadn't found anything.

Remy leaned forward slightly, looking intently at Nora. "Our opinion? You mean, are you going to turn it into the police?" She looked back and forth between Evan and Nora.

"I don't know. Am I?"

Evan answered first, "Yes."

Then Remy answered, "No."

Nora gave them both a devilish smile. "We'll see. Remy, what's your toast?"

Remy held up her glass as she exchanged glances with her two friends. "To destiny or fate or whatever it was that brought us all together. And to coming home."

They each took a long sip, savoring the champagne and the company of true friends. Then Remy turned away from the ocean, toward the enormous wall above her couch. Nora's eyes followed hers. She gasped.

Hanging on the wall, in an obvious place of honor, was the painting she and Remy had fallen in love with on Rocky Neck. Nora remembered how mesmerized she had been by it. She stared at the young woman on the shore. Then she stepped closer, reading aloud the title that had been engraved on the tiny gold plaque in the painting's frame, "*Sweet Homecoming.*"

And yes, it was, thought Nora. It most definitely was.